"Perfect escapism for all teenage boys."
The Times

"Addictive, pacey novels." **Financial Times**

"Adults as well as kids will be hooked on the adventures of Alex Rider ... Harry Potter with attitude." **Daily Express**

"Meaty, thrilling and compelling."
Irish Independent

"This is the kind of book that's designed to grab the reader by the scruff of the neck, pull him into the page and not let go of him until he's well and truly hooked." **The Good Book Guide**

"If you are looking for a thrilling, exciting read, this is it." **Sunday Express**

"Crackling with suspense and daring, this is a fabulous story, showing that a bit of guts will take you a very long way." **Guardian**

"Will last for ever as one of the children's classics of our age." **The Times**

"The series that has re-invented the spy genre."
Independent

Titles by Anthony Horowitz

The Alex Rider series:
Stormbreaker
Point Blanc
Skeleton Key
Eagle Strike
Scorpia
Ark Angel
Snakehead
Crocodile Tears
Scorpia Rising
Russian Roulette

The Power of Five (Book One): *Raven's Gate*
The Power of Five (Book Two): *Evil Star*
The Power of Five (Book Three): *Nightrise*
The Power of Five (Book Four): *Necropolis*
The Power of Five (Book Five): *Oblivion*

The Devil and His Boy
Granny
Groosham Grange
Return to Groosham Grange
The Switch
More Bloody Horowitz

The Diamond Brothers books:
The Falcon's Malteser
Public Enemy Number Two
South by South East
Four of Diamonds

SNAKEHEAD

ANTHONY HOROWITZ

WALKER
BOOKS

For B & CD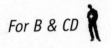

First published 2007 by Walker Books Ltd
87 Vauxhall Walk, London SE11 5HJ

This edition published 2014

2 4 6 8 10 9 7 5 3 1

This book has been typeset in Officina Sans

Printed and bound in Great Britain by Clays Ltd, St Ives plc

British Library Cataloguing in Publication Data: a catalogue record for
this book is available from the British Library

ISBN 978-1-4063-5885-8

www.walker.co.uk

CONTENTS

1	Down to Earth	9
2	"Death Is Not the End"	15
3	Visa Problems	33
4	No Picnic	47
5	On the Rocks	67
6	City of Angels?	84
7	Father and Son	97
8	First Contact	111
9	Once Bitten...	132
10	Wat Ho	147
11	Armed and Dangerous	163
12	The Silent Streets	179
13	Unwin Toys	208
14	The Liberian Star	232
15	Hide-and-Seek	250
16	Made in Britain	275
17	Spare Parts	298
18	Dead of Night	313
19	White Water	327
20	Batteries Not Included	342
21	Attack Force	353
22	Dragon Nine	364
23	Dinner for Three	390
	Afterword	401

DOWN TO EARTH

Splashdown.

Alex Rider would never forget the moment of impact, the first shock as the parachute opened and the second – more jolting still – as the module that had carried him back from outer space crashed into the sea. Was it his imagination or was there steam rising up all around him? Maybe it was sea spray. It didn't matter. He was back. That was all he cared about. He had made it. He was still alive.

He was lying on his back, crammed into the tiny capsule with his knees tucked into his chest. Half closing his eyes, Alex experienced a moment of extraordinary stillness. He was motionless. His fists were clenched. He wasn't breathing. Already he found it impossible to believe that the events that had led to his journey into space had really taken place. He tried to imagine himself hurtling around the earth at seventeen and a half thousand miles an hour. It couldn't have happened. It had surely all been part of some incredible dream.

Slowly he forced himself to unwind. He lifted an arm; it rose normally. He could feel the muscle working. Just minutes before, he had been in zero gravity. But as he rested, trying to collect his thoughts, he realized that once again his body belonged to him.

Alex wasn't sure how long he was on his own, floating in the sea somewhere ... it could have been anywhere in the world. But when things happened, they happened very quickly. First, there was the hammering of helicopter blades. Then the whoop of a siren. He could see very little out of the window – just the rise and fall of the ocean – but suddenly there was a palm slamming against the glass. A scuba-diver. A few seconds later, the capsule was opened from outside. Fresh air came rushing in, and to Alex it smelled delicious. At the same time, a figure loomed over him, his body wrapped in neoprene, his eyes behind a mask.

"Are you OK?"

Alex could hardly make out the words, there was so much noise outside. Did the diver have an American accent?

"I'm fine," he managed to shout back. But it wasn't true. He was beginning to feel sick, and there was a shooting pain behind his eyes.

"Don't worry! We'll soon have you out of there..."

It took them a while. Alex had only been in space a short time but he'd never had any physical training for it, and now his muscles were turning against him, reluctant to start pulling their own weight. He had to be manhandled out of the capsule, into the blinding sun of a Pacific morning. Everything was chaotic. There was a helicopter overhead, the blades beating at the ocean and forming patterns that rippled and vibrated. Alex turned his head and saw – impossibly – an aircraft carrier as big as a mountain looming out of the water less than a quarter of a mile away. It was flying the Stars and Stripes. So he had been right about the diver. He must have landed somewhere off the coast of America.

There were two more divers in the water, bobbing up and down next to the capsule, and Alex could see a fourth man leaning out of the helicopter directly above him. He knew what was going to happen and he didn't resist. First a loop of cable was passed around his chest and connected. He felt it tighten under his arms, and then he was rising into the air, still in his Ark Angel uniform, dangling like a blue-suited puppet as he was winched up.

And already they knew. He had glimpsed it in the eyes of the diver who had spoken to him. The disbelief. These men – the helicopter, the aircraft carrier – had been rushed out to rendezvous with a module that had just re-entered the earth's atmosphere. And inside, they had found a boy. A fourteen-year-old had just plummeted a hundred miles from outer space. These men would be sworn to secrecy, of course. MI6 would see to that. They would never talk about what had happened. But nor would they forget it.

There was a medical officer waiting for him on board the USS *Kitty Hawk*, the ship that had been diverted to pick him up. His name was Josh Cook and he was forty years old, black with wire frame glasses and a pleasant, softly spoken manner. He helped Alex out of his tracksuit and stayed with him when Alex finally did throw up. It turned out that he'd dealt with astronauts before.

"They're all sick when they come down," he explained. "It goes with the territory. Or maybe I should say terra firma. You've certainly come down to earth. You'll be fine by tomorrow morning."

"Where am I?" Alex asked.

"You're about a hundred miles off the east coast of Australia. We were on a training exercise when we got a red alert that you were on your way down."

"So what happens now?"

"Now you have a shower and get some sleep. You're in luck. We've got a mattress made out of memory foam. It was actually developed by NASA. It'll give your muscles a chance to get used to being back in full gravity."

Alex had been given a private cabin in the medical department of the *Kitty Hawk* – in fact a fully equipped "hospital at sea" with sixty-five beds, an operating theatre, a pharmacy and everything else that five and a half thousand sailors might need. The cabin wasn't huge, but he suspected that nobody else on the *Kitty Hawk* would have this much space. Cook went over to the corner and pulled back a plastic curtain to reveal a shower cubicle.

"You may find it difficult to walk," he explained. "You're going to be unsteady on your feet for at least twenty-four hours. If you like, I can wait until you've showered."

"I'll be OK," Alex said.

"All right." Cook smiled and opened the main door. But before he left, he looked back at Alex. "You know – every man and woman on this ship is talking about you," he said. "There are a whole pile of questions I'd like to ask you, but I'm under strict orders from the captain to keep my mouth shut. Even so, I want you to know that I've been at sea for a long, long time and I've never encountered anything like this. A kid in outer space!" He nodded. "I hope you have a good rest. There's a call button beside the bed if you need anything."

It took Alex ten minutes to get into the shower. He had completely lost his sense of balance, and the roll of the ship didn't help. He turned the temperature up as high as he could bear and stood under the steaming water, enjoying the rush of it over his shoulders and through his hair. Then he dried himself and got into bed. The memory foam was only a few centimetres thick but it seemed to mould itself to the shape of his body exactly.

He fell almost instantly into a deep but troubled sleep.

He didn't dream about the Ark Angel space station or his knife fight with Kaspar, the crazed eco-terrorist who had been determined to kill him even though it was clear that all was lost. Nor did he dream about Nikolei Drevin, the billionaire who had been behind it all.

But it did seem to him that, in the middle of his sleep, he heard the whisper of voices which he didn't recognize but which, somehow, he still knew. Old friends. Or old enemies. It didn't matter which, because he couldn't make out what they were saying; and anyway, a moment later they were swept away down the dark river of his sleep.

Perhaps it was a premonition.

Because three weeks before, seven men had met in a room in London to discuss an operation that would make them millions of pounds and would change the shape of the world. And although Alex had never met any of them, he certainly knew who they were.

Scorpia were back.

"DEATH IS NOT THE END"

It was the sort of building you could walk past without noticing: three storeys high, painted white, with perfectly trimmed ivy climbing up to the roof. It stood about halfway down Sloane Street in Belgravia, just round the corner from Harrods, and was one of the most expensive addresses in London. On one side there was a jewellery shop and on the other an Italian fashion boutique – but the customers who came here would no longer be needing either. A single step led up to a door painted black, and there was a window which contained an urn, a vase of fresh flowers and nothing else.

The name of the place was written in discreet gold letters:

Reed and Kelly
FUNERAL DIRECTORS
Death is not the End

At half past ten on a bright October morning, exactly three weeks before Alex landed in the Pacific Ocean, a black Lexus LS 430 four-door saloon drew up outside the front entrance. The car had been carefully chosen. It was a luxury model but there was nothing too special about it, nothing to attract attention. The arrival had also been exactly timed. In the past fifteen minutes, three other vehicles and a taxi had pulled up briefly, and their passengers, either singly or in pairs, had got out, crossed the pavement and entered the parlour. If anyone had been watching, they would have assumed that a large family had gathered to make the final arrangements for someone who had recently departed.

The last person to arrive was a powerfully built man with massive shoulders and a shaven head. There was something quite brutal about his face, with its small, squashed nose, thick lips and muddy brown eyes. But his clothes were immaculate. He was wearing a dark suit, a tailored silk shirt and a cashmere coat, unbuttoned. There was a heavy platinum ring on his fourth finger. He had been smoking a cigar, but as he stepped from the car he dropped it and ground it out with a brilliantly polished shoe. Without looking left or right, he crossed the pavement and entered the building. An old-fashioned bell on a spring jangled as the door opened and closed.

He found himself in a wood-panelled reception

room, where an elderly, grey-haired man sat with folded hands behind a narrow desk. He looked at the new arrival with a mixture of sympathy and politeness.

"Good morning," he said. "How can we be of service?"

"I have come about a death," the visitor replied.

"Someone close to you?"

"My brother. But I hadn't seen him for some years."

"You have my condolences."

The same words had already been spoken six times that morning. If even one syllable had been changed, the bald man would have turned round and left. But he knew now that the building was secure. The meeting that had been arranged just twenty-four hours earlier could go ahead.

The grey-haired man leant forward and pressed a button concealed under the desk. At once, a section of the wooden panelling clicked open to reveal a staircase leading up to the first floor.

Reed and Kelly was a real business. There once had been a Jonathan Reed and a Sebastian Kelly, and for more than fifty years they had arranged funerals and cremations until, at last, the time came to arrange their own. After that, the undertaker's had been purchased by a perfectly legitimate company, registered in Zurich, and it had continued to provide a first-class service for anyone who lived – or rather, *had* lived – in the area. But that was no longer the only purpose of the building in Sloane Street. It had also become the London headquarters of the international criminal organization that went by the name of Scorpia.

The name stood for sabotage, corruption, intelligence and assassination: its four main activities. The organization had been formed some twenty years before in Paris, its members being spies and assassins from different intelligence networks around the world who had decided to go into business for themselves. To begin with, there had been twelve of them. Then one had died of cancer and two had been murdered. The other nine had congratulated themselves on surviving so long with so few casualties.

But recently things had taken a turn for the worse. The oldest member had made the foolish and inexplicable decision to retire, which had, of course, led to his being murdered immediately. But his successor, a woman called Julia Rothman, had also been killed. That had been at the end of an operation – Invisible Sword – which had gone catastrophically wrong. In many ways this was the lowest point in Scorpia's history, and there were many who thought that the organization would never recover. After all, the agent who had beaten them, destroyed the operation and caused the death of Mrs Rothman had been fourteen years old.

However, Scorpia had not given in. They had

taken swift revenge on the boy and gone straight back to work. Invisible Sword was just one of many projects needing their attention, for they were in constant demand from governments, terrorist groups, big business ... in fact, anyone who could pay. And now they were active once again. They had come to this address in London to discuss a relatively small assignment but one that would net them ten million pounds, to be paid in uncut diamonds – easier to carry and harder to trace than banknotes.

The stairs led to a short corridor on the first floor with a single door at the end. One television camera had watched the bald man on his way up. A second followed him as he stepped onto a strange metal platform in front of the door and looked into a glass panel set in the wall. Behind the glass, there was a biometric scanner which took an instant image of the unique pattern of blood vessels on the retina in his eye and matched it against a computer at the reception desk below. Had an enemy agent tried to gain access to the room, he would have triggered a ten-thousand-volt electric charge through the metal floor plate, instantly incinerating him. But this was no enemy. The man's name was Zeljan Kurst and he had been with Scorpia from the beginning. The door slid open and he went in.

He found himself in a long, narrow room with three windows covered by blinds, and plain white walls with no decoration of any kind. There was a glass table surrounded by leather chairs and no sign of any pens, paper or printed documents. Nothing was ever written down at these meetings. Nor was anything recorded. There were six men waiting for him as he took his place at the head of the table. Following the disaster of Invisible Sword, there were now just seven of them left.

"Good morning, gentlemen," Kurst began. He spoke with a strange, mid European accent. The last word had sounded like "chintlemen". All the men at the table were equal partners but he was currently the acting head. A new chief executive was chosen as fresh projects arrived.

Nobody replied. These people were not friends. They had nothing to say to each other outside the work at hand.

"We have been given a most interesting and challenging assignment," Kurst went on. "I need hardly remind you that our reputation was quite seriously damaged by our last failure, and as well as providing us with a much-needed financial injection following the heavy losses we sustained on Invisible Sword, this project will suffice to put us back on the map. Our task is this. We are to assassinate eight extremely wealthy and influential people five weeks from now. They will all be together in one place, which provides us with the ideal opportunity. It has been left to us to decide on the method."

His eyes flickered around the table as he waited for a response. Zeljan Kurst had been the head of the police force in Yugoslavia during the 1980s and had been famous for his love of classical music – particularly Mozart – and extreme violence. It was said that he would interrogate prisoners with either an opera or a symphony playing in the background and that those who survived the ordeal would never be able to listen to that piece of music again. But he had guessed that one day his country would break up, and he had decided to quit before he was out of a job. And so he had changed sides. He had no family, no friends and nowhere he could call home. He needed work and he knew that Scorpia would make him extremely rich.

"You will have read in the newspapers," he continued, "that the G8 summit is taking place in Rome this November. This is a meeting of the eight most powerful heads of government, and as usual they will talk a great deal, have their photographs taken, consume a lot of expensive food and wine … and do absolutely nothing. They are of no interest to us. They are, in effect, irrelevant.

"However, at the same time, another conference will be taking place on the other side of the world. It has been arranged in direct competition with the G8 summit, and you might say that the timing is something of a publicity stunt. Nonetheless, it has already attracted much more attention than G8. Indeed, the politicians have almost been forgotten.

Instead, the eyes of the world are on Reef Island, just off the coast of north-west Australia in the Timor Sea.

"The press have given this alternative summit a name: Reef Encounter. A group of eight people will be coming together, and their names will be known to you. One of them is a pop singer called Rob Goldman. He has apparently raised millions for charity with concerts all over the world. Another is a billionaire, considered by many to be the richest man on the planet. He created a huge property empire but is now giving his fortune away to developing countries. There is an ex-president of the United States. A famous Hollywood actress, Eve Taylor. She owns the island. And so on." Kurst didn't even try to keep the contempt out of his voice. "They are amateurs, do-gooders – but they are also powerful and popular, which makes them dangerous.

"Their aim, as they put it, is 'to make poverty history'. In order to achieve this, they have made certain demands, including the cancellation of world debt. They want millions of dollars to be sent to Africa to fight Aids and malaria. They have called for an end to fighting in the Middle East. It will come as no surprise to those of us in this room that there are many governments and businesses who do not agree with these aims. After all, it is not possible to give to the poor without taking from the rich; and anyway, poverty has its uses.

It keeps people in their place. It also helps to hold prices down.

"A representative from one of the G8 governments contacted us six weeks ago. He has decided that Reef Encounter should end the moment it begins – certainly before any of these meddlers can address the television cameras of the world – and that is our assignment. Disrupting the conference is not enough. All eight are to be killed. The fact that they will all be in one place at one time makes it easier for us. Not one of them must leave Reef Island alive."

One of the other men leant forward. His name was Levi Kroll. He was an Israeli, about fifty years old. Very little of his face could be seen. Most of it was covered by a beard and there was a patch over the eye which he had once, by accident, shot out. "It is a simple matter," he rasped. "I could go out this afternoon and hire an Apache helicopter gunship. Let us say two thousand rounds of 30mm cannon fire and a few Hellfire air-to-ground laser-guided missiles, and this conference would no longer exist."

"Unfortunately it isn't quite as straightforward as that," Kurst replied. "As I said in my opening remarks, this is a particularly challenging assignment because our client does not wish the Reef Island eight to become martyrs. If they were seen to be assassinated, it would only add weight to their cause. And so he has specified that the deaths must seem accidental. In fact, this is critical. There cannot be even the tiniest amount of doubt or suspicion."

There was a soft murmur around the table as the other members of Scorpia took this new information on board. To kill one person in a way that would arouse no suspicion was simple. But to do the same for eight people on a remote island that would doubtless have a tight security system – that was quite another matter.

"There are certain chemical nerve agents..." someone muttered. He was French, exquisitely dressed with a black silk handkerchief poking out of his top pocket. His voice was matter-of-fact.

"How about R5?" a man called Mikato suggested. He was Japanese, with a diamond set in one tooth and – it was rumoured – yakuza tattoos all over his body. "It's the virus we supplied to Herod Sayle. Perhaps we could feed it into the island's water supply."

Kurst shook his head. "Gentlemen, both of these methods would be effective but still might show up in the subsequent investigation. What we require is a natural disaster, but one that we control. We need to eliminate the entire island with everybody on it, but in such a way that no questions will ever be asked."

He paused, then turned to the man sitting opposite him at the end of the table. "Major Yu?" he asked. "Have you given the matter your consideration?"

"Absolutely."

Major Winston Yu was at least sixty years old and although he still had a full head of hair, it had turned completely white – unusual in a Chinese man. The hair looked artificial, cut in a schoolboy style with a straight fringe above the eyes and the whole thing perched on top of a head that was yellow and waxy and that had shrunk like an over-ripe fruit. He was the least impressive person in the room, with circular glasses, thin lips and hands that would have been small on a young boy. Everything about him was somehow delicate. He had been sitting very still at the table, as if afraid he might break. A walking stick with a silver scorpion entwined around the handle rested against his chair. He was wearing a white suit and pale grey gloves.

"I have spent a great deal of time working on this operation," he continued. He had a perfect English accent. "And I am happy to report that although, on the face of it, this seems to be a rather difficult business, we have been blessed with three very fortunate circumstances. First, this island, Reef Island, is in exactly the right place. Five weeks from now is exactly the right moment. And finally, the weapon that we require just happens to be here in England, less than thirty miles from where we are sitting."

"And what weapon is that?" the Frenchman demanded.

"It's a bomb. But a very special bomb – a proto-type. As far as I know, there is only one in existence. The British have given it a code name. They call it Royal Blue."

"Major Yu is absolutely right," Kurst cut in. "Royal Blue is currently in a highly secret weapons facility just outside London. That is why I chose to hold the meeting here today. The building has been under surveillance for the past month and a team is already waiting on standby. By the end of the week, the bomb will be in our possession. After that, Major Yu, I am placing this operation in your hands."

Major Yu nodded slowly.

"With respect, Mr Kurst." It was Levi Kroll speak-ing. His voice was ugly and there was very little respect in it. "I was under the impression that *I* would be in command of the next operation."

"I am afraid you will have to wait, Mr Kroll. Once Royal Blue is in our hands, it will be flown to Bangkok and then carried by sea to its final des-tination. This is a region of the world where you have no working experience. For Major Yu, however, it is another matter. Over the past two decades he has been active in Bangkok, Jakarta, Bali and Lombok. He also has a base in northern Australia. He controls a huge criminal network – his *shetou*, or snakehead. They will smuggle the weapon for us. Major Yu's snakehead is a formidable organization, and in this instance it is best suited to our needs."

The Israeli nodded briefly. "You are right. I apologize for my interruption."

"I accept your apology," Kurst replied, although he didn't. It occurred to him that one day Levi Kroll might have to go. The man spoke too often without thinking first. "Major?"

There was little left to be said. Winston Yu took off his glasses and polished them with his gloved fingers. His eyes were a strange, almost metallic grey with lids that folded in on themselves. "I will contact my people in Bangkok and Jakarta," he muttered. "I will warn them that the machine will soon be on its way. The delivery system has already been constructed close to Reef Island. As to this conference with its high ideals, you need have no worries. I am very happy to assure you that it will never take place."

At six o'clock in the evening, two days later, a blue Renault Megane turned off the M11 motorway, taking an exit marked SERVICE VEHICLES ONLY. There are many such exits in the British motorway system. Thousands of vehicles roar past them every hour and the drivers never give them a second glance. And indeed, the great majority are completely innocent, leading to works depots or police traffic control centres. But the motorway system has its secrets too. As the Megane made its way slowly forward and came to a shuddering halt in front of what looked like a single-storey office compound, it was tracked by three television cameras and the security men inside went into immediate alert.

The building was in fact a laboratory and weapons research centre, belonging to the Ministry of Defence. Very few people knew of its existence and even fewer were allowed in or out. The car that had just arrived was unauthorized and the security men – recruited from the special forces – should have instantly raised the alarm. That was the protocol.

But the Renault Megane is one of the most innocent and ordinary of family cars, and this one had clearly been involved in a bad accident. The front windscreen had shattered. The bonnet was crumpled and steam was rising from the grille. A man wearing a green anorak and a cap was in the driving seat; there was a woman next to him with blood pouring down the side of her face. Worse than that, there were two small children in the back, and although the image on the screen was a little fuzzy, they seemed to be in a bad way. Neither of them was moving. The woman managed to get out of the car, but then she collapsed. Her husband sat where he was, as if dazed.

Two of the security men ran out to them. It was human nature. Here was a young family that needed help; and anyway, it wasn't that much of a security risk. The front door of the building swung shut behind them and would need a seven-digit code to reopen. Both men carried radio transmitters and 9mm Browning automatic pistols underneath their jackets. The Browning is an old weapon but a very reliable one, a favourite with the SAS.

The woman was still lying on the ground. The man who had been driving managed to open the door as the two guards approached.

"What happened?" one of them called out.

It was only now, when it was too late, that they began to realize that none of this added up. A car that had crashed on the motorway would have simply pulled onto the hard shoulder – if it had been able to drive at all. And how come it was only this one car, with these four people, that had been involved? Where were the other vehicles? Where were the police? But any last doubts were removed when the two security men reached the car. The two children on the back seat were dummies. With their cheap wigs and plastic smiles they were like something out of a nightmare.

The woman on the ground twisted round, a machine gun appearing in her hand. She shot the first of the security men in the chest. The second was moving quickly, reaching for his own weapon, taking up a combat stance. He never had a chance. The driver had been balancing a silenced Micro Uzi sub-machine gun on his lap. He tilted it and pulled the trigger. The gun barely whispered as it fired twenty rounds in less than a second. The guard was flung away.

The couple were already up and running towards the building. They couldn't get in yet, but they didn't need to. They made their way towards the back, where a silver box about two metres square had been attached to the brickwork. The man was carrying a toolkit which he had brought from the car. The woman stopped briefly and fired three times, taking out all the cameras. At that moment, an ambulance appeared, driving up from the motorway. It drew in behind the parked Megane.

The next phase of the mission took very little time. The facility was equipped with a standard CBR air filtration system – the letters stood for chemical, biological and radiological. It was designed to counter an enemy attack, but now the exact opposite was about to happen as the enemy turned the system against itself. The man took a miniaturized oxyacetylene torch out of his toolbox and used it to burn out the screws. This allowed him to unfasten a metal panel, revealing a complicated tangle of pipes and wires. From somewhere inside his anorak he produced a gas mask which he strapped over his face. He reached back into his toolbox and took out a metal vial, a few centimetres long, with a nozzle and a spike. He knew exactly what he was doing. Using the heel of his hand, he jammed the spike into one of the pipes. Finally he turned the nozzle.

The hiss was almost inaudible as a stream of potassium cyanide mixed with the air circulating inside the building. Meanwhile, four men dressed as paramedics but all wearing gas masks had approached the front entrance. One of them pressed a magnetized box no bigger than a cigarette packet against the lock. He stepped back. There was an explosion and the door swung open.

It was early evening and only half a dozen people were still working inside the facility. Most of them were technicians; one was the head of security. He had been trying to make an emergency call when the gas had hit him. He was lying on the floor, his face twisted in agony. The receiver was still in his hand.

Across the entrance hall, down a corridor and through a door marked RESTRICTED AREA: the four paramedics knew exactly where they were going. The bomb was in front of them. It looked remarkably old-fashioned, like something out of the Second World War: a huge metal cylinder, silver in colour, flat at one end, pointed at the other. Only a data screen built into the side and a series of digital controls brought it into the twenty-first century. It was strapped down on a power-assisted trolley and the whole thing would fit inside the ambulance with just inches to spare. But that, of course, was why the ambulance had been chosen.

They guided it back down the corridor and out through the front door. The ambulance was equipped with a ramp and the bomb rolled smoothly into the back, allowing room for the driver and one passenger in the front. The other three men and the woman climbed into the car. The dummies were left behind. The entire operation had taken eight and a half minutes. Thirty seconds less than planned.

An hour later, by the time the alarm had been raised in London and other parts of the country, everyone involved had disappeared. They had discarded the wigs, contact lenses and facial padding that had completely changed their appearance. The two vehicles had been incinerated.

And the weapon known as Royal Blue had already begun its journey east.

VISA PROBLEMS

"**A**lex Rider."

The blind man spoke the two words as if they had only just occurred to him. He let them roll over his tongue, tasting them like a fine wine. He was sitting in a soft leather armchair, the sort of furniture that would have been normal in an executive office but which was surprising in a plane, twenty-five thousand feet above Adelaide. The plane was a Gulfstream V executive jet which had been specially adapted for its current use, equipped with a kitchen and bathroom, a satellite link for worldwide communications, a forty-inch plasma TV connected to three twenty-four-hour news services and a bank of computers. There was even a basket for Garth, the blind man's guide dog.

The man's name was Ethan Brooke and he was the chief executive of the Covert Action Division of ASIS – the Australian Secret Intelligence Service. His department was inevitably known as CAD, but only by those who worked in it.

Very few others even knew it existed.

Brooke was a large man, in his mid fifties, with sand-coloured hair and ruddy, weather-beaten cheeks that suggested years spent outdoors. He had been a soldier, a lieutenant colonel with the commandos, until a landmine in East Timor had sent him first into hospital for three months and then into a new career in intelligence. He wore Armani sunglasses, tinted silver, rather than the traditional black glasses of a blind man, and his clothes were casual: jeans, a jacket and an open-necked shirt. A senior minister in the Australian defence department had once complained about the way Brooke dressed. That same minister was now carrying luggage in a three-star Sydney hotel.

Brooke was not alone. Sitting opposite him was a man almost half his age, slim, with short, fair hair. He was wearing a suit. Marc Damon had applied to join Australian intelligence the day after he had left university. He had done this by breaking into the headquarters of ASIS in Canberra and leaving his application on Brooke's desk. The two of them had now worked together for six years.

It was Damon who had produced the file – marked TOP SECRET: CAD EYES ONLY – that lay on the table between them. Although its contents had been translated into Braille, Brooke no longer had any need to refer to them. He had read the report once and had instantly memorized it. He now knew everything he needed about the boy called

Alex Rider. The only part that was missing from his consciousness was a true picture of the fourteen-year-old. There was a photograph attached to the cover, but as always he had been forced to rely on the official report:

PHYSICAL DESCRIPTION/ATTRIBUTES
Height: five feet four inches, still short for his age, but this adds to his operational value.
Weight: one hundred and twenty pounds.
Hair colour: fair.
Eyes: brown.
Physical condition: excellent, but may have been compromised by his recent injury (see *Scorpia* file).
Skills: has been learning karate since the age of six and has reached first *Kyu* grade (black belt). He is known to be fluent in two languages – French and Spanish – and is also proficient in German.
Weapons training: none.
Progress at school: has been slow, with negative feedback from many of his teachers. Spring and summer term reports from Brookland School are attached. However, it must be remembered that he has been absent from class for much of the past eight months.

PSYCHOLOGICAL PROFILE

AR was recruited by MI6 Special Operations
in March of this year, aged fourteen years
and two months. His father was John Rider
– alias Hunter – who was killed in action.
His mother died at the same time and he
was brought up by his uncle, Ian Rider,
also an active agent with MI6 before his
death earlier this year.

It seems certain that the boy was physically
and mentally prepared for intelligence work
from the earliest age. Quite apart from the
languages and martial arts, Ian Rider
equipped him with many skills, including
fencing, mountain climbing, white water
rafting and scuba-diving.

And yet, despite his obvious aptitude
for intelligence work (see below), AR has
shown little enthusiasm for it. Like most
teenagers, he is not a patriot and has
no interest in politics. MI6 (SO) found it
necessary to coerce him to work for them
on at least two occasions.

He is popular at school – when he is
there. Hobbies include football (Chelsea
supporter), tennis, music and cinema.
Evident interest in girls – see separate
file on *Sabina Pleasure* and report by
CIA operative Tamara Knight. Lives with
American housekeeper, Jack Starbright

(note: despite first name, Jack is female).
No ambitions to follow his father and
uncle into intelligence.

PAST ASSIGNMENTS – ACTIVE SERVICE
The British secret service refuses to admit
that it has ever employed a juvenile, and
so it has been difficult to draw together
any concrete evidence of AR's record as an
agent in the field. We believe, however,
that he has worked for them on at least
four occasions. He has also been seconded
to the USA, where he has been employed
by the CIA with equal success at least
twice.

UK: See *Herod Sayle*: Sayle Enterprises,
Cornwall; *Dr Hugo Grief*: Point Blanc
Academy, France; *Damian Cray*: Cray Software
Technology, Amsterdam; *Julia Rothman*
(Scorpia executive): *Operation Invisible
Sword*, London.

USA: FILES CLOSED. Possible links with
General Alexei Sarov: Skeleton Key, Cuba;
Nikolei Drevin: Flamingo Bay, Caribbean
(termination of *Ark Angel* project).

Although it has so far proved impossible
to confirm details, it would appear that in
the space of one year AR has been involved
in six major assignments, succeeding
against impossible odds. He has survived

assassination attempts by both Scorpia and the Chinese triads.

Current status: available.

Footnote: Last year the FBI attempted to recruit a teenage agent to combat drug syndicates operating out of Miami. The boy was killed almost immediately. The experiment has not been repeated.

Secret service files are the same the world over. They are written by people who live in a very black and white world and who, by and large, have no time for creative imagination – certainly not if it gets in the way of the facts. The various pages on Alex Rider had given Brooke a vague impression of the boy. They had certainly been enough to set his mind working. But he suspected that they left out as much as they revealed.

"He's in Australia," he murmured.

"Yes, sir." Damon nodded. "He dropped in on us from outer space."

Brooke smiled. "You know, if anyone else had told me that, I'd swear they were yanking my chain. He really went into space?"

"He was pulled out of the sea a hundred miles off the east coast. He was sitting in the re-entry module of a Soyuz-Fregat. Of course, the Americans aren't telling us anything. But it's probably no coincidence that according to NIWO, the Ark

Angel space station blew up at around the same time."

NIWO is the National Intelligence Watch Office. It employs around two thousand people who keep up a constant surveillance on everything happening in the world – and outside it.

"That was Drevin's big idea," Brooke muttered. "A space hotel."

"Yes, sir."

"I always had a feeling he was up to no good."

There was a moment of turbulence and the plane dipped down. The dog, in his basket, whined. He never had cared much for flying. But then they steadied and continued in their arc over the clouds, heading north-east to Sydney.

"You think we can use him?" Brooke demanded.

"Alex Rider doesn't like being used," Damon replied. "And from what I've read, there's no way he's going to volunteer. But it did occur to me that if we could find some sort of leverage, he'd be perfect for what we need. Put a kid into the pipeline and nobody's going to suspect a thing. It's exactly the same reason the Americans sent him to Skeleton Key – and it worked for them."

"Where is he now?"

"They're flying him over to Perth, sir. A bit of a hike but they wanted him somewhere safe and they've settled on SAS HQ at Swanbourne. He's going to need a couple of days to wind down."

Brooke fell silent. With his eyes permanently

covered, it was always difficult to work out what he was thinking; but Damon knew that he would be turning over all the possibilities, that he would come very quickly to a decision and stick by it. Maybe there was no way that ASIS could persuade this English kid to work for them. But if there was a single weakness, anything they could use to their advantage, his boss would find it.

A moment later, Brooke nodded. "We could pair him with Ash," he said.

And there it was. Simple but brilliant.

"Ash is in Singapore," Damon said.

"Operational?"

"A routine assignment."

"As of now he's reassigned. We'll put the two of them together and send them in. They'll make a perfect team."

Damon couldn't help smiling. Alex Rider would work with the agent they all called Ash. But there was just one problem.

"You think Ash will work with a teenager?" he asked.

"He will if this kid's as good as everyone says he is."

"He'll need proof."

This time it was Brooke's turn to smile. "Leave that to me."

The SAS compound at Swanbourne is a few miles south-west of Perth and has the appearance of a low-rise holiday village, although perhaps one with more security than most. It stretches out next to the white sand and blue water of the Indian Ocean, sheltered from public view by a series of sand dunes. The buildings are clean, modern and unremarkable. But for the rise and fall of the barrier at the main gate, the military vehicles passing in and out, and the occasional sighting of men in khaki with sand-coloured berets, it would be hard to believe that this is the headquarters of Australia's toughest and most elite fighting force.

Alex Rider stood at the window of his room looking out over the main square with the indoor shooting range on one side and the gymnasium and fitness centre on the other. He wanted to go home and wondered how long they were going to keep him here. Certainly his stay on the *Kitty Hawk* had been short enough. He hadn't even had time to eat breakfast before he had been bundled into a Hawkeye jet, an oxygen mask strapped over his face, and then blasted off back into the sky. Nobody had even told him where they were taking him, but he had seen the name written in large letters on the airport terminal: PERTH. There had been a jeep parked on the runway, and the next thing he knew he was bouncing through the very ordinary-looking suburb of Swanbourne. The jeep drove into the SAS compound and stopped. A single soldier was waiting for him, his eyes shielded by sunglasses, his mouth a straight line that gave nothing away. Alex was shown into a comfortable room with a bed, a TV and a view of the sand dunes. The door was closed but it wasn't locked.

And here he was now. They had carried him the entire width of Australia. He wondered what would happen next.

There was a knock on the door. Alex opened it. A second soldier in green and ochre battle fatigues stood in front of him.

"Mr Rider?"

"I'm Alex."

"Colonel Abbott sends his compliments. He'd like to speak to you."

Alex followed the soldier across the compound. There was nobody else around. The sun was beating down on the empty parade ground. It was almost midday and the early Australian summer was already making itself felt. They reached a bungalow standing on its own near the edge of the complex. The soldier knocked and, without waiting for an answer, opened the door for Alex to go in.

A thin, businesslike man in his forties was sitting behind a desk, also wearing fatigues. He had been writing a report but he stood up as Alex came in.

"So you're Alex Rider!" The Australian accent came almost as a surprise. With his short, dark hair and craggy features, Abbott could have been mistaken for an Englishman. He reached out and shook Alex's hand firmly. "I'm Mike Abbott, and

I'm really pleased to meet you, Alex. I've heard a lot about you."

Alex looked surprised and Abbott laughed. "Six months ago, there was a rumour that the Brits were using a teenage agent. Of course, nobody believed it. But it seems they've been keeping you busy; and after you took out Damian Cray ... well, I'm afraid you can't blow up Air Force One in the middle of London without someone hearing about it. But don't worry! You're among friends."

Abbott gestured towards a chair and Alex sat down. "It's very kind of you, Colonel," he said. "But I really want to go home."

Abbott returned to his own chair. "I can understand that, Alex. And I really want to send you on your way. We just need to fix a couple of things."

"What things?"

"Well, you landed in Australia without a visa." Abbott held up his hands before Alex could interrupt. "I know that sounds ridiculous, but it has to be sorted out. As soon as I've got the green light, I'll book you on the first plane back to London."

"There's someone I want to call..."

"I suppose you're thinking about Jack Starbright. Your guardian." Abbott smiled and Alex wondered how he knew about her. "You're too late, Alex. She's been kept fully informed and she's already on her way. Her flight left Heathrow about an hour ago but it'll take her another twenty-five hours to arrive. The two of you will meet up in

Sydney. In the meantime, you're my guest here at Swanbourne and I want you to enjoy yourself. We're right on the beach, and it's the start of the Australian summer. So relax. I'll let you know as soon as there's any news about the visa."

Alex wanted to argue but decided against it. The colonel seemed friendly enough but there was something about him that made Alex think twice before speaking. You didn't rise up through the ranks of the SAS unless you were exceptionally tough – and there was certainly steel behind that smile.

"Anything else you want to know?"

"No thanks, Colonel."

The two of them shook hands.

"I've asked some of the boys to look after you," Abbott said. "They've been looking forward to meeting you. Just let me know if anyone gives you a hard time."

When Alex had been training with the SAS in the Brecon Beacons in Wales, a hard time was exactly what he had been given. But from the moment he left the bungalow, he saw that things were going to be different here. There were four young soldiers waiting for him and they all seemed to be easygoing and keen to introduce themselves. Maybe his reputation had gone ahead of him, but he could see right away that the Australian special forces were going to be the complete opposite of their British counterparts.

"It's great to meet you, Alex." The man who was speaking was about twenty-two and incredibly fit with a green T-shirt stretched tight over finely chiselled pectorals and bulging shoulders. "I'm Scooter. This is Texas, X-Ray and Sparks."

At first Alex thought they were using code names, but he quickly realized that they were just nicknames. All the other men were also in their early twenties and equally fit.

"We're just heading for lunch," Scooter went on. "You want to join us?"

"Thanks." Alex hadn't been given any breakfast and his stomach was empty.

They moved off as a pack. Nobody had even commented on his age. It was clearly no secret who he was. Alex began to feel a little more relaxed. Maybe a day or two here wouldn't be so bad.

From inside the bungalow, Colonel Mike Abbott watched them go. He had an uneasy feeling in his stomach. He was married with three children, and the eldest was only a few years younger than the boy he had just met. He had been impressed. After all he had been through, Alex had a sort of inner calm. Abbott didn't doubt that he could look after himself.

But even so...

He glanced again at the orders which he had received just a few hours ago. It was madness. What was being suggested was simply out of the question. Except that there was no question about it. He had been told exactly what he had to do.

And what if Alex was crippled? What if he was killed?

Not his problem.

The thought didn't comfort him one bit. In twenty years, Mike Abbott had never questioned his commanding officers, but it was with a sense of anger and disbelief that he picked up the telephone and began to issue the instructions for the night ahead.

NO PICNIC

Alex was worn out after all his travelling, and that afternoon he went back to his room and slept. When he was woken up – by the sound of knocking – the day was already drawing to a close. He went over to the door and opened it. The young soldier who had introduced himself as Scooter was standing there. Sparks was with him, holding a cool box.

"How are you doing?" Scooter asked. "We wondered if you'd like to come with us."

"Where are you going?"

"A picnic on the beach. We'll set up a barbecue. Have a few beers. Maybe swim." Scooter gestured at the compound behind him. There was nobody in sight. "There's a big exercise on tonight but we aren't part of it, and the colonel thought you might like to see a bit of the ocean before you leave."

The last three words caught Alex's attention. "I'm leaving?"

"Tomorrow morning. That's what I've heard. So how about it?"

"Sure." Alex had nothing else to do that evening. He didn't particularly want to watch TV on his own.

"Great. We'll pick you up in ten minutes."

The two men walked off, and it was only much later, when he was ten thousand miles away, that Alex would remember the moment and the way they had glanced at each other as if there was something that bothered them. But if he noticed it at the time, he didn't register it.

He went back into the room and pulled on his trainers. The SAS had provided him with some fresh clothes and he took a combat jacket out of the wardrobe. Scooter had talked about swimming but the sun was getting lower and Alex had already felt a cool breeze rolling in. He thought for a moment, then took a towel and a spare pair of boxers that would have to do instead of swimming trunks. Just as he was about to leave, he hesitated. Was this a good idea, heading off down the coast with a group of strangers almost ten years older than him? Suddenly he felt very alone and a long, long way from home. But Jack was on her way. Scooter had told him that he would be leaving the next day. He shook himself out of his mood and left the room, closing the door behind him.

Almost at once, a jeep drew up with Sparks driving and Scooter in the passenger seat. Texas and X-Ray were in the back with bags and cool boxes, blankets and a guitar piled up around them. They had left a narrow space for Alex. As he climbed in, he noticed that Texas was balancing an automatic pistol on his lap, testing the mechanism.

"You ever fired one of these?" Texas asked.

Alex shook his head.

"Well, now's your chance. When we get out there, I'll set up a few targets. See how you do."

Once again, Alex couldn't shake off a vague feeling that something was wrong; but then Sparks turned on the radio and, to a blast of music from some Australian band he had never heard of, they set off. It was going to be a beautiful evening. There were a few streaks of red in the sky but no clouds, and the sun – close to the horizon – was throwing long, stretched-out shadows across the ground. Scooter was slumped in his seat with one foot resting on the dashboard. X-Ray had his hand up, the wind streaming through his fingers. By the time they had passed through the barrier and hit the main road, Alex had relaxed. He only had one evening in Australia. He might as well enjoy it.

They followed the coast for about ten miles, then turned inland. To begin with they passed a number of suburban houses and shopping malls, but they soon left those behind; and by the time they had joined a four-lane motorway, they were driving through open countryside. None of them spoke. It was impossible in the open-top jeep with the wind rushing past. The music pounded out but any words were snatched away and lost.

After about twenty minutes, Scooter turned round and shouted, "You OK?"

Alex nodded. But secretly he was wondering how far they intended to travel and when they would arrive.

The journey lasted over an hour. They came off the motorway and took a road that cut through a wooded area. Then they turned onto a track, and suddenly they were bumping over a rough, uneven surface, eucalyptus and pine trees pressing in on both sides.

X-Ray had taken out a map. He leant forward and tapped Scooter on the shoulder. "Is this the right way?" he shouted.

"Sure!" Scooter shouted back without looking behind him.

"I think we've come too far!"

"Forget it, X-Ray. This is the right way..."

There was a barrier ahead of them, similar to the one at Swanbourne except that it was old and rusted. There was a sign next to it:

MILITARY ZONE
Absolutely no admittance.
Trespassers will be placed under
arrest and may be imprisoned.

Sparks slowed down and, without opening the door, Scooter leapt out of the jeep.

"Where are we?" Alex asked.

"You'll see," Sparks replied. "We come to a load of places around here. You'll like it."

"We've come too far," X-Ray insisted. "We should have turned off a mile back."

Scooter had opened the barrier – it obviously hadn't been locked – and the jeep rolled through. As it passed him, he leapt back into the passenger seat and at once Sparks stepped on the accelerator and they shot forward, bumping over roots and potholes.

It had become very dark. The last of the daylight had slipped away without Alex noticing, and suddenly the trees seemed very close, threatening to block the way ahead. The surface was getting worse and worse. Alex had to cling to the side as he was thrown around, the cool boxes lifting into the air and hanging there before crashing down again. Leaves and branches flickered briefly, a thousand black shadows caught in the headlights, before they whipped into the windscreen and disappeared behind. The track didn't seem to be going anywhere and Alex was having to fight back a sense of unease, wishing he hadn't come, when suddenly they burst through a clump of foliage and came to a shuddering halt, soft sand underneath the wheels. They had arrived.

Sparks turned off the engine and at once the gentler sounds of the evening surrounded them. Alex could hear the whisper of the breeze and the rhythmic breaking of the waves. They had come to a beautiful place: a private beach with perfect white sand that curved round in a crescent, next to a black and silver sea. There was a full moon and a fantastic cluster of stars which seemed to go on for ever, stretching to the very ends of the southern hemisphere.

"Everybody out!" Scooter shouted. He kicked the door open and tumbled out onto the sand. "X-Ray, get me a beer. Texas, it's your turn to cook."

"I always cook!" Texas complained.

"Why do you think we invite you?"

"Here!" X-Ray had produced a can of Foster's. He threw it to Scooter, then turned to Alex. "You want a beer?"

"You got a Coke?" Alex asked.

"Sure!" X-Ray found a can and passed it over.

Meanwhile, Texas had begun to unload the jeep. Alex saw that the SAS men had brought sausages, burgers, steaks and chops – enough meat to feed a small army. But apart from a greasy, blackened steel grill, there was no sign of the promised barbecue.

Scooter must have read his mind. "We're going to build a bonfire, Alex," he said. "You can help collect wood."

Sparks had taken the guitar out of the back. He rested it on his knee and strummed a few chords. The music sounded faint, lost in the emptiness of the night.

"OK. Here's the plan," Scooter said. It seemed that he was the natural leader even if all four men were the same age and rank. "Alex and I will fetch firewood. Texas and X-Ray can start setting things up. Sparks – you keep playing." He took out a torch and threw it to Alex. "If you get lost, just listen out for the music," he said. "It'll guide you back to the beach."

"Right." Alex wasn't sure he would be able to hear the guitar once he was in the wood, but Scooter seemed to know what he was doing.

"Let's go," Scooter said.

He also had a torch, and flicked it on. The beam was powerful; even with the moonlight, it leapt ahead, cutting a path through the shadows. Alex did the same. The two of them moved away from the jeep, heading back up the track that had brought them here. The evening was warmer than Alex had expected. The breeze couldn't penetrate the trees. Everything was very still.

"You all right?" Scooter asked.

Alex nodded.

"We'll build a fire, get things cooking; then we can have a swim."

"Right."

They continued walking. It seemed to Alex that they had left the beach a long way behind them. He could still hear the music, but it was so distant that the notes seemed to have broken up and he couldn't make out any tune.

"See if you can find any dead wood. It burns better."

Alex trained his torch on the forest floor. There were broken branches everywhere and he wondered why they had come so far to collect them. But there was no point arguing. He reached down and gathered a few pieces together, then a few more. It didn't take him long to build up a pile; any more and it would be too heavy to carry. Clutching the wood to his chest, he straightened up and looked around for Scooter.

That was when he realized he was on his own.

"Scooter?"

There was no reply. Nor was there any sign of the SAS man's torch. Alex wasn't worried. It was likely Scooter had already collected his first bundle and was making his way back to the beach. Alex listened out for the sound of the guitar, but it had stopped. Now he felt the first prickle of doubt. He had been so busy collecting the branches that he had lost his sense of direction. He was in the middle of a wood, surrounded by blackness on all sides. Which way was the beach?

Ahead of him he saw a blink of white. A torch. Scooter. Alex called out his name a second time but there was no reply. It didn't matter. He had definitely seen a light, and, as if to reassure him, it flashed again. He headed towards it.

It was only when he had gone twenty or thirty paces that Alex realized he was nowhere near the beach; instead he had been drawn even further into the forest. It was almost as if it had been done on purpose. He was the moth and they had shown him the candle. But now the light had vanished. Even the moon had disappeared. Annoyed with himself, Alex dropped the wood. He could always pick more up later. All he wanted right now was to find his way back.

Ten more steps and abruptly the trees fell away. But he wasn't at the beach. Alex's torch showed him a wide, barren clearing with little hillocks of sand and grass. The forest circled all around him. There was no sign of Scooter or the flickering light that had led him here.

Now what?

Alex decided to go back the way he had come. He might be able to pick up his own footprints. The pile of wood he had dropped couldn't be too far away.

He was about to turn when something – some animal instinct – made him hesitate. About two seconds later, the whole world stopped.

He knew it was going to happen before it actually did. Alex had been in danger so many times that he had developed a sense, a sort of telepathy, that forewarned him. Animals have it – the awareness that makes their hackles rise and sends them running before there is any obvious reason to flee. Alex was throwing himself to the ground even before the missile fell, smashing the trees into matchsticks, scooping up a tonne of earth and hurling it into the sky, shattering the silence of the night and turning darkness into brilliant, blinding day.

The explosion was enormous. Alex had never felt anything like it. The very air had been transformed into a giant fist, a boxing glove that pounded into him, hot and violent; and for a moment he thought he must have broken a dozen bones. He couldn't hear; he couldn't see. The inside of his skull was boiling. Perhaps he was unconscious for a few seconds, because the next thing he knew, he was lying on the ground with his face pressed into a clump of grass and sand in his hair and eyes. His shirt was torn and there was a throbbing in his ears, but otherwise he seemed to be unhurt. How close had the missile fallen? Where had it come from? Even as Alex asked himself these two questions, a third, more unpleasant one, entered his mind. Were there going to be any more?

There was no time to work out what was going on. Alex spat out sand and dragged himself to his knees. At the same moment, something burst in the sky: a white flame that hung there, suspended high above the trees. Alex had tensed himself, expecting another blast, but he quickly recognized it for what it was: a Varey light, a lump of burning phosphorus, designed to illuminate the area for miles around. He was still kneeling. Almost too late he realized that he had turned himself into a target, a black cut-out against the brilliant, artificial glare.

He threw himself onto his stomach a second before a cascade of machine-gun bullets came fanning out of nowhere, pulverizing branches and ripping up the leaves. There was a second explosion, smaller than the first, this one starting at ground level and sending a column of flame shooting up. Alex covered his head with his hands. Earth and sand splattered all around him.

He was in a war zone. It was beyond anything he had ever experienced. But common sense told him that no war had broken out in Western Australia. This was a training exercise and somehow – insanely – he had stumbled into the heart of it.

He heard the blast of a whistle and two more explosions followed. The ground underneath him trembled and suddenly he found that he could no longer breathe. The air around him had been sucked away by the force of the blasts. More machine-gun fire. The entire area was being strafed. Alex glanced up, but even with the Varey light he knew there was no chance he would see anyone. Whoever was firing could be half a mile away. And if he stood up and tried to make himself seen, he would be cut in half before anyone realized their mistake.

And what about Scooter? What about X-Ray and the others? Had they brought him here on purpose? Alex couldn't believe that. What motive could they have to want him dead? He remembered what X-Ray had said in the jeep. *We've come too far. We should have turned off a mile back.* And when they'd invited him along, Scooter had said there was a big training exercise on that night. That was why they'd been free for a picnic on the beach. Some picnic! As insane as it seemed, the four SAS men must have driven to the very edge of the war zone. Alex had managed to stray away from the beach when he was collecting wood and had chosen the worst possible direction. This was the result – a mixture of bad luck and stupidity. But the two of them were going to get him blown apart.

A rhythmic pounding had begun, a mortar bombarding a target that had to be somewhere close by. As each shell detonated, Alex felt a stabbing pain behind his eyes. The power of the weapons was immense. If this was just a training exercise, he wondered what it must be like to get caught up in a real war.

It was time to go. With the mortar still firing, Alex scrambled to his feet and began to move, not sure which way he should go, knowing only that he couldn't remain here. Anyway, he had lost all sense of direction. There was the scream of something falling, and a great whump as it struck the ground somewhere over to Alex's left. That told him all he needed to know. He headed off to the right.

A crackle of machine-gun fire. Alex thought he heard someone shout, but when he looked round, there was no one there. That was the most unnerving thing, to be in the middle of a battle with not a single combatant visible. A tree had caught fire. The entire trunk was wrapped in flames and there were black and crimson shadows leaping all over the ground ahead. Just beyond, Alex caught sight of a wire fence. It wasn't much to aim for but at least it was man-made. Maybe it defined the perimeter of the war zone and he would be safer on the other side. Alex broke into a run. He could taste blood: he must have bitten his tongue when the first bomb went off. He felt bruised all over. He wondered if he might be hurt more than he actually knew.

He reached the fence. It was made of barbed wire and carried another sign: DANGER – KEEP OUT. Alex almost smiled. What danger could there possibly be on the other side that was worse than this? As if to answer the question, there were three more explosions less than a hundred metres behind him. Something hot struck Alex on the back of his neck. Without hesitating, he rolled under the fence, then stood up and continued running across the ground on the other side.

He was in a field. There was still no sign of the ocean. He was surrounded by trees on all sides. He slowed down and tried to take his bearings. His neck hurt. He had been burnt by whatever it was that had hit him. He wondered if Scooter and the others were looking for him. He would certainly have a few things to say to them – if he ever got out of here alive.

He continued. His right foot came down on something small and metallic. He heard – and felt – it click beneath his sole. He stopped. And at the same time, a voice came out of the darkness just behind him.

"Don't move. Don't even move a step..."

Out of the corner of his eye, Alex saw a figure roll under the fence. At first he thought it must be Scooter, but he hadn't recognized the voice and a few seconds later he saw that it was an older man with black curly hair and the beginnings of a rough beard, dressed in full military gear and carrying an assault rifle. The bombs and the shelling seemed to have faded into the distance. They must have been redirected at a target further away.

The man loomed up next to him, looking at Alex with disbelieving eyes. "Who the hell are you?" he asked. "How did you get here?"

"What am I standing on?" Alex demanded. Part of him knew the answer. He hadn't dared look down.

"The field is mined," the man replied briefly. He knelt. Alex felt his hand press gently against his trainer. Then the man straightened up. His eyes were dark brown and bleak. "You're standing on a mine," he said.

Alex was almost tempted to laugh. A sense of disbelief shivered through him and he swayed a little, as if he were about to faint.

"Stay exactly as you are!" the man shouted. "Stand up straight. Don't move from side to side.

If you release the pressure, you're going to kill both of us."

"Who are you?" Alex exclaimed. "What's going on here? Why is there a mine?"

"Didn't you see the sign?"

"It just said DANGER – KEEP OUT."

"What more did you need?" The man shook his head. "You shouldn't be anywhere near this place. How did you get here? What are you doing out here in the middle of the night?"

"I was brought here." Alex could feel a cold numbness creeping through his leg. It got worse the more he thought about what lay beneath his foot. "Can you help me?" he asked.

"Stay still." The man knelt down a second time. He had produced a torch, and he shone it on the ground. It seemed to take an age, but then he spoke again. "It's a butterfly," he said, and there was no emotion in his voice at all. "It's a Soviet PFM-1, a pressure-sensitive blast mine. You're standing on enough high explosive to take your leg off."

"What's it doing here?" Alex cried. He had to fight the instinct to lift his foot off the deadly thing. His entire body was screaming at him to run away.

"They train us!" the man rasped. "They use these things in Iraq and Indonesia. We have to know how to deal with them. How else are they going to do it?"

"But in the middle of a field?"

"You shouldn't be here! Who brought you?" The man straightened up. He was standing very close to Alex, his brown eyes boring into him. "I can't neutralize it," he muttered. "Even if I had the training, I couldn't risk it in the dark."

"So what do we do now?"

"I'm going to have to get help."

"Do you have a radio?"

"If I had a radio, I'd have already used it." The man laid a hand briefly on Alex's shoulder. "There's something else you need to know," he said. He was speaking softly; his mouth was next to Alex's ear. "These things have a delay mechanism ... a separate fuse which you'll have activated when you stepped on it."

"You mean it's going to blow up anyway?"

"In fifteen minutes."

"How long will it take you to find someone?"

"I'll move as quickly as I can. If you hear a click – you'll feel it under your foot – throw yourself flat on the ground. It's your only hope. Good luck."

"Wait..." Alex began.

But the man had already gone.

Alex stood there. He had lost any sense of feeling in his leg but his shoulder was burning and he was beginning to shiver quite violently as the shock set in. He forced himself to bring his body back under control, afraid that the slightest movement might trigger a hideous end to this ordeal. He could imagine the sudden flash, the pain, his leg separated from his body. And there was nothing he could do. His foot was glued to the device that was ticking away, even now, beneath him. He looked around. He noticed that the mine had been placed on top of a ridge, the ground sloping away steeply to a ditch at the bottom. Alex tried to work out the distances. If he threw himself sideways, could he reach the ditch before the mine exploded? And if the force of the blast was above him, would he perhaps escape the worst of it?

The bombing had stopped. Suddenly everything was very quiet. Once again Alex experienced the sense of being completely alone, standing like a scarecrow in the middle of an empty field. He wanted to call out but was afraid to, in case he accidentally shifted his body weight. How long had it been since the man had gone? Five minutes? Ten? And how accurate was the timer anyway? The mine could go off at any moment.

So did he wait? Or did he take his life into his own hands?

Alex made his decision.

He took a deep breath, tensing his body, trying to think of the muscles in his legs as coiled springs that would launch him to safety. His right foot was resting on the mine; the left was on flat ground. That was the one that would have to do most of the work. Alex had to force himself, knowing that he might be making the worst mistake of his life, that seconds from now he could be crippled, in agony.

Do it!

He jumped.

At the very last moment, he changed his mind but continued anyway, launching himself down the slope with all his strength. He thought he felt the mine shudder very slightly as his foot left it. But it hadn't exploded, at least not in the half-second that he had left the ground. Automatically he crossed his arms in front of his face, to protect himself from the fall – and the blast. The slope was rushing past him, a dark streak at the corner of his vision. Then he hit the ditch. Water, cold and muddy, splattered into his face. His shoulder hit something hard. Behind him, there was an explosion. The mine. Clumps of earth and grass rained down on him.

Then nothing. His face was underwater and he pulled his head back, spitting mud. A plume of smoke rose into the night sky. The fuse must have given him three seconds before it detonated the mine. He had taken those three seconds and they had saved him.

He got unsteadily to his feet. Water was dripping from his hair and down his face. His heart was pounding. He felt drained, exhausted. He lost his balance, put a hand out to steady himself and winced as he caught it on the barbed-wire fence. But at least he had found the way out. He rolled underneath and tried to work out which way to go. Seconds later, the question was answered for him. He heard the sound of an engine, saw two beams of light cutting through the trees. His own name was being called out. He hurried forward and found a track.

The four SAS men were in the jeep. This time X-Ray was driving. They were moving slowly through the wood, searching for him. Alex saw that they had left the cool boxes behind, but Sparks had remembered his guitar.

"Alex!"

X-Ray slammed on the brakes and Scooter leapt out of the passenger seat. He looked genuinely concerned, his face white in the glare of the headlamps.

"Are you OK? Jesus! We completely screwed up. We've got to get out of here. We shouldn't be anywhere near this place."

"I told you—" X-Ray began.

"Not now!" Scooter snapped. He grabbed hold of Alex. "As soon as the bombs went off, I knew what had happened. I looked for you but we must have got separated. You look terrible, mate. Are you hurt?"

"No." Alex didn't trust himself to say any more.

"Get in. We'll get you home. I don't know what to say to you. We're complete idiots. We could have got you killed."

This time Alex took the front seat. Scooter climbed in the back with the others and they set off back down the track and out towards the main road. Alex still wasn't sure what had just happened

– how the SAS men had managed to get themselves into this mess. Nor did he care. He allowed the noise of the engine to drift away on the cool night air, and seconds later he was sound asleep.

ON THE ROCKS

Two days later, Alex had put his experiences at Swanbourne behind him. He was sitting outside a café in Sydney, the Opera House on one side, the great stretch of the Harbour Bridge on the other. It was the world's favourite picture postcard view and he had seen it many times. But now he was actually in it, eating vanilla and strawberry ice cream and watching as the Manly ferry came grinding into the quay, scattering the smaller craft. The sun was beating down and the sky was a dazzling blue. It was hard to believe that he was really here.

And he wasn't alone. Jack had joined him the day before, bleary-eyed with jet lag but awake and bursting with excitement the moment she saw him. It had taken her twenty-six hours to get here and Alex knew she would have been worrying all the way. Jack was meant to look after him. She hated it when he was away – and this time he had never been further. As soon as she'd arrived, she had made it clear that all she wanted was to get him on a plane and take him back to London. Yes, it was cold and drizzling there; the English winter had already arrived. Yes, they both deserved a holiday. But it was time to go home.

Jack was also eating ice cream, and although she was twenty-eight she suddenly looked younger with her untidy red hair, lopsided smile and her brightly coloured kangaroo T-shirt. More a big sister than a housekeeper. And above all a friend.

"I don't know why it's taking so long," she was saying. "It's ridiculous. By the time you get back, you'll have missed half the term."

"They said they'd have it this afternoon."

"They should have had it two days ago."

They were talking about Alex's visa. That morning, Jack had received a call at the hotel where they were staying. They had been given an address, a government office in Macquarie Street, just past the old parliament building. The visa would be ready at four o'clock. Alex could pick it up then.

"Could we stay here a couple more days?" Alex asked.

Jack looked at him curiously. "Don't you want to go home?"

"Yes." Alex paused. "I suppose so. But at the same time ... I'm not quite sure I'm ready to go back to school. I've been thinking about it. I'm worried I'm not going to be able to fit in."

"Of course you'll fit in, Alex. You've got lots of friends. They've all been missing you. Once you're back, you'll forget any of this stuff ever happened."

But Alex wasn't so sure. He and Jack had talked about it the evening before. After all he had been through, how could he go back to geography lessons and school lunches and being told off for running too fast down the corridor? The day MI6 had recruited him, they had built a wall between him and his past life and he wondered if there was now any way back.

"I've hardly been to school this year," he muttered. "I'm way behind."

"Maybe we can get Mr Grey to come in this Christmas," Jack suggested. Mr Grey was the teacher who had given Alex extra tuition during the summer. "You got on well with him, and he'd soon help you catch up."

"I don't know, Jack." Alex looked at the ice cream melting on his spoon. He wished he could explain how he felt. He didn't want to work for MI6 again. He was sure of that. But at the same time...

"It's half past three," Jack said. "We ought to get going."

They got up and made their way along the side of the Opera House and up into the Royal Botanic Gardens – the incredible park that seemed to contain the city rather than the other way round. Looking back at the harbour, the bustle of life below and the gleaming skyscrapers stretched out behind, Alex wondered how the Australians had managed to get it all so right. It was impossible not to love Sydney, and despite what Jack had said, he knew he wasn't yet ready to leave.

Together, the two of them made their way up past the Art Gallery of New South Wales and into Macquarie Street, where the parliament building stood, two storeys high, an elegant construction of pink and white that somehow reminded Alex of the ice cream he had just eaten. The address they had been given was just beyond, a modern glass block that was presumably filled with minor government offices. The receptionist already had visitor passes waiting for them and directed them to the fourth floor and a room at the end of a corridor.

"I don't know why they couldn't have just put you on a plane and sent you out of here," Jack grumbled as they left the lift. "It seems a lot of fuss about nothing."

There was a door ahead of them. They walked through without knocking and stopped dead in their tracks. There had obviously been some sort of mistake. Wherever they were, it certainly wasn't a visa office.

Two men were talking to each other in what looked like a library with antique furniture and a Persian rug on a highly polished wooden floor. Alex's immediate impression was that the room didn't belong to the building it was in. A golden Labrador lay curled up on a cushion in front of a fireplace. One of the men was behind a desk. He was the elder of the two, wearing a shirt and jacket and no tie. His eyes were concealed behind designer sunglasses. The other man was standing by the window with his arms folded. He was in his late twenties, thin and fair-haired, dressed in an expensive suit.

"Oh ... I'm sorry," Jack began.

"Not at all, Miss Starbright," the man behind the desk replied. "Please come in."

"We're looking for the visa office," Jack said.

"Sit down. I take it Alex is with you? The question may seem odd, but I'm blind."

"I'm here," Alex said.

"Who are you?" Jack asked. She and Alex had moved further into the room. The younger man came over and closed the door behind them.

"My name is Ethan Brooke. My colleague here is Marc Damon. Thank you very much for coming in, Miss Starbright. Do you mind if I call you Jack? Please – take a seat."

There were two leather chairs in front of the desk. Feeling increasingly uncomfortable, Jack and Alex sat down. The man called Damon walked across and took a third seat at the side. The dog's tail thumped twice against the wooden floor.

"I know you're in a hurry to get back to London," Brooke began. "But let me explain why the two of you are here. The fact of the matter is, we need a little help."

"You want our help?" Jack looked around her. Suddenly it all made sense. "You want Alex." She spoke the words heavily. She knew now who the men were – or at least what they represented. She had met their type before.

"We'd like to put a proposition to Alex," Brooke agreed.

"Forget it. He's not interested."

"Won't you at least listen to what we have to say?" Brooke spread his hands. He looked completely reasonable. He could have been a bank manager advising them on their mortgage, or a family lawyer about to read a will.

"We want the visa."

"You'll have it. As soon as I'm done."

Alex had said nothing. Jack looked at him, then turned to Brooke and Damon with anger in her eyes. "Why can't you people leave him alone?" she demanded.

"Because he's special. In fact, I'd say he's unique. And right now we need him, just for a week or two. But I promise you, Jack. If he's not interested, he can walk out of here. We can have him on a plane tonight. Just give me a minute to explain."

"Who are you?" Alex asked.

Brooke turned towards Damon. "We work for ASIS," the younger man replied. "The Australian Secret Intelligence Service."

"Special Operations?"

"Covert Action. The two are more or less the same. You could say we're the rough equivalent of the outfit Alan Blunt runs in London."

"I've read your file, Alex," Brooke added. "I have to say, I'm impressed."

"What do you want me for?" Alex demanded.

"I'll tell you."

Brooke folded his hands, and to Alex it seemed somehow inevitable, unsurprising even. It had happened to him six times before. Why not again?

"Have you ever heard the term 'snakehead', or '*shetou*'?" Brooke began. There was silence, so he went on. "All right, let me start by saying that the snakehead groups are without doubt the biggest and most dangerous criminal organizations in the world. Compared to them, the Mafia and the triads are amateurs. They have more influence – and they're doing more damage – than even al-Qaeda, but they're not interested in religion. They have no beliefs. All they want is money. That's the bottom line. They're gangsters, but on a huge scale.

"Have you ever bought an illegal DVD? The chances are that it was manufactured and distributed by a snakehead. And the profits they'll have made out of it will have gone straight into one of their other concerns, which you may not find so amusing. Maybe it's drugs or slaves or body parts. You need a new kidney or a heart? The snakeheads operate the biggest market in illegal organs, and they're not fussy about where they get them. Or weapons. There have been at least fifty wars around the world that have used weapons supplied by the snakeheads: shoulder-launched missiles,

AK-47s, that sort of thing. Where do you think terrorists go if they want a bomb or a gun or something nasty and biological that comes in a test tube? Think of it as an international supermarket, Alex. But everything it sells is bad.

"What else can you buy? You name it! Paintings stolen from museums. Diamonds mined illegally using slave labour. Ancient artefacts plundered from Iraq. Elephant tusks or tiger-skin rugs. A few years ago a hundred kids died in Haiti because someone had sold them cough medicine that happened to contain antifreeze. That was a snakehead – and I don't think it offered anyone their money back.

"But the biggest moneymaker for the snakeheads is people smuggling. You probably have no idea how many people there are being smuggled from one country to another all around the globe. These are some of the poorest families in the world, desperate to build themselves a new life in the West. Some of them are fleeing from hopelessness and starvation; others are threatened in their own countries with prison and torture." Brooke paused and looked directly at Alex, fixing him with his sightless eyes. "Half of them are under the age of eighteen," he said. "About five per cent are younger than you – and they're travelling on their own. The lucky ones get picked up by the authorities. What happens to the rest of them ... you don't want to know.

"People smuggling is a huge problem for Australia. We have illegal immigrants coming in from Iraq and Afghanistan. They come in boats from Bali, Flores, Lombok and Jakarta. My country used to welcome immigrants. We were all immigrants ourselves once. That's all changed now – and I have to say the way we treat these people leaves a lot to be desired. But what can we do? The answer is, we have to stop them coming. And to do that, we have to take on the snakeheads, face to face.

"There's one snakehead in particular. It operates throughout Indonesia, and it's more powerful and more dangerous than all the rest. As it happens, we know the name of the man in charge. Major Yu. But that's all we've managed to find out. We don't know what he looks like or where he lives. Twice now we've tried to infiltrate the organization. That is, we put agents inside, pretending to be customers."

"What happened to them?" Jack asked.

"They both died." It was Damon who had answered the question.

"And so now I suppose you're thinking about using Alex."

"We have no idea how our agents were discovered," Brooke went on. It was as if Jack hadn't spoken. "Somehow this man – Yu – seems to know everything we're doing. Either that or he's very careful. The trouble is, these gangs operate under a system known as *guanxi*. Basically, it means everyone knows everyone. They're like a family. And the fact is, a single agent coming in from outside and operating on his own is too obvious. We need to get inside the snakehead in a way that is completely original and also above suspicion."

"A man and a boy," Damon said.

"We have an agent in Bangkok now. We're going to set him up as a refugee from Afghanistan planning to be smuggled into Australia. He'll meet with the snakehead and gather names, faces, phone numbers, addresses – anything he can. But he won't be on his own. He'll be travelling with his son."

"We'll fly you to Bangkok," Damon continued, speaking directly to Alex. "You'll join our agent there and the two of you will be passed down the pipeline back here. And here's the deal. As soon as you're back on Australian soil, we'll send you first class, direct to England. You won't have to do anything, Alex. But you'll provide perfect cover for our man. He'll get the information we need and maybe we'll be able to break up Yu's network once and for all."

"Why Bangkok?" There were a hundred questions Alex could have asked. This was the first one that came to his mind.

"Bangkok is a major centre for the sale of false documents," Damon replied. "In fact, we'd very much like to know who supplies Yu's people with fake passports, export certificates and the rest of it. And now we have a chance. Our agent has been told to wait there until he is contacted. He'll be given the papers he needs and then he'll continue the journey south."

There was a brief silence.

Then Jack Starbright shook her head. "All right," she said. "We've listened to your proposition, Mr Brooke. Now you can listen to my answer. And it's no. Forget it! You said it yourself. These people are dangerous. Two of your spies have already been killed. There's no way I'm going to let Alex get mixed up in that."

"I'd have thought after all Alex has been through, he could make up his own mind," Brooke replied.

"He can make up his own mind. I'm just telling you what he's going to say. The answer's no!"

"There is one thing we haven't mentioned." Brooke rested his hands on the desk. His face gave nothing away but Damon knew what was about to come. His boss was the consummate poker player, only now preparing to show his hand. "I didn't tell you the name of our agent in Bangkok."

"And who is that?" Jack asked.

"You know him, I think. His name is Ash."

Jack sat back, unable to keep the shock out of her eyes. "Ash?" she faltered.

"That's right."

Alex had seen the effect the name had had on her. "Who's Ash?" he demanded.

"You don't know him?" Brooke was enjoying

himself now, though only Damon was aware of it. He turned to Jack. "Maybe you'd like to explain?"

"Ash was someone who knew your dad," Jack muttered.

"He was rather more than that," Brooke corrected her. "Ash was John Rider's closest friend. He was the best man at your parents' wedding, Alex. He's also your godfather."

"My..." Alex couldn't believe what he was hearing. He didn't even know he had a godfather.

"And for what it's worth, he was the last person to see your parents alive," Brooke went on. "He was with them, the morning they died. He was at the airport when they got on the plane for the South of France."

The plane had never arrived. There had been a bomb on board, placed there as an act of revenge by Scorpia. That much Alex knew.

Alex gazed at Jack. "Did you meet him?" He was feeling completely disorientated, as if the ground had just been stolen from under his feet. She looked exactly the same.

"I saw him a few times," she replied. "It was just after I started working for your uncle. Ash came to visit. He was checking up on you. After all, he was your godfather."

"How come you've never mentioned him?"

"He disappeared. You were still very young. He told me he was going away for good and I never saw him again."

"Ash was an agent with MI6," Brooke explained. "That was how he and your father met. They worked together as a team. Your dad even saved his life once – in Malta. You can ask him about that ... if you meet. I'd have thought the two of you would have a lot to talk about."

"How can you do this?" Jack whispered. She was looking at Brooke with utter contempt.

"Ash left MI6 a few months after your parents died, and emigrated here," Brooke continued. "He came with great references so we were happy to take him on at ASIS. He's been with us ever since. Right now he's in Bangkok, about to go undercover – like I said. But there's nobody better placed to pretend to be your father, Alex. I mean, he's almost that already. He'll look after you. And I think you'll find him interesting. What do you say?"

Alex said nothing. He had already made up his mind, but somehow he knew that Brooke wouldn't need to be told. He had figured that out for himself.

"I need time," he said, at length.

"Sure. Why don't you and Jack go and talk about it?" Brooke nodded and Damon produced a white card. He must have had it ready in his pocket from the very start. "Here's a number where you can reach me. We'll need to fly you into Bangkok tomorrow. So maybe you could call me this evening?"

"I know what you're thinking, but you can't possibly go," Jack said. "It's wrong."

Alex and Jack had wandered over to the Rocks, the little cluster of shops and cafés that nestled on the very edge of the harbour, right underneath the bridge. Jack had brought them here purposely. She wanted to mingle with the crowds somewhere bright and ordinary, a world apart from the hidden truths and half-lies of the Australian secret service.

"I think I have to," Alex replied.

And it was true. Earlier that afternoon, he had promised himself that he would never work for MI6 again. But this was different – and not just because it was the Australians that were asking him this time. It was Ash. Ash made all the difference, even though the two of them had never met and it was a name he had only just heard for the first time.

"Ash can tell me who I am," he said.

"Don't you know who you are?"

"Not really, Jack. I thought I knew. When Ian was alive, everything seemed so simple. But then, when I found out the truth about him, it all went wrong. All my life he was training me to be something I never wanted to be. But maybe he was right. Maybe it was what I was always meant to be."

"You think Ash can tell you?"

"I don't know." Alex squinted at Jack. The sunlight was streaming over her shoulders. "When did you meet him?" he asked.

"It was about a month after I started working for your uncle," she said. "At the time, it was just meant to be a vacation job, to support myself while

I was doing my studies. I didn't know anything about spies and I certainly didn't know I'd be sticking with you for ever!" She sighed. "You were about seven years old. Do you really not remember him?"

Alex shook his head.

"He was in London for a few weeks, staying in a hotel. But he came over to the house two or three times. Now I come to think of it, he never did talk to you very much. Maybe he felt awkward with kids. But I got to know him a bit."

"What was he like?"

Jack thought back. "I liked him," she admitted. "In fact, if you want the truth, I even went out with him a couple of times, though he was quite a lot older than me. He was very good-looking. And there was something dangerous about him. He told me he was a deep-sea diver. He was fun to have around."

"Is Ash his real name?"

"It's what he calls himself. A.S.H. are his initials – but he never told me what they stood for."

"And he's really my godfather?"

Jack nodded. "I've seen photos of him at your christening. And Ian knew him too. The two of them were friends. I never knew what he was doing in London but he was keen to check up on you. He wanted to be sure you were OK."

Alex drew a deep breath. "You don't know what it's like, not having parents," he began. "It's never bothered me, because I never knew them. I was so small when they died. But even so, I've often wondered about them. And it sometimes feels like there's a hole in my life, a sort of emptiness. I look back but there's nothing there. Maybe if I spend a bit of time with this man – even if I do have to dress up like an Afghan refugee – it'll fill something in for me."

"But, Alex..." Jack looked at him and he could see she was afraid. "You heard what Brooke said. This could be terribly dangerous. You've been lucky so far, but your luck can't last for ever. These people – the snakehead – they sound horrible. You shouldn't get involved."

"I have to, Jack. Ash worked with my dad. He saw my parents the day they died. I didn't know he existed until today, but now I do, I've got to meet him." Alex forced a smile. "My dad was a spy. My uncle was a spy. And now it turns out I've got a godfather who's a spy. You have to admit, it certainly runs in the family."

Jack rested her hands on Alex's shoulders. Behind them the sun was already setting, reflecting blood red in the water. The shops were beginning to empty. The bridge hung over them, casting a dark shadow.

"Is there anything I can say to stop you?" she asked.

"Yes." Alex looked her straight in the eye. "But please don't."

"All right." She nodded. "But I'll be worried sick about you. You know that. Just make sure you look after yourself. And tell Ash from me that I want you home by Christmas. And maybe this time, just for once, he'll remember to send a card."

Quickly she turned round and continued walking. Alex waited a minute, then followed.

Bangkok. The snakehead. Another mission. The truth was that Alex had always suspected it might happen – but even he hadn't thought it would come so soon.

CITY OF ANGELS?

Twenty-four hours later, Alex touched down at Suvarnabhumi International Airport in Bangkok. Even the name warned him that he had arrived at the gateway to a completely alien world. For all his travels, he had never been to the East. Now, following the nine-hour flight from Sydney, he was here – on his own. Jack had wanted to travel with him but he had decided against it. He'd found it easier to say goodbye to her at the hotel. He knew he needed time to prepare himself for what might lie ahead.

He had met once more with Brooke and Damon the night before. There hadn't been much more to say. Alex was booked into a room at the Peninsula Hotel in Bangkok. A driver would pick him up from the airport and take him there. Ash would meet him as soon as he'd arrived.

"You realize we'll have to disguise you," Brooke said. "You don't look anything like an Afghan."

"And I don't speak their language," Alex added.

"That's not a problem. You're a child and a refugee. No one will be expecting you to say anything."

The flight had seemed endless. ASIS had booked him into business class, but in a way that made him feel all the more alienated and alone. He watched a film, ate a meal and rested. But nobody spoke to him. He was in a strange, metal bubble, surrounded by strangers, being carried once again towards danger and possible death. Alex looked out of the window at the brilliant sunlight bouncing off a seemingly solid carpet of cloud and wondered. Was he making a mistake? He could board another plane at Bangkok and be back in London in twelve hours. But he had made his decision. This wasn't about ASIS or the snakehead.

He was the last person to see your parents alive.

Alex remembered what Brooke had told him. He was about to meet his father's best friend. His god-father. This wasn't just a flight from one country to another. It was a journey into his own past.

The 747 rumbled into its stall. The FASTEN YOUR SEAT BELT signs blinked off and the passengers stood up as one, scrabbling for the overhead lockers. Alex had one small suitcase and quickly passed through immigration and customs and out into the hot, sticky air of the arrivals hall. Suddenly he found himself in a crowd of jabbering, gesticulating people.

"Taxi! Taxi!"

"You want hotel?"

It felt strange emerging from business class into this. He was suddenly back in the noise and chaos of the real world. Down to earth in more senses than one.

And then he saw his name on a placard being held by a Thai man – black-haired, short, casually dressed like almost everyone around him. Alex went over to him.

"Are you Alex? Mr Ash sent me to collect you. I hope you had a good flight. The car is outside."

It was as they made their way out of the airport that Alex noticed the man with the poppy in his buttonhole. It was the poppy that first drew his attention. Of course, it was November. It would soon be Remembrance Day back in England. It was just strange to see any sign of it out here.

The man was wearing jeans and a leather jacket. He was European, in his twenties, with black hair cut short and dark, thoughtful eyes. He had very square features with high cheekbones and thin lips. The man had stopped dead in his tracks and seemed to be staring at something on the other side of the arrivals lounge. It took Alex a moment to realize that the man's attention was actually fixed on him. Did they know each other? He was just asking himself that question when a crowd of people moved between them, making for the exit. When the floor cleared again, the man had gone.

He must have imagined it. He was tired after the long flight. Maybe the man had simply been one of the other passengers on the plane. Alex followed the driver to the car park and a few minutes later they were on the wide, three-lane motorway that led into Bangkok – or, as the Thai people call it, Krung Thep. City of Angels.

Sitting in the back of the air-conditioned car, gazing out of the window, Alex wondered how it had got that name. He certainly wasn't impressed by his first sight of the city, a sprawl of ugly, old-fashioned skyscrapers, blocks of flats piled up on top of each other like discarded boxes, electricity pylons and satellite towers. They stopped at a pay toll where a woman sat in a cramped cubicle, her face hidden behind the white mask that protected her from the traffic fumes. Then they were off again. Alex saw a huge portrait of a man next to the road: black hair, glasses, open-necked shirt. It was painted on the entire side of a building, twenty storeys high, covering both the brickwork and the windows.

"That's our king," the driver explained.

Alex looked again at the portrait. What would it be like, he wondered, to work at a desk inside that office? To pound away at a computer for eight or nine hours a day but to look out at Bangkok through the eyes of a king.

They left the motorway, driving down a ramp into a dense, chaotic world of shrubs and food stalls, traffic jams and policemen at every intersection, their whistles screaming like dying birds. Alex saw tuk-tuks – motorized rickshaws – bicycles and buses that looked as if they had been welded together from a dozen different models. He felt a hollow feeling in his stomach. What was he letting himself in for? How was he going to adapt to a country that was, in every last detail, so different from his own?

Then the car turned a corner. They had entered the driveway of the Peninsula Hotel and Alex learnt something else about Bangkok. It was actually two cities: one very poor and one very rich, living side by side and yet with a great gulf between them. His journey had brought him from one to the other. Now he was passing through a beautifully tended tropical garden. As they drew up at the front entrance, half a dozen men in perfect white uniforms hurried forward to help – one to take the luggage, one to help Alex out, two more bowing to welcome him, two holding open the hotel doors.

The cold embrace of the hotel's air conditioning reached out to welcome him. Alex crossed a wide marble floor towards the reception area, piano music tinkling somewhere in the background, and was handed a garland of flowers by a smiling receptionist. Nobody seemed to have noticed that he was only fourteen. He was a guest; that was all that mattered. His key was already waiting for him. He was shown into a lift, itself the size of a small room. The doors slid shut. Only the pressure in his ears told him that they had begun the journey up.

His room was on the nineteenth floor.

Ten minutes later, he stood in front of a floor-to-ceiling window, looking at the view. His suitcase was on his bed. He had been shown the luxury bathroom, the widescreen TV, the well-stocked fridge and the complimentary basket of exotic fruit. Alex tried to shrug off the heavy fingers of jet lag. He knew he had little enough time to prepare himself for what lay ahead.

The city was spread out on the other side of a wide, brown river that curved and twisted as far as he could see. Skyscrapers towered in the far distance. Nearer by, there were hotels, temples, palaces with perfect lawns and – standing alongside them – shacks and slum houses and warehouses so dilapidated they looked as if they might fall over at any time. All manner of boats were making their way up and down the murky water. Some were modern, carrying coal and iron; some were ferries with strange, curving roofs, like floating pagodas. The nimblest were elongated, long and wafer thin with the driver leaning wearily over the tiller at the stern. The sun was setting, and the sky was huge and grey. It was like looking at a television screen with the colour control turned down.

The telephone rang. Alex went over and picked it up.

"Hello? Is that Alex?" It was a man's voice. Alex could make out a slight Australian accent.

"Yes," he replied.

"You arrived OK, then?"

"Yes, thanks."

"I'm in reception. You feel like a bit of dinner?"

Alex wasn't hungry but that didn't matter. Even though the man hadn't introduced himself, he knew who he was talking to. "I'll come straight down," he said.

He hadn't had time to shower or change after the flight. It would just have to wait. Alex left the room and took the lift back down. It stopped twice on the way, letting people in on the ninth and seventh floors. Alex stood silently in the corner. He was suddenly nervous, though he wasn't quite sure why. Finally they arrived. The lift doors opened.

Ash was standing in the reception area, dressed in a blue linen jacket, a white shirt and jeans. There were plenty of other people around but Alex recognized him instantly, and somehow he wasn't even surprised.

They had met before.

Ash was the soldier in the forest, the man who had told him he was standing on a mine.

"It was all a set-up, wasn't it?" Alex said. "The training exercise. The minefield. All of it."

"Yeah." Ash nodded. "I expect that must make you pretty annoyed."

"You could say that," Alex growled.

There was an eating area just outside the hotel,

softly lit, with the river in front and a long, narrow swimming pool to one side. The two of them were sitting at a table, facing each other. Ash had a Singha beer. He had ordered Alex a fruit cocktail: orange, pineapple and guava blended with crushed ice. It was almost dark now but Alex could still feel the heat of the evening pressing down on him. He realized it was going to take time to get used to the climate in Bangkok. The air was like syrup.

He looked again at his godfather, the man who had known him when he was a baby. Ash was leaning back with his legs stretched out, untroubled by the trick that had been played in the forest near Swanbourne. Out of uniform, with his shirt open and a silver chain glinting around his neck, he looked nothing like a soldier or a spy. He was more like a film star with his curly black hair, rough beard and suntanned skin. Physically he was slim – wiry was the word that sprang to Alex's mind. Fast-moving rather than particularly strong. He had brown eyes that were very dark and Alex guessed he could easily play the part of an Afghan. He certainly didn't look European.

There was something else about him that Alex found harder to place. A certain guarded quality in the eyes, a sense of tension. He might look relaxed but he never would be. He had been touched by something at some time and it would never let him go.

"So why did you do it?" Alex asked.

"It was a test, Alex. Why do you think?" Ash had a soft, lilting voice. The fourteen years he had spent in Australia had given him an accent but Alex could hear the English there too. "We weren't going to use a fourteen-year-old boy – not even you. Not unless we were damn sure you weren't going to panic at the first sign of danger."

"I didn't panic with Drevin. Or with Scorpia..."

"The snakeheads are different. You have no idea what sort of people we're up against. Didn't Brooke tell you? They've already killed two of our agents. The first one came home minus his head. They sent the second back in an envelope. They'd had him cremated to save us the trouble." Ash drank his beer and signalled to the waiter for another. "I had to see for myself that you were up to the job," he went on. "We created a situation that would have terrorized any normal kid. Then we watched how you got on with it."

"I could have been killed." Alex remembered how the first bomb had blown him off his feet.

"You weren't in any real danger. All the missiles were launched with pinpoint accuracy. We knew exactly where you were all the time."

"How?"

Ash smiled. "There was a beacon inside the heel of one of your trainers. Colonel Abbott arranged that while you were asleep. It sent out a signal to the nearest millimetre."

"What about the mine?"

"It had less explosive in it than you probably thought. And it was activated by remote control. I set it off a couple of seconds after you made that dive. You did pretty well, by the way."

"You were watching me all the time."

"Just put it behind you, Alex. It was a test. You passed. That's all that matters."

The waiter arrived with the second beer. Ash lit a cigarette – Alex was surprised to see that he smoked – and blew smoke out into the warm evening air.

"I can't believe we're finally meeting," he said. He examined Alex closely. "You look a hell of a lot like your dad."

"You were close to him."

"Yeah. We were close."

"And my mother."

"I don't want to talk about them, Alex." Ash shifted uncomfortably, then reached out and drank some of his second beer. "Do you mind? It was all a long time ago. My life's moved on since then."

"It's the only reason I'm here," Alex said.

There was a long silence. Then Ash smiled briefly. "How's that housekeeper of yours?" he asked. "Jack what's-her-name. Is she still with you?"

"Yes. She said hello."

"She was an attractive girl. I liked her. I'm glad she stuck by you."

"You didn't."

"Well ... I moved on." Ash paused. Then suddenly he leant forward. His face was deadly serious and Alex saw that this was a tough, cold-hearted man and that he was going to have to watch himself when they were together.

"All right. This is how we're going to play it," he began. "You're in this smart, luxury hotel because I wanted to ease you in. But tomorrow that all comes to an end. We're going to have breakfast and then we're going up to your room and you're going to become an Afghan boy, a refugee. We're going to change the way you look, the way you walk and even the way you smell. And then we're going out there..." He pointed across the river. "You enjoy your bed tonight, Alex, because where you sleep tomorrow night is going to be very different. And trust me. You're not going to like it."

He lifted the cigarette and inhaled. Grey smoke curled out of the corner of his mouth.

"We should make contact with the snakehead in the next few days," he went on. "I'll explain all that tomorrow. But this is what you've got to understand. You do nothing and you say nothing unless I tell you. You play dumb. And if I think the situation is getting out of hand, if I think you're in danger, you'll clear out. With no argument. Do you understand?"

"Yes." Alex was taken aback. This wasn't what he had expected. It wasn't what he'd flown five thousand miles to hear.

Ash softened. "But I'll make you this promise. We're going to be spending a lot of time together, and when I feel I know you better, when the time is right, I'll tell you everything you want to know. About your father. About what happened in Malta. About your mother and about you. The only thing I'll never talk to you about is the way they died. I was there and I saw it and I don't want to remember it. Is that OK with you?"

Alex nodded.

"Right. Then let's get some food in us. I forgot to mention – the stuff you'll be eating from now on may not be to your taste either. And you can tell me a bit about yourself. I'd like to know what school you go to and if you have a girlfriend, and things like that. Let's enjoy the evening. There may not be a lot of fun ahead."

Ash picked up his menu and Alex did the same. But before he could read it, a movement caught his eye. It was just chance really. The hotel had a private ferry that ran between the two banks of the river – a wide, spacious boat with antique chairs placed at intervals on a polished wooden floor. It had just arrived, and it was the roar of the engine going into reverse that had made Alex look up.

A man was just climbing aboard. Alex thought he recognized him, and his suspicion was confirmed when the man turned round and looked purposefully in his direction. The poppy had gone but it was the man from the airport. Alex was sure of it.

A coincidence? The man hurried on board, disappearing beneath the canopy as if anxious to get out of sight, and Alex knew that there was no chance about it. The man had spotted him in the arrivals lounge and followed him here.

Alex wondered if he should mention it to Ash. Almost at once he decided against it. It was impossible for the snakehead to know that he was here, and if he made a fuss, if Ash decided he had been compromised, he might be sent home before the mission had even begun. No. Much better to keep quiet. If he saw the man a third time, then he would speak out.

So Alex said nothing. He didn't even watch as the ferry began its crossing back to the other side. Nor did he hear the click of the camera with its special night scope and long-distance lens trained on him as his picture was taken, again and again, in the dwindling light.

FATHER AND SON

The next morning, Alex ate the best breakfast of his life. He had a feeling he was going to need it. The hotel offered a hot and cold buffet that included just about every cuisine – French, English, Thai, Vietnamese – with dishes ranging from eggs and bacon to stir-fried noodles. Ash joined him but spoke little. He seemed to be deep in thought, and Alex wondered if he was already having reservations about what lay ahead.

"You've had enough?" he asked as Alex finished his second croissant.

Alex nodded.

"Then let's go up to your room. Mrs Webber will be here soon. We'll wait for her there."

Alex had no idea who Mrs Webber was and it didn't seem that Ash wanted to tell him. The two of them went back up to the nineteenth floor. Ash hung the DO NOT DISTURB SIGN on the door and pointed Alex to a seat next to the window. He sat down opposite.

"OK," he began. "Let me tell you how this works. Two weeks ago, working with the Pakistani authorities, ASIS managed to pick up a father and a son heading into India on their way here. We interrogated them and discovered they'd paid the snakehead four thousand American dollars to smuggle them into Australia.

"Originally we were just going to send them back. But now we've decided to use them. The father's called Karim; the son is Abdul. Get used to the names, Alex, because from now on that's you and me. Karim and Abdul Hassan. We're taking their place, which means staying here in Bangkok. They were given an address and told to wait there until they were contacted by a man called Sukit."

"Who's he?"

"It took us a while to find out. But it turns out we're talking about a Mr Anan Sukit. He works for Major Yu. One of his lieutenants, you might say. Very high up. Very dangerous. It means we're one step down the pipeline, Alex. We're on our way."

"So we wait for him to get in touch."

"Exactly."

"What about the real Abdul?" Alex asked. He wondered how he could pretend to be someone he had never even met.

"You don't need to know much about him or his father. The two of them are Hazaras – a minority group within Afghanistan. The Hazaras have been persecuted for centuries. They get the worst education and the poorest jobs – in fact, most people think of them as hardly better than animals. *Kofr* – that's the word they use for them. It means 'infidel' and in Afghanistan it's the worst four-letter word you can call anyone."

"So where did they get their money?" Alex asked.

"They had a business in Mazar-e-Sharif which they managed to sell just before it was taken from them. They hid out in the Hindu Kush until they made contact with a local agent for the snakehead, paid the money and began their journey south."

"I don't suppose I look anything like an Afghan," Alex said. "What do these Hazara people look like?"

"Most of them are Asian – Mongol or Chinese. But not all. In fact, a lot of them managed to survive in Afghanistan precisely because they didn't look too Eastern. Anyway, you don't need to worry. Mrs Webber will take care of that."

"How about language?"

"You won't talk. Ever. You're going to pretend to be a simpleton. Just stare into the corner and keep your mouth shut. Try and look scared – as if I'm about to beat you. Maybe I will, from time to time. Just to make us look authentic."

Alex wasn't sure if Ash was being serious or not.

"I speak Dari," Ash went on. "That's the majority language in Afghanistan and it's the language the snakehead will use. I speak a few words of Hazaragi too, but we shouldn't need them. Just remember. Never open your mouth. If you do, you'll kill us both."

Ash stood up. While he had been talking, he had been grim – almost hostile. But now he turned to Alex with something close to desperation in his dark brown eyes. "Alex..." He paused, scratching at his beard. "Are you sure you want to do this? ASIS has got nothing to do with you. People smuggling and all the rest of it – you should be at school. Why don't you just go home?"

"It's a bit late now," Alex said. "I agreed. And I want you to tell me about my dad."

"Is that the main reason you agreed to this?"

"It's the only reason."

"I don't think I could forgive myself if anything happened to you. I'd be dead if it wasn't for your father. That's the truth of it." Ash looked away, as if trying to avoid the memory. "One day I'll tell you about it ... Malta, and what happened after Yassen Gregorovich had finished with me. But I'll tell you this right now. John wouldn't thank me for getting you into trouble. So if you'll take my advice, you'll call Brooke. Tell him you've changed your mind. And get out now."

"I'm staying," Alex said. "But thanks anyway."

In fact, what Ash had just said – the mention of Yassen Gregorovich – had only made Alex determined to learn more. Suddenly things were beginning to come together.

Alex knew that his father, John Rider, had pretended to be an enemy agent, working for Scorpia. When MI6 wanted him back, they had arranged for him to be "captured". That had been in Malta. It had all been a set-up. And Yassen Gregorovich had been there. Yassen was an international assassin and Alex had met him fourteen years later – first when he was working for Herod Sayle, a second time inside the evil empire of Damian Cray. Yassen was dead now but it seemed that he was still destined to be part of Alex's life. Ash had met him in Malta. And whatever had happened on that island was part of the story that Alex wanted to know.

"You're sure?" Ash asked him one last time.

"I'm sure," Alex said.

"Very well." Ash nodded gravely. "Then I'd better teach you this: *Ba'ad az ar tariki, roshani ast.* It's an old Afghan proverb, and there may come a time when you need to remember it. 'After every darkness, there is light.' I hope it will be true for you."

There was a knock at the door.

Ash went over and opened it and a short, rather dumpy woman walked in, carrying a suitcase. She could have been a retired matron or perhaps a very old-fashioned schoolteacher. She was wearing an olive-green two-piece suit and heavy stockings that only emphasized the fact that she had very shapeless legs. Her hair hung loose with no particular colour or style. Her face could have been made of putty. She was wearing no make-up. There was a single brooch – a silver daisy – pinned to her lapel.

"How are you doing, Ash?" She smiled as she came in and that, along with her broad Australian accent, seemed to bring her to life.

"Good to see you, Cloudy," Ash replied. He closed the door. "This is Mrs Webber, Alex," he explained. "She works for ASIS – a specialist in disguise. Her name is Chloe but we call her Cloudy. We think it suits her better. Cloudy Webber, meet Alex Rider."

The woman stumped over to Alex and examined him. "Hmm..." she muttered disapprovingly. "Mr Brooke must need his head examined if he thinks we're going to get away with this one. But I'll see what I can do." She heaved the suitcase onto the bed. "Let's have all those clothes off you, boy. T-shirt, boxers, the lot. The first thing we're going to start with is your skin."

"Wait a minute—" Alex began.

"For heaven's sake!" the woman exploded. "You think I'm going to see anything I haven't seen before?" She turned to Ash, who was watching. "It's the same for you, Ash. I don't know what you're grinning about. You may look a bit more like an Afghan than him, but I'm going to need all your clothes too."

She unzipped the suitcase and took out half a dozen plastic bottles filled with various dark liquids. Next came a hairbrush, a vanity bag and several tubes that might have contained toothpaste. The rest of the case was packed with clothes that looked – and smelled – as if they had come off a skip.

"The clothes are all from Oxfam," she explained. "Donated in England and picked up in the market in Mazar-e-Sharif. I'll give you two sets each, which is all you'll need: you'll wear them day and night. Ash, go and run a bath." She unscrewed one of the bottles. The smell – seaweed and white spirit – reached Alex even on the other side of the room. "Cold water!" she added sharply.

In the end she let Alex take a bath on his own. She had mixed two bottles of brown dye with half a bath of cold water. Alex was instructed to lie in it for ten minutes, submerging both his face and his hair. He was shivering by the time he was allowed out, and he didn't dare look in the mirror as he dried himself – but he noticed that the hotel towels now looked as if they'd been dragged through a sewer. He pulled on a pair of ragged, shapeless boxers and came out.

"That's better," Mrs Webber muttered. She noticed the raw scar just above his heart. It was where Alex had been shot and nearly killed by a sniper following his encounter with Scorpia. "That might be useful too," she added. "A lot of Afghan boys have got bullet wounds. Together, the two of you make quite a pair."

Alex didn't know what she meant. He glanced at Ash – and then he understood. Ash was just pulling on a loose, short-sleeved shirt and for a moment his chest and stomach were exposed. He too had a scar – but it was much worse than Alex's, a distinct line of white, dead skin that snaked across his belly and down below the waistline of his trousers. Ash turned away, buttoning up the shirt, but he was too late. Alex had seen the terrible injury. It was a stab wound. He was sure of that. He wondered who had been holding the knife.

"Come and sit down, Alex," Mrs Webber said. She had produced a tarpaulin which she had spread underneath a chair. "Let me deal with your hair."

Alex did as he was told and for the next few minutes he heard only the click of scissors and watched as uneven clumps of his hair tumbled to the floor. From the way she worked, he doubted that Mrs Webber had received her training in a London salon. A sheep-shearing farm was more likely. When she had finished cutting, she opened one of the tubes and smeared a thick, greasy ointment over his head. Finally she stepped back.

"He looks great," Ash said.

"The teeth still need work. They'd give him away in a minute."

There was another tube of paste for his teeth. She rubbed it in, using her finger. Lastly she produced two small plastic caps. They were both the size of a tooth but one was grey and one was black.

"I'm going to glue these in," Mrs Webber warned him.

Alex opened his mouth and allowed her to fix the fake teeth into place. He grimaced. His mouth no longer felt like his own.

"You'll notice them for a day or two but then you'll forget them," she said. She stepped back. "There! I'm all done. Why don't you get dressed and take a look at yourself?"

"Cloudy, you're damn good," Ash muttered.

Alex pulled on a faded red T-shirt and a pair of jeans – both of them dirty and full of holes. Then he went back into the bathroom and stood in front of the full-length mirror. He gasped. The boy he was looking at certainly wasn't him. He was olive-skinned with hair that was short, dark brown and matted in thick strands. Somehow the clothes made him look thinner than he really was. He opened his mouth and saw that two of his teeth seemed to have rotted and the rest were ugly and discoloured.

Mrs Webber came in behind him. "You won't need to worry about the skin colour for two weeks," she said. "Not unless you bath – and I don't think you'll be doing that. You'll have to check on the hair and teeth every five or six days. I'll make sure Ash has plenty of supplies."

"It's amazing," Ash said. He was standing at the door.

"I've got some trainers for you," Mrs Webber added. "You won't need socks. I doubt a refugee boy would wear any."

She went back into the bedroom and produced

a pair of trainers that were stained and torn. Alex tried to slip them on.

"They're too small," he said.

Mrs Webber frowned. "I can cut a hole for your toes."

"No. I can't wear them."

She scowled at him, but even she could see that the trainers were far too small. "All right." She nodded. "You can hang on to your own. Just give me a minute."

She dug around in the suitcase and produced a razor, some old paint and another bottle of some sort of chemical. Two minutes later, Alex's own trainers looked as if they'd been thrown away ten years before. As he slipped them on, she set to work on Ash. He too had completely changed. He didn't need to dye his skin, and his beard would have suited a Hazara tribesman. But his hair had to be hacked around and he needed new clothes as well. It was strange, but by the time she had finished, Alex and Ash really could have been father and son. Poverty had brought them closer together.

Mrs Webber packed all the clothes that Alex and Ash had been wearing into her suitcase. She zipped her bag shut and straightened up. She jabbed a finger in Ash's direction.

"You look after Alex," she commanded. "I've already had words with Mr Brooke. Sending a boy this age into the field: I don't think it's right. Just you make sure he comes back in one piece."

"I'll look after him," Ash promised.

"You'd better. Take care, Alex!"

And with that, she was gone.

Ash turned to Alex. "How are you feeling?"

"Grimy."

"It's going to get worse. Are you ready? It's time we left."

Alex moved towards the door.

"We'll take the service lift," Ash said. "And we'll find the back way out. If anyone sees us looking like this in the Peninsula Hotel, we'll be arrested."

The driver who had met Alex at the airport was waiting for them outside the hotel, and he took them over the river and then upstream towards Chinatown. Alex felt the air conditioning blowing cold against his skin and knew that it was a luxury he wasn't going to enjoy again for a while. The car dropped them off at a corner, and at once the heat, the grime and the noise of the city hit him. He was sweating before the door was even closed. Ash dragged a small battered case out of the boot and that was it. Suddenly they were on their own.

Bangkok's Chinatown was like nowhere Alex had ever been before. When he looked up, it seemed to have no sky – all the light had been blocked out by billboards, banners, electric cables and neon signs: TOM YUM KUNG RESTAURANT. THAI MASSAGE. SENG HONG DENTAL CLINIC (GREAT SMILE START HERE). The pavements were equally cluttered, every inch of them taken up by stalls spilling food and cheap clothes and electronics into the street. There were people everywhere, hundreds of them, weaving their way between the traffic, which seemed frozen in an endless, diesel-infested jam.

"This way," Ash muttered, keeping his voice low. From now on, whenever he spoke in English, he would make sure he wasn't overheard.

They pushed their way into the chaos, and in the next few minutes Alex passed vegetables that he had never seen before and meats he hoped he would never see again: hearts and lungs bubbling in green soup and brown intestines spilling out of their cauldrons as if trying to escape. Every scent on the planet seemed to be mixed together. Meat and fish and rubbish and sweat – every step brought another smell.

They walked for about ten minutes until they came to an opening between a restaurant – with a few plastic tables and a single glass counter displaying plastic replicas of the food it served – and a paint works. Here at last was an escape from the main road. A soiled, narrow alleyway led down between two blocks of flats piled up on top of one another as if thrown there at random. There was a miniature altar at the entrance, the incense adding another smell to Alex's collection. Further along, two cars had been parked next to a dozen crates of empty Pepsi bottles, a pile of old gas canisters and a row of tables and chairs. A Chinese woman was sitting cross-legged in the gutter, fixing ribbons to baskets of exotic fruit. Alex remembered the complimentary fruit basket in his hotel room. Maybe this was where it had come from.

"This is the place," Ash said.

It was the address that Karim Hassan and his son had been given by the snakehead. This was where they were expected to stay.

All the flats opened directly onto the alley and Alex could see straight in. There were no doors or curtains. In one front room, a Chinese man sat smoking at a table, dressed in shorts and glasses, his huge stomach bulging over his knees. In another, a whole family were eating lunch, crouching on the floor with chopsticks. They came to a room that looked derelict but was occupied. An old woman was standing beside a stove. Ash signalled to Alex to wait, then went over and spoke to her, relying on sign language as much as words and waving a sheet of paper in front of her face.

She understood and pointed to a staircase at the back. Ash grunted something in Dari and, pretending to understand, Alex hurried forward.

The stairs were made of cement with pools of murky water on at least half of them. Alex followed Ash to the third floor and a single door with no handle. Ash pushed it open. On the other side was a bare room with a metal bed, a spare mattress on the floor, a sink, a toilet and a grimy window. There was no carpet and no light. As Alex walked in, the biggest cockroach he had ever seen climbed over the side of the bed and scuttled across the wall.

"This is it?" Alex muttered.

"This is it," Ash said.

Outside in the alleyway, the man who had followed them all the way from the hotel made a note of the building. As he turned away he took out a mobile phone and dialled a number. By the time he had been connected he had disappeared into the crowd.

FIRST CONTACT

"Suppose they don't come," Alex said.

"They'll come."

"How much longer do you think we're going to have to wait?"

They had been living in Chinatown for nearly three days and Alex was feeling hot, frustrated ... and bored. Ash wouldn't let him have a newspaper or a book in English. There was always the chance that he might be caught reading it by someone entering the room. Nor was he able to see very much of Bangkok. There was no way of knowing when the snakehead might show up and they couldn't risk being out.

But Alex had been allowed to spend a couple of hours early each morning wandering on his own through the streets. It amused him that nobody treated him like a tourist – indeed, tourists stepped aside to avoid him. Mrs Webber had done her job well. He looked like a street urchin from somewhere far away, and after more than fifty hours without a shower or a bath – without even changing his clothes – he imagined he could be smelled long before he could be seen.

Slowly he managed to get to grips with the city, the way the shops and the houses, the pavements and the streets, all tumbled into each other, the clammy heat, the never-ending noise and movement. There seemed to be a surprise round every corner. A cripple with withered legs, scuttling past on his hands like a giant spider. A temple sprouting out of nowhere like an exotic flower. Bald-headed monks in their bright orange robes, moving in a crowd.

He also learnt a little more about Ash.

Ash slept badly. He had given Alex the bed and taken the mattress for himself, but sometimes in the night he would begin muttering and then jerk awake. He would clasp his hand to his stomach, and Alex knew that he was remembering the time he had been stabbed and that it was hurting him even now.

"Why did you become a spy?" Alex asked one morning.

"It seemed like a good idea at the time," Ash growled. He hated being asked questions and seldom gave straightforward answers. But that day he was in a better mood. "I was approached while I was in the army."

"By Alan Blunt?"

"No. He was there when I joined, but he wasn't

in the top spot. I was recruited a short while after your dad. I'll tell you why he joined, if you like."

"Why?"

"He was a patriot." Ash grimaced. "He really thought he had a duty to serve queen and country."

"Don't you?"

"I did ... once."

"So what happened? What made you change your mind?"

"It was a long time ago." Ash had a way of cutting off a conversation if he didn't want to say more. Alex had come to learn that when that happened, there was no point trying to go on. Ash could wrap silence around him like a coat. It was infuriating but he knew he would just have to wait. Ash would talk in his own time.

And then, on the fourth day, the snakehead came.

Alex had just got back with food from the local market when he heard the stamp of feet on the concrete steps. Ash threw him a look of warning and swung himself off the bed just as the door crashed open and one of the ugliest men Alex had ever seen walked into the room.

He was short, wearing a suit that looked as if it had shrunk in the wash to fit him. He was bald and unshaven so that both the top and bottom of his head were covered in a thin black stubble. On the other hand, he didn't seem to have any eyebrows – as if his skin were too thick and pock-marked to grow through. His mouth was impossibly wide, like an open wound, with as many gaps as teeth. Worst of all, he had no ears. Alex could see the discoloured lumps of flesh that remained. The rest had at some time been cut off.

This had to be Anan Sukit. There was a second man with him, dressed in a white T-shirt and jeans, carrying a camera – a clunky wooden box that could have come out of an antique shop. A third man followed. He looked similar to Ash – presumably an Afghan brought along to translate. Alex had quickly sat down in the corner. He glanced at the three men but tried not to show too much interest, as if he didn't want to be noticed himself.

Sukit snapped a few words at the translator, who then spoke to Ash. Ash replied in Dari and a three-way conversation began. As it continued, Alex noticed Sukit examining him. The snakehead lieutenant had tiny pupils which moved ceaselessly, darting left and right. The cameraman had started his work, and Alex sat still as several shots were taken of him. Then it was Ash's turn. He had already explained to Alex what sort of papers would be prepared. Passports, possibly with visas for Indonesia. A police arrest form for Ash. A hospital report showing that he had been injured during questioning. Perhaps an old membership card for the Communist Party. All these things would help them get refugee status once they arrived in Australia.

The photographer finished but the discussion went on. Alex became aware that something was wrong. Sukit nodded in his direction a couple of times; he seemed to be making some sort of demand. Ash was arguing, and he looked unhappy. Alex heard his name – Abdul – mentioned several times.

Then, suddenly, Anan Sukit walked over to him. He was sweating and his skin smelled of garlic. Without warning, he reached down and dragged Alex to his feet. Ash stood up and shouted something. Alex couldn't understand a word that was being said but he did what Ash had told him and stared with unfocused eyes as if he were a simpleton. Sukit slapped him, twice, on each side of his face. Alex cried out. It wasn't just the pain. It was the casual violence, the shock of what had happened. Ash let loose a torrent of words. He seemed to be pleading. Sukit spoke one last time. Ash nodded. Whatever had been demanded, he'd agreed. The three men turned and left the room.

Alex waited until he was sure they had gone. His cheeks were stinging. "I take it that was Anan Sukit?" he muttered.

"That was him."

"What happened to his ears?"

"A gang fight five years ago. Maybe I should have mentioned it to you before. Someone cut them off."

"He's lucky he doesn't need glasses." Alex

rubbed the side of his face with a grimy hand. "So what was all that about?" he asked.

"I don't know. I don't understand..." Ash was deep in thought. "They're getting the papers for us. They'll be ready this evening."

"That's good. But why did he hit me?"

"He made a demand. I refused. So he got angry – and he took it out on you. I'm sorry, Alex." Ash ran a hand through his curly dark hair. He looked shaken by what had just taken place. "I didn't want him to hurt you, but there was nothing I could do."

"What did he want?"

Ash sighed. "Sukit insisted that you collect the papers. Not me. He just wants you."

"Why?"

"He didn't say. He told me they'd pick you up at Patpong at seven o'clock this evening. You've got to be on your own. If you're not there, we can forget it. The deal's off."

Ash fell silent. He had lost control of the situation and he knew it.

Alex wasn't sure how to respond. His first encounter with the snakehead had been short and unpleasant. The question was, what did they want with him? Had they seen through his disguise? If he turned up at this place – Patpong – they could bundle him into a car and he might never be seen again.

"If they wanted to kill you, they could have

done it here and now," Ash said. It was as if he'd read Alex's thoughts. "They could have killed both of us."

"Do you think I should go?"

"I can't make that decision, Alex. That's up to you."

But if he didn't go, there would be no forged papers, no way for Ash to find out where they were being manufactured. Nor would the two of them be able to continue down the pipeline. The mission would be over before it had even begun. And Alex would have learnt nothing from Ash – nothing about his father, about Malta, about Yassen Gregorovich.

It was a risk. But it was one worth taking.

"I'll do it," Alex said.

Patpong showed Alex another side of Bangkok – and not one that he wanted to see. It was a tangle of bars and strip clubs where backpackers and businessmen gathered to drink the night away. Through the doorways he glimpsed half-naked dancers writhing in time to Western pop music. Fat men in floral shirts strolled past with Thai girlfriends. The neon lights flickered and the music pounded out, and the air was thick with the smell of alcohol and cheap perfume. It was the last place on earth that a fourteen-year-old English boy would want to find himself, and Alex was feeling distinctly uncomfortable, standing at the entrance to the main square. But he'd only been there a few minutes when a beaten-up black Citroën pulled over with two men inside. He recognized one of them. The man in the passenger seat had been carrying the camera and had taken the pictures of him and Ash.

So this was it. He had come to Thailand to investigate the snakehead and now he was delivering himself to them with no weapons, no gadgets – nothing to help him if things went wrong. Were they simply going to hand over the papers as promised? Somehow he doubted it. But it was too late for second thoughts. He climbed into the back of the car. The seat was plastic – and it was torn. Furry dice swung beneath the driver's mirror.

Nobody spoke to him – but then, of course, they didn't know his language. Ash had warned him not to say anything, no matter what happened. One word of English would mean an immediate death sentence for both of them. He would pretend he was simple, that he understood nothing at all. If things got out of hand, he would try to break away.

The Citroën joined the sluggish flow of traffic and suddenly they were surrounded by cars, lorries, buses and tuk-tuks. As always, everyone was hooting at everyone else. The heat of the evening only intensified the noise and the smell of exhaust fumes that hung thick in the air.

They drove for about thirty minutes. It was dark and Alex had no idea in which direction they were heading. He tried to pick out a few landmarks – a neon sign, a skyscraper with a strange gold dome on the roof, a hotel. Part of his job was to find out as much about the snakehead as he could, and the following day he might have to show Ash exactly where he'd been taken. The car turned off the main road and suddenly they were travelling down a narrow alleyway between two high walls. Alex was liking this less and less. He had the feeling that he was delivering himself into some sort of trap. Sukit had said he would hand over the papers but Alex didn't believe him. There had to be another reason for all this.

And then they broke out and he saw the river in front of him, the water black and empty but for a single rice barge making its way home. In the far distance, a tower block that he recognized caught his eye. It was the Peninsula Hotel, where he had spent his first night in Bangkok. It was less than half a mile upstream but it might as well have belonged to a different world. The car slowed down. They had come right to the river's edge. The driver turned off the engine and they got out.

The smell of sewage. That was what hit him first: thick, sweet and heavy. The surface of the water was covered with a layer of rotting vegetables and rubbish that rocked back and forth with the current like a living carpet. One of the men pushed him, hard, in the small of his back and Alex made his way over to a broken-down jetty where a boat was waiting to ferry them across, another hard-faced Thai man at the rudder. Alex climbed in. The other men followed.

They set off. The moon had risen, and out in the open everything was suddenly bright. Ahead of him Alex could see their destination. There was a long, three-storey building with a green painted sign advertising it to any passing river traffic: CHADA TRADING COMPANY. Alex didn't like the look of it one bit.

The building was on the very edge of the river, half falling into it, propped up on a series of concrete posts that held it about two metres above the water. It was made of wood and corrugated iron: a slanting, leaning assembly of roofs, verandas, balconies and walkways that looked as if it had been hammered together by a child. It seemed to have few doors and fewer windows. As they drew closer, Alex heard a sound: a low shouting that suddenly rose up like the noise of a crowd at a football match. It was coming from inside.

The boat arrived. A ladder led up to a landing platform and once again Alex felt a fist jabbing into his lower back. It seemed to be the only way these people knew how to communicate. He got unsteadily to his feet and grabbed the ladder. As he did so, he heard a splash and saw a streak of movement out of the corner of his eye. Something was living in the dark space underneath the building. There was another roar from inside and the chime of a bell. How had he got himself into this? Alex gritted his teeth and climbed up.

He went through a door and found himself in a narrow corridor that sloped down with doorways on each side. Naked bulbs dangled at intervals, throwing out a damp, yellow light. The whole place smelled of the river. Halfway down they stopped at one of the doors, which was thrown open to reveal a room that was like a cell, a couple of metres square with a tiny barred window, a bench and a table. There was a pair of brightly coloured shorts lying on the bench. Camera Man – Alex didn't know his name – picked up the shorts and spat out a sentence in Thai. This time the meaning was clear.

The door slammed shut. There was another roar from somewhere near by, the sound echoing outwards. Alex picked up the shorts. They were made of silk, recently laundered, but there were still dark spots embedded in the material. Old bloodstains. Alex clamped down the rising sense of fear. He looked at the window, but there was no way he was going to be able to climb out. He had no doubt the men were standing guard on the other side of the door. He heard the whine of a mosquito and slapped it against the side of his head. He began to undress.

Ten minutes later, they led him further along the corridor to a flight of steps that seemed to have collapsed in on itself like a house of cards. Alex was now wearing the shorts and nothing else.

They started high on his body, above the waist, and came down to his knees. They were the kind worn for a boxing or wrestling match. Which of them was it going to be? Or was he being led towards something worse than either?

He could hear music playing. The crackle of a loudspeaker and a stream of words, amplified, all in Thai. Laughter. The soft babble of many people talking. At last he emerged into a scene that was like nothing he had ever experienced before – and something he would never forget.

It was an arena, circular in shape with dozens of narrow pillars holding up the ceiling, a raised boxing ring in the middle and wooden seating slanting up around the sides. It was lit by neon strips that dangled on chains and there were twenty or thirty fans turning slowly, trying to redistribute the hot, sticky air. Thai music was blaring out of speakers and, bizarrely, there were old television sets facing outwards, each one showing a different programme.

The ring itself was surrounded by a wire fence which had been built to keep either the players in or the audience out. There must have been about four hundred people in the room, chattering excitedly among themselves as they swapped bright yellow slips of paper. Alex had read somewhere that betting was illegal in Thailand but he recognized at once what was going on here. He had arrived just at the end of a fight. A young man was being dragged feet first across the ring, his arms splayed out, his shoulders painting a red streak along the canvas as he was hauled away. And the members of the audience who had bet on his opponent were collecting their winnings.

Alex was at the very back of the arena. As he arrived, another man – dressed like him in shorts – was led down to the ring, his entire body taut with fear. Seeing him, the audience laughed and applauded. More yellow betting slips changed hands. Someone put a hand on Alex's shoulder and pushed him down onto a plastic seat. There was a crack in the floor and he caught a glimpse of silver, the river water lapping at the concrete posts underneath. He was sweating and the mosquitoes had picked up his scent. He could hear them right inside his ear. His skin crawled as he was bitten again and again.

The new challenger had passed through the audience and reached the wire fence. Someone had placed a string of flowers around his neck, and he looked as if he were about to be sacrificed. It occurred to Alex that in a sense he was. Two burly Thai men led him through an opening in the fence and helped him climb into the ring. They forced him to bow to the audience. Then, in the far corner, the champion appeared.

He wasn't big – but he emanated power and speed. Alex could see every single muscle on his body. They were locked together like metal plates and he didn't have a single spare ounce of fat.

His hair, very black, was cut short. His eyes were black too. He had a boy's face, completely smooth, but Alex guessed he was in his mid twenties. His name – Sunthorn – was written in white letters on his shorts. He bowed to the audience and danced on his feet, raising his fists to acknowledge their applause.

The challenger awaited his fate. The flower garland had been removed and the other men had left the ring. The music stopped. A bell rang.

At once Alex understood what he was seeing. He had been expecting the worst and this was it. Muay Thai, also known as the science of eight limbs, one of the most aggressive and dangerous martial arts in the world. Alex had learnt karate but he knew that it was a world apart from Muay Thai, which permitted strikes by the fists, elbows, knees and feet with no fewer than twenty-four targets – from the top of the head to the rear calf – on your opponent. And this was a dirty, illegal version. Neither of the fighters had hand wraps, shin pads or abdomen protectors. The fight would continue until one of them was carried out unconscious – or worse.

Alex watched the first round with a mixture of fascination and horror, knowing that he was going to be next. The fight had begun with both men weaving around, weighing up each other's weaknesses. Sunthorn had struck out a few times, first with a right side elbow attack, then twisting his body round in a fast knee strike. But the challenger was faster than he looked, dodging both blows and even trying a counter-kick, slicing his left foot into the air and missing Sunthorn's neck by centimetres, a move that sparked a roar of excitement from the crowd.

But then, at the end of the first round, he made his fatal mistake. He had allowed his guard to drop, as if waiting for the bell. Suddenly Sunthorn lashed out, a rear leg push kick that slammed into the other man's chest, winding him and almost throwing him off his feet. It was only the chime of the bell a second later that saved him. He staggered into the corner, where someone forced a bottle of water between his lips and flannelled down his face. But he was barely conscious. The next round wouldn't last long.

In the brief interval, more music blasted out of the speakers and the televisions flickered back on. Yellow slips were exchanged and Alex noticed people gesturing wildly, angrily tapping their watches. He was feeling sick. He realized now that the spectators weren't betting on who was going to win the fight. With Sunthorn in the ring, there could be no doubt of that. They were betting on how long a fighter could last against him.

The bell rang for the next round, and as expected it was all over very quickly. The challenger moved forward as if he knew he was walking to his execution. Sunthorn examined him with a cruel smile then finished the fight in the most vicious way he could: a kick to the stomach followed by a second, much harder kick straight into the face. A great flower of blood erupted into the ring. The audience howled. The challenger crashed down on his back and lay still. Sunthorn danced around him, waving his fists in triumph. The cleaners climbed into the ring to clear away the mess.

And now it was Alex's turn.

He was suddenly aware of a man leaning over him – a weird, stretched-out face like a reflection in a fairground mirror. It was Anan Sukit. The snakehead lieutenant spoke to him first in Thai, then in another language. Once again, Alex smelled the stale scent of garlic. Sukit paused. Alex stared straight ahead, as if he hadn't even heard what had just been said. Sukit leant forward. He said something in bad French. Then he repeated it in English.

"You fight, or I kill you."

Alex had to force himself to pretend that he hadn't understood. The man couldn't possibly have known who he was or where he came from. He was simply saying the same thing in as many languages as possible. And finally he used the most effective language of all, grabbing Alex by the hair and pulling him out of his seat and then propelling him down the aisle towards the ring.

As he walked down between the audience, Alex felt himself being examined and evaluated on every side. Once again the yellow markers were being handed out, and he could imagine the bets being placed. Fifteen seconds ... twenty seconds – it was obvious that this foreign boy wouldn't last long. His heart was pounding – he could actually see the movement in his naked chest. Why had he been chosen for this? Why not Ash? He could only assume that these people got a sick satisfaction out of ringing the changes. During the course of the evening, they had seen a number of men beaten up. Now they were going to watch the same thing happen to a teenager.

He passed through the opening in the fence. The two seconds were waiting for him, grinning and offering to help him up into the ring. One of them was carrying a garland of flowers to put around his neck. Alex had already made up his mind about that. As their hands reached towards him, he struck out at them, drawing laughter and jeers from the crowd. But he wasn't going to be touched by them and nor was he going to parade in their flowers. He pulled himself into the ring just as two cleaners climbed out, lowering themselves between the ropes. They took with them the bloody rags that they had used to clean the canvas floor.

Sunthorn was waiting in the opposite corner.

It was only now that he was closer that Alex could see the arrogance and the cruelty of the man he was about to face. Sunthorn had probably been training all his life and knew that this next fight was going to be over as soon as it began. But he didn't care. Presumably he was being paid and would cheerfully maim Alex, provided he got his cheque. Already he was smiling, showing cracked lips and uneven teeth. His nose had been broken at some time and it had set badly. He might have had the body of a world-class athlete but he had the face of a freak.

A plastic bottle of water was forced between Alex's lips and he drank. It was horribly warm in the arena and that would only sap his strength. He wondered how Sunthorn had managed to continue for so long. Perhaps he was given some sort of drug. The military music was blasting out all around him. The fans were turning. Alex clung to the rope, trying to work out some sort of strategy. Would it be easier just to take a dive the moment the fight began? If he allowed himself to be knocked out in the opening seconds, at least it would be over. But there was a risk in that too. It would all depend how hard Sunthorn hit him. He didn't want to wake up with a broken neck.

The music stopped. The bell rang. The spectators fell silent. It was too late to work out any plan. The first round had begun.

Alex took a couple of steps forward. He could feel the eyes of the crowd boring into him, waiting for him to go down. Sunthorn looked completely relaxed. He had taken up the standard stance with his body weight poised on his front foot – the basic defence in almost every martial art – but he barely looked interested. It occurred to Alex that if he had any chance at all in this fight, it would be in the opening seconds. Nobody in the arena could possibly know that he was a first grade *Dan* – a black belt in karate. The fight was completely unfair. Sunthorn had the advantages of size, weight and experience. But Alex had the advantage of surprise.

He decided to use it. He continued forward and, at the last second, when he knew he was close enough, he suddenly twisted round and lashed out with all his strength. He had used the back kick, one of the most powerful blows in karate, and if he had made contact he would have taken his opponent out then and there. But to his dismay his foot hit only empty air. Sunthorn had reacted with fantastic speed, springing back and twisting so that the kick missed his abdomen by a centimetre.

The audience gasped, then chattered with new excitement. Alex tried a front jab but this time Sunthorn was ready. He blocked the attack with his right arm, then followed through with a counter-kick that slammed into Alex's side, propelling him back against the ropes. Alex was bruised and winded. Red spots danced in front of his eyes. If Sunthorn hit him a second time, it would be over. Alex rested with the ropes against his shoulders and waited for the end.

It didn't come. Sunthorn was smiling again, enjoying himself. The foreign boy hadn't been the easy kill that everyone expected and he knew he could enjoy himself here. The audience wanted blood but they wanted drama too. He could play with the boy for a while, weaken him before the final blow that would put him in hospital. He reached out with his hand, bending his fingers as if to say "Come on!" The crowd roared their approval. Even the gamblers who had already lost and were tearing up their yellow slips wanted to see more.

Alex drew a deep breath and straightened up. There was a red mark where Sunthorn's foot had caught him, just above the waist. The man had a sole that could have been made of the toughest leather and leg muscles like steel rods. How could Ash have got him into this? But Alex knew it wasn't his godfather's fault. He should have listened to Jack when he was in Sydney. Right now he could have been safely back at school.

For the next couple of minutes, the two of them circled each other, throwing a few feints, but neither landing a real punch. Alex tried to keep his distance while he recovered his breath. How long did each round last? He had seen that there were intervals and he desperately needed a few seconds on his own, unthreatened: time to think. The sweat was dripping off him. He wiped his eyes, and that was when Sunthorn attacked, a whirl of jabbing elbows, knees and fists, any one of which could have knocked Alex down.

In the next thirty seconds, Alex used every defence technique he had ever been taught, but he knew that in truth he was simply relying on his instincts, dodging and weaving as the arena seemed to spin around him, the audience shouting, the fans turning and the sluggish heat weighing down on him from all sides. A right hook caught him on the side of the face and his whole head jerked round, a spasm of pain travelling down his neck and spine. Sunthorn followed through with a side knee to the ribs. Alex doubled up, unable to help himself. He hit the canvas just as the bell rang for the end of the first round.

There was applause and cheering. The music blared out. Sunthorn leapt back, grinning and waving, enjoying the fight. Alex felt he had no strength left. He was aware of the two men acting as his seconds shouting at him, gesturing for him to return to his corner. Somehow he forced himself to his feet. His nose was bleeding. He could taste the blood as it trickled into his mouth.

He wasn't going to last another round: that much was obvious. All the odds were against him. But he had come to a decision. Sunthorn was older, taller, heavier and more experienced than he was, and there was only one way Alex was going to beat him.

He was just going to have to cheat.

ONCE BITTEN...

One of the men who had been chosen to look after Alex while he was fighting wiped away the blood with a wet sponge. The other helped him drink. Alex felt the cold water trickle down the sides of his face and over his shoulders. Both men were grinning at him, muttering words of encouragement as if he could understand a single word they were saying. They had probably done exactly the same during the previous fight – and Alex had seen the result. Well, he wasn't going to let that happen to him. These people were in for a surprise.

He felt the water bottle being forced one last time between his lips and sucked in as much as he could. A moment later, a bell rang and the bottle was whisked away. The interval music stopped. There were shouts from different parts of the audience. Glancing to one side, Alex saw Anan Sukit striding down to take a place in the front row. Presumably he wanted a closer view of the final knockout.

Alex moved forward cautiously, fists raised, weight evenly distributed on the balls of his feet. Sunthorn was waiting for him. That was good. The one thing Alex had most feared was a fast, direct attack. That wouldn't leave him time for what he had in mind. But Alex had shown his true colours in the first round. Sunthorn knew that he had trained in at least one martial art and he was planning his moves carefully. Alex had come close to knocking him out; Sunthorn wasn't going to give him a second chance.

In the end Sunthorn went for a straight clinch, the wrestling grip that, in Muay Thai, is also known as the standard tie-up. Suddenly they were face to face, their feet almost touching. Sunthorn had locked his hands behind Alex's head and he was sneering, utterly confident. With his extra height, he had the complete advantage. He could throw Alex off balance or finish him with an explosive strike from his knee. The audience saw that the last seconds of the fight had arrived and roared their approval.

It was exactly what Alex wanted. It was exactly what he had been inviting. Before Sunthorn could make his move, he acted. What nobody knew – not Sunthorn, nor the seconds nor the audience – was that Alex's mouth was still full of water and had been since the round began. Now he spat it out, straight into Sunthorn's face.

Sunthorn reacted instinctively, jerking his head

back in surprise and loosening his grip. For a second, he was blinded. Alex acted instantly, striking out with a savage uppercut that sent his fist crashing into his opponent's jaw. But that wasn't enough. He wouldn't get a second chance: he had to finish this now. Alex swung round, putting all his strength into a single powerhouse kick, his bare foot landing square in the man's solar plexus.

Even Sunthorn's advanced muscle structure wasn't up to such a blow. Alex heard the breath explode from his lips. All the colour left his face. For a moment, he stood there, hands hanging limply beneath him. The crowd had fallen silent, as if in shock. Then Sunthorn collapsed onto his knees and finally slammed face down, unconscious, on the canvas.

The entire arena erupted with cries of anger and outrage. The audience had seen what had happened – and they couldn't believe it. The foreign boy had been brought here to entertain them but he had cheated them instead. They had lost money. And their champion – Sunthorn – had been humiliated.

It was only now, hearing the shouting all around him, that Alex realized he had put himself in fresh danger. If he had played his part as expected, he might have been carried out on his back with a broken nose – or worse. But presumably there would have been a consolation prize. He would have been driven home with the false documents that Ash had sent him here to collect. There was no longer any chance of that. He had offended the snakehead, taken out their prize fighter. Somehow he doubted that they were going to thank him and give him a gold cup.

He stepped over the unconscious body and made as if to climb out of the ring. But he saw at once that he was right. Anan Sukit was back on his feet, his face dark with fury, his eyes ablaze. He had pulled a gun out of an inside pocket of his suit. Unbelieving, Alex watched as he brought it round and aimed. Sukit was going to shoot him, right there, in front of all these people – a punishment for the trick that had just been played. And there was nothing Alex could do, nowhere to hide. He watched as the cold eye of the muzzle focused on his head.

Then all the lights went out.

The darkness was absolute. It seemed to fold in from all sides, like a collapsing box. Sukit had chosen that moment to fire. Alex saw two bursts of orange flame and heard the shots. But he was already moving. The bullets had been aimed at his head but he had dropped down onto the canvas and was rolling away, searching for the ropes on the other side of the ring. He found them. Reaching up with one hand, he swung himself through, then down into the ringside area below.

The spectators had reacted to the blackout with silence, but the sound of the two shots had provoked instant panic. They were suddenly blind and someone had a gun! Alex heard screams, the clatter of seats being pushed to the ground. Someone ran into him, then tumbled back. There were more cries of protest. Alex crouched where he was, waiting for his eyes to get used to the dark.

At least that happened quickly. As Alex had approached the building from the river, he had seen how dilapidated it was; and although there were few windows, the roof and the walls were full of cracks. The moon was still shining and the light was spilling in everywhere, not enough to distinguish faces but Alex was in no mood to make new friends. All he wanted was the way out and he could see it, straight in front of him, up a flight of concrete steps.

He got to his feet and ran, immediately crashing into the wire fence that surrounded the ring. Where was the opening? Desperately he felt his way along, using his palms against the wire. He found the gap and stumbled through, forcing himself on towards the raked seating which climbed steeply up to the door where he'd come in. There was a third shot and a man standing next to him twisted round and fell. Sukit had spotted him, which was hardly surprising. Alex's bare shoulders and brightly coloured shorts made him a target even in the dark. He scrambled on, fighting his way through the crowd. His skin was slippery, covered in sweat, and at least that made it difficult for anyone to grab hold of him. A Thai man stepped in front of him, muttering something in his own language. Alex raised a hand, driving the heel straight into his face. The man grunted and fell backwards. The knife he had been holding clattered to the floor. Now Alex understood the rules. He was to be captured and killed. That seemed to be the price of winning the fight.

Alex was unarmed. He was half naked. And members of the snakehead were all around him. He knew that only speed and the darkness were on his side. He had to find his way out of this building in the next few minutes. And that meant retrieving his own clothes first. He reached the door – and it was then that the lights flashed back on.

Sukit saw him at once. He pointed with a stubby finger and shouted. Alex saw half a dozen young men running towards him, all of them black-haired, dressed in black shirts. They were coming at him from both sides. Sukit fired. The bullet hit a pillar and ricocheted into one of the television sets. The glass shattered and there was a crackle of electricity. Alex saw a tongue of flame and wondered if the whole place might catch light. That would help him. But the walls were too damp. The river was everywhere, even in the air he was breathing.

He hurled himself through the doorway and down the wooden staircase on the other side, almost losing his balance on the crazy fairground steps. A splinter buried itself in his toe. Alex ignored the pain. He was back in the corridor.

Which way had they led him? Left or right? He had less than a second to make a decision and the wrong choice might kill him.

He went right. That way, the corridor sloped upwards and he remembered that, coming in, he had gone down. Behind him he heard a burst of gunfire: not one gun but several. That was strange. He was out of sight now, so who were they firing at? The dull yellow light bulbs flickered overhead. It seemed that war had broken out in the arena. Was it possible...? Alex wondered if Ash could have somehow followed him here. Certainly there seemed to be someone on his side.

He found the room where he had undressed and ran in, swinging the door shut behind him. His clothes were where he'd left them, and gratefully he pulled them on. At least he looked normal again – and he needed the trainers if he was going to run over any more wooden floors. When he was dressed, he went back to the door and slowly opened it. Sweat trickled down his face. His hair was drenched. But there didn't seem to be anyone outside.

The end of the corridor and the exit to the jetty were about twenty metres away. But as he made his way towards the open air, Alex heard the roar of an engine, and knew that a boat had just pulled in. He guessed what was going to happen next. Luckily he was outside one of the other rooms. He threw himself inside just as the main door crashed open and the new arrivals began to make their way down the corridor. There were two of them. They were both carrying old-fashioned, Russian-made RPK-74 light machine guns. The barrels had been modified to make them shorter. As Alex crouched in the shadows, he heard them move towards him. They were searching the changing rooms, one by one. In less than a minute they would be here.

Alex looked around him. This room was almost identical to the one he had left, with no cupboards, nowhere to hide and a single window, securely barred. But there was one difference. Part of the floor had rotted away; he could just make out the water churning underneath. Could he fit through? There was a crash as the door of the room next to his was thrown open. He heard one of the men call out in Thai. They would be here in a few seconds. Alex didn't like to think what he might be getting himself into. The water was a long way down and the current might suck him beneath the surface. But if he stayed here, he would die anyway. He went over to the hole, took a deep breath, and dropped through it.

He fell into darkness, and just had time to put a hand over his nose before he hit the river. The water was warm and sluggish, covered by a layer of filth and rotting vegetation. The stink was almost unendurable. It was like plunging into the oldest, dirtiest bath in the world. As Alex broke back through the surface, he could feel the liquid, like oil, running down his cheeks and over his lips. Some sort of slime was clinging to his face. He tore it off, forcing himself not to swallow.

He was out of the arena but he still hadn't escaped. He could hear voices above him. It was almost impossible to see anything. He was underneath the building, treading water, surrounded by the concrete pillars that held the place up. In the distance he could just make out the shape of the boat that must have brought the two men with machine guns. It was alongside the jetty, its engines still running. There was the stamp of footsteps and he looked up as two flickering shadows passed above his head. They belonged to men running along the veranda outside the arena. Sukit must have given the order to surround the place. Presumably they were still searching it inch by inch.

And then something climbed onto his shoulder.

It was only now that he remembered the movement he had seen when he had arrived: something living in the water and the shadows beneath the building. Alex reached out and grabbed one of the pillars, steadying himself. Then, very slowly, he turned his head.

It was a rat, heavy and bloated, over thirty centimetres long, with vicious yellow teeth and eyes the colour of blood. Its tail, curling round behind Alex's neck, added another twenty-five centimetres to its length and it was clinging to his shirt with little claws, scrabbling feverishly at the material. And it wasn't alone. As Alex froze in utter horror, two more rats appeared, then a fourth. Soon the water was swarming with them. Another one climbed onto the side of his face, scratching the skin as it pulled itself on top of his head. Alex wanted to scream – but it was the one thing he couldn't do. There were armed men standing above him, only a few metres away. If he so much as splashed too loudly, it would all be over.

Were the rats going to bite him? That was the terrible thought. Was he going to be eaten alive? He felt something nudge his shirt. One of the creatures had dived underwater and was trying to dig its way inside. He could feel its nose and claws burrowing against the soft flesh of his stomach. With a feeling of nausea, he reached down and gently pushed it away. If he was too rough the rat would bite him, and once the others got a scent of his blood...

He stopped himself. Better not even to imagine.

His only hope was to do nothing. Let the rats decide that he was just another bit of pollution that had been dumped in the river. He tried to send his thoughts out to the pack. I'm not edible. You wouldn't like me.

The rat that had climbed onto his head was now nestling in his hair. Alex winced as it pulled out a few strands and began to chew on them, checking out the taste. The first rat, the one that had started all this, was still on his shoulder. Without moving, Alex glanced down and saw a pointed nose twitching right beside his jugular. Behind it he could make out two eyes, gleaming with excitement, fascinated by the rapid pulsing – in exact time with Alex's heart. All it had to do was bite through the flesh, find the vein. Alex was certain it was about to strike.

He was saved by an explosion, a fireball that erupted in the very centre of the building, reflecting down into the water. At once, all the rats took fright, leaping off him and disappearing behind the pillars. What the hell was going on? Had he perhaps wandered into some war between two rival snakeheads? That didn't matter now. He had to move before the rats came back. Alex launched himself away from the pillar and swam through the muck, trying to keep his face out of the water.

The arena was on fire. He could hear voices yelling and saw the flicker of red. A piece of blazing wood tumbled out of nowhere and fell, hissing and spitting, into the river. Alex glanced upwards. The building had been rickety to begin with. He didn't want it collapsing now – not when he was underneath. The jetty was straight ahead of him. Even if there were men standing on guard, Alex doubted he would be noticed. With all that was going on inside, nobody would be looking down into the water. Anyway, he didn't care any more. He'd had enough of this. It was time to go.

He reached the side of the boat, a sheer metal wall rising up into fresh air and freedom. There was a net hanging over the side and Alex grabbed it gratefully. Somehow he found the last reserves of strength he needed to climb up. The boat was one of the old river ferries, with a red roof to show that it crossed continually from one side to the other. There was one man on board – presumably the driver – a Thai wearing jeans and a jacket but no shirt. He was leaning against the side, watching the fire with a look of astonishment.

The wooden building was crackling loudly. Flames had caught hold of the roof and the back wall and were leaping up into the night sky. The wood was splintering, pieces of it splashing down. Alex didn't even try to be quiet. He hauled himself over the rail on the other side of the ferry, behind the driver. The man didn't turn round. Alex ran across the deck and grabbed him by his collar and belt. He was lucky. The man weighed very little. Alex heaved him up over the rail and into the river. Then, still dripping wet, water running into his eyes, he went over to the controls and slammed the throttle down as far as it would go.

This was going to be his way out of here. Once he was downriver, nobody would be able to find him.

The engines roared and the propellers thrashed at the water, turning it white. The boat surged forward. Alex grinned. But a second later, he was almost thrown off his feet as the boat seemed to slam into a brick wall. Still gripping the steering wheel, he turned round and saw, to his dismay, that the boat had been moored to one of the pillars supporting the building. The propellers were churning up the water. If the rats were anywhere near, they would be chopped to pieces. But the boat wasn't going anywhere. A length of rope almost as thick as Alex's arm stretched between the stern and the pillar.

And he didn't have time to untie it. Alex eased the throttle back, afraid the engines would explode, and the rope sagged. Then somebody shouted something, and with a heavy heart he saw Anan Sukit appear on the walkway outside the arena, anger stretching his mouth even further across his hideous face. He had seen Alex. He still had his gun. Once again he took aim. He was about twenty metres away but he had a clear shot.

Alex did the only thing he could. Once again he slammed down the throttle, and suddenly it seemed to him that everything happened at once.

There were three shots. But Alex wasn't hit. And it wasn't Sukit who had fired. The snakehead lieutenant seemed to throw his own gun into the river, as if he no longer had any use for it. Then he followed it in, pitching head first into the water. He had been shot from behind, the bullets hitting him between the shoulders. Alex thought he saw a shadowy figure standing in a doorway, but before he could make out who it was, the boat surged forward again. And this time it took the pillar with it, ripping it out from beneath the burning building.

Alex felt himself propelled into the middle of the river incredibly fast. He risked a last look back and saw the arena consumed by fire, sparks dancing above it. In the distance he could hear fire engines. But they weren't going to be needed. He had torn out a vital part of the structure. Even as he watched, the entire building slumped to its knees, as if in surrender, then slid off the bank and into the river. All of it went. The water rushed in through the rotting wood, eager at last to reclaim it. Alex heard screams coming from inside. Another burst of gunfire. And then the Chada Trading Company had disappeared as if it had never existed. Only the green sign remained, floating on the surface, surrounded by other pieces of splintered wood and debris. The flames sat briefly on the river before extinguishing themselves. Dozens of shadowy figures thrashed and shouted in the water, trying to reach dry land.

Alex dragged at the steering wheel and brought the ferry under control. It was incredible, but he really was the only person on board. So which way now? North would take him to familiar territory. He could see the Peninsula Hotel in the far distance. He wondered what he must look like. Bruised, scratched, soaked, in rags – he didn't think they'd be too happy to let him check in.

And anyway, there was still Ash, presumably waiting for him in Chinatown. Alex steered the ferry towards the next public jetty. They would have to do without the forged papers. He just hoped Ash would understand.

WAT HO

Major Winston Yu selected an egg and cress sandwich and held it delicately between his gloved fingers. He was at the Ritz Hotel in London, which – even if they did allow too many tourists into the main rooms – was still his favourite hotel in the world. And tea was definitely his favourite meal. He loved the little sandwiches, cut in perfect triangles, with a scone served with jam and cream to follow. It was all so very English. Even the bone china teapot and cup had been made by Wedgwood, the Staffordshire family firm established in 1759.

He sipped his tea and dabbed his lips with a serviette. The news from Bangkok, he had to admit, was not good. But he wasn't going to let that spoil his tea. His mother had always told him that every cloud has a silver lining and he was looking for one now. It was true that it wouldn't be easy to replace Anan Sukit. But on the other hand, every organization – even a snakehead – needs a change of personnel from time to time. It keeps people on their toes. There were plenty of young lieutenants who deserved promotion. Yu would make a choice in due course.

Much less welcome was the man sitting opposite him. It was very rare for two members of Scorpia to be seen together in public, but Zeljan Kurst had telephoned him and insisted on a meeting. Major Yu had suggested the Ritz, but now he felt it had been a mistake. The big Yugoslavian with his bald head and wrestler's shoulders couldn't have looked more out of place. And he was drinking mineral water! Who drank mineral water at five o'clock in the afternoon?

"Why didn't you report to us about the boy?" Kurst asked.

"I didn't think it was relevant," Yu replied.

"Not relevant?"

"This is my operation. I have everything under control."

"That's not what I've heard."

It didn't surprise Yu that the executive board had already learnt about the destruction of the Chada Trading Company offices and the death of Sukit. They were always watching one another's backs, doubtless working out where to place the knives. It was sad that criminals weren't the same any more. No one trusted anyone.

"We're still not sure what has just happened," Yu said. It might be teatime in England but it was midnight in Bangkok. "It's not even clear the boy was responsible."

"This is Alex Rider," Kurst snapped. "We underestimated him once before and it was an expensive mistake. Why haven't you killed him already?"

"For obvious reasons." Yu's hand hovered over another sandwich but he changed his mind. He had rather lost his appetite. "I was aware of Alex Rider's presence in Bangkok the moment he landed," he continued. "I knew they were coming – a boy and a man – even before they arrived."

"Who told you?"

"That's my secret and I intend to keep it that way. I could have arranged to have the Rider child gunned down at Suvarnabhumi Airport. It would have been simple. But that would have told ASIS I was aware of their plans. They already suspect I have inside information. This would have confirmed it."

"So what do you intend to do?"

"I want to play with him. The fight at the arena was just the beginning, and there's no real harm done. The place was falling down anyway. But if you ask me, the situation is quite amusing. Here's the famous Alex Rider, dressed up as an Afghan refugee. He thinks he's so clever. But I have him in the palm of my hand and I can crush him at any time."

"That was what Julia Rothman thought."

"He's a child, Mr Kurst. A very clever child, but a child all the same. I think you're overreacting."

Something deadly flickered in Kurst's eyes and Yu made a mental note not to eat anything more. He wouldn't put it past Scorpia to slip a radioactive pellet into an egg and cress sandwich. After all, they had done it before.

"We will be monitoring the situation," Kurst said at length. "And I'm warning you, Major Yu, if we feel that things are getting out of hand, you will be replaced."

He got up and left.

Yu stayed where he was, thinking about what had just been said. He suspected that Levi Kroll was behind this. The Israeli had been playing power games ever since Max Grendel had retired. He had also volunteered for the Reef Island business. He would be itching to move in if Yu failed.

He was not going to fail. Royal Blue had been thoroughly tested by Yu's operatives in Bangkok. The detonation system had been adapted. And in less than two days' time it would set off on the next leg of its journey. All according to plan. But Yu decided to take out a little insurance. He and he alone would set off the bomb. He was the one who would take the credit for the worldwide destruction that would follow.

So how to stop Kroll from seizing control?

It was very simple. A little technological tinkering and nobody would be able to replace him. Yu smiled to himself and called for the bill.

*   *   *

"I should never have let you go," Ash exclaimed. "I can't believe I let them do that to you."

It was one o'clock in the morning in Bangkok and Alex and Ash were in their room on the third floor.

Alex had abandoned the ferry downriver on the other side of an ugly, modern bridge. From there he'd had to find his way across the city on foot, dripping wet, without money and relying only on his sense of direction. He had stopped twice to ask for directions from a monk and from a stallholder closing up for the night. They spoke little English but were able to understand enough to point him in the right direction. Even so, it had been well after midnight by the time he had reached China-town. Ash had been pacing the room like a lion in a cage, sick with worry, and had grabbed hold of Alex when he finally arrived. He had listened to the story with disbelief.

"I shouldn't have let you go," he said again.

"You weren't to know."

"I've heard about these fights. The snakeheads hold them all the time. Anyone who crosses them can end up in the ring. People get crippled – or killed."

"I was lucky."

"You were smart, Alex." Ash looked at him approvingly, as if seeing him in a new light. "You say someone was there, shooting. They attacked the building. Did you see who they were?"

"I got a glimpse of someone. But I'm sorry, Ash. It was dark and it was all happening too quickly."

"Were they Thai or European?"

"I didn't see."

Alex was sitting on the bed, wrapped in a blanket. Ash had laid his clothes out to dry – not that there was much chance of that. The night itself was damp, on the edge of a tropical storm. He had also brought Alex a bowl of chicken broth from the restaurant at the end of the alley. Alex needed it. He hadn't eaten since late that afternoon. He was starving and exhausted.

Ash examined him. "I remember the first time I met your father," he said suddenly. The change of subject took Alex by surprise. "I'd been sent out on a routine operation in Prague. I was just back-up. He was in charge – for the first time, I think. He was about the same age as me." He took out a cigarette and rolled it between his fingers. "Anyway, everything that could go wrong did go wrong. A building blown to smithereens. Three ex-KGB agents dead in the street. The Czech police crawling all over us. And he was just like you are now."

"What do you mean?"

"I mean you take after him," Ash explained. "John always had the luck of the devil. He'd walk into trouble and somehow he'd get out of it in one piece. And then he'd sit there – the same as you – as if nothing had happened. Untouched by it."

"His luck ran out in the end," Alex said.

"Everyone's luck runs out in the end," Ash replied and turned away, a haunted look in his eyes.

They didn't talk much more after that. Alex finished his soup and fell asleep almost immediately. The last thing he remembered was Ash, hunched over a cigarette, the red tip winking at him in the darkness as if sharing a secret.

Despite everything, Alex woke early the next morning. There were a couple of fat cockroaches crawling up the wall right next to him, but by now he had got used to them. They didn't bite or sting; they were just ugly. He ignored them and got out of bed. Ash had already been out, taking Alex's wet clothes to a laundry to be spin-dried. He dressed quickly and the two of them went out for a bowl of jok, the rice porridge which many of the stalls served for breakfast.

They ate in silence, squatting on two wooden crates at the edge of the road, the traffic rumbling past. It had rained in the night and there were huge puddles everywhere, which somehow slowed the city down even more. Once again Ash had slept badly, and there were dark rings under his eyes. His wound was hurting him. He did his best not to show it, but Alex noticed him wince as he sat down and he looked more ragged and drawn out than ever.

"I'm going to have to cross the river," Ash said at last.

"The Chada Trading Company?" Alex shrugged. "You won't find very much of it left."

"I was thinking the same thing about our assignment." Ash threw down his spoon. "I'm not blaming you for what happened last night," he said. "But it may well be that our friends in the snakehead have no further interest in smuggling us into Australia. One of their main lieutenants is dead. And it has to be said, you took out a large chunk of their operation."

"I didn't set fire to the building!" Alex protested.

"No. But you pulled it into the river."

"That put the fire out."

Ash half smiled. "Fair point. But I need to find out how things stand."

"Can I come?"

"Absolutely not, Alex. I think that's a bad idea. You go back to the room – and watch out for yourself. It's always possible they'll send someone round to settle the score. I'll be back as soon as I can."

He walked off. Alex thought back over what he'd just said. Was Ash angry with him? It was difficult to read his moods, as if a life in the secret service had put any display of emotion under wraps. But Alex could see that things hadn't quite gone as expected. His job was to infiltrate the snakehead, not start a war with it. And the fake papers that were so important to Ash might well be sitting on the bottom of the river – and the rest of the Chada Trading Company with them.

Alex got to his feet and began to walk slowly along the street, barely glancing at the brightly coloured silks that every shop in this area seemed to sell. Thai high streets certainly weren't like English ones. In England things were spread out. Here you had whole clusters of shops all selling the same thing: whole streets of silk, whole streets of ceramics. He wondered how people chose where to go.

He wished Ash had let him go with him. The truth was, he didn't want to spend any more time on his own and he'd had enough of Bangkok. As for his hopes that meeting Ash would tell him anything about himself, so far all he had been given was a few glimpses of the past. He was beginning to wonder if his godfather would ever open up enough to say anything meaningful at all.

Alex was just approaching the top of the alley-way when he realized that the entrance was being watched.

Ash had warned him to keep his eyes open, and perhaps it was thanks to him that Alex spotted the man on the other side of the road, half hidden behind a vegetable stall. He didn't need to look twice. The man had changed his clothes. Gone were the red poppy and the leather jacket. But Alex was absolutely certain. This was the same square, hard-edged face that he had already seen at the airport and then again at the Peninsula Hotel. Now he was here. He must have been trailing Alex for days.

The man had disguised himself as a tourist, complete with camera and baseball cap, but his attention was fixed on the building where Alex and Ash were staying. Perhaps he was waiting for them to come out. Once again Alex had the feeling that he knew the man from somewhere. But where? In which country? Could this be one of his old enemies catching up with him? He examined the cold dark eyes beneath the fringe of black hair. A soldier? Alex was just about to make the connection when the man turned and began to walk away. He must have decided that there was no one at home. Alex made a snap decision. To hell with what Ash had told him. He was going to follow.

The man had set off down Yaowarat Road, one of the busiest streets in Chinatown with huge signs carrying Chinese characters high into the air. Alex was confident he wouldn't be seen. As ever, the pavement was cluttered with stalls, and if the man glanced back he could find somewhere to hide in an instant. The real danger was that Alex might lose him. Despite the early hour, the crowds were already out – they formed a constantly shifting barrier between the two of them – and the man could disappear all too easily into a dozen entrances. There were shops selling gold and spices. Cafés and restaurants. Arcades and tiny alleys. The trick was to stay close enough not to lose him but far enough away not to be seen.

But the man didn't suspect anything. His pace

hadn't changed. He took a right turn, then a left, and suddenly they were out of Chinatown and heading into the Old City, the very heart of Bangkok, where every street seemed to contain a temple or a shrine. The pavements were emptier here and Alex had to be more careful, dropping further back and hovering close to doorways or parked cars in case he had to duck out of sight.

They had been walking for about ten minutes when the man turned off, passing through the entrance to a large temple complex. The gateway itself was decorated with silver and mother-of-pearl and opened onto a courtyard filled with shrines and statues: a fantastic, richly decorated world where myth and religion collided in a cloud of incense and a blaze of gold and brilliantly coloured mosaic.

The Thai word for a Buddhist monastery or temple is *wat*. There are thirty thousand of them scattered across the country, hundreds in Bangkok alone. There was a sign outside this one, giving its name in Thai and – helpfully – in English. It was called Wat Ho.

Alex only had a few moments to take in his surroundings: the ornamental ponds, and the Bodhi trees which grow in every wat because they once gave shelter to the Buddha. He glanced at the golden figures, half woman half lion, that guarded the main temple, the delicate slanting roofs and the mondops – incredible, intricate towers with hundreds of tiny figures that must have taken years to carve by hand. A group of monks walked past. Everywhere there were people kneeling in prayer. He had never been anywhere so peaceful.

The man he was following had disappeared behind a bell tower. Alex was suddenly afraid that he was going to lose him, at the same time wondering what it was that had brought him here. Could he have been mistaken? Could the man be a tourist after all? He hurried round the corner and stopped. The man had gone. A crowd of Thai were kneeling at a shrine. A couple of backpackers were having their photograph taken in front of one of the terraces. Alex was angry with himself. He had been too slow. The entire journey had been a waste of time.

He took a step forward and froze as a shadow fell across him and a hand pressed something hard into his back.

"Don't turn round," a voice commanded, speaking in English.

Alex stood where he was, a sick feeling in his stomach. This was exactly what Ash had warned him against. The snakehead had sent someone after him and he had allowed himself to be led straight into a trap. But why here, in a Thai temple? And how did the man know he spoke English?

"Walk across the courtyard. There's a red door on the other side of the shrine. Do you see it?"

Alex nodded. The man had a Liverpudlian

accent. It sounded weird in the context of a Bangkok temple.

"We're going through the door. I'll give you more instructions on the other side. Don't try anything."

Another jab with the gun. Alex didn't need any further prompting. He walked away from the bell tower, skirting round the Thai people lost in their prayers. Briefly he considered starting a fight, out here, while there were still witnesses. But it would do him no good. The man could shoot him in the back and disappear before anyone realized what had happened. The moment would come ... but not yet.

The red door was set in the wall of a cloister, somewhere for the monks to walk in silent contemplation. It was surrounded by images of the Ramakien, the great story of gods and demons known to every child in Thailand. Gods or demons? He had little doubt to which group this man belonged.

As he approached, the door clicked open automatically. There had to be a surveillance camera somewhere but, looking around, Alex couldn't see it. There was a modern corridor on the other side, with bare brick walls slanting down towards a second door. This one opened too. All the sounds of the wat had faded away behind him. He felt as if he were being swallowed up.

Alex wasn't going to let that happen. He timed his move very carefully. The second doorway was narrow, leading into a square-shaped hall that could have been the reception area of a solicitor's office or a smart private bank. The walls were covered in wooden panels. There was an antique table with a lamp, a fan turning overhead. And, more bizarre than anything, on the opposite wall, a picture of Queen Elizabeth II. As Alex made his way in he hesitated, allowing the man to catch up, then suddenly punched backwards with his elbow and brought his fist swinging round.

It was a move he had been taught when he was training with the SAS in the Brecon Beacons in Wales. The elbow jab winds your man; the fist carries the gun aside, giving you time to spin round and kick out with all your strength. Never try it in the open because you'll end up getting shot. It only works in a confined space.

But not this time. The man seemed to have been expecting the manoeuvre. He had simply stepped aside the moment Alex began his move. Alex's first strike didn't make contact with anything, and before he could even begin to turn he felt the cold farewell of the gun pressed against the side of his head.

"Nice try, Cub," the man said. "But much too slow."

And that was when Alex knew.

"Fox!" he exclaimed.

The gun didn't matter any more. Alex turned to face the man – who was now grinning at him like an old friend. Which, in a sense, he was. The two of them had actually met in the Brecon Beacons. There had been four men in the unit to which Alex had been assigned: Wolf, Eagle, Snake and Fox. None of them had been allowed to use their real names. While he was with them, Alex was Cub. And now that he thought about it, there had been one with a Liverpudlian accent. It seemed incredible that the two of them should have met up again in Bangkok, but there could be no doubt about it. Fox was standing in front of him now.

"You were at the airport," Alex said. "I saw you, wearing a poppy."

"Yes. I should have taken that off. But I'd just flown in from London."

"And you were at the Peninsula Hotel."

Fox nodded. "I couldn't believe it was you when I first saw you, so I followed you to be sure. I've been keeping an eye on you ever since, Alex. Lucky for you..."

"Last night." Alex's head swam. "Was that you at the arena? You set the place on fire!"

"I followed you over to Patpong and I was there when those men picked you up. Then I followed you down to the Chada Trading Company. It wasn't easy, I can tell you. And it took me ages to weasel my way in. When I arrived you were already in the ring. I thought you were going to be beaten to a pulp. But I'd seen where the main fuses were, so I nipped back and turned out all the lights. Then I came looking for you. Things got a bit dodgy when the lights came back on; I had to shoot a few of the opposition and chuck a couple of grenades. The last time I saw you, you were in a ferry, trying to get away. It might have helped if you'd untied it first."

"You shot Anan Sukit."

"Was that his name? Well, he was trying to shoot you. It was the very least I could do."

"So what is this place?" Alex looked around him. "What are you doing in Bangkok? And what's your real name? You can't go on expecting me to call you Fox."

"My real name's Ben Daniels. You're Alex Rider. Of course, I know that now."

"You've left the SAS?"

"I got seconded to MI6 Special Operations. And since you ask, that's where you are now. This is what you might call the Bangkok office of the Royal & General Bank."

The words were hardly out of his mouth when a door opened on the other side of the hallway and a woman walked out. Alex caught it at once – the faint smell of peppermint.

"Alex Rider!" Mrs Jones exclaimed. "I have to say, you're the last person I expected to see. Come into my office immediately. I want to know – why aren't you at school?"

ARMED AND DANGEROUS

The last time Alex had seen Mrs Jones, she had been visiting him in a north London hospital. Then she had seemed unsure of herself, regretful, blaming herself for the security lapse that had left Alex close to death on the pavement outside the MI6 offices in Liverpool Street. She had also been at her most human.

Now she was much more like the woman he had first met, dressed severely in a slate-coloured jacket and dress with a single necklace that could have been silver or steel. Her hair was still cut short, and her face – with those night-black eyes – was utterly serious. Mrs Jones was not attractive, but then she did not try to be. In a way, her looks exactly suited her work as deputy head of MI6 Special Operations, one of the most secretive departments of the British secret service. They gave nothing away.

Once again she was sucking a peppermint. Alex wondered if she had given up smoking at some point. Or was the habit also related to her job?

When Mrs Jones spoke, people sometimes died. It wouldn't surprise him if she felt the need to sweeten her breath.

The two of them were sitting in an office on the first floor of the building that stood directly behind Wat Ho. It was a very ordinary room with a wooden table and three leather chairs. Two large, square windows looked out over the temple court-yard. Alex knew that all this could be deceptive. The glass was probably bulletproof. There would be hidden cameras and microphones, and how many agents were there, mingling among the orange-robed monks? When it came to MI6, nothing was ever quite what it seemed.

Ben Daniels, the man he had known as Fox, was also there. He was younger than Alex had first thought, no more than twenty-two or twenty-three, laid-back and thoughtful. He was sitting next to Alex. The two of them were opposite Mrs Jones, who had taken her place behind the table.

Alex had told her his story, from the time he had splashed down off the Australian coast to his recruitment by ASIS, his meeting with Ash in Bangkok and his first encounter with the snakehead. He noticed that she reacted uncomfortably at the mention of Ash. But then, of course, she must have known him. She had been at MI6 when his father was undercover with Scorpia. She might even have been involved in the operation in Malta that had brought him safely home.

"Well, Ethan Brooke certainly has a nerve," she remarked when he had finished. "Recruiting you without so much as a by-your-leave! He could have talked to us first."

"I don't work for you," Alex said.

"I know you don't, Alex. But that's not the point. At the very least you're a British citizen, and if a foreign agency is going to use you, it ought to ask." She softened slightly. "For that matter, what ever prompted you to go back into the field? I thought you'd had enough of all this."

"I wanted to meet Ash," Alex said. Another thought occurred to him. "Why did you never tell me about him?" he asked.

"Why should I have?" Mrs Jones replied. "I haven't seen him for years."

"But he worked for you."

"He worked for Special Operations at the same time as me. In fact, I had very little to do with him. I met him once or twice. That's all."

"Do you know what happened in Malta?"

Mrs Jones hesitated. "You'd have to ask Alan Blunt," she said. "That was his operation. You know it was all a set-up. John – your father – was pretending to work for Scorpia and we had to get him back. We set up a fake ambush in a place called Mdina, but it went wrong and Ash was nearly killed. After that he was confined to desk duty, and not long after your parents died he left the service. That's all I can tell you."

"Where is Mr Blunt?"

"He's in London."

"So why are you here?"

Mrs Jones looked at Alex curiously. "You've changed," she said. "You've grown up a lot. I suppose we're to thank for that. You know, Alex, we weren't going to use you again. Alan and I had agreed: after what happened with Scorpia, that was going to be the end of it. But the next thing we learn, you're in America, up to your neck in it with the CIA. I ought to congratulate you, by the way. That business with the Ark Angel space station was quite remarkable."

"Thank you."

"And now ASIS! You certainly get around." Mrs Jones reached forward and flipped open a file lying on the table in front of her. "It's strange that we should have run into you this way," she went on. "But it may be less of a coincidence than you think. Major Yu. Does that name mean anything to you?"

"He's in charge of the snakehead." Ethan Brooke had told Alex the name when he was in Sydney.

"Well, to answer your question, we're investigating him. That's why I'm here. That's why Daniels is here too." Mrs Jones tapped the file with her index finger. "How much did ASIS tell you about Major Yu?"

Alex shrugged. He felt uncomfortable suddenly, caught in the middle of two rival intelligence agencies. "Not very much," he admitted. "They don't seem to know a lot about him. That's part of my job..."

"Well, maybe I can help you." Mrs Jones paused. "We've been interested in Major Winston Yu for some time, although we haven't managed to find out too much about him ourselves. We know he had a Chinese mother. His father is unknown. He was brought up in poverty in Hong Kong – his mother worked in a hotel – but cut forward eight years and you find him being privately educated in England. He went to Harrow School, for heaven's sake! How his mother managed to afford the fees is another question.

"He was an average student. We have copies of his reports. On the other hand, he seems to have fitted in quite well, which is surprising, considering his background. There was a question mark over a rather nasty incident that took place at the end of his second term – a boy killed in a car accident – but nothing was ever proved. He was also very good at sport, a triple house blood, whatever that means.

"He left with reasonable A levels and read politics at London University. Gained a second-class degree. After that he went into the army. Trained at Sandhurst and did much better there. He seems to have taken to the army life and achieved the highest score in military, practical and academic studies, for which he received the Queen's Medal.

He joined one of our country's most distinguished regiments – the Household Cavalry – and did three tours in Northern Ireland.

"Unfortunately he developed a bone condition which brought an end to his army career. But he was snapped up by intelligence, and for a time he worked for MI6 – not Special Operations. He was fairly low-grade, gathering and processing information, that sort of thing. Well, eventually he must have had enough of it, because one day he disappeared. We know he has been active in Thailand and Australia, but there's no record of his activities; and it's only recently that we've been able to identify him as the leader of one of the most powerful snakeheads in the region."

Mrs Jones paused. When she looked up again, her eyes were bleak. "This may put you off, Alex. It may even persuade you to go home – and believe me, I wouldn't blame you. According to our sources, Major Yu may have contacts with Scorpia. It's even possible that he's on the executive board."

Scorpia. Alex had hoped he would never hear that name again. And Mrs Jones was right. If Ethan Brooke had given him that information, he might have thought twice about the whole thing. He wondered if the head of ASIS Covert Action had known. Almost certainly. But he'd needed Alex so he'd decided to keep it under his hat.

"You still haven't told me why you're interested in him," Alex said.

"That's top secret." Mrs Jones gestured with one hand. "But I'll tell you. Apart from anything else, it may well be that you're in a position to help us – assuming that's something you'd even consider. Anyway, I'll explain and you can make up your own mind.

"Have you ever heard of the daisy cutter?"

Alex thought for a moment. "It's a bomb." He remembered talking about it once at school, during history. "The Americans used it in Vietnam."

"They've also used it in Afghanistan," Mrs Jones said. "The daisy cutter, also known as BLU-82B or the Blue Boy, is the largest conventional bomb in existence. It's the size of a car – and I mean a five-seater. Each bomb contains twelve and a half thousand pounds of ammonium nitrate, aluminium powder and polystyrene, and it's powerful enough to destroy an entire building, easily. In fact, it'll probably take out a whole street."

"The Americans used it because it's terrifying," Daniels muttered. He was speaking for the first time. "It may not compare to a nuclear bomb, but there's nothing on earth like it. The shock wave that it releases is unbelievable. You have no idea how much damage it can do."

"They used it in Vietnam to clear landing sites for helicopters," Mrs Jones went on. "Drop one on the jungle and you have no jungle for half a mile around. They called it the daisy cutter because that was the pattern the explosion made. It was used in Afghanistan to scare the Taliban, to show them what they were up against."

"What's this got to do with Major Yu?" Alex asked. He was also wondering, with a sense of growing unease, what it might have to do with him.

"For the last few years, the British government has been developing a second generation of daisy cutters," Mrs Jones explained. "Scientists have managed to create a similar type of bomb, except it's a little smaller and it's more powerful, with an even greater shock wave. They gave it a code name, Royal Blue, and they built a prototype at a secret laboratory just outside London." She took out a peppermint and twisted off the wrapper with a single movement of her thumb and forefinger. "Four weeks ago the prototype was stolen. Eight of our people were killed. Three of them were security guards; the rest were technicians. It was a very professional operation: perfectly timed, ruthlessly executed." She slid the peppermint between her lips.

"And you think Major Yu...?"

"These things aren't easy to transport, Alex. They need to be carried in a Hercules MC-130 transport plane. We lost sight of the bomb, but two days later a C-130 took off with a flight plan that brought it to Bangkok via Albania and Tajikistan. We were able to identify the pilot; his name was Feng. He in turn had been employed by a criminal based here in Bangkok, a man called Anan Sukit—"

"—and he works for the snakehead!" Alex finished the sentence.

"He *worked* for the snakehead," Mrs Jones remarked sourly. "Until Daniels put three bullets into him."

It was all beginning to make sense. MI6 Special Operations were chasing a missing bomb which had led them to the snakehead. Alex was investigating the snakehead and that had led him to MI6. It was as if they had met in the middle.

"We were planning to put Daniels into the snakehead," Mrs Jones said. "We'd arranged a cover story for him. He was a rich European who'd flown out from London, hoping to put together a big drug deal. Of course, everything changed the moment he spotted you. As soon as we realized you were here, we decided to keep an eye on you and find out what you were up to. I have to say, we were very surprised when you changed your appearance." She ran an eye over Alex. "If we hadn't seen you at the airport, we wouldn't have recognized you."

"I like the teeth," Daniels muttered.

"So what now?" Alex asked. "You said you wanted me to help you."

"You and Ash have already penetrated the snakehead. You've also shaken things up a bit – no surprises there. Maybe you can find Royal Blue for us."

"It shouldn't be too hard to spot," Daniels said.

"It's bloody huge. And if it goes bang you'll hear it ten miles away."

Alex considered. Getting involved with MI6 again was the last thing he wanted; but, in a way, what Mrs Jones had told him changed nothing. He was still working for ASIS. And if he did come across a bomb the size of a family car, there would be no harm in reporting it.

"What do they want it for?" he asked.

"That's what most worries us," Mrs Jones replied. "We've got no idea. Obviously they must be planning something big – but not that big. A nuclear bomb would be about a thousand times more powerful."

"So they're not out to destroy a whole city," Daniels added.

"But if this is a Scorpia operation, you can be pretty sure it's serious and large-scale. These people aren't bank robbers – you know that better than anyone. I have to admit, we're in the dark. Anything you can find out will be helpful to us."

Once again Alex fell silent. But he had made up his mind. "I'll have to tell Ash," he said.

Mrs Jones nodded. "I don't see any harm in that. And in return, we can help you. You and Daniels already know each other. There's no point trying to put him in undercover now. But he can continue to watch over you."

Ben smiled. "I'd be happy to do that," he said.

"We can give you something to contact him

at any time. Have ASIS provided you with any equipment?"

Alex shook his head.

Mrs Jones sighed. "That's the trouble with the Australians. They rush into everything without a second thought. Well, we can give you what you need."

"Gadgets?" Alex's eyes lit up.

"You've got an old friend here; I think you ought to meet."

Smithers was down the corridor in a room that was a cross between a library, an office and a workshop. He was sitting at a desk, surrounded by bits of machinery – like a destructive child on Christmas Day. There was a half-dismantled alarm clock, a laptop computer with its insides spilling out, a video camera divided into about fifty different pieces and a whole tangle of wires and circuits. Smithers himself was wearing sandals, baggy shorts and a bright yellow short-sleeved shirt. Alex wondered how he could possibly carry so much weight around in this heat. But he looked perfectly composed, sitting with his great stomach stretching out towards his knees and two very plump, pink legs tucked away below. He was fanning himself with a Chinese fan decorated with two interweaving dragons.

"Alex? Is that you?" he exclaimed as Alex came into the room. "My dear chap! You don't look like yourself at all. Don't tell me! You must have spent some time with Cloudy Webber."

"Do you know her?" Alex asked.

"We're old friends. The last time we met was at a party in Athens. We were both in disguise, as it happened, and we chatted for half an hour before we recognized each other." He smiled. "But I can't believe you're back again. So much has happened since I last saw you. That was in America. Did my Stingo mosquito lotion come in useful?"

Now it was Alex's turn to smile. The liquid that Smithers had invented attracted insects instead of repelling them and it had been very useful indeed, helping him to get past a checkpoint on Flamingo Bay. "It was great, thanks," he said. "What are you doing here?"

"Mrs Jones asked me to think up a few gadgets for our agents out here in the East," Smithers replied. He lifted the fan. "This is one of them. It's very simple but I rather like it. You see, it looks like an ordinary fan but actually there are very thin plates of galvanized steel hidden under the silk. And when you bring them together" – he folded the fan, then brought it smashing down onto the desk and the wood shattered – "it becomes a useful weapon. I call it—"

"—the fan club?" Alex suggested.

Smithers laughed. "You're getting used to my little ways," he said. "Anyway, I've had all sorts of ideas since I came to Bangkok." He rifled around the surface of the desk and finally found a packet with a dozen sticks of incense. "Everyone burns incense out here," he explained. "It comes in jasmine and musk and it's rather lovely – but my incense has no smell at all."

"So what's the point?"

"After thirty seconds it will make a whole room of people throw up. It's quite the most disgusting gadget I've ever invented, and I have to say we had no fun at all testing it. But it's still quite useful, I think."

He unfolded a sheaf of drawings. "I'm also working on one of these local three-wheeled taxis. They call them tuk-tuks, but this one has got a missile launcher built into the front headlight and a machine gun directly controlled by the handlebars, so I suppose you could say it's an attack-tuk."

"What's this?" Alex asked. He picked up a small bronze Buddha sitting in the lotus position. With its round stomach and bald head, it reminded him a little of Smithers.

"Oh, do be careful with that!" Smithers exclaimed. "That's my Buddha hand grenade. Twist the head twice and throw it, and anyone within ten metres can say their prayers."

He took it back and placed it carefully in a drawer.

"Mrs Jones said you're taking on a snakehead," he continued, and suddenly he was serious. "You be careful, Alex. I know you've done tremendously well in the past, but these people are extremely nasty."

"I know." Alex thought back to his first meeting with Anan Sukit and the fight in the riverside arena. He didn't need to be told.

"There are all sorts of things I'd love to equip you with," Smithers said. "But as I understand it, you're working undercover as an Afghan refugee. Which means you won't be carrying very much. Is that right?"

Alex nodded. He was disappointed. Smithers had once given him a Nintendo DS jammed with special devices, and he would have felt more confident having something like that with him now.

Smithers opened an old cigar box. The first object he took out was a watch, a cheap fairground thing on a plastic strap. He handed it to Alex.

Alex looked at the time. According to the watch, it was half past six. He shook it. "This doesn't work," he said.

"We have to think about the psychology," Smithers explained. "A poor Afghan refugee wouldn't own many possessions, but he would be very proud of the few he did have – even a broken watch. But this watch will work when it matters. There's a powerful transmitter and a battery inside. If you get into trouble, set the hands to eleven o'clock and it will send out a signal which will repeat every ten minutes until it runs out of power. We'll be able to pick you up anywhere on the globe."

Smithers rummaged around in the box again and took out three coins. Alex recognized them. They were Thai currency: one baht, five baht and ten baht, worth about twenty-five pence in total.

"I don't think anyone would worry about a few local coins," he said, "and these are rather fun. They're actually miniature explosives. Let me show you how you detonate them."

He produced a half-empty packet of chewing gum. At least, that was what it looked like. But then he turned it round in his podgy fingers and slid open a secret panel. There were three tiny switches on the other side, marked with the figures 1, 5 and 10.

"This is how it works," he explained. "The coins are magnetic so you can stick them to a metal surface when you want to use them. They won't be activated until you flick the appropriate switch – just make sure you get the right value. The coins will blow open a lock or even smash a hole in a wall. Think of them as miniature landmines. And do try not to spend them!"

"Thanks, Mr Smithers."

"And finally, I've got something that might come in very useful if you find yourself off the beaten track." Smithers pulled open a drawer in the desk and took out an old belt with a heavy silver buckle. "You can slip it into your jeans. There's a particularly sharp knife hidden inside the buckle. It's made out of toughened plastic and is rather cunningly designed so it won't show up on X-ray machines if you go through an airport. And if you slice open the belt, you'll find matches, medicine, water-purifying tablets and knockout pills that are guaranteed to work on eleven different varieties of snake. I developed it for use in the jungle, and although you're not heading that way, you never know." He handed it across. "It's a shame, really. I'd love to give you the trousers that go with it. The legs are highly inflammable."

"Exploding jeans?" Alex asked.

"Flares," Smithers replied. He reached out and shook Alex's hand. "Good luck, old bean. And one last word of advice." He leant forward as if afraid of being overheard. "I wouldn't trust these Australians if I were you. They're not a bad lot. But they are a bit rough, if you know what I mean. They don't play by the rules. Just keep your wits around you." He tapped the side of his nose. "And call for help the moment you need us. That Ben Daniels is a good chap. He won't let you down."

Alex gathered up his few weapons. As he left, he heard Smithers humming behind him. The song was that old Australian favourite, "Waltzing Matilda". Alex wondered what Smithers had meant by his warning. Did he really know something that Alex didn't or was he just being mischievous?

Ben Daniels was waiting outside.

"Are you ready, Cub?" he asked.

"Armed and dangerous," Alex replied.

The two of them left together.

THE SILENT STREETS

Ash was already in the room when Alex got back. At first he was angry.

"Where the hell have you been, Alex?" he growled. "I was worried about you. I told you to wait for me here." Then his eyes narrowed. He glanced down at Alex's waist. "That's a nice belt. Where did you get it?"

Alex was impressed. His godfather had spent nearly half his life as a spy, and of course he had been trained to notice every detail. Despite everything that had happened in the last twenty-four hours, Ash had immediately picked up on this one tiny change in Alex's appearance.

"It was given to me," Alex said.

"Who by?"

"I met some old friends..."

Quickly Alex described what had happened: how he had seen Ben Daniels in the crowd, followed him to Wat Ho and found himself in the MI6 stronghold. Mrs Jones had given him permission to tell Ash about Royal Blue and he mentioned the possible link between Major Yu and Scorpia. Ash's eyes grew dark when he heard the name.

"Nobody told me they were involved," he muttered. "I don't like this, Alex. And nor will Ethan Brooke. You and I are meant to be gathering information. Nothing more, nothing less. Now it's getting messy."

"That's not my fault, Ash."

"Maybe I should go to this temple, have a word with Mrs Jones." Ash thought for a moment, then shook his head. "No. There's no use arguing with her. Go on..."

Alex went on with his story. It seemed he was now working for not one but two secret services. He supposed Ash had a point. The mission had already been bent out of shape, and suddenly there was a ticking bomb at the heart of it. Why did Scorpia need Royal Blue? If Scorpia were involved, it was bound to be something messy – they wouldn't care how many people died. But why this bomb? Why not any other?

Alex tried to put it out of his head. He finished by describing how once again Smithers had equipped him.

"So Smithers is still with MI6!" Ash smiled briefly. "He's quite a character. And he supplied the belt? What does it do – besides keeping your trousers up?"

"I haven't had a chance to examine it yet," Alex admitted. "But there's a knife in the buckle. And there's stuff hidden inside. Some sort of jungle survival kit."

"Who said you were heading into the jungle?"

Alex shrugged.

Ash shook his head. "I'm not sure you should have it."

"Why not?"

"Because it may not fit in with your cover. It didn't come from Afghanistan like everything else you're wearing. If we get into any more trouble, it could be noticed."

"Forget it, Ash. I'm keeping it. But if you like, I'll make sure it's out of sight." Alex untucked his shirt and let it hang over the belt.

"What about the watch? Did Smithers give you that too?"

"Yes." Alex wasn't surprised that Ash had also noticed the watch. He held out his wrist. "In case you're wondering, the hands don't move. It's got a transmitter in it. I can contact MI6."

"Why would you want to do that?"

"I might need help."

"If you need help, you can call me."

"I don't have your number, Ash."

Ash scowled. "I'm not sure ASIS would be too happy about any of this."

Alex held his ground. "That's too bad," he said.

Ash could see that Alex was in no mood for an argument. "All right," he said. "Maybe it's for the best. I won't have to worry about you so much if

I know you've got back-up. But don't contact MI6 without telling me, OK? Promise me that. I don't work for them any more and when all is said and done, I've got my reputation to consider."

Alex nodded. He had decided not to mention the three exploding coins and the detonators concealed in the chewing gum packet. Ash might try to take those too. He changed the subject. "How did you get on?" he asked. "Did you go to the river?"

Ash lit a cigarette. It still surprised Alex that a man who looked after himself so carefully in every other respect chose to smoke. "It's all good news," he said. "I found the arena where you were taken – or what was left of it – and spoke to a guy called Shaw. You may remember him. He was the one who took the photographs. Richard Shaw. Or Rick to his friends."

"What was he doing there?"

"There were dozens of them, salvaging what they could out of the wreckage. Papers, computer disks, that sort of thing. Our late friend Mr Sukit had his offices there, and there was plenty of stuff they wouldn't want the police to find."

"What did Shaw say?"

"I got him to take me to Sukit's deputy. Another charming guy. Looked like he'd been in a street fight – face all over the place. He obviously had a lot on his mind, but I persuaded him to send us on the next step of our journey. After all, we'd paid the money. And you'd done what they wanted. You'd taken part in their fight, even if you had humiliated their champion."

"What about the fire and all the rest of it?"

"Nothing to do with you. They think the Chada Trading Company was hit by a rival gang. The long and the short of it is that they're happy to get us out of the way. We leave for Jakarta tonight."

"Jakarta?"

"We're moving further down the pipeline, Alex. They're smuggling us into Australia via Indonesia. I don't know how, but it'll almost certainly involve some sort of ship. Jakarta's only about forty-eight hours by sea from Darwin. Maybe it'll be a fishing boat, or possibly something bigger. We'll find out soon enough."

"How do we get to Jakarta?"

"We fly just like anyone else." Ash produced a folder containing two plane tickets, passports, visas and a letter of credit written on smart paper with the name UNWIN TOYS printed across the top. "We're being met at Jakarta Soekarno-Hatta International Airport," he went on. "I'm now a sales manager for Unwin Toys. Flying in to look at their new range and bringing my son with me."

"Unwin Toys ... I've heard of them."

The name had seemed familiar the moment he saw it. Now Alex remembered. He had seen their products all over London, often on market stalls or bargain basements on Oxford Street. They specialized in radio-controlled cars, building kits and water pistols – always made out of brightly coloured plastic, manufactured in the Far East and guaranteed to fall apart a few days after they were opened. Unwin Toys wasn't a great name but it was a well-known one, and he found it hard to believe that it could be tied in with the snakehead.

It was as if Ash knew what was in his mind. "Think about it, Alex," he said. "A big company like Unwin Toys would be a perfect cover for a smuggling operation. They're moving goods all over the world, and the fact that they're for little kids – it's the last place you'd think of looking."

Alex nodded. He could imagine it. A crate full of plastic trucks, each one loaded with a stash of heroin or cocaine. Water pistols that were actually the real thing. Teddy bears with God knows what inside. All sorts of unpleasant secrets could hide behind such an innocent facade.

"We're making real progress," Ash said. "But we still have to be careful. The more we know, the more dangerous we become to the snakehead." He thought for a moment. "What you said just now, about calling me. You're right. I want you to remember a phone number. Write it on your hand."

"What phone number?"

"If anything happens, if we get separated, call the number before you contact anyone else. It's my mobile. But the number's special, Alex. It was given to me by ASIS. You can call from anywhere in the world and you'll be put through instantly. It will cost you nothing. The numbers will override any security system in any telephone network so you can reach me any time, anywhere. What do you say?"

Alex nodded. "Fine."

Ash gave him the number. There were eleven digits but otherwise it was like no phone number Alex had ever heard before. He wrote them on the back of his hand. The numbers would soon fade, but by then he would have memorized them.

"What now?" he asked.

"We rest. Then we get a taxi to the airport. It's going to be a long night."

Alex realized the moment had come. They might not be able to speak to each other in Jakarta or on the way to Australia – certainly not in English – and very soon after that, the whole business would be over. Once they had arrived in Darwin, Alex wouldn't be needed any more.

"All right, Ash," he said. "You promised you'd tell me about my mum and dad. You were the best man at their wedding and they made you my god-father. And you were there when they died. I want to know all about them because, for me, it's like they didn't exist. I want to know where I came from, that's all … and what they thought about me." He paused. "And I want to know what happened in Malta. You said that Yassen Gregorovich was there. Was he the one who gave you that scar? How did that happen? Was my dad to blame?"

There was a long silence. Then Ash nodded slowly. He stubbed out his cigarette.

"All right," he said. "On the plane."

They were thirty thousand feet above the Gulf of Thailand, heading south on the short flight to Jakarta. The plane was only half full. Alex and Ash had a whole row to themselves, right at the back. Ash had smartened himself up a little with a white shirt and a cheap tie. He was, after all, meant to be a sales manager. But Alex hadn't changed. He was grubby and a little ragged, still wearing the clothes he had been given in Bangkok. Perhaps that was why the two of them had been seated on their own. In front of them the other passengers were dozing in the strange half-light of the cabin. Outside, the sun had set. The plane hung in the darkness.

Ash hadn't spoken while they took off and climbed into the sky. He had accepted two miniature whisky bottles from the stewardess but he was still sitting in silence, his dark eyes darker than ever, fixed on the ice in his glass as it slowly melted. He looked even more exhausted than usual. Alex had noticed him swallow two tablets with his drink. It had taken him a while to realize that Ash was in constant pain. He was beginning to wonder if his godfather really was going to tell him what he wanted to know.

And then, without warning, Ash began to speak.

"I met your dad on my first assignment for

Special Operations. He joined just before me, but he was completely different. Everyone knew John Rider. Top of his class. Golden boy. On the fast track to the top." There was no rancour in Ash's voice. There was no emotion at all. "He couldn't have been more than twenty-six. Recruited out of the Paras. Before that he'd been at Oxford University. A first-class degree in politics and economics. And did I mention that he was also a brilliant athlete? Rowed for Oxford – and won. A good tennis player too. And now he was in Prague, in charge of his first operation, and I was a nobody sent along to learn the ropes.

"Well, as it turned out, the whole thing was a shambles. It wasn't John's fault. Sometimes it just happens that way. But afterwards, at the debriefing, I met him properly for the first time, and you know what I liked most about him? It was how calm he was. We had three agents dead – not ours, thank God. The Czech police were going crazy. And the Museum of East European Folk Art and Antiquities had burnt down. Actually, it wasn't really a museum, but that's another story. Your dad wasn't much older than me and he wasn't even worried. He didn't shout at anyone. He never lost his temper. He just got on with it.

"After that we became friends. I'm not sure how it happened. We lived near each other – he had a flat in an old warehouse in Blackfriars, set back from the river. We started playing squash together.

In the end we must have played about a hundred games, and you know what? I won at least a couple of them. Sometimes we met for a drink. John liked black velvet: champagne and Guinness. He was away a lot, of course, and he wasn't allowed to tell me what he'd been doing. Even though we were in the same service, I didn't have clearance. But you heard things, and I looked in on him a couple of times when he was in hospital. That was how I met your mother."

"She was a nurse."

"That's right. Helen Beckett. That was her maiden name. She was very attractive. Same colour hair as you. And maybe the same eyes. I actually asked her out, if you want to know. She turned me down very sweetly. She was already going out with your dad. She knew him from Oxford; they'd met when she was studying medicine."

"Did she know then what my dad did?"

"I don't know how much he told her, but of course she knew something. When you're treating someone with two broken ribs and a bullet wound, you don't imagine they fell over playing golf. But it didn't bother her. The next thing I knew, she had moved in with him and we weren't playing squash quite so often."

"Did you ever get married, Ash?" Alex asked.

Ash shook his head. "Never met the right girl, although I had fun with quite a few wrong ones. I'm actually quite glad, Alex. I'll tell you why.

"You can't afford to get scared in our business. Fear's the one thing that will kill you faster than anything, and although it's true to say that all agents are fearless, generally what that means is that they're not afraid for themselves. All that changes when you get married, and it's even worse when you have kids. Alan Blunt didn't want your dad to marry. He knew that in the end he'd be losing his best man."

"He knew my mother?"

"He had her investigated." Alex looked shocked and Ash smiled. "It was standard procedure. He had to be sure she wasn't a security risk."

So somewhere inside MI6 Special Operations there was a file on his mother. Alex made a mental note of it. Maybe one day it would be something he would dig out.

"I was quite surprised when John asked me to be his best man," Ash went on. "I mean, he was such a hotshot and nobody had even noticed I existed. But he didn't really have much choice. His brother, Ian, was away on an assignment ... and there's something else you might as well know. Spies don't have many friends. It goes with the territory. John was still in touch with one or two people from university – he'd told them he was working for an insurance company – but friendship doesn't really work when you have to lie all the time."

Alex knew that was true. It was the same for him at school. Everyone at Brookland had been told he had been struck down by a series of illnesses in the past eight months. He'd been back at school a bit and he'd even joined a school trip to Venice. But he'd felt like an outsider. Somehow his friends knew that something wasn't adding up, and the knowledge had soured their relationship.

"Did he have any other family?" he asked.

"Apart from his brother?" Ash shook his head. "There was no family that I knew of. The wedding was at a registry office in London. There were only half a dozen people there."

Alex felt a twinge of sadness. He would have liked his mother to have had a white wedding in a country church with a big party in a marquee and speeches and dancing and too much to drink. After all, he already knew that her happiness wasn't going to last long. But he understood that he was getting a glimpse of a secret agent's life. Friendless, secretive and a little empty.

The plane trembled briefly in the air, and further down the aisle one of the call lights blinked on. Outside the window, the sky was very black.

"Tell me more about my mother," Alex said.

"I can't, Alex," Ash replied. He twisted in his seat and Alex noticed a flicker of pain in his eyes. The tablets hadn't kicked in yet. "I mean, she liked to read. She went to the cinema a lot – she preferred foreign films if she had a choice. She never bought expensive clothes but she still looked good." Ash sighed. "I didn't know her that well.

And she didn't really trust me, if you want the truth. Maybe she blamed me. I was part of the world that put John in danger. She loved your dad; she hated what he did. And she was smart enough to know that she couldn't talk him out of it."

Ash opened the second miniature and poured the contents into his plastic glass.

"Helen found out she was expecting you when John was in the middle of his toughest assignment," Ash continued. "The timing couldn't have been worse. But a new organization had come to the attention of MI6. I don't need to tell you its name. I guess you know more about Scorpia than I do. Anyway, there it was: an international network of ex-spies and assassins. People who'd gone into business for themselves.

"At first they were useful. You have to remember that MI6 actually welcomed them at the beginning. If you wanted information about what the CIA were up to or how the Iranians were getting on with their nuclear programme, Scorpia would sell it to you. If you wanted to do something outside the law with no way of having it traced back to you, there they were! That was the whole point about them. They were loyal to no one. They were only interested in money. And they were bloody good at their job. Until you came along, Alex, they had never really failed.

"But MI6 became worried about them. They could see that Scorpia were getting out of control, particularly when a couple of their own agents were murdered in Madrid. All around the world, intelligence agencies are regulated, which is to say they play by the rules – at least, to a certain extent. But not Scorpia. They were growing bigger and more powerful, and at the same time they were becoming more ruthless. They didn't care how many people they killed so long as they got their cheque.

"So Alan Blunt – who'd just become the chief executive of MI6 Special Operations – decided to put your father into Scorpia. The idea was to place him inside the organization, to get them to recruit him. Once he was there, he'd find out everything he could about them. Who was on the executive board? Who was paying them? Who were their connections within the intelligence agencies? That sort of thing. But to do that, MI6 had to put your dad into deep cover. That meant faking everything about him."

"I know about this," Alex interrupted. "They pretended he'd been in jail."

"They actually sent him to jail for a time. They had to be thorough. There were newspaper stories about him. Everyone turned against him. It looked like he lost all his money and he had to sell the flat. He and Helen moved to some dump in Bermondsey. It was very hard on her."

"But she must have known the truth."

"I can't tell you that. Maybe your dad told her. Maybe he didn't."

Alex couldn't believe that. Somehow he was sure his mother would have known. "He was recruited by Scorpia," he said.

"That's right. They sent him to their training facility on the island of Malagosto, just a few miles from Venice."

The name made Alex shiver. He had been sent there himself when Scorpia had tried to recruit him.

"As far as Scorpia were concerned, John Rider was a gift," Ash said. "He was a brilliant operator. He had an excellent track record inside British intelligence. And he was desperate. He was also a very good-looking man, by the way. One of the board members at Scorpia took a fancy to him."

"Julia Rothman." Alex had met her too. She had talked about his father over dinner in Positano.

"The very same. She quickly saw John's potential, and soon he was a senior training officer with special responsibility for some of Scorpia's younger recruits. And she gave him a code name. He was called Hunter."

"How do you know all this?" Alex asked.

"That's a good question." Ash smiled. "Because, finally, someone had noticed I existed. Alan Blunt sent me out to shadow John in the field. I was his back-up. My job was to stay close but not too close, to be there if he needed to make contact. And that's how I came to be there when it all ended."

"In Malta."

"Yeah. In Malta."

"What happened?"

"Your dad was coming in. He'd had enough of Scorpia *and* MI6. You had just been born. John wanted a normal life; and anyway, he'd achieved what he'd set out to do. Thanks to him, we knew a great deal about the structure of command within Scorpia. We had the names of most of their agents. We knew who was paying them and how much.

"The job now was to bring him home without arousing suspicion. We knew Julia Rothman would kill him if she found out he was a spy. The plan was to get him back to England and then let him disappear. A new home. A new identity. The whole works... He'd start a new life in France with you and your mum. I should have mentioned that he spoke fluent French, by the way. If things had gone the way they'd planned, you'd be speaking French now. You'd be in a *lycée* in Marseilles or somewhere and you wouldn't know anything about all this.

"Well, it was right at this time that Scorpia unwittingly provided an opportunity for us to get John out. There was a man called Caxero. He was a petty criminal: a drug dealer, a money launderer ... that sort of thing. But he must have rubbed someone up the wrong way, because someone had paid Scorpia to hit him. Your dad was sent to do the job.

"Caxero lived in Mdina in the middle of Malta. It's an old citadel, completely surrounded by walls.

Caxero's home town has another name too. It is so quiet and full of shadows, even in the winter, that the locals call it the Silent City. And MI6 realized it was the perfect place for the ambush that would bring John home.

"Your dad wasn't sent there alone. He was accompanied by a young assassin, one of the best who ever came out of Malagosto. I understand you met him. His name was Yassen Gregorovich."

Alex shivered again. He couldn't help himself. They were certainly digging deep into his past tonight.

He remembered the slim, fair-haired Russian with the ice-cold eyes. Alex had met Yassen on his first mission. Yassen could have killed him then but had chosen not to. And then they had met a second time in the South of France. It had been Yassen who had led him into the nightmare world of Damian Cray. Alex thought back to the last moments they had been together. Once again Yassen had refused to kill him, and this time it had cost him his own life.

"What can you tell me about Yassen?" he asked.

"An interesting young man," Ash replied, but there was a sudden coldness in his voice. "He was born in a place called Estrov. You won't have heard of it, but it was certainly of interest to us. The Russians had a secret facility there – biochemical warfare – but one day the whole place blew up. Hundreds were killed – and Yassen's father was one of them. His mother was injured, and died six months later.

"The Russians tried to hush the whole thing up. They didn't want to admit anything had happened, and even now we don't know the whole truth. But one thing was certain. By the end of the year, Yassen was totally alone. He was just fourteen years old, Alex. The same age as you are now."

"How did Scorpia find him?"

"He found them. He crossed the whole of Russia on his own, with no money and no food. He worked in Moscow for a while, living on the street and running errands for the local mafiya. We still don't know how he managed to find his way to Scorpia, but all of a sudden he turned up at Malagosto. Curiously, your dad was in charge of his training for a time. He told me the boy was a natural. It's funny, isn't it? In a way, the two of you and Yassen had a lot in common." Ash turned to Alex and he seemed suddenly ghost-like in the artificial light of the plane. A strange look came into his eyes. "John had a soft spot for Yassen," he said. "He really liked him. What do you make of that? The spy and the assassin. A bit of an odd couple, I'd say..."

And fifteen years after his father had saved his life, Yassen had sacrificed himself for Alex, repaying the debt of an old friendship. But Alex didn't tell Ash that. For some reason, he wanted to keep it to himself.

"This was the deal in Malta," Ash said. Suddenly

he sounded tired, as if he wanted to get this over with. "Caxero was a man of habit – and that's dangerous if you're in crime. He liked to have a black coffee and a cognac every night at a little café in the square opposite St Paul's Cathedral in Mdina. That was where they were going to kill him. John let me know when the hit was arranged. It was going to be at eleven o'clock at night on 11 February. We'd be there waiting. We'd wait until they'd killed Caxero – he was a nasty piece of work and we decided we might as well let Scorpia get him out of the way – and then we'd move in and grab John. But we'd let Yassen escape. He'd report back to Scorpia. He'd tell them that their man had been captured.

"It had to look good. I was in charge of the operation. This was the first time I had been given command. I had nine men, and even though John was our target we were all carrying live ammunition – not blanks. Yassen might have been able to tell the difference. He was that smart. We were all wearing concealed body armour. John wouldn't be aiming at us when we moved in but Yassen would. And we already knew he was a crack shot.

"I'd put a couple of my people in place that morning. The cathedral had these two bell towers – one on either side – and I put a man in each. I remember it also had two clocks. One of them was five minutes slow. I thought it was strange, the faces showing different times. Anyway, the

197

men in the towers had night-vision glasses and radios. They could see the whole town from up there. They'd make sure that nothing went wrong."

Ash paused.

"Everything went wrong, Alex. Everything."

"Tell me."

Ash sipped his whisky. All the ice had melted.

"We arrived at Mdina just after half past ten. It was a beautiful night. This was February, before the tourist season had started. There was a sliver of a crescent moon and a sky full of stars. As we came in through the south gate, it was like stepping back a thousand years in time. The roads in Mdina are narrow and the walls are high. And all the bricks are different shapes and sizes. You can almost imagine them being laid, one by one.

"The whole place felt deserted. The shutters were closed on the houses and the only light seemed to come from the wrought-iron lamps hanging over the corners. As we made our way up the Triq Villegaignon – the main street – a horse-drawn carriage crossed in front of us. They use them to ferry tourists, but this one was on its way home. I can still hear the echo of the horse's hooves and the rattle of the wheels on the cobbles.

"I got a whisper in my earpiece from one of the lookouts in the towers. Caxero was in his usual place, drinking his coffee and smoking a cigar. No sign of anyone else. It was a quarter to eleven.

"We crept forward, past an old chapel on one

side of the road, a crumbling palazzo on the other. All the shops and restaurants were closed. I had seven men with me; we were all dressed in black. We'd spent half the day studying the map of Mdina and I signalled them to spread out. We were going to surround the square, ready to move in.

"Ten to eleven. I could see the time on the cathedral clock. And there was Caxero. He was a short, round man in a suit. He had a fancy moustache and he was holding his coffee cup with his little finger pointing into the air. There were a couple of cars parked in the square next to some cannons and a waiter standing in the doorway of the café. Otherwise, nothing.

"But then, suddenly, they were there, John Rider and Yassen Gregorovich – or Hunter and Cossack. Those were the names they used. They were five minutes early ... or so I thought. That was my first mistake."

"The clocks..."

"The cathedral clocks. Yes. One was right and one was wrong, and in all the tension I'd been looking at the one that was five minutes slow. As for Yassen, it was like some trick in a film. One minute he wasn't there, the next he was, with John next to him. It was a ninja technique – how to move and stay invisible – and the irony was, it was probably your dad who'd taught him.

"I don't think Caxero saw them coming. They walked straight up to him and he was still holding his coffee cup in that stupid way. He looked up just as a complete stranger shot him in the heart. Yassen didn't do it quickly. I remember thinking that I'd never seen anyone so relaxed.

"I was worried that my men wouldn't be in place yet, that not all the exits from the square would be covered. But in a way that didn't matter. Don't forget we wanted Yassen to escape. That was part of the plan.

"I stepped out of my hiding place. Yassen saw me and all hell broke loose.

"Yassen fired at me. Two of his bullets missed but I felt the third slam into my chest. It was like being hit by a sledgehammer, and if I hadn't been wearing an armour-plated vest, I'd have been killed. As it was, I was blown off my feet. I went smashing down into the cobbles, almost dislocating my shoulder. But I didn't hang around, Alex. I got straight back up again. That was my second mistake. I'll come to that later.

"Anyway, suddenly everyone was firing at once. The waiter turned round and dived for cover. About half a second later, the plate-glass window of the café shattered. It came down like a shower of ice. The men high up in the cathedral were using rifles. The others were entering the square from different sides. Your dad and Yassen had separated – as I knew they would. It was standard procedure. Staying together would have just made it easier for us to catch both of them. For a moment, I thought everything was going to work out all right after all.

"It didn't.

"Three of my men grabbed hold of John. They'd cornered him and it really did look as if there was nothing he could do. They made him throw down his weapon and lie flat on the ground. That left three others to go after Yassen. Of course, they'd let him get away. But it would still be close. That was the plan.

"Yassen Gregorovich had plans of his own. He was halfway across the square, making for one of the side streets. But then suddenly he stopped, turned round and fired three times. The gun had a silencer; it hardly made any sound. And this time he wasn't aiming for the chest. His bullets hit one of my men between the eyes, one in the side of the neck and one in the throat. Two of them died instantly. The third went down and didn't move.

"There was still one agent left. His name was Travis and I'd chosen him personally. He was on the far side of the square and I saw him hesitate. He didn't know what to do. After all, I'd given him orders not to shoot Yassen. Well, he should have disobeyed me. The situation was out of control. Enough people had already died that night. He should have shot Yassen or got the hell out of there, but he did neither. He just stood there and Yassen gunned him down too. A bullet in the leg to bring him down and then another in the head to finish him off. The square was littered with bodies.

And this whole thing was meant to be bloodless!"

Ash fell silent.

Alex noticed he had finished his whisky. "Do you want another drink, Ash?" he asked.

Ash shook his head. Then he went on.

"Yassen had gone. We had John. So, in a way, we'd succeeded. Maybe I should have left it at that. But I couldn't. This was my first solo operation and Yassen Gregorovich had wiped out almost half my task force. I went after him.

"I don't know what I was thinking. Part of me knew that I couldn't kill him. But nor could I just let him go. I pulled off my body armour; it had a quick release and I couldn't run with it on. Then I started across the square and towards the northern wall. I heard someone shout after me – it might even have been John. But I didn't care. I turned a corner. I remember the pink stone and a balcony like something in an opera house. I couldn't see anyone. I thought Yassen must have got away.

"And then, without any warning, he stepped out in front of me.

"He'd waited! A whole town crowded with MI6 agents and he just stood there like he owned the place and none of us could touch him. I ran straight into him. I couldn't stop myself. His hand moved so fast that I didn't see it. I felt it smash into the nerve points in my wrist. I lost my gun; it went spinning away into the darkness. At the same time, his gun pressed against my neck.

"He was ten years younger than me. A Russian kid who'd got sucked into all this because his parents had died in an accident. And he'd beaten me. He'd taken out nearly half my team. I was going to be next.

"Who are you?

"MI6.

"There was no point lying. We wanted Scorpia to know.

"How did you know we would be here?

"I didn't answer that. He pushed harder with the gun, hurting me. But that didn't matter. It would all be over soon anyway.

"You should have stayed at home.

"And then he turned and ran.

"To this day, I don't know why he didn't shoot me. Maybe his gun had jammed. Or perhaps it was simpler than that. He'd killed Caxero, Travis and three more of my men: maybe he'd run out of ammunition. I watched him disappear down the next alleyway and that was when I realized he'd had a knife as well as a gun. The hilt was sticking out of my stomach. I didn't feel anything. But looking down... There was so much blood. It was pouring out of me. It was everywhere."

Ash stopped. The soft scream of the plane's engines rose in pitch for a moment. Alex wondered if they were coming into Jakarta.

"The pain came later," Ash said. "You have no idea how bad it was. I should have died that night.

Maybe I would have, but your dad had come after me. He'd feared the worst – and he'd put his own life at risk, because if Yassen had seen him, he would have known that the whole thing was a set-up. By then I was on the ground. I was slipping away fast. And I was cold. I've never felt so cold.

"Your father didn't take the knife out. He knew that would kill me straight away. He put pressure on the wound and kept it there until the ambulance came. I was airlifted to Valletta, where I stayed on critical for a week. I'd lost five pints of blood. In the end I came through, but ... you've seen the scar. I'm missing about half my stomach. There wasn't anything they could do about that. There are about a hundred things I'm not meant to eat because there's nowhere for them to go. And I have to take pills ... a lot of pills. But I'm alive. I suppose I should be grateful for that."

There was a long silence.

"Scorpia got my dad in the end," Alex said.

"Yeah. A couple of months later. Just after you were christened, Alex. It was almost the last time I saw your dad – and if it makes you feel any better, I'd never seen him look happier than when he was holding you that day. He and your mother. It was like you made them real people again. You brought them out of the shadows."

"You went with them to the airport. They were on their way to France. You said they were going to Marseilles."

"That's right. They had to leave you behind. You had an ear infection, so you couldn't fly. Otherwise you'd have been with them."

"You were there when the bomb went off on their plane."

Ash looked away. "I said I wouldn't talk about that and I meant it. Somehow Scorpia found out they'd been tricked and they took revenge. That's all I know."

"What happened to you, Ash? Why did you leave MI6?"

"I'll tell you that, Alex, and then that's the end of it. I think I've lived up to my side of the bargain."

Ash crumpled his plastic glass and shoved the broken pieces into the compartment in front of him.

"I didn't come out of the Malta operation too well if you want the truth," he said. "I was on sick leave for six weeks and the day I returned to Liverpool Street, Alan Blunt called me into his office. He then gave me a bollocking for everything that had gone wrong.

"First of all, there was the thing with the time. The wrong clock. But it turned out that the most stupid mistake I'd made was to stand up after Yassen had shot me. You see, that had told him we were all wearing body armour, and that was the reason why he'd shot Travis and the others in the head. It was all my fault – at least, according to Blunt."

"That wasn't fair," Alex muttered.

"You know what, mate? I thought more or less the same thing. And then, chasing after Yassen when the whole point was to let him get away. That was the final nail in my coffin. Blunt didn't fire me. But I was demoted. He made it clear that I wouldn't be heading up any more operations. It didn't matter that I'd almost been killed. In a way, that just made it worse. A nice guy, Mr Blunt. All heart!"

Ash shook his head.

"It was soon afterwards that your parents died together on that plane, and after that my heart sort of went out of it. I told you when we were in Bangkok: it was your dad who was the patriot, serving his country. Maybe I felt like that for a time, but by the end I'd had enough. I did a few more months' desk duty, but then I handed in my resignation and headed down under. ASIS were keen to have me. And I wanted to start again.

"I saw you a few times, Alex. I looked in on you to see that you were OK. After all, I was your godfather. But by then Ian had started adoption proceedings. I had a drink with him the night before I left England and he told me he was going to look after you. It was obvious you didn't need me. In fact, if truth be told, you were probably better off without me. I hadn't been much help, had I!"

"You shouldn't blame yourself," Alex said. "I don't."

"Anyway, I saw you again. I was in London, working with the Australian embassy. You were still at primary school – and Jack was looking after you."

"You went out with her."

"A couple of times. We had a laugh together." Ash glanced briefly at Alex as if searching for something. "I couldn't believe it when I heard that MI6 had recruited you," he muttered. "Alan Blunt certainly is a cold-hearted son of a bitch. And then, when you wound up in Australia! But I still wish you hadn't come on this mission, Alex. I don't want you to get hurt."

"A bit late now, Ash."

The lights in the cabin came back on, and the stewardesses began to move up the aisle. At the same time, Alex felt his stomach lurch as they began to come down.

They had arrived in Jakarta, the next step on their journey. The end of the pipeline was in sight.

UNWIN TOYS

Sometimes Alex wondered whether all the airports in the world had been designed by the same architect: someone with a love of shops and corridors, plate-glass windows and potted plants. Here he was at Soekarno-Hatta, the international airport of Jakarta, but it might just as well have been Perth or Bangkok. The floors might be more polished and the ceilings higher, and every other shop seemed to be selling rattan furniture or the colourful printed cloth known as batik. But otherwise he could have been right back where he started.

They came through passport control quickly. The official in his glass-fronted booth barely glanced at the forged documents before stamping them, and without a word being spoken they were in. Nor did they have to wait at baggage claim. They had just one suitcase between them and Ash had carried it on and off the plane.

Alex was tired. It was as if the events of the last five days in Bangkok had finally caught up with him and all he wanted to do was sleep – although somehow he doubted he would be spending the night in a comfortable bed. Most of all, he wanted time on his own to reflect on what Ash had told him. He had learnt more about his past in the last hour than he had in his entire life, but there were still questions he wanted to ask. Had his father blamed Ash for the mistakes that had been made in Mdina? Why had he been with them at the airport? And what had he seen that he was so unwilling to talk about?

They passed into the arrivals lounge, and once again they were surrounded by a crowd of touts and taxi drivers. This time there were two men waiting for them, both Indonesian, slim and athletic in jeans and short-sleeved shirts. One of them was holding a placard that read KARIM HASSAN. Alex stared at it for a few seconds before the name registered, and he was annoyed with himself. He had completely forgotten that it was the name under which Ash was travelling. Ash was Karim; he was Abdul. It didn't matter how tired he was. A mistake like that could get them both killed.

Ash went over to them and introduced himself using a mixture of Dari and sign language. The two men didn't even try to be friendly. They simply turned and walked away, expecting Ash and Alex to follow.

It was ten o'clock, and outside, away from the artificial climate of the air conditioning, the heat was thick and unwelcoming. Nobody spoke as they crossed the main concourse to the kerbside, where a dirty, white van was parked with a third man in the driving seat. The van had double doors at the back with no windows. Alex glanced nervously at Ash. He felt as if he were about to be swallowed up, and he remembered the last time he had got into a car with members of the snakehead. But Ash didn't look worried. Alex followed him in.

The doors slammed shut. The two men got in the front with the driver and they moved off. Alex and Ash sat on a metal bench that had been welded to the floor. Their only view was out of the front windscreen, and that was so filthy Alex wondered how the driver could see where they were going. The van was at least ten years old and had no suspension at all. Alex felt every bump, every pothole. And there were plenty of both.

The airport was about twelve miles from the city, connected by a motorway that was clogged with traffic even at this time of the night. Squinting over the driver's shoulder, Alex barely saw anything until, at last, Jakarta came into sight. It reminded him at first of Bangkok, but as they drew closer he saw that it was uglier and somehow less sure of itself, still struggling to escape from the sprawling shanty town it had once been.

The traffic was horrible. They were carried into Jakarta on a concrete flyover, and suddenly there were cars and motorbikes above them and below them as well as on both sides. Skyscrapers – bulky rather than beautiful – rose up ahead, a thousand light bulbs burning uselessly in offices that were surely empty, colouring the night sky yellow and grey. There were brightly coloured food stalls – *warungs* – along the pavements, but nobody seemed to be eating. The crowds were drifting home like sleepwalkers, pushing their way through the noise and the dirt and the heat.

They turned off the flyover, leaving the main sprawl of the city as quickly as they had entered it. Suddenly the van was rumbling over a dirt track, splashing through puddles and weaving around loose bricks and rubble. There were no street lamps, no signs, no illumination from a moon that had been blocked out by cloud. Alex saw only what the headlights showed him. This was some sort of suburb, a slum area with narrow streets, houses with tin roofs and corrugated iron patches, walls held up by wooden scaffolding. Strange spiky shrubs and stunted palm trees grew at the side of the road. There was no pavement. Somewhere a dog barked. But nowhere was there any sign of life.

They came to gates that seemed to have been cobbled together from pieces of driftwood. Two words – in Indonesian – had been scrawled across them in red paint. As they approached, the driver pressed a remote control in the van and the gates opened, allowing them into a large, square compound with warehouses and offices, lit by a couple of arc lamps and fenced in on all sides. The van stopped. They had arrived.

There didn't seem to be anyone else there. The doors of the van were flung open and the two men led Alex and Ash into one of the warehouses. Alex saw crates stacked high, some of them open, spilling out straw and plastic toys. There was a pile of scooters, tangled together, and a Wendy house lying on its side. A furry monkey was slumped with its legs apart, foam hanging out of a gash in its stomach, staring at them with empty glass eyes. Alex hoped it wasn't an omen. He had never seen a collection of toys that looked less fun. From the state of them – dusty and dilapidated – they could have been here for years.

Two thin mattresses spread out on the floor told him the worst. This was where they were supposed to sleep. There was no sign of any toilet or anywhere to wash. Ash turned to the men and signalled, cupping his hands to his mouth. He was thirsty. The men shrugged and walked out.

It was to be the longest nine hours of Alex's life. He had no sheets or blankets and the mattress did almost nothing to protect him from the stone floor underneath. He was sweating. His clothes were digging into him. The whole of Jakarta was in the grip of a storm that refused to break and the air seemed to be nine parts water. Worst of all were the mosquitoes. They found him almost immediately and refused to leave him alone. There was no point slapping at his face, and after a while Alex stopped bothering. The mosquitoes didn't seem to care. The only escape would be sleep, but sleep refused to come.

Ash couldn't talk to him. There was always a chance there might be microphones in the room. Anyway, he was used to this. To Alex's annoyance, his godfather was asleep almost at once, leaving him on his own to suffer through every minute of the night.

But at last the morning came. Alex must have drifted into some sort of half-sleep because the next thing he knew, Ash was shaking him and grey daylight was seeping in through the windows and the open door. Someone had brought them two glasses of sweet tea and a basket of bread rolls. Alex would have preferred eggs and bacon but decided it was probably better not to complain. Squatting on his mattress, he began to eat.

What was going on? Alex realized that the false passports they had been given in Bangkok had been enough to get them into Indonesia, but Australia, with far stricter border controls, would prove more difficult. Here on the island of Java was about as near as they could get to Australian soil, and the last part of their journey would be across the sea – a passage of approximately forty-eight hours, Ash had said. The place they were in now was connected to Unwin Toys – a storage depot and office complex, from what Alex had seen the night before. They were going to have to wait here until their boat was ready. And what sort of boat would that be? He would find out in good time.

Shortly after nine o'clock, one of the two men who had met them at the airport came for them and led them out of the warehouse where they had slept. The morning light was thick and gloomy but at least it allowed Alex to take better stock of his surroundings. Unwin Toys reminded him of an old-fashioned prisoner-of-war camp, something out of a Second World War film. The buildings were made of wood and seemed to have been bashed together in a hurry, using whatever was at hand. Rickety staircases led up to the first floor. The main square was cracked and uneven with weeds sprouting out of the concrete. It was hard to imagine that a brightly coloured toy wrapped up under a Christmas tree in England might have begun its life here.

By now there were a dozen or so men and women in the complex. Some of them were office staff, sitting behind windows and tapping away at computers. A truck had arrived and there were people unloading it, passing cardboard boxes from hand to hand. Two guards stood by the gates. They seemed to be unarmed, but, noticing the wire fence surrounding them, the arc lamps and the security cameras, Alex suspected they were carrying guns. This was a secret world. It wanted to keep its distance from the city outside.

He looked up. The clouds were thick, an ugly shade of grey. He couldn't see the sun but he could feel it, pressing down on them. Surely it would rain soon. The entire atmosphere was like a balloon filled with water. At any second it could burst.

It was time to go. The white van was there with its engine running. The back doors were open. Somebody called out to them. Ash took a step forward.

Alex would remember the moment later. It was like a flash photograph – a few seconds caught in time when everything was normal and everyone in the picture was still unaware of the approaching danger. He heard a vehicle coming towards the main gates. It occurred to him that it was being driven far too fast, that it would surely have to slow down so that the gates could be opened. Then the realization came that the car wasn't going to slow down, that the driver didn't need open gates to enter.

Without any further warning the gates of the complex were smashed to pieces, one flying open, the other hanging drunkenly off its hinges as first one then a second huge Jeep Cherokee burst through. Each vehicle carried five men, who came tumbling out almost before the Jeeps had stopped. They were all armed with CZ-Scorpion sub-machine guns or AK-47 assault rifles. Some also carried knives. They were dressed in combat outfits and most of them wore red berets, but they didn't look like soldiers. Their hair was too long and they hadn't shaved. Nobody seemed to be in charge. As they spread out across the square, waving their weapons from side to side and screaming out orders, Alex was convinced that he had stepped into the middle of an armed robbery and that he was about to witness a shoot-out between different Jakarta gangs.

Ash had stopped dead. He turned to Alex and muttered a single word. "Kopassus." It meant nothing to Alex. So, making sure that nobody could hear him, Ash added in English, "Indonesian SAS."

He was right.

Kopassus was an abbreviation of Komando Pasukan Khusus, one of the most ruthless fighting forces in the world. It consists of five different groups specializing in sabotage, infiltration, direct action, intelligence and counter-terrorism. The men who had just broken into the compound came from Group 4, a counter-intelligence group based in the south of Jakarta with special responsibility for smuggling operations in and out of the city. It might have been luck that had brought them here, or it could have been the result of a tip-off. But either way, the result would be the same. They were under arrest, and even if they were able to talk their way out of jail – Ash would only have to prove that he worked for ASIS – their work would be over. They would have destroyed their cover. They would never find out how the snakehead had planned to get them into Australia. And, Alex reflected bitterly, he would never catch up with the stolen weapon that Mrs Jones was looking for – Royal Blue. He would have failed twice.

But there was nothing he could do. The Kopassus soldiers had taken up positions across the square so that every angle was covered and nobody could move without being seen. They were still shouting in Indonesian. It didn't really matter what they were saying. Their aim was to confuse and intimidate the opposition, and they seemed to have succeeded. The civilians inside the compound were standing helplessly. Some of them had raised their arms. Kopassus was in control.

They were made to line up. Alex found himself between Ash and one of the men who had met them at the airport. They were covered by at least half a dozen guns. At the same time, three of the soldiers were searching inside the offices and warehouses, making sure nobody was hiding. One of the toy workers had decided to do exactly that. Alex heard a scream, then the smash of breaking glass as the unfortunate man was hurled, head first, through a window. He came crashing into the courtyard, blood streaming from his face. Another of the soldiers lashed out with a foot and the man howled, then staggered to his feet and limped over to join the line.

One last man had climbed out of the Jeep. This was presumably the commanding officer. He was unusually tall for an Indonesian with a long, slender neck and black hair down to his shoulders; Alex heard one of the soldiers refer to him as *kolonel*. Slowly he made his way along the line, shouting out instructions. Alex guessed he was asking for ID.

One after another the toy workers produced scraps of paper, driving licences or work permits, the man who had been thrown out of the window holding his up with shaking hands. The colonel didn't seem interested in any of them. Then he reached Ash. Alex tried not to look as Ash took out the fake passport he had been given in Bangkok. He was afraid his eyes might give something away. He glanced down as the colonel opened the passport and held it up to the light. On the edge of his vision, he saw the colonel hesitate. Then suddenly the man struck out, hitting Ash on both sides of the face with the offending document and screaming at him in Indonesian. Two soldiers appeared from nowhere, pinning Ash's arms behind his back and forcing him to his knees. The barrel of a sub-machine gun was pressed into his neck. The colonel handed the passport to one of his subordinates. For a moment, he examined Ash's face, gazing into his eyes as if his true identity might be found there. Then he moved on.

He stopped in front of Alex.

Alex looked up. He was scared and he didn't care if it showed. Maybe the man would decide that he was just a kid and leave him alone. But the colonel didn't care how old he was. He smelled blood. Something like a smile spread across his face and he rapped out a sentence in Indonesian, holding out a hand for Alex's ID. Alex froze. He didn't have his own passport. That was in Ash's pocket. But even if he was able to produce it, the colonel would know it was fake. Should he tell the man who he was? Just a few words in English would do the trick. End the danger.

End the mission too.

It began to rain.

No. It wasn't quite like that. In London rain has a beginning, a few drops that send people scattering for cover and allow time for umbrellas to rise. In Jakarta, there was no warning. The rain fell as if a dam had burst. In an instant it was flooding down, warm and solid, an ocean of rain that spluttered out of the drainpipes, hammered against the roofs and turned the earth to mud.

And with the flood came a brief moment of confusion. Up until then, Kopassus had been in complete control of the complex, working to a plan that allowed the soldiers to cover every inch of ground. The sudden downpour changed things. Alex didn't even see where the gunfire began. But someone must have decided that they had too much to lose and that the rain would give them enough cover to risk shooting their way out. There were half a dozen shots from somewhere near the warehouse where Alex had slept. They came from a single gun, fired carefully, at precise intervals.

The Kopassus men reacted instantly, diving for cover, returning fire even as they went. The sound of their sub-machine guns was deafening. They didn't seem to care where they were aiming. Alex saw an entire wall ripped apart, the wooden planks shredded. A man who had been standing near the warehouse was blown off his feet by the first volley. Alex had seen him just minutes before, sweeping the yard.

But the Kopassus soldiers were falling too. At least three guns were now being fired at them. As Alex turned, searching for cover, the soldier whose gun had been pressed against Ash's neck fell back, a mushroom of blood erupting from his shoulder. Immediately a second man stepped into his place, firing in the direction from which the bullets had come, the nozzle of his sub-machine gun flashing white behind the rain.

The colonel had pulled out a pistol, a Swiss-made SIG-Sauer P226 and one of the ugliest 9mm weapons on the market. Alex saw him take aim at Ash. His intention was clear. He had been about to arrest a man and that had provoked a firestorm – at least, that was what he thought. Well, whoever the man was, the colonel wasn't going to let him get away. Rough justice. He would execute him here and now and bring an end to all this.

Alex couldn't let it happen. With a cry he hurled

himself sideways, his shoulder slamming into the colonel's stomach. The gun went off, the bullet firing into the air. Carried by Alex's velocity, the two of them came crashing down into a puddle. The colonel tried to bring the gun round to aim at Alex. Alex caught hold of his wrist and slammed it down, smashing the back of his hand against the concrete. The colonel cried out. Rain was driving into Alex's face, blinding him. He forced the colonel's hand up and down a second time. The fingers opened and the gun fell free.

Part of him knew that this was all wrong. He was on the same side as Kopassus, both of them fighting the snakehead, the true enemy. But there was no time to explain. Alex saw a soldier throw something – a round, black object about the size of a cricket ball – through the deluge. He knew at once what it was, even before the explosion that tore open the side of a warehouse, smashed three windows and blew a hole in the roof. A tongue of flame leapt up, only to be driven back by the rain.

More gunfire. The man who had thrown the grenade cried out and reeled backwards, clutching his shoulder. The white van was moving. Alex heard the engine rev, then saw the van begin a clumsy three-point turn. Ash grabbed hold of his arm. His hair was matted; water was streaming down his face.

"We have to go!" he shouted. With the noise of the rain and the shooting, there was no chance of his being overheard.

The colonel lunged sideways, trying to reach the gun. Ash kicked it away, then brought a fist crashing down into the man's head.

"Ash—" Alex began.

"Later!"

The van had completed its first turn. It was being brought round to face the shattered gates. Ash started forward and Alex followed. They caught up with the van just as it began to pick up speed. The driver wasn't waiting for them. Ash reached out and wrenched open the back doors. There was a burst of machine-gun fire and Alex cried out as a line of bullet holes stitched themselves across the side of the van, right in front of him.

"Go!" Ash shouted.

Alex threw himself through the doors into the back of the van. A second later, Ash followed, landing on top of him. The driver didn't seem to notice them. All he cared about was getting away. One of the wing mirrors exploded, the glass shattering and the metal casing tearing free. The engine screamed as the driver pressed his foot on the accelerator. They leapt forward. There was an explosion, so close that Alex felt the flames scorch the side of his face. But then they were away, shooting out through the gates and into the street beyond.

The van skidded all over the road. It slammed into a wall and one side crumpled, sparks flickering as metal and brickwork collided. Alex glanced back. One of the van's doors had been blown off and he saw two soldiers – they looked like ghosts – kneeling in the gateway, firing at them. Bullets, burning white, sliced through the rain. But they were already out of range. The van hurtled up the track they had come down the night before; by now it was little more than a brown river of mud and debris. Alex looked back again, expecting Kopassus to be following. But the rain was falling so hard that the warehouse complex had already disappeared; if the two Jeep Cherokees were after them, it was impossible to tell.

The driver was the same man who had brought them from the airport. He was clutching the steering wheel as if his life depended on it. He looked in the mirror and caught sight of his two unwanted passengers. At once he let loose a torrent of Indonesian. But he didn't slow down or stop. Alex was relieved. It didn't matter where they were heading. All that mattered was that they hadn't been left behind.

"What was that about?" he demanded. His mouth was right next to Ash's ear and he was confident that the driver wouldn't be able to hear what he said or what language he was speaking.

"I don't know." For once, Ash had lost his composure. He was lying on his side, trying to catch his breath. "It was routine ... bad luck. Or maybe someone hadn't paid. It happens all the time in Jakarta."

"Where are we going?"

Ash looked out of the back. It was hard to see anything in the half-light and swirling water of the storm, but he must have recognized something. "This is Kota. The old city. We're heading north."

"Is that good?"

"The port is in the north."

They had joined the morning traffic, and now they were forced to slow down, falling in behind a line of cars and buses. All the food stalls had disappeared beneath a sea of plastic sheeting and the people were crowded in doorways or squatting under umbrellas, waiting for the storm to pass.

The driver turned round and shouted something. Even if it had been in English, Alex doubted that he would have been able to hear.

"He's taking us to the boat," Ash explained.

"You speak Indonesian?"

Ash nodded. "Enough to understand."

The van emerged from a side street and cut across a main road. Alex saw a taxi swerve to avoid them, its horn blaring. Behind them an old house loomed out of the rain. It reminded him of something he might have seen in Amsterdam, but then the whole city had belonged to the Dutch once, a far outpost of their East India Company. They crossed a square. It was lined with cobblestones and, lying in the back of the van, Alex felt every one of them. A crowd of cyclists swerved to avoid them, crashing into each other and tumbling over in a tangle of chains and obscenities. A man pushing a food stall threw himself out of the way with seconds to spare.

Then they were on another main road. There was more traffic here – an endless procession of lorries, each one piled up with goods that were concealed beneath garish plastic tarpaulins. The lorries looked overloaded, as if they might collapse at any time under the weight.

Finally, just ahead, the buildings parted and Alex saw fences, cranes and ships looming high above them. There were warehouses, guard posts and offices made of corrugated iron, huge gantries and great stretches of empty concrete with more lorries and vans making their way back and forth. It was almost impossible to see anything through the endless rain, but this was the port. It had to be. There was a security barrier straight ahead of them, and beyond that a stack of containers behind a barbed-wire fence. The van slowed down and stopped. The driver turned round and explained something in a torrent of Indonesian. Then he was gone.

"Ash—" Alex began.

"This is Tanjung Priok Docks," Ash cut in. "They must be taking us on a container ship." He pointed. "You see those fenced-off areas? They're EPZs: export processing zones. Stuff comes into Jakarta. It gets assembled there and then it's shipped out again. That's our way out of here. Once we're in an EPZ, we'll be safe."

"How do we get in there?" Alex had seen the barriers ahead of them. There were guards on duty, even in the driving rain.

"We pay." Ash grimaced. "This is Indonesia! The docks are run by the military; but the military are in the pay of the Indonesian mafia. Small beer compared to the snakeheads, but still in control around here. You can do anything, so long as you pay." Ash got to one knee and peered out of the window. There was nobody in sight. He glanced at Alex. "Thank you for what you did back there."

"I didn't do anything, Ash."

"The colonel was about to shoot me. You stopped him." Ash shrugged. "That's Kopassus for you. Kill the wrong guy and send flowers to the funeral. Really charming."

"What happens when we get to Australia?"

"Then it's over. I get a pat on the back from Ethan Brooke. You go home."

"Will we see each other again?"

Ash looked away. Like Alex he was completely drenched, his clothes dripping and forming a pool around him. The two of them both looked like shipwrecks. "Who knows?" he growled. "I haven't been much of a godfather, have I? Maybe I should have sent you a Bible or something."

But before Alex could respond, the driver returned and this time he wasn't alone. There were three men with him, their faces hidden under the hoods of their plastic anoraks. They were all talking at once, jabbing their fingers at Alex and Ash, gesticulating wildly. Slowly their meaning became clear, and Alex felt a chasm open up beneath him. They wanted Alex to go with them. But Ash was to stay behind.

The two of them were being separated.

He wanted to cry out, to argue – but even one word would be fatal and he forced himself to keep his mouth shut. He tried to resist, pulling away from the hands that grabbed at him. It was useless. As he was bundled out of the van, he took one last look at Ash. His godfather was watching him almost sadly, as if he had guessed that something bad was going to happen and knew that he was powerless to stop it now that it had.

Alex was half dragged onto the road. Ahead of him a gate had swung open, and he was marched through with a man on each side of him and one ahead. A security guard appeared briefly but the men shouted at him and he quickly turned away.

It was hard to see anything in the driving rain. There was a quayside ahead of them, and a ship, bigger than any Alex had ever seen, the equivalent of about three football pitches in length. The ship had a central section where the crew worked and lived. Alex could see the bridge with four or five huge windows and giant windscreen wipers swinging back and forth, fighting against the rain. The ship had a name, printed in English along the bow: *Liberian Star*. It was being loaded with containers, the rectangular boxes dangling from the huge spreader which loomed over them like some sort of monster in a science-fiction film. A man in a cabin was controlling the cables and pulleys, lowering each box into place with incredible precision.

They entered the EPZ where the next lorryloads of containers were waiting their turn, each one painted a different colour, some displaying the names of the companies that owned them. Alex saw a yellow box sitting on one of the lorries and knew that it was his destination. The name was painted in black: UNWIN TOYS. He looked back, hoping against hope that Ash would be following him after all. But they were alone. Why had the two of them been separated like this? It made no sense. After all, they were supposed to be father and son. He just hoped that Ash would be in a second container and that somehow they would meet up again when they arrived in Darwin. He turned his hand over. The phone number that Ash had given him had almost vanished, reduced to an inky blur by the constant rain. Fortunately Alex had committed it to memory – or at least he hoped so. He would know for sure soon enough – if he ever found a phone.

They reached the yellow container and Alex saw at once that it was locked. More than that, there was a steel pin connected to the door. He guessed its purpose. All containers had to be checked by customs officials both going on and coming off a ship. Obviously they couldn't be opened on their journey, or anything – guns, drugs, people – could be added. The steel pin would have a code number which would already have been checked; it would be checked a second time when they arrived in Australia. If the pin had been tampered with or broken, the entire container would be impounded and examined.

So how was he expected to get in? Alex could see that this was how he was going to travel. Presumably it was too dangerous for him to have a cabin on board the ship; and anyway, as far as the snakehead was concerned, this was all he was: cargo, to be dumped along with all the other merchandise. The man who had been leading the way turned and put a hand on his shoulder, urging him to get down. Alex realized that he was expected to clamber underneath the lorry, between the wheels.

A moment later, he saw why. The container had a secret entrance, a trapdoor that was open, hanging down. He could climb in without touching the main door or the pin that secured it, and once the container was in place, part of a tower with dozens more on top and below, there would be no way that anyone could examine it. The whole thing was simple and effective, and part of him even admired the snakehead. It was certainly a huge business, operating in at least three countries. Ethan Brooke had been right. These people were much more than simple criminals.

He started to crawl under the lorry. Immediately he felt claustrophobic. It wasn't just the weight of the container pressing down on him. He could see that the trapdoor would be locked from the outside. There was a single, solid bolt that slid across. Once that happened, he would be trapped. If the ship sank or if they simply decided to drop the whole thing overboard, he would drown in his own oversized metal coffin. He hesitated and at once the man jabbed him between the shoulders, urging him forward.

Alex turned, pretending to be scared, pleading with his eyes to be reunited with Ash. But how could he make himself understood when he couldn't utter a single word? One of the other men thrust something into his hands: a plastic bag with two bottles of water and a loaf of bread. Supplies for the long journey ahead. The first man pushed him again and shouted.

Alex couldn't delay any longer. He crawled over to the trapdoor. The men gestured and he pulled himself up. But as he went, he stumbled. One of his hands caught hold of the sliding bolt and he steadied himself.

That was his last sight of Indonesia. Mud, dripping rain and the undercarriage of a lorry. He pulled himself into the container and seconds later the trapdoor slammed shut behind him. He heard the bolt slide across with a loud clang. Now there was no way out.

It was only as he straightened up that he realized he could see. There was light inside the container. He looked around. A crowd of anxious faces stared at him.

It seemed he wasn't going to make this part of the journey alone.

THE LIBERIAN STAR

In fact, there were twenty people inside the container, huddled together in the half-light thrown by a single battery-operated lamp. Alex knew at once that they were refugees. He could tell from their faces: not just foreign but afraid, far removed from their own world. Most of them were men, but there were also women and children, a couple of them as young as seven or eight. Alex remembered what Ethan Brooke had told him about illegal immigrants when he was in Sydney. *Half of them are under the age of eighteen*. Well, here was the proof. There were whole families locked together in this metal box, hoping and praying that they would arrive safely in Australia. But they were powerless and they knew it, utterly dependent on the good will of the snakehead. No wonder they looked nervous.

A gaunt, grey-haired man, wearing a loose, brightly coloured shirt and baggy trousers, made his way forward. Alex guessed he was in his sixties. He might once have been a farmer; his hands were coarse and his face had been burnt dry by the sun. He muttered a few words to Alex. He could have been speaking any language – Dari, Hazaragi, Kurdish or Arabic – it would have made no difference. Alex knew that without Ash he was exposed. He had no way of communicating and nobody to hide behind. What would these people do if they discovered that he was an impostor? He hoped he wouldn't have to find out.

The man realized that Alex hadn't understood him. He tapped his chest and spoke a single word. "Salem." That was presumably his name.

He waited for Alex to reply; and when none came he gestured to a woman, who came forward and tried a second language. Alex turned away and sat in a corner. Let them think he was shy or unfriendly. He didn't care. He wasn't here to make friends.

Alex drew his legs up towards him and buried his face against his knees. He needed to think. Why had he been separated from Ash? Had the snakehead somehow found out that the two of them were working for ASIS? All in all, he doubted it. If the snakehead even suspected who they were, they would have dragged them out together and shot them. There had to be another reason for the last-minute decision at the harbour, but try as he might Alex couldn't work out what it was.

There was a sudden jolt. The whole container shook and one of the children began to cry. The other refugees drew closer together and stared around them as if they could somehow see through the flat metal walls. Alex knew what had happened. One of the huge machines – the spreaders – had picked them up, lifting them off the lorry and loading them onto the *Liberian Star*. Right now they could be fifty metres above the quay, dangling on four thin wires. Nobody moved, afraid of upsetting the balance. Alex thought he heard the hum of machinery somewhere above his head. There was a second jolt, and the electric lamp flickered. And that was a horrible thought. Suppose it went out! Could they endure the entire voyage in pitch darkness? The container was swaying very slightly. Somebody shouted, a long way away. They began the journey down.

Alex hadn't been able to see very much of the *Liberian Star* in the rain and the confusion of their arrival, but he had taken in the great metal boxes piled on top of one another with seemingly no space in between. Where would they end up? On top, in the middle or buried somewhere deep in the hold? Once again he had to fight back a sense of claustrophobia. There were no holes drilled in the walls. The only air would come in through the cracks around the door and the secret trapdoor. The container had already reminded Alex of a coffin. Now he felt as if he and the twenty other occupants were about to be buried alive.

They came to a halt. Something clanged against

the outer wall. Two of the children whimpered and Salem went over to them, putting his arms round their shoulders and holding them close. Alex took a deep breath. There could be no going back now – that much was certain. They were on board.

And what next? Ash had said it would take them forty-eight hours to reach northern Australia, and by the time they had waited to be unloaded it could be as much as three or four days. Alex wasn't sure he could bear to sit in here all that time, locked up with these strangers. The two bottles of water and the bread that he had been given at the last moment were all he had. Presumably the other refugees had brought their own supplies. There was a chemical toilet in the far corner, but Alex knew that conditions inside the container would soon become disgusting. For the first time, he understood how desperate these people must be to make such a journey.

For his own part, he knew he couldn't just sit here. He was worried about Ash – and he was going to learn nothing about the snakehead locked up in the dark. Of course, there was always the watch that Smithers had given him. But despite everything, there was no real reason to send out a distress signal. There was still a chance that Ash was somewhere on board the *Liberian Star*. Alex was just going to have to find him.

He had made up his mind. There was nothing he could do until the ship had left Jakarta, but once

235

they were at sea, there was every possibility that the container would be unguarded. Why bother when there was no chance of escape? Alex closed his eyes and tried to sleep. He needed to gather his strength. He wasn't going to use the watch but there was another gadget Smithers had given him. Alex had already slipped it into position. When the time was right, he would use it to break out.

He waited until he guessed they were at least half-way into their journey before he made his move.

Over twenty-four hours had passed, night blending into day with no difference between the two inside this blank, airless box. The smell was getting worse and worse. At least no one had been seasick, but the chemical toilet was barely adequate for so many people. Nobody was talking. What was there to say? The crossing had become a sort of living death.

Alex had caught up on some of the sleep he'd missed in Jakarta, although he'd had bad dreams ... Ash, Thai boxing, sardines! Now he'd had enough.

He dug into his pocket and took out the packet of chewing gum, then slid open the panel in the side. He had to hold it against the light to see properly, but there were the three numbers: 1, 5 and 10, each with its own switch.

The five-baht coin was already in position. When Alex had climbed into the container he had pretended to stumble, and as he reached out to steady himself he had slipped it behind the sliding bolt. So long as none of the snakehead members had seen it, it would still be there, magnetically held in place underneath him. Now was the time to find out. He would just have to hope that the noise of the engines and the sea swell would cover any sound made by the explosion.

He went over to the trapdoor and knelt beside it. He couldn't hear anything outside, but that was hardly surprising. The other refugees were looking at him, wondering what he was doing. There was no point waiting any longer. Alex pressed the switch marked 5.

There was a sharp crack under the trapdoor and a wisp of acrid smoke rose up inside the container. One of the women began to gabble at Alex but he ignored her. He pressed down with one hand and to his relief the trapdoor fell open, forming a small chute that angled out into darkness. The bolt had snapped in half. There was just enough room for Alex to slither out – but into what? It was always possible that he would find himself in the very depths of the hold, hemmed in on all sides, with nowhere else to go.

He had caused a minor panic inside the container. Everyone was talking at once, at least half a dozen languages fighting with one another all around him. Salem came over to him and tugged at his shirt, pleading with him not to do whatever it was he had planned. He looked bewildered. Who was this boy, travelling on his own, who dared to antagonize the snakehead by attempting to leave without permission? And how had he done it? They had heard the bolt shatter but that was all. It seemed to have happened by magic.

Alex looked Salem in the eye and pressed a finger against his lips. He was pleading with the old man to be silent and not to let the others give him away. It was the most he could hope for. These people were here to make a journey. He was nothing to do with them. With a bit of luck, none of them would try to follow him out or, worse still, tell the ship's crew what had happened. But if he waited any longer, one of them might try to stop him. It was time to go.

Still not sure what he was letting himself in for, Alex slid through the trapdoor head first, easing himself into the black square that had opened up below. It was much cooler outside. He had been sharing the same air with twenty people for an entire day and night and he had been unaware how stifling it had become. It was noisier too. He could hear the hum of the ship's engines, the grinding of machinery in constant motion.

But at least there was a way out. Alex found himself in what was effectively a long, flat tunnel. The containers were piled up on top of him and he could sense their huge weight pressing down. But there was a crawl space about half a metre high between the floor above him and the ceiling of the container below. He could see the daylight bleeding in – a narrow strip like a crack in a brick wall. Using his knees and elbows, he pushed himself towards it. It was a painful process, Alex constantly scraping his legs and banging his shoulders on the rusty metal above and below him.

At last he reached the edge, only to find himself high above the deck, caught three storeys up a tower of containers with no obvious way to climb down. Alex could see the ocean rushing past on the other side of the ship. There was no sign of land. For a moment, he was tempted to crawl back inside. He had nowhere to run. He would be safer with Salem and the others.

And was there really any chance of finding Ash? The *Liberian Star* was huge. It probably held more than a thousand containers. Ash could be stuck in any one of them, locked up with his own crowd of refugees. Alex felt helpless. But going back would be admitting defeat. Ever since he had first encountered the snakehead in Bangkok, he had allowed them to push him around. He'd had enough. It was time to fight back.

He had come out at one of the long sides of the container, and there was a sheer drop to the deck below. There was no way down so he crawled all the way along the edge and round to the front. Here he had more luck. The container doors were fastened with long steel rods that formed a climbing frame, and there were the metal security pins and padlocks that would provide perfect footholds. Alex knew he had to move quickly. It was still light – he guessed it must be late afternoon – and he would be seen by anyone who happened to appear on deck. On the other hand, he would have to be careful. If he slipped, there was a long way to fall.

Holding on to one of the rods, he began the journey down, trying to ignore the sea spray that whipped into his back and made every surface slippery. His worst fear was that a crew member would come out, and despite the danger he forced himself to move faster, finally dropping the last few metres and crashing down onto the deck, anxious to get himself out of sight. Nobody had seen him. He looked back up, checking the position of the container in case he needed to return. There was the name, UNWIN TOYS, in great black letters. Alex thought about the secret it concealed. He had to admit that he had never come across a criminal organization – or a crime – quite like this.

He looked around him. It was only now, crouching in the open air, that he realized quite how enormous the *Liberian Star* actually was. It measured at least three hundred metres in length and it must have been about forty metres across. The containers were piled up like metal office blocks, surrounded by decks, gantries and ladders that allowed the crew to scurry around in what little space was left. Alex was at the stern of the ship, where the huge anchor chains disappeared into a cavity below. In front of him the bridge rose up, the eyes and brain of the entire ship. Behind him the water boiled, churned up by the propellers below. He guessed they must be travelling at about thirty-five knots – forty miles per hour.

He had already accepted the fact that he had no hope at all of finding Ash. But now that he was out, he decided to explore. They could only be about twenty-four hours from Darwin. If he could survive that long without being seen, he might be able to get off the ship there and find a telephone. The number that Ash had given him was still just visible on the back of his hand. All he wanted to do was make contact. Assuming, of course, that Ash was still able to take his call.

In the next couple of hours, Alex explored a large part of the ship. He quickly realized that despite its great size, it was almost entirely made up of containers and the layout was actually very simple, with two decks running all the way from fore to aft and only a limited area for the crew to live and work in. The crew seemed surprisingly small. Only once did he spot a couple of crewmen – Filipinos in blue overalls, leaning against a handrail, smoking cigarettes. Alex slipped behind a ventilation shaft and waited until they left. That was something else to his advantage in this strange, entirely metal world. There were a thousand places to hide.

It was more dangerous inside, where the clean, brightly lit passageways were lined with dozens of doors, any one of which could open at any time. Alex was looking for the food store – he was hungry – but just as he came upon it, another crewman appeared and he had to duck down the nearest stairway. The stairs led to a cargo hold. As he waited for the man to disappear, Alex heard voices. They were speaking in English. Intrigued, he continued down.

He came to a platform perched on the edge of an area that was like an oversized metal cube with sheer walls rising to the deck above. A single container had been stored here. It was also marked UNWIN TOYS and was locked with the same security pin as the others. Four men were standing in a semicircle, deep in conversation. One of them was obviously in charge. He was standing with his back to Alex, and from his position high above, all Alex could make out was a thin, rather frail-looking body and strange white hair. The man was leaning on a walking stick. He was wearing grey gloves.

Alex assumed they were going to unlock the container, but what happened next took him completely by surprise. One of the men lifted something that looked like a television remote control and pressed a button. At once one side of the container opened electronically, the sections separating like lift doors. There was a click and then the floor of the container slid forward, bringing the contents out where they could be examined.

Alex knew at once what he was looking at. There could be no mistaking it.

Royal Blue.

That was the name Mrs Jones had given it. She had told him it was the most powerful non-nuclear weapon on the planet. Alex's first impression was that the bomb was so bomb-shaped it was almost like a cartoon. In the great emptiness of the hold it looked small, but he guessed that it was about the size of a car, just as Mrs Jones had said. He wondered what it was doing out here – and where were they taking it? Australia? Was Major Yu planning to set it off there?

Right now it was surrounded by a bank of machinery, and as soon as the container had clicked into position two of the men set to work, connecting it all up. There was some sort of scanner – it looked like an office photocopier – and a laptop. A third man was explaining something. He was black with a pock-marked face, very white teeth and cheap plastic spectacles that were too heavy for his face. He was wearing a short-sleeved shirt with half a dozen pens in the breast pocket. Alex edged forward to hear what he was saying.

"...we had to modify the bomb to change the method of detonation." The man had an accent that Alex couldn't quite place – French, perhaps. "It would normally explode one metre above the ground. But this one will be required to explode one kilometre below it. So we have made the necessary adaptations."

"A radio signal?" the white-haired man asked.

"Yes, sir." The black man indicated a piece of equipment. "This is how you communicate with the bomb. The timing is crucial. I estimate that Royal Blue will only be able to function at that depth for around twenty minutes. You must send the signal during that time."

"I want to be the one who sends the signal," the white-haired man said. He spoke perfect English, like an old-fashioned newsreader.

"Of course, sir. I received your email from London. And as you can see, I've arranged a fairly simple device. It allows you to scan your fingerprints into the system. From that moment on, you will have sole control."

"That's absolutely top-hole. Thank you, Mr Varga."

The white-haired man pulled off one of his gloves, revealing a hand that was small and withered; it could have belonged to a dead person. Alex watched as he placed it against the scanner. Varga pressed a few buttons on the laptop. A green bar of light appeared underneath the hand, travelling across the palm. It only took a couple of seconds and then it was over.

One of the other men was overweight, with thinning ginger hair. He was about fifty years old, dressed in trousers and a white shirt with blue and gold bands on the shoulders. The white-haired man now turned to him.

"You can put Royal Blue back into the container, Captain de Wynter," he said. "It'll be unloaded the moment we arrive at East Arm."

"Yes, Major."

"And one other thing—"

But the white-haired man – the major – never finished the sentence. There was a scream from a siren, so loud that Alex was almost knocked off the platform and had to cover his ears to protect himself from the noise. It was an alarm signal. The fourth man, who had so far said nothing, swung round revealing a machine gun – a lightweight Belgian M249 – hanging at his waist. Captain de Wynter pulled out a mobile phone and speed-dialled.

The siren stopped. The captain listened for a few seconds, then reported what he had heard, speaking in a low voice. Half deafened, Alex couldn't hear a word he said.

The white-haired man shook his head angrily. "Who is he? Where did he come from?"

"They are holding him on the deck," de Wynter replied.

"I want to see him for myself," the major exclaimed. "Come with me!"

The four of them made for a door set in the side of the hold. A moment later, they were gone, and to his astonishment Alex found himself alone with the bomb. It seemed a heaven-sent opportunity and, without even hesitating, he clambered down the staircase and went over to the container.

And there it was right in front of him. MI6 were searching for Royal Blue all over Thailand but he had found it in the middle of the Indian Ocean. He had found Winston Yu at the same time – for that was surely who the white-haired man must be. After all, he had just heard the captain call him Major. But why were they both here? What did the major want with the bomb? Alex wished he had heard more.

He ran his eyes over it. Close up, it struck him as one of the ugliest things he had ever seen – blunt and heavy, built only to kill and destroy. For a fleeting moment, he wondered if he could detonate it. That would put an end to Yu's plans, whatever they were. But Alex had no wish to die; and anyway, there were at least twenty refugees, some of them children, concealed on the ship. They'd be killed too.

Perhaps he could disarm it. But there was no point. Yu or the man called Varga would soon see what he had done and simply reverse it. Could he use another of the exploding coins? No – even if they could penetrate the thick shell of Royal Blue, what then? Anything he damaged, Yu could easily replace.

He had to do something. The four men might be back at any time. He glanced at the laptop and that was when he saw the instruction, printed in capital letters, on the screen.

> PLACE HAND ON SCREEN

The laptop was still connected to the scanner. Alex could see the outline of a human hand, positioned exactly to read the user's fingertips. Acting on impulse, he placed his own hand on the glass surface. There was a click and the green light rolled underneath his palm. On the laptop, the readout changed.

> FINGERPRINT PROFILE ACCEPTED
> ADD FURTHER AUTHORIZATION? Y/N

Alex reached out and pressed the Y. The screen returned to its first message.

> PLACE HAND ON SCREEN

So that was interesting. He had given himself the power to override the system if he ever happened to come across it again – and with a bit of luck neither Major Yu nor Mr Varga would notice.

There was nothing more he could do. Alex made his way back to the staircase and went up, intending to find somewhere to hide. He would wait until he got to Darwin. Then he would contact Mrs Jones and tell her about her precious bomb.

If she asked him nicely, he could even defuse it for her.

He reached the deck. Major Yu had arrived there ahead of him – Alex could hear his voice although he couldn't make out any of the words. Quickly he climbed a ladder that led to a narrow passageway dividing two of the container towers. There was no chance of anyone spotting him here. Feeling bolder, he made his way to the end and found himself looking down on the foredeck, where a single communications mast rose up amid a tangle of winches and cables.

What he saw there chilled him.

He had thought the siren was a useful diversion, perhaps announcing some problem in the engine room. It had got Major Yu and his men out of the way at exactly the right moment. But now he realized that it hadn't been good news at all. In fact, it could hardly have been worse.

The old man from the container – Salem – had decided to follow Alex out. He must have squeezed through the trapdoor and found his way onto the deck. But there his luck had run out. A couple of the crew had discovered him. They were holding him now with his hands pinned behind his back, while Major Yu questioned him. Captain de Wynter and Varga were watching. Salem was having difficulty making himself understood. He had been beaten. One of his eyes was swollen half shut, and there was blood trickling from a cut on his cheek.

He finished speaking, a gabble of words swept away by the wind. It wasn't cold out on the deck but Alex found himself shivering. Major Yu still had his back to him. Alex watched as he carefully removed one of his gloves and reached into his jacket pocket. He took out a small pistol. Without hesitating, without even pausing to aim, he shot the old man between the eyes. The single report of the bullet was like the crack of wood. Salem died on his feet, still held up by the two crewmen. Yu nodded and the men tilted him backwards, tipping his lifeless body over the rails. Alex saw it fall into the water and disappear.

Then Major Yu spoke again, and somehow his words carried up as if amplified.

"There is a child on this ship," he exclaimed. "He has escaped from the container; I don't know how. He must be found immediately and brought to me. Do not kill him unless absolutely necessary."

Alex was on his own, unarmed, on a ship many hundreds of miles from dry land. He had nowhere to run. There were going to be thirty men looking for him and he had no doubt that they would all be armed. They would start at one end and sweep all the way to the other. And when they found him, he knew exactly what to expect.

He backed away and set about finding somewhere to hide.

HIDE-AND-SEEK

The captain of the *Liberian Star* was not normally a nervous man, but right now he was sweating. Standing in front of the stateroom door, he tried to compose himself, mopping his forehead and tucking his cap under his arm. He was aware that he might have only a few minutes to live.

Hermann de Wynter was Dutch, unmarried, out of shape and saving up for a retirement somewhere in the sun. He had been working for the snakehead for eleven years, transporting containers all over the world. Never once had he asked what was inside. He knew that in this game the wrong question could prove fatal. So could failure. And now it was his duty to tell Major Yu that he had failed.

He took a deep breath and knocked on the door of the stateroom that Yu occupied on the main deck.

"Come!"

The single word sounded cheerful enough, but de Wynter had been present the day before. Yu had smiled as he killed the Afghan refugee.

He opened the door. The room was well appointed with a thick carpet, modern English furniture and soft lighting. Yu was sitting at his desk, drinking a cup of tea. There was also a plate of shortbread, which de Wynter knew was organic and came from Highgrove, the estate belonging to the Prince of Wales.

"Good day, Captain." Yu motioned for him to come in. "What news do you have for me?"

De Wynter had to force the words into his mouth. "I am very sorry to have to report, Major Yu, that we have been unable to find the boy."

Yu looked surprised. "You've been searching for nearly eighteen hours."

"Yes, sir. None of the crew have slept. We've spent the whole night searching the ship from top to bottom. Frankly, it's incredible that we have found no trace of him. We've used motion detectors and sonic intensifiers. Nothing! Some of the men think the child must have slipped overboard. Of course, we still haven't given up..."

His voice trailed off. There was nothing more to say and he knew that making too many excuses would annoy Major Yu all the more. De Wynter stood there, waiting for whatever might come. He had once seen Yu shoot a man simply for being late with his tea. He just hoped his own end would be as quick.

But to his amazement, Major Yu smiled pleasantly. "The boy certainly is trouble," he admitted.

"I must say, I'm not at all surprised that he's managed to give you the slip. He's quite a character."

De Wynter blinked. "You know him?" he asked.

"Oh yes. Our paths have crossed once before."

"But I thought..." De Wynter frowned. "He's just a refugee! A street urchin from Afghanistan."

"Not at all, Captain. That's what he'd like us to believe. But the truth is, he's unique. His name is Alex Rider. He works for British intelligence. He's what you might call a teenage spy."

De Wynter sat down. This was in itself remarkable. After all, Major Yu hadn't offered him a seat.

"Forgive me, sir," he began. "But are you saying that the British managed to smuggle a spy on board? A child...?"

"Exactly."

"And you knew?"

"I know everything, Captain de Wynter."

"But ... why?" De Wynter had completely forgotten his earlier fear. Somewhere in the back of his mind it occurred to him that he had never spoken to Major Yu so familiarly, or for such a length of time.

"It amused me," Yu replied. "This boy is rather full of himself. He travelled to Jakarta and disguised himself as a refugee. His mission was to infiltrate my snakehead. But all along I knew who he was and I was simply choosing the moment when I would bring his young life to a fitting end. I have friends who wanted me to do it sooner rather than later. But the timing was my choice."

Yu poured himself some more tea. He picked up a shortbread biscuit, holding it between his gloved fingers, and dipped it into the cup.

"My intention was to allow him to travel as far as Darwin," he continued. "I was going to deal with him then. Unfortunately the old man was unable to tell me how he managed to break out of the container, and it's certainly an unwelcome surprise. But I am still confident that you will be able to locate him eventually. After all, we have plenty of time."

The Dutchman felt his mouth go dry. "I'm afraid not, sir," he muttered. "In fact, it may already be too late."

Major Yu's eyebrows rose behind the round wire frames. "Why is that?"

"Look out of the window, sir. We've arrived at Darwin. They've already sent out a couple of tugs to tow us in."

"Surely we can delay docking for a few more hours."

"No, sir. If we do that, we could be stuck here for a week." De Wynter ran a hand over his jaw. "The Australian ports run like clockwork," he explained. "Everything has to be very precise. We have an allocated time for arrival and it's a small window. If we miss it, another ship will take our place."

Yu considered. Something very close to anxiety appeared in his shrunken, schoolboy face. This was exactly what Zeljan Kurst had warned him about in London. Like it or not, Alex Rider had taken on Scorpia once before and beaten them. Yu had thought it impossible that such a thing could happen a second time. And yet the boy did seem to have the luck of the devil. How had he managed to get out of the container? It was a shame nobody had been able to understand the old man before he had died.

"Even if we dock, the boy cannot possibly leave the ship," de Wynter said. "There is only one exit – the main gangway – and that will be guarded at all times. He can jump into the sea but I will have men on lookout. We can cover every angle with rifles. We'll pick him off in the water. A single shot. No one will hear anything. We'll only be in Darwin for a few hours. Our next port is Rio de Janeiro. We'll have three weeks to flush him out."

Major Yu nodded slowly. Even as de Wynter had been speaking, he had made up his mind. In truth he had little choice. Royal Blue had to be disembarked immediately in order to continue its journey. He couldn't wait. But there was something that Alex Rider didn't know. Whatever happened, all the cards were in Yu's hand.

"Very well, Captain," he muttered. "We'll tie up at Darwin. But if the boy does slip through your fingers a second time, I suggest you kill yourself." He snapped a biscuit in half. "It will spare me the trouble and it will, I assure you, cause you a great deal less pain."

*   *   *

Alex Rider had heard everything that Major Yu had said.

The man who sat on the executive board of Scorpia and who was in charge of the most powerful snakehead in South East Asia would have been horrified to know that Alex was hiding in perhaps the most obvious place in the world. Under his own bed.

Alex had known what he was up against. The moment he had seen the refugee killed on the deck and had heard Yu give the order for the crew to hunt him down, he had realized he needed to find somewhere on the ship where nobody would even dream of looking. It was true there were hundreds of hiding places – ventilation shafts, the crawl spaces between the containers, cabins, cable housings and storage units. But none of these would be good enough, not with the entire crew searching for him non-stop through the night.

No ... it had to be somewhere completely unthinkable – and the idea had come to him almost at once. Where was the last place he would go? It had to be the captain's cabin, or better still Major Yu's own quarters. The crew almost certainly weren't allowed in either. It wouldn't even occur to them to look inside.

He'd only had a few minutes' head start. As the crew members organized themselves and the various listening devices were handed out, Alex was racing. The layout of the ship was fairly easy to understand. He had seen much of it already. The engine room and the crew's cabins were somewhere down below. Yu, the captain and the senior officers – anyone important – would surely be housed above sea level, somewhere in the central block.

Breathless, imagining the crewmen fanning out behind him, Alex stumbled on a door that led to one of the spotlessly clean, brightly lit corridors that he had explored. He was on the right track. The first door he came to after that opened into a conference room full of charts and computers. Next came a living space with a bar and TV. He heard the clatter of saucepans and ducked back as a man wearing a chef's hat suddenly crossed the corridor and disappeared into a room opposite. A moment later, he emerged again and went back the way he had come, carrying a box of canned food.

Alex hurried forward. The chef had clearly entered some sort of larder and Alex wasted a few seconds pulling out a bottle of water for himself. He was going to need it. Continuing down the corridor, he passed a laundry, a games room, a miniature hospital, and finally a lift. There were six floors on the *Liberian Star*. Alex noticed the numbers as he ran past.

He came upon Yu's stateroom at the very end of the corridor. It wasn't locked – but there wasn't a man on board the *Liberian Star* who would have dared enter even if the door had been open and Yu miles away. Alex slipped inside. He saw a desk with a number of files and documents spread across the surface and wished he had time to examine them. But he didn't dare touch anything. Moving even one page a fraction of an inch might give him away.

He looked around him, taking in the pictures on the walls – scenes of the English countryside with, in one image, a traditional hunt setting out across what might be Salisbury Plain. A sophisticated stereo system and a plasma TV. A leather sofa. This was where Yu worked and relaxed when he was on board.

The bedroom was next door. Here was another bizarre touch: Yu slept in an antique four-poster bed. But Alex knew at once that it was perfect for his needs. There was a silk valance that trailed down to the floor and, lifting it up, he saw a space half a metre high that would conceal him perfectly. It reminded him of being seven years old again, playing hide-and-seek with Jack on Christmas Eve. But this wasn't the same. This time he was on a container ship in the middle of the Indian Ocean, surrounded by people who wouldn't think twice about killing him.

Same game. Different rules.

Alex took a swig of the water he had stolen and slid under the bed, easing the silk valance back into position. Very little light bled through. He prepared himself, trying to find a comfortable position. He knew he wouldn't be able to move a muscle once Yu entered the room.

He was suddenly struck by the craziness of his plan. Could he really stay here all night? How stupid would he look if Yu found him! He was briefly tempted to crawl out and find somewhere else. But it was already too late. The search would have begun and he couldn't risk starting again.

In fact, it was several hours before Yu came in. Alex heard the outer door open and close again. Footsteps. Then music. Yu had turned on the stereo system. His taste was classical: Elgar's *Pomp and Circumstance*, the music they played at the Albert Hall in London every summer. He listened to the piece while he ate his dinner. Alex heard one of the stewards deliver it to him and caught a faint scent of roast meat. The smell made him hungry. He sipped a little more water, glumly reflecting that it was all he had to last the night.

Later Yu turned on the television. Somehow he had managed to tune into the BBC, and Alex heard the late night news.

"The pop singer Rob Goldman was in Sydney this week, before the conference taking place on Reef Island, which has been nicknamed Reef Encounter and which has been scheduled to take place at exactly the same time as the G8 summit in Rome.

"Goldman played to a packed-out Sydney Opera House and told an enthusiastic crowd that peace and an end to world poverty were possible – but that they would have to be achieved by people, not politicians.

"Speaking from 10 Downing Street, the British prime minister said he wished Sir Rob every success but insisted that the real work would be done in Rome. It's a view not many people seem to share..."

Much later, Major Yu went to bed. Alex barely breathed as he came into the bedroom. Lying in the semi-darkness with muscles that were already aching, he heard the major undress and wash in the adjoining bathroom. And then came the inevitable moment: the creak of wood and shifting metal springs as Yu climbed into bed, just inches above the boy he was so determined to find. Fortunately he didn't read before going to sleep. Alex heard the click of a light switch and the last glimmer of light was extinguished. Then everything was silent.

For Alex, the night was yet another long, dreary ordeal. He was fairly sure that Major Yu was asleep but he couldn't be certain, and he didn't dare sleep himself in case the sound of his breathing or an accidental movement gave him away. All he could do was wait, listening to the hum of the engines and feeling the pitch of the ship as they drew ever closer to Australia. At least that was one consolation. Every second that he remained undiscovered brought him a little closer to safety.

But how was he to get off the *Liberian Star*? One exit – guarded. The decks watched. Alex didn't like the idea of diving overboard and swimming, even assuming he could manage it without being crushed or drowned. And there would be a dozen or more men waiting to take a potshot at him. Well, he would just have to worry about that when the time came.

The ship ploughed on through the darkness; the minutes dragged slowly past. At last the first streak of light crept across the floor, pushing away the shadows of the night.

Yu woke up, washed, dressed and took his breakfast in the stateroom. That was the worst part for Alex. He had barely moved for ten hours and all his bones were aching. Still Yu refused to leave. He was working at his desk. Alex heard the rustle of pages turning and, briefly, the rattle of computer keys. And then the steward brought tea and shortbread, and soon after that de Wynter arrived with the news of his failure.

So Major Yu knew who he was – and had known from the start! Alex tucked that information away, hoping he would be able to make sense of it later. For now, all that mattered was that his plan had worked and the long hours of discomfort had been worth it. They were docking at Darwin. Surely, any minute now, Yu would go out on deck to see dry land.

But it was another two hours before Yu left. Alex

waited until he was quite sure that he was alone, then rolled out from under the bed. He glanced into the stateroom. Yu had gone but he had left some of the biscuits and Alex wolfed them down. He tried to ease some feeling back into his muscles. He had to prepare himself. He knew that he had one chance to get away. They would set off to sea again in just a few hours' time, and if he was still on board he would be finished.

He went over to the window. The *Liberian Star* had already berthed at the section of the Port of Darwin known as the East Arm Wharf. To his dismay, Alex realized that they were still a very long way from land. The East Arm was an artificial, cement causeway stretching far out into the ocean with the usual array of gantries, cranes and spreaders waiting to receive the ships. It was a different world from the docks at Jakarta. Quite apart from the blinding Australian sun, everything seemed very clean and ordered. There were two long rows of parked cars, and beyond them a neat, modern warehouse and some gas tanks – all of them painted white.

A van drove by, heading up the quay. Two men walked past in fluorescent jackets and hard hats. Even assuming Alex could get off the ship, he still wouldn't be safe. It was at least a mile to the mainland and presumably there would be security barriers at the far end. Yu wouldn't dare gun him down in plain sight. That was one consolation. But however Alex looked at it, this wasn't going to be as easy as he had hoped.

Even so, he couldn't wait any longer.

Alex crept over to the door and opened it an inch at a time. The corridor was empty, lit by the same hard light that made it impossible to tell if it was night or day. He had already worked out a strategy based on what he had overheard in the stateroom. Everyone was waiting for him to break out. That meant their attention would be fixed on the main deck and the gangplank. So the rest of the ship was his. Right now he needed a diversion. He set out to create one.

He hurried past the lift and found a staircase leading down. He could hear a deep throbbing coming from below and guessed that he was heading the right way – to the engine room. He came upon it quite suddenly, a strangely old-fashioned tangle of brass valves and silver pipes and pistons, all connected to one another in a steel framework like an exhibition in an industrial museum. The air was hot down here; there was no natural light. The machinery seemed to stretch on for a mile and Alex could imagine that a ship the size of the *Liberian Star* would need every inch of it.

The control room was raised slightly above the engines, separated from them by three thick glass observation windows and reached by a short flight of metal stairs. Alex crept up on his hands and feet and found himself looking at a much more modern room with rows of gauges and dials, TV screens, computers and intricate switchboards. A single man sat in a high-backed chair, tapping at a keyboard. He looked half asleep. He certainly wasn't expecting trouble down here.

Alex saw what he was looking for: a metal cabinet about fifteen metres high with thick pipes leading in and out and a warning sign:

AIR SUPPLY
DANGER: DO NOT CUT OFF

He didn't know what needed the air or what would happen if it didn't get it, but the bright red letters were irresistible. He was going to find out.

He reached into his pocket and took out the one-baht coin that Smithers had given him. Using it would leave him with only the ten-baht coin. With a bit of luck, he wouldn't be needing it. Alex watched the man in the chair for a minute, then slipped into the control room and placed the coin against the pipe just where it entered the cabinet. The man didn't look up. The coin clicked into place, activating the charge inside. Alex tiptoed out again.

He found the chewing gum packet, slid the side open and pressed the switch marked 1. The bang was very loud and, to his surprise and relief, highly destructive. The explosion not only tore open the pipe, it wrecked the electrical circuits inside the cabinet. There was a series of brilliant sparks, and something like white steam gushed out into the control room. The man leapt up. Another alarm had gone off and red lights were flashing all around him. Alex didn't wait to see what would happen next. He was already on his way out.

Down the stairs, past the engines and back up again. This time he took the lift, guessing that in an emergency the crew would be more likely to use the stairs. He pressed the button for the sixth floor and the lift slid smoothly up.

He knew where he was heading. He had seen the bridge when he was being loaded into the container at Jakarta, and had noticed that it had its own deck, a sort of balcony with a railing and a view over the entire ship. This was going to be his way off the *Liberian Star*. For – once again – Yu's guns might be pointing everywhere else, but surely they wouldn't be pointing here.

The lift reached the sixth floor and the doors slid open. To Alex's dismay, he found himself facing a squat Chinese crewman. The man was even more shocked than Alex and reacted clumsily, scrabbling for the gun that was tucked into the waistband of his trousers. That was a mistake. Alex didn't give him time to draw it, lashing out with his foot, aiming straight between the man's legs. It wasn't so much a karate strike, more an old-fashioned kick in the groin, but it did the trick. The man gurgled and collapsed, dropping the gun. Alex scooped it up and continued on his way. Now he was armed.

Alarms were going off everywhere and Alex wondered what damage he had done with the second coin. Good old Smithers! He was the one person in MI6 who had never let him down.

The corridor led directly to the bridge. Alex passed through an archway, climbed three steps and found himself in a narrow, curving room, surprisingly empty, with large windows overlooking the decks, the containers and, to one side, the port.

There were two men on duty, sitting in what could have been dentist's chairs in front of a bank of television screens. One was a second officer that Alex hadn't seen before. The other was Captain de Wynter. He was on the telephone, talking in a voice that sounded strained and hoarse with disbelief.

"It's the reefers," he was saying. "We're going to have to shut them all down. The whole ship could go up in flames..."

The reefers were refrigerated containers. There were three hundred of them on the *Liberian Star*, storing meat, vegetables and chemicals that needed to be transported at low temperatures. The containers themselves needed constant cooling and Alex had smashed the pipes that provided exactly that. At the very least, he was going to cause Major Yu tens of thousands of pounds' worth of losses as the contents deteriorated. He might even have set the whole ship on fire.

The second officer saw Alex first. He muttered

something in Dutch and de Wynter looked round, the phone still in his hand.

Alex raised the gun. "Put it down," he said.

De Wynter went pale. He lowered the phone.

What did he do now? Alex realized that he had made it this far without any real plan at all. "I want you to get me off this ship," he said.

De Wynter shook his head. "That's not possible." He was afraid of the gun, but he was even more afraid of Major Yu.

Alex glanced at the phone. Presumably it could be connected to Darwin. "Call the police," he said. "I want you to bring them here."

"I cannot do that either," de Wynter replied. He looked a little sad. "There is no way I will help you, child. And there is nowhere for you to go. You might as well give yourself up."

Alex looked briefly out of the window. One of the containers bound for Australia was already being lifted off the ship, dangling on wires beneath a metal frame so huge that in comparison it seemed no bigger than a matchbox. The spreader was controlled by a man in a glass-fronted cabin, high up in the air. The container rose up. In a few seconds it would swing across and down to the piles that were already mounting on the quayside.

Alex judged the distance and the timing. Yes – he could do it. He had arrived at the bridge at exactly the right moment. He pointed the gun directly at de Wynter. "Get out of here," he snapped.

The captain stayed where he was. He didn't believe Alex had the nerve to pull the trigger.

"I said – get out!" Alex swung his hand and fired at a radar screen right next to the chair where de Wynter was sitting.

The sound of the gunshot was deafening inside the confined space. The screen shattered, fragments of glass scattering over the work surface. Alex smiled to himself. That was another piece of expensive equipment on the *Liberian Star* that was going to need replacing.

De Wynter didn't need telling again. He got up and hurried away from the bridge, following the second officer, who was already clambering down the stairs. Alex waited until they had gone. He knew they would call for help and come back with half a dozen armed men, but he didn't care. He had seen his way out. With a bit of luck he would be gone long before they arrived.

A glass door led onto the outer walkway. Alex opened it and found himself about twenty metres above the nearest container, far enough to break his neck if he fell. The sea was another thirty metres below that. Diving into the water was out of the question. He could see Yu's men on the main deck, waiting for him to try. But he was too high. They wouldn't need to shoot him. The impact would kill him first.

The container he had seen being lifted was now nearly above him, moving closer all the time as it travelled over the deck. Alex climbed onto the railing in front of him and tensed himself. The container loomed over him. He jumped – not down, but up, his arms stretching out. For a moment, he was suspended in space and he wondered if he was going to make it. He grimaced, trying not to imagine the crushing pain, his legs smashing into the deck, if he fell. But then his hands caught hold of the lashings beneath the container and he was being carried outwards, his legs dangling in the air, his neck and shoulder muscles screaming. The man operating the spreader couldn't see him. He was like an insect, clinging to the underbelly of the container. And Yu's men hadn't noticed him either. They were following orders, their eyes fixed on the deck and the sea below.

Alex had thought the container was moving quickly when he was on the bridge. Now that he was desperately holding on, it seemed to take for ever to reach the quay and he was certain that at any moment one of Yu's men would glance up and see him. But he was already over the side of the ship and now he saw another danger. Drop too early and he would break a leg. Leave it too late and he risked being crushed as the container was set down.

And then someone saw him.

He heard a yell of alarm. It was a docker on the wharf. He probably wasn't working for Yu but that didn't matter – as far as Alex was concerned he was just as much of a threat. Alex couldn't wait any longer. He let go with both hands and fell through the air for what seemed like an eternity. He had been hanging over a container with a tarpaulin cover. The tarpaulin provided a soft landing – even if the wind was knocked out of him as his back slammed into it. He didn't stop to recover his breath but rolled over and climbed down the side.

As he ran down the quay, dodging behind containers, Alex tried to work out a strategy. The next few minutes were going to be vital. If he was captured by the port authorities, there was always a chance that he might be handed back to Major Yu. Or if he was locked up, Yu would know where to find him. Either way, Alex knew what the result would be. He would end up dead. He had to stay out of sight until he had reached the mainland itself. So long as he was on East Arm Wharf, he would never be safe.

But luck was on his side. As he came round the corner of the last container tower, a pick-up truck drew up in front of him, the back filled with old cartons and empty petrol cans. The driver rolled down the window and yelled something at another dock worker. The man replied and the two of them laughed. By the time the truck rumbled forward again, Alex was in the back, lying on his stomach, concealed among the cartons.

The truck followed a railway line, curving round on the edge of the water, and stopped at a barrier as

Alex had expected. But the security guards knew the driver and waved him through. The truck picked up speed. Alex lay there, feeling the warm Australian breeze on his shoulders as they drove away.

He had done it! He had achieved everything that Ethan Brooke and ASIS had demanded. He had been smuggled illegally into Australia, and on the way he had uncovered much of Major Yu's network: the Chada Trading Company in Bangkok, Unwin Toys, the *Liberian Star*. For that matter, he had also located Royal Blue for Mrs Jones. If he could just reach Darwin in one piece and contact Ash, his mission would be over and he could finally go home. All he had to do was find a phone.

Twenty minutes later, the truck stopped. The engine cut out and Alex heard the driver's door open and shut. Cautiously he looked out. The port was out of sight. They had parked outside a café, a brightly coloured wooden shack beside an empty road. It was called Jake's and it had a hand-painted sign that read: THE BEST PIES IN DARWIN. Alex was desperate for food. He had barely eaten anything for two days. But it was what he saw next to the café that mattered more to him right now. It was a public telephone.

He waited until the driver had disappeared into the building, then climbed out and ran over to the phone. Apart from the last coin that Smithers had given him he had no money, but according to Ash he wouldn't need any to make a call. Now, what was the number? For a horrible moment, the separate digits danced in his head, refusing to come together. He forced himself to concentrate: 795... No ... 759... Somehow the full number took shape. He punched it in and waited.

He'd got it right. The numbers were able to override the system and Alex heard the connection being made. The phone rang three times before it was answered.

"Yes?"

Alex felt a wave of relief. It was Ash's voice. "Ash, it's me. Alex."

"Alex ... thank God! Where are you?"

"I'm in Darwin, I think. Or somewhere near it. There's a café called Jake's. About twenty minutes from the port."

"Stay where you are. I'm coming to get you."

"Are you here too? How did you get here?"

A pause, then Ash replied, "I'll tell you when I see you. Just watch out for yourself. I'll be with you as soon as I can."

He hung up, and it was only in the silence that followed that Alex realized something was wrong. It had definitely been Ash on the phone but he hadn't sounded himself. His voice had been strained and there had been something in that last pause. It was almost as if he had been waiting to be told what to say.

Alex made a decision. He had contacted Ash first as he had promised. But that might not be enough.

He twisted his wrist and looked at the watch that Smithers had given him, then deliberately moved the hands to eleven o'clock. According to Smithers, the watch would send out a signal every ten minutes. Ash might not be happy about it but Alex didn't care. He wasn't going to take any more chances. He just wanted to know that MI6 were on their way.

After that he waited for Ash to arrive. Alex couldn't think what else to do. He was exhausted after three nights with almost no proper sleep and weak from lack of food. He crept round the side of the café and sat in the shade, keeping himself out of sight. It was likely that Major Yu's men were still looking for him, and apart from the knife concealed in his belt he had no way of defending himself. He had left the gun behind on the bridge. He wished he had it with him now.

Ten minutes later, the door of the café opened and the driver who had brought him here came out, carrying a brown paper bag. He got into the pick-up truck and drove off again, leaving a plume of dust behind him.

More time passed. There were flies buzzing around Alex's face but he ignored them. The café seemed to be in the middle of nowhere, surrounded by scrubland and on the edge of a road with little traffic. The sun was beginning to dip down to the horizon and Alex had to struggle not to doze off. But then he saw a car heading towards him, a black four-by-four with tinted windows. It pulled in outside the café. Ash got out.

But he wasn't alone. He hadn't been driving. His hands were chained in front of him. His black hair was in disarray and his shirt was torn; a streak of blood ran down the side of his face. He looked dazed. He hadn't seen Alex yet.

Major Yu got out of the back of the car. He was wearing a white suit with a lavender shirt buttoned at the neck. He moved slowly, supporting himself on his walking stick. As always his hands were gloved. At the same time, the driver and another man got out. They were taking no chances. The three of them surrounded Ash. Yu took out the pistol he had used to kill the old man on the *Liberian Star*. He held it against Ash's head.

"Alex Rider!" he called out in a thin voice filled with hate. "You have three seconds to show yourself. Otherwise you will see your godfather's brains all over the tarmac. I am counting now!"

Alex realized he wasn't breathing. They had Ash! What was he to do? Give himself up and they would both be killed. But could he forgive himself if he turned and ran?

"One..."

He regretted now that he hadn't used the phone to call ASIS, the police, anyone. He had known something was wrong. How could he have been so stupid?

"Two..."

He had no choice. Even if he tried to run, they would catch him. There were three of them. They had a car. He was in the middle of nowhere.

He stood up, showing himself.

Major Yu lowered the gun and Alex began to walk forward, worn out and defeated. Ash must have been on the *Liberian Star* all the time, a prisoner like him. He seemed to be in pain. His eyes were empty.

"I'm sorry, Alex," he rasped.

"Well, here you are at last," Major Yu said. "I have to say, you've caused me a great deal of time and inconvenience."

"Go to hell," Alex snarled.

"Yes, my dear Alex," Yu replied. "That's exactly where I'm taking you."

Yu raised the hand with the walking stick, then swung it with all his strength. This was the last thing that Alex remembered – a silver scorpion glinting brilliantly as it swooped towards him out of the Australian sun. He didn't even feel it as it smashed into the side of his head.

"Pick him up!" Yu commanded.

He turned his back on the unconscious boy and climbed back into the car.

MADE IN BRITAIN

There was a vase of roses on the table. Alex smelled them first ... sweet and slightly cloying. Then he opened his eyes and allowed them to come into focus. The roses were bright pink, a dozen of them arranged in a porcelain vase with a lace mat underneath. Alex felt sick. The side of his head was throbbing and he could feel the broken skin where the walking stick had hit him. There was a sour taste in his mouth. It was dark outside and he wondered how long he had been here.

And where was he? Looking around at the antique furniture, the grandfather clock, the heavy curtains and the stone fireplace with two sculpted lions, he would have said he was back home in Britain – although he knew that wasn't possible. He was lying on a bed in what could have been a country hotel. A door to one side opened into an en suite bathroom. There were bottles of Molton Brown shampoo and bubble bath beside the washbasin.

Alex rolled off the bed and staggered into the

bathroom. He splashed water on his face and examined himself in the mirror. He looked terrible. Quite apart from the dark hair and skin colour and the two fake teeth, his eyes were bloodshot, there was a huge bruise next to his eye and generally he looked as if he had been dumped here by a rubbish truck. On an impulse, he reached into his mouth and pulled the two plastic caps off his teeth. Major Yu knew perfectly well who – and what – he was. There was no need for any further pretence.

He ran himself a bath, and while the tub was filling he went back into the bedroom. The main door was locked, of course. The window looked out onto a perfect lawn with – bizarrely – a set of croquet hoops arranged in neat lines. Beyond, in the moonlight, he could see a rocky outcrop, a jetty and the sea. He turned back. Someone had left him a snack: smoked salmon sandwiches, a glass of milk, a plate of McVitie's Jaffa Cakes. He ate the lot greedily. Then he stripped off and got into the bath. He didn't know what was going to happen next – and he didn't like to think – but whatever it was, he might as well be clean.

He felt a lot better after half an hour in the hot, scented water, and although he hadn't been able to get off all the make-up Mrs Webber had given him, at least some of his own colour had returned. There were fresh clothes in the wardrobe: a Vivienne Westwood shirt and Paul Smith jeans and underwear – both London-based designers. He still had his old clothes, but the belt Smithers had given him had been removed. Alex wondered about that. Had Major Yu discovered the knife in the buckle or the jungle supplies hidden inside the leather itself? He was sorry he hadn't had the chance to use it. Maybe there would have been something inside that could have helped him now.

Luckily nobody had searched the pockets of his jeans – or if they had, they had missed the ten-baht coin and the chewing gum packet with the secret detonators. The watch was also untouched, the hands fixed at eleven o'clock, and that gave Alex a sense of reassurance. The eleventh hour indeed. Major Yu might think he held all the cards but the watch would still be transmitting, and even now MI6 Special Operations had to be closing in.

Alex got dressed in the new clothes and sat down in a comfortable armchair. He had even been supplied with some books to read: Biggles, the Famous Five and Just William. They weren't quite to his taste but he supposed he should appreciate the thought.

A few minutes later, there was a rattle of a key turning in the lock and the door opened. A maid wearing a black dress and a white apron came in. She looked Indonesian.

"Major Yu would like to invite you to dinner," she said.

"That's very kind of him," Alex replied. He closed

Biggles Investigates. "I don't suppose there's any chance of our eating out?"

"He's in the dining room," the maid replied.

Alex followed her out of the room and down a wood-panelled corridor with oil paintings on the walls. They were all scenes of the English country-side. Briefly he thought of overpowering the maid and making another bid for freedom, but he decided against it. There was a part of him that reacted against the idea of attacking a young woman; and anyway, he had no doubt that – following the events on the *Liberian Star* – Yu would be taking no chances. Security here would be tight.

They reached a grand staircase that swept down to a hall with a suit of armour standing beside a second, monumental fireplace. More English landscape paintings everywhere. Alex had to remind himself that he was still in Australia. The house didn't fit here. It felt as if it had been imported brick by brick, and he was reminded for a moment of Nikolei Drevin, who had transported his own fourteenth-century castle from Scotland to Oxfordshire. It was strange how very bad men felt a need to live somewhere not just spectacular but slightly insane.

The maid held back and gestured Alex through a door and into a long dining room with floor-to-ceiling windows looking out over the sea. The room was carpeted, and had a table and a dozen chairs suitable for a medieval banquet. The paintings in this room were modern: a portrait by David Hockney and a wheel of colour by Damien Hirst. Alex had seen similar works in galleries in London and knew that they had to be worth millions. Only one end of the table had been laid. Major Yu was sitting there, waiting for him, the walking stick leaning against his chair.

"Ah, there you are, Alex," he said in a pleasant voice, as if they were old friends meeting up for the weekend. "Please come and sit down."

As he walked forward, Alex examined the snake-head boss properly for the first time, taking in the round, shrunken head, the wire frame glasses, the white hair that sat so oddly with the Chinese features. Yu was wearing a striped blazer with a white open-necked shirt. There was a silk handkerchief poking out of his top pocket. His gloved hands were crossed in front of him.

"How are you feeling?" Yu asked.

"My head hurts," Alex replied.

"Yes. I'm afraid I must apologize. I really don't know what came over me, hitting you like that. But the truth is, I was angry. You did a lot of damage on the *Liberian Star* and made it necessary for me to kill Captain de Wynter, which I didn't really want to do."

Alex filed the information away. So de Wynter was dead. He had paid the price for failing a second time.

"Even so, it was unforgivable of me. My mother

used to say that you can lose money, you can lose at cards but you should never lose your temper. Can I offer you some apple juice? It comes from High House Fruit Farm in Suffolk and it's quite delicious."

"Thank you," Alex said. He didn't know what was going on here but he decided he might as well play along with this madman. He held out his glass and Yu poured. As he did so, the Indonesian maid came in with the dinner: roast beef and Yorkshire pudding. Alex helped himself. He noticed that Yu ate very little and held his knife and fork as if they were surgical implements.

"I'm very glad to have this opportunity to meet you," Major Yu began. "Ever since you destroyed our operation, Invisible Sword, and caused the death of poor Mrs Rothman, I've been wondering what sort of boy you were..."

So Mrs Jones had been right. Major Yu was indeed part of Scorpia. Alex understood with a sense of dread that it gave Yu another reason to want to kill him – to settle an old score.

"It's just a shame that we have so little time together," Yu went on.

Alex didn't like the sound of that. "I have a question," he said.

"Please go ahead."

"Where is Ash? What have you done with him?"

"Let's not talk about Ash." Yu gave him a thin smile. "You don't have to worry about him. You'll never see him again. How is the beef, by the way?"

"A little bloody for my taste."

Yu sighed. "It's organic. From Yorkshire."

"Where else?" Alex was getting a bit fed up with all this. He toyed with his knife, wondering if he had the speed and the determination to stick it into the man's heart. It might be five or ten minutes before the maid came back. Enough time to find a way out of here...

Yu must have seen the idea forming in Alex's eyes. "Please don't try anything foolish," he remarked. "There is a pistol in my right-hand jacket pocket and, as the Americans would say, I am very quick on the draw. I could shoot you dead before you had even left your chair, and that would spoil a perfectly pleasant meal. So come now, Alex. I want to know all about you. Where were you born?"

Alex shrugged. "West London."

"Your parents were both English?"

"I don't want to talk about them." Alex looked around him. Suddenly the paintings, the furniture, the clothes, even the food, made sense. "You seem to like England, Major Yu," he remarked.

"I admire it greatly. If I may say so, Alex, I have enjoyed having you as my adversary because you are British. It is also one of the reasons I have invited you to dine with me now."

"But what about Invisible Sword? You tried to kill every schoolchild in London."

"That was business, and I really was very unhappy about it. You might also like to know, by the way, that I voted against sending a sniper to kill you. It seemed so crude. Some more apple juice?"

"No, thank you."

"So where do you go to school?"

Alex shook his head. He'd had enough of this game. "I don't want to talk about myself," he said. "And certainly not to you. I want to see Ash. And I want to go home."

"Neither of which is possible."

Major Yu was drinking wine. Alex noticed even that was English. He remembered Ian Rider once describing English wine as unnatural, undesirable and undrinkable. But Yu sipped it with obvious enthusiasm.

"I love England, as a matter of fact," he said. "Since you won't talk about yourself, perhaps you will permit me to tell you a little about me. My life has been remarkable. Maybe one day someone will write a book about me..."

"I've never much cared for horror stories," Alex said.

Yu smiled again – but his eyes were cold. "I like to think of myself as a genius," he began. "Of course, you might remark that I have never invented anything or written a novel or painted a great painting, and despite what I've just said, it is unlikely that I will become a household name. But different people are talented in different ways, and I think I have achieved a certain greatness in crime, Alex. And it's not surprising that my life story is a remarkable one. How could someone like me have anything other?"

He coughed, dabbed his lips and began again.

"I was born in Hong Kong. Although you wouldn't believe it to look at me now, I began with nothing. My cot was a cardboard box filled with straw. My mother was Chinese. She lived in a single room in a slum and worked as a chambermaid at the famous Victoria Hotel. Sometimes she would smuggle home soaps and shampoos for me. It was the only luxury I ever knew.

"My father was a guest there, a businessman from Tunbridge Wells, in Kent. She never told me his name. The two of them began an affair, and I have to say that she fell hopelessly in love with him. He used to talk to her about the place where he lived, this country called Great Britain. He promised her that as soon as he had enough money, he would take her with him and he would turn her into an English lady with a thatched cottage and a garden and a bulldog. For my mother, who had nothing, it was like an impossible dream.

"I'm sure you have no attachment to your country, being young; but the truth is, it's a remarkable place. At one time, this tiny island had an empire that stretched all around the world. You have to remember that when I was born, you even owned Hong Kong. Think how many inventors and explorers, artists and writers, soldiers and statesmen, have come out of Britain. William Shakespeare! Charles

Dickens! The computer was a British invention – as was the World Wide Web. It's sad that much of your country's greatness has been squandered by politicians in recent years. But I still have faith. One day Britain will once again lead the world.

"Anyway, my mother's affair came to an unhappy end. I suppose it was inevitable. As soon as he found out that she was pregnant, the businessman abandoned her and she never saw him again. Nor did he ever pay a penny towards my upkeep. He simply disappeared.

"But my mother never lost sight of her dream. If anything, it became more intense. She was determined that I should grow up with full recognition of my English blood. She named me Winston, of course, after the great wartime leader Winston Churchill. The first clothes I wore had been made in Britain. As the years went on, she became more and more fanatical. One day she decided that I should be educated at a British public school – even though it was obviously quite impossible when she was earning only a few pounds an hour changing beds and cleaning toilets. But nonetheless, when I was six years old, she left her job and began to look for other ways to make money.

"It took her just two years – a tribute, I think, to her single-mindedness and courage. And that was how I found myself at a prep school in Tunbridge Wells itself, and later at Harrow, dressed in that smart blue jacket with the marvellous straw hat. All the boys wore them. On Sundays we dressed in cut-off tailcoats – bum freezers we used to call them. It's Winston Churchill's old school, and I found it hard to believe I was there. I mean, I could actually imagine I might be sitting at his desk or reading a book that had once belonged to him. It was thrilling, and my mother was so proud of me! I did sometimes wonder how she could possibly afford it all, but it wasn't until the end of my second term that I found out – and I must say it came as a bit of a surprise.

"This is what happened..."

He poured himself some more wine, swirled it round the glass and drank.

"You might imagine that I was bullied at Harrow," he said. "After all, this was back in the fifties and there weren't many half-Chinese boys there, particularly with a single parent. But by and large everyone was very kind to me. However, there was one boy, a chap by the name of Max Odey. He had a brother called Felix, and I must say I liked both of them. Max was a pleasant enough chap, very good with money. Anyway, I don't quite know what I did to upset him but he made a lot of rather hurtful remarks and for a couple of terms, thanks to him, life was very uncomfortable. But then my mother heard about it and I'm afraid she dealt with him very severely. A hit-and-run and they never found the driver. But I knew who it was and I was horrified. It was a side of my mother I had never seen before. And that was when I discovered the truth.

"It turned out that when I was just six years old, she had managed to track down one of the main snakeheads operating in Hong Kong and had volunteered her services as a paid assassin. I know it sounds remarkable, but I suppose that being abandoned so cruelly had changed her. She no longer had any respect for life. And the fact was, she was extremely good at her new job. She was very small and Chinese, so nobody ever suspected her; and she was utterly without mercy – because mercy, of course, wouldn't pay the school fees. And that was how she was supporting me at Harrow! Every time a bill arrived at the start of a new term, she would have to go out and kill someone. It's strange to think that fifteen men died to make my education possible – sixteen, in fact, when I decided to take up horse-riding.

"After she'd finished with Max, I never had any more trouble. Even the teachers went out of their way to be pleasant to me. I was made head boy in my last term, although between you and me I was the second choice."

"What happened to the first choice?"

"He fell off a roof. From Harrow I went to London University, where I studied politics, and after that I joined the army. I was sent to Sandhurst, and I will never forget the day of my passing out parade, when I received a medal from the Queen. I'm afraid it was all too much for my mother. A few weeks later, she died quite suddenly. A massive heart attack, they said. I was shaken to the core because I loved her very much – and here's something you might like to know. I bribed one of the gardeners and had her ashes scattered in the grounds of Buckingham Palace ... in the roses. I knew it was something she would have appreciated."

Major Yu had finally finished eating and the maid suddenly appeared to clear the dishes. Alex wondered how she had known when to arrive. Pudding was a rhubarb crumble served with cream. At the same time, the maid brought in a cheese-board: Cheddar, Stilton and Red Leicester. All English, of course.

"There is not much more to tell," Yu continued. "I served with distinction in Northern Ireland and was given a letter of commendation. I was as happy in the army as I had been at Harrow – happier, in fact, as I had discovered that I rather enjoyed killing people, particularly foreigners. I rose to the rank of major, and it was then that the great tragedy of my life occurred. I was diagnosed with a quite serious illness, a rare form of osteoporosis known as brittle bone disease. The name tells you everything you need to know. What it meant was that my bones had become very fragile. In recent years the condition has got considerably worse. As you can see, I need a stick to walk. I am forced to wear gloves to protect my hands. It is as if my entire skeleton is made of glass and the slightest blow could cause a terrible injury."

"You must be all broken up about that," Alex remarked.

"I shall ignore your lame attempts at humour," Yu remarked. "Soon you will have cause to regret them."

He poured himself another glass of wine.

"I was forced to leave active service but that was not the end of my career. I still had an excellent mind and I was recommended for a job in intelligence – in MI6. That's quite a coincidence, don't you think? In other circumstances, you and I could have been working together. Unfortunately it didn't quite work out that way.

"You see, at first I thought it was all going to be very exciting. I imagined myself as quite the young James Bond. But I was never invited to be part of Special Operations like you, Alex. I never met Alan Blunt or Mrs Jones. I was sent to the communications centre at Cheltenham. A desk job! Can you imagine someone like me, slaving away from nine to five in a boring little office, surrounded by secretaries and coffee machines? It was miserable. And all the while I knew that my disease was getting worse and that it was only a matter of time before I would be thrown out onto the scrap heap.

"And so I decided to look out for myself. Despite everything, a lot of the information that passed my way at Cheltenham was highly sensitive and confidential. And of course there was a market for stuff like that. So, very carefully, I began to steal secrets from British intelligence – and guess where I took them! I went to the very snakehead which had employed my mother when she was in Hong Kong. They were delighted to have me – like mother, like son.

"In the end I had to resign from MI6. The snakehead were paying me a fortune and they were offering me all sorts of career opportunities. Very quickly, I rose up the ladder until – by the early eighties – I had become number two in what was now the most powerful criminal organization in South East Asia."

"And I suppose number one fell off a roof," Alex said.

"As a matter of fact, he drowned ... but you seem to have got the general idea." Yu smiled. "Anyway, it was about this time that I heard rumours of a new organization that was being formed by people who were, in their own way, quite similar to me. I decided to diversify, and using my snakehead connections I managed to contact them; and eventually we met up in Paris to finalize details. That, of course, was the birth of Scorpia, and I was one of the founding members."

"So what are you doing now? Why do you need Royal Blue?"

Major Yu had been helping himself to cheese.

He froze with a piece of Cheddar on the end of his knife. "You saw the bomb?" he asked.

Alex said nothing. There was no point denying it.

"You really are a very capable young man, Alex. I see now that we were quite unwise to underestimate you last time." Major Yu dropped the cheese onto his plate and reached for a biscuit. "I'm going to tell you what the bomb is for because it will amuse me," he went on. "But then I'm afraid you must be on your way." He looked at his watch. "We've chatted for quite long enough."

"Where am I going, Major Yu?"

"We'll get to that in a minute. Cheese?"

"Do you have any Brie?"

"Personally, I find French cheese disgusting." He ate silently for a moment. "There is an island in the Timor Sea, not very far from the north-west coast of Australia. Its name is Reef Island. You may have heard of it."

Alex remembered the news report he had heard on board the *Liberian Star*. A conference was to take place there in a few days' time. The alternative to the G8 summit. A meeting of famous people who were trying to make the world a better place.

"Scorpia have been given the job of destroying the island and the eight so-called celebrities who will be on it," Yu went on. He sounded pleased with himself. Alex imagined one of the problems of being a criminal was that you could never tell anyone about your crimes. "But what makes the task particularly interesting is that we have to make it look like an accident."

"So you're going to blow them up," Alex said.

"No, no, no, Alex. That wouldn't work at all. We have to be much more subtle. Let me explain." He swallowed a piece of cheese and dabbed his lips with his napkin. "As it happens, Reef Island is located in what is known as a subduction zone. Perhaps you've studied that in geography. What it means is that, under the sea, a few hundred miles north of the island, there are two tectonic plates pushing against each other with a fault line between them.

"Among its many business interests, the Chada Trading Company is involved in deep-sea oil exploration and leases an oil platform in the Timor Sea. In the last couple of months, I have arranged for a shaft to be driven into the seabed precisely over the fault line. This was quite a feat of engineering, Alex. We used the same reverse circulation system that was developed to build the ventilation shafts for the Hong Kong underground railway. And I'm delighted to say that it was designed by Seacore, a British company – once again, one step ahead of the world.

"Normally the pipe running down from the rig would be no more than thirteen centimetres in diameter by the time it hit the oilfield. However, our shaft will have ample room for Royal Blue. We will place the bomb one kilometre below the surface of the seabed. I will then travel to the oil platform and personally detonate it."

But what was the point? Alex went through what he had just been told and suddenly he understood. He knew exactly what the result would be. Not just an explosion. Something much, much worse.

He couldn't keep the horror out of his voice. "You're going to cause a wave," he said. "A huge wave..."

"Go on, Alex." Yu couldn't keep the glee out of his voice.

"A tsunami..." Alex whispered the word.

He could see it clearly. That was what had happened on 26 December 2004. An earthquake underneath the sea. A tsunami that had hit first Sumatra, and even reached the coast of Somalia. More than two hundred thousand people had died.

"Exactly. The bomb will have the effect of lubricating the fault line." Yu rested one hand on top of the other. "This will force one of the plates to rise." He lifted the upper hand a few centimetres. "The result will be a deep water wave, just one metre high. You wouldn't think it could do much harm. But as it approaches the coastline, where the seabed begins to rise, the front will slow down and the rest of the water will pile up behind. By the time it hits Reef Island, a thirty-metre wall of water will have formed, travelling at about five hundred and fifty miles an hour – the speed of a jumbo jet. One cubic metre of water weighs about one tonne, Alex. Imagine hundreds of cubic metres rushing in. There will be no warning. The island will be destroyed. It is low-lying; there will be nowhere to hide. Every building will be smashed. Every single person on the island will be killed."

"But the tsunami won't stop there!" Alex exclaimed. "What will happen to it after that?"

"That's a very intelligent observation. No. The tsunami will unleash the same amount of energy as several thousand nuclear weapons. It will continue on its way until it hits Australia. We'll be all right up here in Darwin, but I'm afraid a very large section of the western coast will disappear. Everything from Derby to Carnarvon. Fortunately there's nowhere very important or even attractive in that part of the country. Broome, Port Hedland ... few people have even heard of these places. And they're not exactly overpopulated. I wouldn't expect more than about ten or twenty thousand people to die."

"But I don't understand." Alex could feel his chest tightening. "You're going to do all this just to kill eight people?"

"Perhaps you didn't hear what I said. Their deaths have to look accidental. Our job is to make the world forget that this stupid conference was ever organized. And so we will provide a natural disaster on a massive scale. Who will care about the extinction of eight people when the number of deaths rises into the thousands? Who will remember a little island when an entire continent has been hit?"

"But they'll know it was you! They'll know it was all started with a bomb."

"That would be true if we used a nuclear bomb. There is an international network of seismographs: the Poseidon satellite in outer space, the Pacific Tsunami Warning Center, and so on. But the blast made by Royal Blue won't register. It will be lost as the tectonic plates shift and the devastation begins."

Alex tried to make sense of what he was hearing. He had been sent to uncover a smuggling operation, and somehow, instead, he had stumbled into this terrible nightmare – another attempt by Scorpia to change the world. He had to stop himself glancing at his watch. Hours had passed since he had set the hands to eleven o'clock. Surely MI6 were on their way.

"I expect you're wondering whether such a relatively small bomb will really be able to cause such havoc," Major Yu continued. "Well, there is one other thing you need to know. As luck would have it, in four days' time a rather special event is taking place. I'm afraid I don't know the astronomical term for it, but what we're talking about is the alignment of the sun, the earth and the moon. And the moon is going to be particularly close. At midnight, in fact, it will be as close as it ever is.

"As a result, there will be a particularly strong gravitational pull on the earth's surface. I'm sorry,

Alex. I'm beginning to sound like a schoolteacher. Let me put it more simply. The sun will be pulling one way; the moon will be pulling the other. And for just one hour, from the moment of midnight, the tectonic plates will be at their most volatile. A single explosion on the stroke of midnight will be more than enough to begin the process I have described. Royal Blue is the perfect weapon for our needs. Undetectable. Invisible. And above all, British. I'm very proud of that."

Yu fell silent, and in that moment Alex heard the drone of a plane. He looked out of the window and saw that a series of floodlights had been turned on. There was a seaplane circling, a tiny two-seater with floats instead of wheels. It could land on the water right outside the house and tie up on the jetty that Alex had seen from his room. He knew it had come for him.

"Where are you taking me?" he demanded.

"Ah, yes. Now we come to the rub." Major Yu sat back and suddenly the gun was in his hand, pointing at Alex. He had certainly moved quickly; Alex hadn't even seen him draw it. "The easiest and perhaps the most sensible thing would be to shoot you now," he said. "In half an hour you could be at the bottom of the ocean and neither Mrs Jones nor Mr Ethan Brooke would ever know what had happened to you.

"But I'm not going to do that. Why? Two reasons. The first is that I really don't want to get blood on the carpet. You may have noticed that it's an Axminster – from the town of Axminster in Devon. The second is more personal. You owe me a great deal of money, Alex. You have to pay for the damage you caused on the *Liberian Star*. And there is still the rather more considerable debt that you owe to Scorpia following the collapse of Invisible Sword. The truth is, although you may not realize it, right now you are worth a great deal to me alive.

"How much were you told about my snakehead? People smuggling, weapons, drugs – these are all part of my organization. But I have another highly profitable business based a couple of hundred miles from here in a facility hidden in the heart of the Australian jungle. This facility deals in the sale of human organs."

Alex said nothing. No words would come.

"Do you know how hard it is to find a kidney donor, even if you are rich and live in the West?" Yu pointed the gun at Alex's stomach. "I will be able to sell your kidney for one hundred thousand pounds. And the operation won't even kill you. You will live through it; and after that we'll be able to come back, perhaps, for your eyes." The gun rose up to the level of Alex's head. "Your eyes will sell for twenty thousand pounds each, leaving you blind but otherwise in good health." The gun dropped again. "You can live without your pancreas. It will make me a further fifty thousand pounds. While you are recovering from each operation, I will drain off your blood and your plasma. They will be kept frozen and sold at five hundred pounds a pint.

"And finally, of course, there is your heart. The heart of a young, healthy boy could fetch up to a million. Do you see, Alex? Shooting you does me no good at all. But keeping you alive is good for business; and you might even get some satisfaction in knowing, when you do eventually die, that you have restored the health of quite a few people around the world."

Alex swore. He spat out every foul word he knew. But Major Yu was no longer listening. The door to the dining room had opened again but this time it wasn't the maid who came in. Two men. Indonesian, like the maid. Alex hadn't seen them before. One of them placed a hand on his shoulder but Alex shrugged it off and stood up on his own. He wasn't going to let them drag him out of here.

"We'll fly you out tomorrow morning," Major Yu said. He glanced briefly at the two men. "Make sure he's locked up. Don't let him out of your sight." One last look at Alex. "Would you like an After Eight before you leave?"

Alex said nothing. Major Yu signalled. The two men took him away.

SPARE PARTS

The plane was a two-seater Piper PA-18-150 Super Cub with a top speed of just one hundred and thirty miles an hour – but Alex had already been told that they wouldn't be travelling very far. He was sitting behind the pilot in the cramped cockpit with the buzz of the propeller wiping out any chance of conversation. Not that Alex had anything to talk about. His wrists and ankles were shackled. The seat belt had been fastened in such a way that he couldn't reach the release buckle.

He wondered briefly about the balding, red-necked man in front of him – paid to carry a boy to an unspeakable death. Was he married? Did he have children of his own? Alex considered trying to bribe him. ASIS might pay twenty thousand dollars or more for his safe return. But he never even got a chance. The pilot only glanced at him once, revealing black sunglasses and a blank face, then put on headphones. Alex guessed he would have been chosen carefully. Major Yu wasn't going to make any more mistakes.

But his worst mistake had already been made. He had left the watch on Alex's wrist: the same watch that was even now – surely – sending out a distress signal to MI6. It had to be. Inside him Alex knew that without this one hope, if he didn't believe that despite everything he still had the advantage, he would be paralysed with fear. Major Yu's plan for him was the most evil thing he had ever heard – turning him from a human being into a bag of spare parts. Ash had certainly been right about the snakehead, and maybe Alex should have listened to his warnings. These people were death itself.

And yet...

Alex had been locked up at Yu's house through-out the night and for much of the morning. It was now almost midday. How long had it been since he had begun sending the signal? Sixteen hours at the very least. Maybe longer. MI6 would have received the signal in Bangkok; it would take them time to reach Australia. Surely they would be tracking him even now, watching him every inch of the way as he moved eastwards.

But Alex had to force himself to ignore the little voice in his ear that told him they should have been here by now. Perhaps they had decided not to bother. After all, he had called them once before when he had been a prisoner in Point Blanc Academy. That time, the panic button had been concealed in a CD player. He had pressed it and they had done nothing. Was it happening again?

No. Don't go there. They would come.

He had no idea where they were heading, and the pilot's body was effectively blocking out the compass and any of the other controls which might have given him a clue. He had assumed at first that they would stick to the coast. After all, the plane had no wheels; it had to land on water. But for the last hour, they had been flying inland and only the position of the sun gave him any idea of the direction. He looked out of the window, past the blur of the propeller. The landscape was flat and rocky, covered in scrub. A brilliant blue river snaked down like a great crack in the surface of the world. Wherever this was, it was huge and empty. There was no sign of any roads. No houses. Nothing.

He tried to make out more of the pilot's features but the man's eyes were fixed on the controls as if he were making a deliberate effort to ignore his passenger. He pulled on the joystick and Alex leant to one side as the plane dipped. Now he saw a canopy of green ... a band of rainforest. Yu had spoken of the Australian jungle. Was this what he had meant?

The plane dipped down. Alex had been in rainforests before and recognized the extraordinary chaos of leaves and vines, a thousand different shades and sizes, each one of them endlessly fighting for a place in the sun. Surely there would be nowhere for them to land here? But then they flew over the edge of the canopy, and Alex saw a clearing and a river that swelled suddenly into a lake with a cluster of buildings around the edge and a jetty reaching out to welcome them.

"We're landing," the pilot said – for no obvious reason. It was the first time he had spoken throughout the flight.

Alex felt his stomach shrink, and his ears popped as they circled round and began their descent. The sound of the engine rose as they neared the surface of the water. They touched down, sending spray in two directions. An osprey, frightened by the sudden arrival, leapt out of the undergrowth in a panic of beating wings. The pilot brought the plane round and they headed smoothly towards the jetty.

Two Aboriginal men had come out. They were both muscular, unsmiling, dressed in dirty jeans and string vests. One of them had a rifle slung over his bare shoulder. The pilot cut the engine and opened the door. He had unhooked a paddle from the side wall of the cockpit and used it to steer the plane the last few metres. The two men helped tie it to the jetty. One of them opened the door and released Alex from his seat. Nobody spoke. That was perhaps more unnerving than anything else.

Alex took a look around him. The compound was clean and well ordered with neat flower beds and lawns that had recently been mown. All the buildings were made of wood, painted white, with low roofs stretching out over long verandas. There were four houses, square and compact, with open shutters and fans turning within; each of them had a balcony on the first floor with views down to the lake. One of the buildings was an office and administration centre connected to a metal radio tower with two satellite dishes. There was a water tower and an electric generator with a fence running round it, topped with razor wire.

The last building was the hospital itself, long and narrow with a row of windows covered in mosquito nets and a red cross painted on the front door. This was where Alex would be sent when the time came ... not once but again and again, until there was nothing of him left. The thought made him shiver despite the damp heat of the afternoon and he turned his head away.

At first sight, there didn't seem to be too much security – but then Alex noticed a second fence, this one on the edge of the compound and about ten metres high. It was painted green to blend in with the forest beyond. There were no boats moored to the jetty and no sign of any boathouse, so an escape downriver would be impossible too – unless he swam. And what would be the point of breaking out of here? He had seen from the plane. He was in the middle of the outback with nowhere to go.

The two guards had each clamped hold of an arm and now they led him towards the administrative building. As they reached the door a young woman appeared, dressed as a nurse. She was short, plump and blonde. She had put on bright red lipstick, which seemed strangely at odds with her starched white uniform. One of her stockings was laddered.

"You must be Alex," she said. "I'm Nurse Hicks. But you can call me Charleen."

Alex had never heard such a broad Australian accent. And what the woman was saying was simply crazy. She was welcoming him as if he might actually be glad to be here.

"Come straight in," she continued. Then she noticed the cuffs. "Oh, for heaven's sake!" she exclaimed in a voice full of indignation. "You know we don't need those here, Jacko. Will you please remove them?"

One of the men produced a key and freed Alex's hands and feet. The nurse tut-tutted at them, then opened the door and led Alex down a corridor that was clean and simple with rush matting and white-washed walls. Fans were turning overhead and there was music playing somewhere, a Mozart opera.

"The doc will see you now," the nurse said cheerfully, as if Alex had booked an appointment weeks ago.

There was another door at the far end and they went through. Alex found himself in a sunny, sparsely furnished room – little more than a desk and two chairs. There was a screen to one side, a small fridge and a trolley with some bottles, a stethoscope and two scalpels. The window was open with a view of the jetty.

A man was sitting behind the desk, dressed not in a white coat but jeans and a brightly coloured open-necked shirt with the sleeves rolled up. He was in his forties, with thick blond hair and a craggy, weather-beaten face. He didn't look like a doctor. He hadn't shaved for a couple of days and his hands were grubby. There was a glass of beer on his desk and an ashtray filled with butts.

"Good day, Alex." He also spoke with an Australian accent. "Take a seat!"

It wasn't an invitation. It was a command.

"I'm Bill Tanner. We're going to be seeing a lot of each other over the next few weeks, so I might as well get a few things clear from the start. Fancy a beer?"

"No," Alex replied.

"You'd better drink something anyway," the nurse said. "You don't want to get dehydrated." She went over to the fridge and produced a bottle of mineral water. Alex didn't touch it. He had already decided he wasn't going to play these people's game.

"How was the flight?" Tanner asked.

Alex didn't answer.

The doctor shrugged. "You're feeling sore. That's OK. I'd be pretty sore if I were in your shoes. But maybe you should have thought about the consequences before you took on the snakehead."

He leant forward and Alex knew, with a sense of revulsion, that he'd had this conversation many times before. Alex wasn't the first person to be brought unwillingly to this secret hospital. Others had sat right where he was sitting now.

"Let me tell you how this works," Dr Tanner began. "You're going to die. I'm sorry to have to tell you that, but you might as well get used to it. We all have to die sometime, although for you it's probably a little sooner than expected. But you have to look on the upside. You're going to be well looked after. We have a really qualified team here and it's in our interests to keep you going as long as possible. You're going to have a lot of surgery, Alex. There are some bad days ahead. But you'll come through ... I know you will. We'll help you to the finishing line."

Alex glanced briefly at the trolley, measuring the distance between himself and the scalpels. He thought about making a grab for one of them, using it as a weapon. But that wouldn't help him. Better to take it with him, to find a use for it later. He realized that the doctor was waiting for him to reply. He answered with a single, ugly swear word. Tanner just smiled.

"Your language is a little ripe, son," he said. "But that's no worries. I've heard it all before." He gestured out of the window. "Now, you're probably wondering how you can escape from here. You've seen the fence and you're thinking you can climb over it. Or maybe you've looked at the river and decided you can try swimming. It all looks pretty easy, doesn't it! No TV cameras. Just the seven of us in the compound. Me, four nurses, Jacko and Quombi. Not much security – that's what you're thinking.

"Well, I'm sorry to tell you, mate, but you're wrong. You go out at night and you'll have to reckon with Jacko's pit bull. His name is Spike and he's a nasty piece of work. He'll rip you apart as soon as look at you. As for the fence, it's electrified. Touch it and it'll take you a week to wake up. And you're not getting anywhere near the generator – not unless you know how to bite your way through razor wire – so you can forget about tampering with the current.

"And even if you did manage to get out, it wouldn't do you much good. We're on the edge of the Kakadu National Park – two thousand million years old and as bad as the world was when it began. The start of Arnhem Land is about a mile from here, but that's a mile of tropical rainforest and you'd never find your way through. Assuming a death adder or a king brown didn't get you, there are spiders, wasps, stinging nettles, biting ants and – waiting for you on the other side – saltwater crocodiles." He jerked a thumb. "There are a hundred ways to die out there and all of them are more painful than anything we've got lined up for you here.

"That leaves the river. Looks pretty tempting, doesn't it! Well, there are no boats here. No canoes or kayaks or rafts or anything else you can get your hands on. We even keep the coffins locked up after one guy tried to bust out in one of those. You remember that, Charleen?"

The nurse laughed. "He was using the lid as a paddle."

"But he didn't get very far, Alex, and nor would you. Because this is the pre-monsoon season, what the Aboriginals call Gunumeleng. The water's swollen and fast-moving. About ten minutes downriver you'll hit the first rapids, and after that it just gets worse and worse. You try to swim, you'll be cut to pieces on the rocks. You'll almost certainly drown first. And waiting for you a mile downstream are the Bora Falls. A fifty-metre drop with a tonne of water crashing down every minute. So do you get what I'm saying? You're stuck here, mate, and that's that."

Alex said nothing but he was storing away everything Tanner was telling him. It was just possible that the doctor was giving away more than he realized. Outside, he heard a sudden whirring. The engine of the Piper had started again. He glanced out and saw the seaplane moving away from the jetty, preparing to take off.

"We're not going to lock you up, Alex," Tanner went on. "The grub's good and if you want a beer, just help yourself. There's no TV but you can listen to the radio, and I think we've got a few books. The point I'm trying to make is that, right now, you're here as our guest. Soon you'll be here as our patient. And after we've begun work, you won't be going anywhere. But until then, I want you to take it easy."

"We have to watch your blood pressure," the nurse muttered.

"That's right. And now, if you don't mind, I'd like you to roll up a sleeve so I can take a blood sample. It doesn't matter which arm. I also want a urine sample. It looks to me like you're pretty fit but I need to get it all down on the computer."

Alex didn't move.

"It's your choice, son," Tanner said. "You cooperate or you don't cooperate. But if you want to play hardball, I'll have to call Jacko and Quombi in. They'll rough you up a little and then they'll tie you down and I'll get what I want anyway. You don't want that, do you? Make it easy on yourself..."

Alex knew there was no point refusing. Although it made him sick, he allowed Tanner and the nurse to give him a thorough examination. They checked his reflexes, probed his eyes, ears and mouth, weighed and measured him and took the various samples. At last they let him go.

"You've looked after yourself, Alex," Tanner said. "For a Pom, you're in great shape." He was obviously pleased. "Your blood type is A positive," he added. "That's going to be an easy match."

It was as he was putting his clothes back on that he did it. Tanner was typing something into his computer; the nurse was looking over his shoulder. Alex was pulling on his trainers, leaning against the trolley as if to support himself. He allowed one hand to cover a scalpel, then slid it sideways and dropped it into his trouser pocket. He would have to walk very carefully or he'd give himself a nasty cut. He just hoped nobody would notice what he had done.

The nurse looked up and saw that he was dressed. "I'll take you to your room," she volunteered. "You should rest. We'll bring you supper in about an hour."

The sun had almost set. The sky was a deep grey with a streak of red like a fresh wound above the horizon. It had begun to rain, fat drops of water bursting one at a time on the ground.

"There's going to be another storm," the nurse said. "I'd tuck up and have an early night if I were you. And remember – stay indoors. The dog's trained not to come into the buildings. I mean, this *is* a medical facility. But take one step outside and he'll go for you – and we don't want you losing too much of that blood of yours, do we! Not at five hundred pounds a pint!"

She left Alex alone in a small room on the ground floor. It had a bed, a table and a single fan rotating in the centre of the ceiling; in one corner, there was a heavy silver filing cabinet. Alex opened it but there was nothing inside. A second door led into a small shower room, which also contained a toilet and a sink. Alex slid the scalpel out of his pocket and hid it inside the hanging roll of toilet paper. He didn't know if he would have any use for it, but at least it made him feel better having taken it. Maybe these people weren't quite as clever as they thought.

He went back into the bedroom. A single window looked down to the lake. With the Piper Super Cub gone, somehow Alex felt more abandoned than ever.

He sat down on the bed and tried to collect his thoughts. Only the day before, he had been in Darwin, congratulating himself on what he had achieved, thinking that his mission was over. And now this! How could he have been so stupid? He wondered what was happening to Ash. He still didn't understand why the two of them had been separated. If Yu knew that Ash was working for ASIS, why hadn't he sent him here too? Alex was filled with a longing to see his godfather again. It made everything even worse, being here alone.

About an hour later, the door opened and a second nurse came in, carrying a tray. She was dark-haired and slim and would have been pretty except that she had a rash over the lower part of her face. She was younger than Charleen but equally welcoming.

"I'm Isabel," she said. "I'm going to be looking after you. I've got a room just past the stairs, halfway down the corridor, so if you need anything just yell."

She set the tray down. Alex's dinner consisted of steak and chips, fruit salad and a glass of milk, but the sight of the food sickened him. He knew they were only building him up for what lay ahead.

He noticed two pills in a plastic cup. "What are these?" he asked.

"Just something to help you sleep," Isabel replied. "Some of our patients have difficulty nodding off, especially the first couple of nights. And it's important you get your rest." She paused at the door. "You're the youngest we've ever had," she said, as if Alex wanted to know. "Leave the tray outside the door. I'll collect it later."

Alex picked at the food. He wasn't hungry but he knew he had to keep his strength up. Outside, the rain fell more heavily. It was the same tropical rain that he had experienced in Jakarta. He could hear it hammering on the veranda roof and splashing into ever-widening puddles. There was a flicker of lightning and for a couple of seconds he saw the rainforest, black and impenetrable. It seemed to have moved closer, as if it were trying to swallow him up.

Later, somehow, he slept. He didn't take off any of his clothes. He couldn't bear to. He simply lay down on the bed and closed his eyes.

When he opened them again, the first light of the morning was already slanting in. His clothes felt damp. His muscles ached. He lifted his wrist and examined the watch. The hands were still set at eleven o'clock.

Almost thirty-six hours had passed since he had called for help. He listened to the world outside. The harsh cry of some sort of bird. The rustle of the grasshoppers. The last drip of the water as it fell from the branches. There was nobody out there. MI6 still hadn't arrived, and Alex couldn't fool himself any longer.

Something had gone wrong. The watch wasn't working.

They were never going to come.

DEAD OF NIGHT

The following afternoon, the silence of the rain-forest was punctured by the drone of the engine. The Piper Super Cub had returned.

By now Alex had fallen into a strange mood and one that he could barely understand. It was almost as if he had accepted his fate and could no longer find the strength or even the desire to escape it. He had met the two other women working at the hospital: Nurse Swaine and Nurse Wilcox, who had proudly told him that she would be his anaesthetist. Nobody had been unkind to him. In a way, that was what made it all so nightmarish. They were always checking that he had food and water. Would he like something to read? Would he like to listen to some music? Soon the very sound of their voices made his skin crawl. He couldn't break free of the feeling that they owned him and always would.

But he hadn't given up completely. He was still searching for a way out of this hideous trap. The river was impossible. There were no boats; nothing that would pass as a boat. He had followed the fence all the way round. There were no gaps, no convenient overhanging branches. He had considered blowing a hole in it. He still had one of the three coins that Smithers had given him. But the fence was connected to an electrical circuit. The guards would know instantly what he had done, and without a map, a compass or a machete, Alex doubted he would be able to find a way through the rainforest.

He thought about sending a radio message. He had seen the radio room in the administration building, and it was neither locked nor guarded. He soon realized why. The radio transmitter was connected to a numeric keypad: you had to punch in a code to activate it. Major Yu really had thought of everything.

Alex watched as the plane hit the surface of the lake and began a slow, lazy turn towards the jetty. He had been expecting it. Dr Tanner had told him it would be coming the night before.

"It's your first customer, Alex," he had said cheerfully. "A man called R. V. Weinberg. You may have heard of him."

As usual, Alex said nothing.

"He's a reality TV producer from Miami. Very successful. But he's contracted a serious eye disease and he needs two transplants. So it looks as if we'll be starting with your eyes. We'll operate first thing tomorrow morning."

Alex examined the American from a distance as he was helped out of the plane. Dr Tanner had warned him not to approach or try to speak to the "customer". It was one of the house rules. But, looking at him, Alex found himself filled with more hatred than he had ever felt for any human being.

Weinberg was overweight in a soft, flabby way. He had curling grey hair and a face that could have been made of putty, with sagging cheeks and jowls. He was a millionaire yet he dressed shabbily, his gut pressing against his Lacoste shirt. But it wasn't just his appearance that disgusted Alex. It was his selfishness, his complete lack of heart. Tomorrow Alex would be blind. This man would take his sight without thinking about it, simply because it was what he wanted and he had the money to pay for it. Major Yu, Dr Tanner and the nurses were evil in their own way. But Weinberg, the successful businessman from Miami, made him physically sick.

Alex waited until the man had disappeared into the house that had been prepared for him, then walked down to the edge of the lake. So this was it. He had just one night to make his escape. After that it really would be impossible.

But the anger that Alex felt had broken through his sense of hopelessness. It had come like a slap in the face and suddenly he was ready to fight back. These people thought he was helpless. They thought they'd covered everything. But they hadn't noticed the missing scalpel. And there was something even more important that they'd overlooked – despite the fact that it was sitting there right in front of them.

The plane.

The pilot had climbed out, dragging a kitbag with him. It looked as if he was going to stay until Weinberg was ready to leave. Alex had no doubt that the Piper would be incapacitated, the engine closed down and the keys locked away. And Dr Tanner would be fairly certain that no fourteen-year-old boy knew how to fly.

But that was his mistake: to leave the plane, and everything inside it, moored to the jetty.

Alex examined it, working out the angles, thinking about what lay ahead.

He might have found the way out.

They sent Alex to bed at half past eight and Nurse Isabel came into the room once he was tucked up. She was carrying two sleeping pills and a little cardboard cup of water.

"I don't want to sleep," Alex said.

"I know, dear," Isabel replied. "But Dr Tanner says you've got to get your rest." She held out the pills. "It's going to be a big day for you tomorrow," she went on. "You need your sleep."

Alex hesitated, then took the pills. He threw them into his mouth and swallowed the water.

The nurse smiled at him. "It won't be too bad,"

she said. "You'll see." She put a hand to her mouth. "Or rather, you won't..."

They checked Alex's room an hour later and again at eleven. Both times they saw him lying, utterly still, in bed. Dr Tanner was surprised. He had been expecting Alex to try something. After all, Major Yu had warned him to take extreme care with this particular boy, and tonight was his last chance. But it sometimes happened that way. It seemed that – despite his reputation – Alex had accepted the hopelessness of his situation and had chosen to find a brief escape in sleep.

Even so, Dr Tanner was a cautious man. Before he went to bed himself, he called the two guards, Quombi and Jacko, into his office.

"I want the two of you outside the boy's room all night," he ordered.

The two men looked at each other in dismay.

"That's crazy, boss," Jacko said. "The kid's asleep. He's been asleep for hours."

"He can still wake up."

"So he wakes up! Where's he going to go?"

Tanner rubbed his eyes. He liked to get a good night's sleep before he operated and he was in no mood for a lengthy debate. "I've got my orders from Major Yu," he snapped. "You want to argue with *him*?" He thought for a moment, then nodded. "All right. Let's do it this way. Jacko, you take the first shift until four o'clock. Quombi, you take over then. And make sure that dog stays outside the

317

whole time too. I want to be sure that no one goes anywhere tonight. OK?"

The two men nodded.

"Good. I'll see you tomorrow..."

At half past three that night, Jacko was sitting on the veranda outside Alex's room, flicking through a magazine he had read fifty times before. He was in a bad mood. He had passed Alex's window at least a dozen times, listening out for the faintest sound. There'd been nothing. It seemed to Jacko that everyone had got themselves into a complete panic about this kid. What was so special about him? He was just one of the many who had passed through the hospital. Some had screamed and cried; some had tried to buy their way out. All of them had ended up the same way.

The last thirty minutes of his guard duty ticked by. He stood up and stretched. A few metres away, lying on the grass, Spike cocked an ear and growled.

"It's all right, dog," Jacko said. "I'm going to bed. Quombi will be here soon."

He belched, stretched a second time and walked off into the darkness.

Ten minutes later, Quombi took his place. He was the younger of the two men and had spent almost a third of his life in jail until Dr Tanner had found him and brought him here. He liked his work at the hospital, and enjoyed taunting the patients as they got weaker and weaker. But he was in a bad mood right now. He needed his sleep. And he didn't get paid overtime for working through the night.

As he reached the building, his eye was caught by something glinting in the grass, just in front of the door. Some sort of foreign coin. Quombi didn't even wonder how it had got there. Money was money. He walked straight over and bent down to pick it up.

He was faintly aware of something falling out of the sky but he didn't look up quickly enough to see it. The silver filing cabinet could have crushed him but he was lucky. One corner struck him a glancing blow on the side of the head. Even so, it was enough to knock him out instantly. Fortunately the cabinet made little sound as it thudded onto the soft grass. Quombi fell like an axed tree. The dog got up and whined. It knew that something was wrong but it had never been trained for this. It went over and sniffed at the motionless figure, then sat on its hind legs and scratched.

On the first-floor balcony, Alex Rider looked down at his handiwork with grim satisfaction.

He had never been asleep. He had palmed the pills and swallowed only water and had been waiting quietly ever since. He had got up several times in the night, waiting for Jacko to leave, and had heard the words he had spoken to the dog. That was when he had got dressed and set to work.

Carrying the heavy filing cabinet up one flight

of stairs had almost been beyond him, and it was probably only desperation that had lent him strength as he clutched it in both arms and balanced it on his knee. The worst part had been making sure the metal frame never banged against the walls or the wooden steps. Nurse Isabel had a room on the ground floor, halfway down the corridor, and the slightest sound might wake her. He had dragged the cabinet into the room over the front door, and with one last effort had somehow managed to heave it up onto the balcony rail, balancing it there while he fumbled in his pocket.

He had only just been in time. Quombi had made his appearance a few seconds after Alex had dropped the ten-baht coin that Smithers had given him onto the lawn as bait. From that moment, the trap had been set.

And it had worked. Jacko was in bed. From the sound of it, Nurse Isabel hadn't woken up. Quombi was unconscious. With a bit of luck, he might even have fractured his skull. And the dog hadn't spoilt it all by barking.

The dog was next.

Alex crept back downstairs and went over to the main door. As he appeared, Spike began to growl, its hackles rising and its ugly brown eyes glaring out of the darkness. But – like Dr Tanner – Nurse Hicks had told him more than she should have. She had said that the dog was trained not to come into the buildings. The animal was clearly lethal. Even for a pit bull it was ugly. But it wouldn't harm him as long as he didn't step outside.

"Nice dog," Alex muttered.

He stretched out his hand. He was holding the piece of steak that he had been given on the first night. It had been kind of Dr Tanner to warn him that there was a dog. Cut into the meat were the six sleeping pills that he had been given over the last three days. The question was – would the dog take the bait? It didn't move, so Alex threw the meat onto the grass, close to the sprawled-out body of the guard. The animal ran over to it, its stubby tail wagging. It looked down, sniffed and scooped up the meat greedily, swallowing it without even chewing.

Just as Alex had hoped.

It took ten minutes for the pills to take effect. Alex watched as the dog grew more and more lumpen, until finally it collapsed onto one side and lay still, apart from the rise and fall of its stomach. At last things seemed to be going his way. Even so, he stepped outside cautiously, expecting either the dog or Quombi to wake up at any time. But he had no need to worry. He scooped up the coin – it was lying a few centimetres from the edge of the filing cabinet – and hurried into the night.

There was a soft echo of thunder that trembled through the air like a drum rolling down a hill. It wasn't raining yet but there was going to be another storm. Good. That was exactly what Alex wanted. He checked left and right. The compound was kept permanently lit by a series of arc lamps. The rest of the hospital staff, the pilot and the American television producer would all be fast asleep. Alex hesitated for just a few seconds, thinking how wonderful it would be if MI6 – perhaps Ben Daniels and a platoon of SAS men – chose this moment to make their appearance. But he knew that wasn't going to happen. It was all down to him.

He hurried towards the jetty. If only he had learnt how to fly! He might have been able to get the Piper started up, and in minutes he would have been out of here, on his way to freedom. But at fourteen, and despite all the other skills his uncle had taught him, he had been too young for flying lessons. Never mind. The plane was still going to be useful to him – for that was Dr Tanner's big mistake. The security at the hospital had been thoroughly checked – *but only when the Piper had been away*. Right now it was back; and even though he couldn't fly it, the seaplane was still going to help him escape.

Alex reached the jetty without being seen and crouched in the shadow of the plane, which was sitting on its two floats, rocking gently in the water. There was another rumble of thunder, louder this time, and a few drops of water splashed on his shoulders. The storm was going to break very soon. Alex examined the Piper Super Cub. There were two metal struts on each side, supporting the weight of the cockpit and fuselage. They tapered to a point where they were bolted into the long, fibreglass floats. Just as he remembered.

Alex reached into his pocket and took out the ten-baht coin again. It was the last one Smithers had given him, and it occurred to him that, if this went according to plan, all three would have saved his life. He placed it against the larger of the metal struts and looked up at the sky. There were few stars tonight, the clouds swirling overhead. Behind them the lightning flickered, white and mauve. Alex had the chewing gum packet in his hand. He waited for the thunder and pressed the switch at exactly the right moment.

There was a flash and a small explosion. Even without the storm it might not have been heard. But the coin had done its job. One of the struts had been ripped apart; the other had come free from the float. The Piper sagged in the water. Alex lay down on the jetty and pressed his feet against the float, pushing with all his strength. Slowly the float moved away from the main body of the plane. Alex pushed harder and the float came free. The plane sagged uselessly in the water. Moving more quickly now, Alex grabbed hold of the float and dragged it to the shore.

What he had was something almost exactly the same shape and size as a kayak or a canoe. He had even managed to blow a hole in the top which would allow his legs to fit inside. Admittedly the float had no foot braces, no thigh hooks and no support for his lower back. The hull was too flat. That would make it stable in the water but with such a wide footprint it would be hard to control. It was also much too heavy. Most modern kayaks are made of Kevlar or graphite cloth, glued together and strengthened with resin. The float from the Piper would be as nimble as a London bus. But at least it would carry him. It would just have to do.

Alex had gone kayaking three times in his life. Twice with his uncle, Ian Rider, in Norway and Canada; and once in Wales with Brookland School when he was doing his Duke of Edinburgh's Award. He'd had some experience of rapids – the pillows and eddies, the holes and the pourovers that made the journey such a white-knuckle ride. But the truth was, he was no expert. Far from it. All he could remember of his last trip was speed, screams and exploding water. He had been thirteen at the time and had thought himself lucky to come out alive.

The scalpel was back in his pocket, wrapped in toilet paper to prevent the blade cutting him. Now he took it out and unwrapped it, glad that he'd decided to take it from Dr Tanner's office. Being careful not to slip and slice open the palm of his hand, he cut away the jagged edges of the hole, trying to make a smooth line. He knew that the journey ahead was going to be tough; he didn't want his stomach and hips to be cut to pieces. The blade was small but very sharp. Soon the float was ready, and he left it on the shoreline.

Now he needed a paddle.

That was the easy part. For all his smug jokes about coffin lids, Dr Tanner had overlooked the obvious. The Piper Super Cub itself carried a paddle as part of its safety equipment. Alex had noticed it when he had flown in, clipped to the side wall of the cockpit. The pilot had used it to steer the plane ashore.

Alex went back to the edge of the lake, where the plane seemed to have tilted even further below the surface of the water. Eventually it would sink. He found a piece of the broken strut and twisted it free. Now he had a makeshift crowbar. He waited for another roll of thunder, then used it to smash a window. Opening the passenger door from the inside, he reached in and took the paddle.

Alex was tempted to get under way at once, but he made himself wait. If the rapids were as bad as Tanner had described, he couldn't possibly risk hitting them in the dark. He needed the first light of dawn. It was raining harder now, and Alex was soaked through. But in a way he was glad. The rain would provide him with cover if anyone chanced to look outside. While he was on the wide section of the lake he would be exposed. It would take him about five minutes of hard paddling to reach the cover of the rainforest.

He needed a diversion, and it suddenly occurred to him that the Piper could provide it. Once again he worked out the various possibilities. He had at least another hour until he would have enough light to take on the river. He might as well put the time to good use. And he wanted to leave his mark on Dr Tanner, R. V. Weinberg and this entire set-up.

Alex smiled grimly. These people were poison but they'd been in control for too long.

Now it was time to bite back.

WHITE WATER

Alex went back to the plane and, rummaging around in the hold, soon found what he was looking for: two empty jerrycans which might have been used to carry water or fuel. He needed a length of rubber tubing and tore it out of the engine itself. It didn't matter: this plane wasn't going anywhere. He opened the cap under the wing and put one end of the rubber tube into the fuel tank and the other into his mouth and sucked, reeling back, gagging as the acrid taste of aviation fuel cut into his throat. Nothing happened. He forced himself to try again and this time it worked. He had created a vacuum and the liquid was flowing out. He dragged over the jerrycans and filled them both.

By the time he had finished, the cans were almost too heavy to lift. Gritting his teeth, he set off across the lawn, heading back to the hospital. He knew he was taking a risk but he didn't care. He wondered how many other people had been brought here, poor refugees who had set out in hope of a better life but who had never arrived. He wanted to wipe this place off the face of the earth. Someone should have done it years ago.

The biggest risk of all was creeping into Dr Tanner's office. The first thin cracks of light were appearing in the sky and one of the nurses might wake up at any time. But he found what he was looking for in a drawer of the doctor's desk. A cigarette lighter. Tanner should have known that smoking could be harmful to his health. It was certainly going to prove expensive.

Moving faster but still being careful not to make any sound, Alex splashed the fuel over the side of the hospital, the veranda, the porch. It sat on top of the rainwater, not mixing with it. He saw it in the puddles, a strange mauve colour that almost seemed to glow. When he had just half a can left, he went back to the lake, leaving a trail of fuel behind him. He threw the empty can into the water, then climbed into his makeshift kayak, resting the paddle across his legs.

He was almost ready.

The paddle was too short and the kayak hopelessly unbalanced. It should have been trimmed out, the bow and the stern holding the same position in the water, but unfortunately the hole he had made wasn't central. He tried to shift his weight. At once he found himself wavering helplessly and thought he was going to capsize, but at the last minute he managed to right himself. He tried again more cautiously, and this time he succeeded. The float sat evenly on the surface. He dropped a shoulder. The fibreglass dug into his back but the kayak tilted slightly. He had it under control.

He took a deep breath and pushed off.

At the last minute, he flicked the lighter on. The tiny flame leapt up, battling against the falling rain. Alex touched it against the grass and at once the fire took hold, rushing up towards the hospital, which was now clearly visible in the rapidly breaking day. Alex didn't wait to see it arrive. He was already paddling, leaning forward and driving with his shoulders to give each stroke more power. He wobbled a couple of times as he got used to the weight, but the float was living up to its name. It was carrying him away.

Behind him, the line of flames reached the hospital.

The result was more spectacular than Alex could have hoped for. The rainwater had spread the aviation fuel everywhere, and although the wood was wet on the surface, years of Australian sunshine had baked it dry inside. Alex heard the soft explosion as the fire caught hold and felt the heat on his shoulders. He glanced back and saw that the entire building had become a fireball. The rain was actually steaming as it hit the roof and there was an epic struggle going on between the falling water and the rising flames.

Nobody had come outside yet, but a moment later Jacko was there, shocked out of his sleep and unable to take in what was happening. He was followed by Dr Tanner. By now, it wasn't just the hospital that was on fire. The administrative centre and one of the houses had also caught alight. The whole compound was being torn apart. Suddenly the American, R. V. Weinberg, appeared, dressed ridiculously in striped pyjamas, his trouser legs on fire. Alex smiled grimly as he hopped about, screaming, in the rain. It wasn't just his eyes that were going to need medical treatment.

Tanner looked around him and saw Quombi lying motionless on the grass, next to the great bulk of the filing cabinet. He understood at once.

"The boy!" he shouted. "Find the boy!"

Weinberg had thrown himself into a puddle and lay there whimpering. The rest of them ignored him, scattering around the complex searching for Alex. But even if they had thought to look out at the lake, they would have been too late. Alex was already out of sight, behind the curtain of rain.

There was a deafening crack and the generator shuddered to a halt with a series of sparks and a plume of black smoke. Unable to contend with the joint attack of water and fire, the electricity had failed. Tanner howled.

"Sir – the plane!" Jacko had noticed the Piper resting lopsidedly on its single float.

With the rain streaming down his face, Tanner gazed at it and pieced together what had happened. Now he knew where Alex had gone. He scanned the river, searching for him, but the smoke, the rain and the half-light had blotted out the world. The kid couldn't have gone far, though. It wasn't over yet.

Dr Tanner dragged his mobile phone out of his pocket and began to dial.

Alex heard the first rapids before he saw them. The lake wasn't a lake at all – it was simply a widening of the river. There was probably a word for it, but it had been a long time since he had sat in a geography lesson. At the far end, it became narrower again, the banks closing in like a letter V, and Alex could feel the current driving him on. He hardly had any need to paddle. At the same time, the rainforest pressed in on both sides, the trees towering above him, the foliage squeezing out the very air. And there was a sound which he remembered well. It was distant and elemental and immediately filled him with dread. Rushing water, somewhere round the corner, daring him to come on.

He dipped the paddle into the water, testing his makeshift kayak, knowing that he would have to be able to twist and turn, reacting to whatever the river threw at him with split-second timing. He could see already that he wasn't going to be able to stop. The current was too strong and the banks too steep. The nearest trees simply disappeared into the water, their roots trailing down with ugly-looking rocks behind. But at least he was putting distance between himself and the compound – or what was left of it. And Dr Tanner had already told him that there were no boats. The Piper was a wreck. Smoke was still rising from the hospital – he could see it over the line of the trees. There was no way that anyone would be able to follow him.

He turned the corner and came to the first section of rapids. The sight reminded him that he wasn't safe yet. The worst still lay before him, and he might only have exchanged one death for another.

Ahead of him the river dipped steeply down-wards, hemmed in by massive boulders and tree trunks on both sides. A series of jagged ledges had created a sort of natural staircase. If he landed where the water was too shallow, the kayak would be snapped in half – and Alex with it. White water was frothing and foaming, thousands of gallons thundering down from one level to the next. To make matters worse, the whole stretch was dotted with boils, areas where the water was rushing to the surface as if it were being heated in a sauce-pan. Hit one of those and he would lose all control, and then he'd be completely at the mercy of the river.

The thing is, Alex, you're never really in control, whatever you may think. Just keep paddling and never fight the current, because the current will always win.

The words of his uncle, spoken what seemed like a lifetime ago, came to his mind. Alex wished he could grasp some comfort from them. He felt like a loose button in a washing machine. His fate was out of his hands. Gritting his teeth, he tightened his hold on the paddle and charged forward.

Nothing quite made sense after that. He was fighting, thrown left and right, blind. Water was shooting past him, smashing into his face, pounding him from above. He dug down, using a forward sweep to turn the float, missing a black boulder with vicious razor-sharp edges by a matter of centimetres. The green canopy spun around him. The trees had all blurred into one another. He couldn't hear. His ears were full of water and when he opened his mouth, gasping for air, water rushed down his throat. Two more sweep strokes, dodging the rocks, then a terrible crash as the kayak slammed into one of the shelves. Mercifully it stayed in one piece. A huge blanket of water fell on him and he went under. He was drowning.

But then suddenly, somehow, he was through. He felt battered and exhausted, as if he had just been in hand-to-hand combat with the river, which in a sense he had. His stomach and back were on fire where the broken edges had cut into him. Alex slid a hand under the sodden rag that was his shirt and felt the damage. When he took it out, his fingers were bloody. Behind him the white water leapt and hurled itself against the rocks, displaying its fury that the kayak had got through.

Alex knew he wouldn't be able to take much more. It was only desperation – and pure luck – that had brought him this far. From the moment he had entered the white water, he had lost all sense of his centre of gravity, which really meant that he had lost everything. He might as well have been a piece of driftwood being swept no matter where. It wasn't just that the kayak was the wrong shape. It wasn't a kayak at all. It was a float ripped off a seaplane, and if Alex had decided, after all, to steal a coffin for the journey, he doubted he would have had any less control.

He tried to remember what Dr Tanner had told him about the river. After the first rapids, it got worse. And then, a mile downstream, came something called the Bora Falls. Alex didn't like the sound of that. He would have to find somewhere to come ashore and take his chances in the rainforest. He had already covered a fair amount of ground. With a bit of luck he might even have reached the edge of the flood plain on the other side. There had to be some civilization somewhere in the area: a ranger, a flying doctor, somebody! Somehow he would find them.

But there was still nowhere to land. The banks climbed steeply, rocks forming an almost unbroken barrier. When he looked up, the tops of the trees seemed a long way away. As wet as he was, Alex wasn't cold. The rainforest throbbed with its own muddy heat. He was moving swiftly, still being swept along by the current. He was listening out for the next stretch of rapids – but that wasn't what he heard. Instead it was the last thing he had expected.

A helicopter.

If he had still been in the rapids he wouldn't have been able to hear the chatter of the blades, but right now he was in one of the straits where the water was fast-moving but silent. Even so, he had to look up to make sure he wasn't imagining it. Somehow it seemed unlikely, early in the morning, in the middle of an Australian rainforest. But there it was. It was still a small speck, some distance behind, but drawing nearer with every second.

Alex's first thought was that MI6 had finally arrived, almost when it was too late. He looked back a second time and felt his hopes shrivel and die. There was something mean and sinister about the helicopter, the way it was zeroing in on him like an insect about to sting. If MI6 were coming, they would have been here days ago. No. This was something else. And it wasn't on his side.

The helicopter was a Bell UH-1D, a "Huey", one of the most famous flying machines in the world ever since the Americans had sent hundreds of them to Vietnam back in the sixties. Alex recognized the long, slim fuselage with the extended tail. The cargo door was open and there was a man sitting with his legs hanging out and some sort of weapon on his lap. It had to be nothing more than bad luck. Dr Tanner couldn't have summoned up support in the few minutes that Alex had been gone. The helicopter must have been on its way anyway, perhaps dropping off supplies, and Tanner had simply redirected it after him.

Alex had nowhere to hide. He was in the middle of the river and he wasn't moving fast enough to get away. At least the helicopter didn't seem to be equipped with door guns, rocket launchers or anti-tank missiles. And the man only had a rifle. That was good too. If it had been a machine gun, Alex would have had no chance at all. But even so, a half-decent marksman would be able to pick him off with no trouble. Suddenly Alex's back and shoulders felt horribly exposed. He could almost feel the first bullet slamming into them.

He lowered his head towards the water, changing his centre of gravity and tilting the float onto its side. His left shoulder was touching the water now as he lanced forward, pounding down with the paddle, heading for the nearest bank. It was a stroke known as the low brace and Alex hoped that as well as giving him extra momentum through the water, it would also present less of a target to the sniper up above.

Something snapped against the surface centimetres from his head, and a microsecond later he heard the discharge of the rifle. The bullet had reached him faster than its sound. Alex jerked upright again. Water dripped off the side of his face. But he had reached his destination: a clump of trees hanging over the river, forming a green tunnel for him to go through. At least he would be out of sight for about fifty metres.

The next stretch of white water was about fifty metres in front of him, directly ahead. The rapids had been his enemy, but now, in a strange way, they had become his friend. The churning water, the spinning current and the waves tossing him from side to side would make him more difficult to hit. But could he reach them? The helicopter was directly above. The leaves and branches were thrashing around madly, tearing themselves apart. The downdraught was beating at the river and the howl of the Huey's engine was shattering the very air.

Alex emerged from the tunnel and dug down, using all the strength of his upper body and shoulders to propel himself forward. There were two more shots. One of them hit the kayak and Alex found himself staring at a hole right in front of him. It had been fired at an angle, boring through the fibreglass and exiting just above the waterline. It must have missed his leg with barely a centimetre to spare.

Left and then right, two more power strokes and he was into the rapids. He hadn't had time to pick a line – or form any strategy for surviving the next section. And this stretch was even worse than the first one, with faster water, a bigger slope, rocks that seemed purpose-built to impale him or tear him in half.

Even the sniper seemed to hesitate, letting the river do its work for him.

When in doubt, keep paddling. That had been another of Ian Rider's instructions and Alex did just that, swinging the paddle automatically, first one side, then the other, battling his way through. The helicopter had disappeared. The spray had wiped it out. Surely that meant they couldn't see him. There was an ear-splitting bang but it wasn't the rifle. The nose of the kayak had slammed into a rock, jerking Alex round in a crazy circle so that for the next few seconds he found himself travelling down the river backwards. He jammed the paddle in, using the current to turn. His arms were almost torn off by the strain but the float came round, then shot forward. All the water in the world fell on him. But then it was over. He was through.

Ahead of him the river was wider, and this time the vegetation was set further back, providing no cover. The kayak was being carried at speed. In fact, the river seemed to be moving faster and faster. Why? But Alex had no time to find an answer. He glanced up and saw the sniper taking aim. He was so close that Alex could make out the stubble on his chin, the finger closing on the trigger.

There was only one thing he could do, one last trick he could play. It might easily kill him but Alex was fighting back and he wasn't just going to sit there and let this anonymous man gun him down. The sniper fired. Alex felt the bullet crease the side of his neck, just above his shoulder. He wanted to scream. It was as if someone had drawn a kitchen knife across his flesh. But at that exact moment, he took a deep breath, threw himself sideways, jerked up a knee and turned the kayak upside down.

He wanted the sniper and the helicopter pilot to think that they had got him. From the air, all they would be able to see was the upturned hull of the kayak. Alex was dangling beneath, his face and shoulders buffeted by the current, the paddle gripped tightly in his hands. He was still travelling at speed. If he hit a rock, he would be killed. It was as simple as that. But it was either that or a bullet from above.

The next minute was the longest of Alex's life. He could feel himself moving but he could see nothing. When he tried to look, everything was a swirl of dark grey and the water beat against his eyes. He could hear strange echoes of the river and, far away, the helicopter hovering in the air. His legs were trapped, locked above his head inside the kayak. His heart was pounding. His lungs were beginning to demand fresh air.

But he had to stay underwater. How long would

the helicopter follow him before the sniper decided that his work was done? His chest was getting tighter. There were bubbles escaping from his mouth and ears, precious oxygen leaking out of him. He had no idea how long he had been submerged. He felt the kayak hit something, sending a shudder down his spine. This was madness. He was drowning. If he waited much longer, he wouldn't have the strength to flip himself back up.

At last, at the very end of his endurance, on the edge of a blackout, he acted. The move was called the hip snap. Alex curled his face into his body and pushed with the paddle. At the same time, he rolled his hips, forcing the kayak to turn.

Everything happened at once. His head and shoulders cleared the surface, water streaming down his face. Daylight burst all around him. The float swayed, then righted itself. Gasping, dazed, Alex found himself in the middle of the river, moving faster than ever.

And he was alone. The helicopter had gone. He could see it looping away towards the column of black smoke still rising from the hospital compound. So it had worked. They thought he was dead.

Alex looked ahead of him. And saw that he was.

Now he understood why they had left him. It wouldn't have mattered if he was still alive underneath the kayak, because what lay in front of him would kill him anyway.

He had reached the Bora Falls.

A straight line that marked the end of the world. The river was rushing over it, hundreds and thousands of gallons. There was a white cloud, a mist hanging over the abyss. And beyond that – nothing. He could hear the water thundering down endlessly and knew that there could be no going back. There was no power on earth that could stop him now.

Alex Rider opened his mouth and yelled as he was swept helplessly over the edge.

BATTERIES NOT INCLUDED

For a long-drawn-out second, he hung in space with the roar of the Bora Falls in his ears, the spray in his eyes and the certainty that he couldn't possibly survive. The water was like some huge, living thing, rushing and exploding over the side of the rock face. And there would be no safe landing. Looking down, Alex saw a boiling cauldron, fifty metres below, waiting to receive him.

There was no time to think, no time to do anything but react instinctively, half remembering lessons taught long ago. Somehow he had to lessen the impact when he hit the surface below. Be aggressive! Don't let the waterfall just take you. At the very last moment, before he fell, Alex tensed himself, took a deep breath and then pulled hard with a single, powerful stroke.

The world tilted.

The roar in his ears was deafening. He was blind. His head was being hammered. He was only aware of his hands gripping the paddle, the wrists locked, his muscles seizing up.

Lean forward. You don't want to fight the water – you have to go with it. The higher the drop, the more angle you'll need when you hit the bottom. And – he remembered when it was almost too late – turn your head to one side or the impact will smash every bone in your face.

He was falling. Half in the water, half in the air. Faster and faster.

Try to aim for the white. That's where there's the most air in the water and the air will cushion your fall. Don't shout. You have to hold that breath.

How much further could it be? And how deep was the basin? God – he would be smashed to pieces if he hit a rock. Too late to worry about that now. The spray was stinging his eyes. He closed them. Why watch his own death?

The kayak hit the cauldron nose first and was instantly sucked inside, dragging Alex with it. He felt his legs and stomach take the full force of the impact before the water overwhelmed him. It was pounding down on his shoulders, crushing him. His head was thrown back and he felt the whiplash on his neck. The paddle was torn free. And then he was floundering, scrabbling desperately with his hands, trying to free himself from the kayak, which was dragging him into the depths below. His elbow struck a rock, almost breaking the bone. The shock made him release his breath and he knew he had only seconds to reach the surface. But his legs were trapped. He couldn't pull them free. The kayak was sinking, taking him with it. Using all his strength, he twisted his lower body and somehow his hips cleared the edge of the float. He pulled. First one leg, then the other. He was swallowing water. He no longer knew which way was up and which was down. His feet were free. He lashed out once and then again. The water was spinning him, throwing him violently from side to side. He couldn't take any more. One last try...

...and his head and shoulders burst up into the air. He was already far downstream. The Bora Falls were behind him, impossibly high. There was no sign of the float. It must have been smashed to pieces. But as Alex sucked in fresh air, he knew that he had done everything right and that by a miracle he had survived. He had taken on the falls and he had beaten them.

The current had slowed down. Alex's arms and legs were completely limp. All his strength had gone, and the best he could manage was to keep himself afloat, tilting his head back so that his mouth stayed in the air. He felt as if he had swallowed a gallon of water and vaguely wondered about cholera, yellow fever or whatever else this tropical river might contain. ASIS hadn't bothered giving him any injections before he flew to Bangkok. Well, he'd have to worry about that later. Complain to them when the time came...

He had never felt so exhausted. The water had

become a cushion and he almost wanted to lie back and go to sleep. How far had he travelled? Dr Tanner had said that the falls were a mile from the compound, but he felt he had gone twice that distance. No sign of the helicopter. That was a good thing. They thought he was dead. So they'd leave him alone.

Sometime later, he found himself lying on a riverbank made up of shingle and sand. He had been washed up without even noticing and must have nodded off, because the sun was now much higher in the sky. He allowed the warmth to creep into him. As far as he could tell, none of his limbs were broken. His neck and back were badly bruised and hurting – his spine had taken the full force of the impact – and there were cuts and scratches all over his torso, hips and legs. But he knew he had got off lightly. The chances of his surviving the waterfall had been tiny, but to have done so without a major injury was a miracle. He remembered what Ash had told him about his father. *The luck of the devil.* Well, that was something Alex seemed to have inherited.

Ash.

Reef Island.

The tsunami heading for Western Australia.

Alex had been so worried about himself that he had lost sight of the bigger picture. How long did he have before Major Yu set off the bomb that would have such a devastating effect on the earth's tectonic plates? Was he already too late? Alex forced himself into a sitting position, trying to get life back into his battered frame as he warmed himself in the sun. At the same time, he worked it out. Yu had spoken of four days. At midnight on the fourth day the earth was going to be in the grip of some sort of gravitational pull and the fault line deep down below the seabed would be at its most vulnerable.

Four days. Alex had spent three of them as a prisoner. So it was going to happen tonight! Right now it couldn't be much later than ten o'clock in the morning. So Alex had just over twelve hours to prevent a terrible catastrophe, the murder of eight people on Reef Island and the deaths of thousands more in Australia.

And that was when the complete hopelessness of his situation hit him. It was true he had managed to escape from the horrific death Major Yu had planned for him. But where was he? Looking around him, Alex saw that he had left the rainforest behind. He was on the edge of a flood plain with mountains in the far distance, perhaps fifty miles away. He was surrounded by stubby, dwarf-like trees that he couldn't name, a few boulders and some termite mounds. There was a sweet smell – something like mouldering wood – in the air. And that was all. If nowhere had a middle, this was it.

There was nothing he could do. Nobody was going to operate on him, but he would die anyway

- from either starvation or disease. Assuming, of course, that a saltwater crocodile didn't get him first. Alex wiped a grimy hand across his face. It seemed to him that from the moment this mission had begun, nothing had gone right. He had never been in control. He cast his mind back to the office in Sydney and Ethan Brooke outlining what he would have to do. He would be there to provide cover, that was all. It would be easy. Instead of which, he had been thrown into the worst two weeks of his life. God! He should have listened to Jack!

He looked again at the mountains. It would take him a day to reach them at the very least. Too long. And why should he assume anyone lived there? He hadn't seen any roads or houses from the plane. If only he could get in touch with MI6. He glanced at his wrist. Miraculously, despite the battering it had taken, the watch was still in one piece. The question was – why hadn't it worked? Smithers had built it for him personally. The watch *had* to be sending out a signal. So what possible reason could MI6 have to ignore it? Alex remembered his meeting with Mrs Jones and Ben Daniels – Fox as he had once been known. He couldn't believe that the SAS man would let him down. So what had gone wrong?

He took the watch off and examined it. Although it looked cheap and tacky, something he might have got in a street market in Afghanistan, the watch would have been built to last. The strap must have been strong to survive the journey over the Bora Falls, and Alex guessed the case was waterproof. The hands were still showing eleven o'clock. He turned the watch over. There was a groove running all the way round the underside: the back screwed off. He pressed his thumb against it and twisted, and the case opened with surprising ease.

The watch contained some complicated microcircuitry which Smithers must have designed and installed. It was completely dry. There was no evidence of any water seeping in. The whole thing was powered by a battery that should have been sitting in a circular compartment, right in the middle.

But there was no battery. The compartment was empty.

So there was his answer. That was the reason why his signal hadn't been heard. There had been no signal. But how could it have happened? Smithers had always been on his side. It was completely unlike him to forget something so basic. Alex fought back a wave of fury. His whole life snatched away from him simply because of a missing battery!

And how would he find a replacement? Somehow he doubted he was going to discover a Boots in the middle of the outback. For a moment, Alex was tempted to fling the watch into the river. He never wanted to see the bloody thing again.

For a long time he didn't move. He let the sun beat down on him, drying out his clothes. A fly buzzed around his head and he swatted it away.

He found himself playing back everything that had happened to him: the waterfall, the flight through the rapids, the moment he had set the hospital ablaze. Had it really all been for nothing? And before that, his dinner with Major Yu, the chase on the *Liberian Star*, the discovery of Royal Blue, the sudden appearance of Kopassus, the toy warehouse in Jakarta.

No battery!

He remembered his time in Bangkok and what Ash had told him about his parents. That was the only reason he had agreed to all this, to learn something about himself. Had it been worth it? Probably not. The truth was, Ash had disappointed him. His godfather. Alex had hoped he would become a friend, but despite all the time they had spent together, he had never really got to know him. Ash was too much of a mystery – and from the very start he had set out to trick Alex, with that business in the forest near Swanbourne.

He remembered his first sight of Ash, dressed as a soldier and carrying an assault rifle, looming out of the darkness as Alex stood on a fake mine in the middle of a fake barrage. How could they have done that to him?

You weren't in any real danger. We knew exactly where you were all the time.

That was what Ash had told him that night at the Peninsula Hotel, sitting out by the swimming pool. Alex remembered it now.

And how had they known?

There was a beacon inside the heel of one of your trainers.

His trainers.

Alex looked down at them. All the colour had faded and they were ragged, full of holes. Was it possible, what he was thinking? He had been given the trainers when he was on the aircraft carrier that had picked him up when he landed in the Pacific. The beacon had been added by Colonel Abbott when he was staying with the SAS in Swanbourne.

He was wearing the same trainers now.

He had been given a complete change of clothes by Cloudy Webber when she had dressed him as an Afghan – but the shoes hadn't fitted him so she had allowed him to keep his own. He hadn't changed again until his dinner with Major Yu. He had worn the English designer shirt and jeans until he had arrived at the hospital, where there had been fresh clothes in his room. But neither Major Yu nor Dr Tanner had provided him with new footwear. So the beacon that had been planted in Swanbourne had to be on him still. It wouldn't be working. It had been designed for short-range use.

But it might be battery operated.

Alex fought back the surge of excitement. He was too afraid of being disappointed. He leant down and pulled the trainers off so that he could examine them. Ash had told him the beacon was inside one of the heels. Alex turned the shoes over.

The soles were made of rubber and he couldn't see any openings or anything that looked like a secret compartment. He pulled out the insoles. And that was when he found it. It was in the left shoe, directly over the heel: a flap that had been cut into the fabric and then sealed.

It took Alex ten minutes to prise it open, using his fingers, his teeth and a sharp stone from the riverbank. As he worked, he knew that this might all be for nothing. The battery had been there for two weeks. It might be dead. It surely wouldn't fit the transmitter in the watch anyway. But the chances of finding a battery in the Australian outback had been zero to begin with.

He pulled open the flap and there it was – the little pack of circuitry that had been designed to save his life during the bombardment in the forest. And there was the power source too: a straight-forward lithium battery, about twice the size of the one that should have been in the watch. Alex eased it out and held it in the palm of his hand as if it were a nugget of pure gold. All he had to do was connect it. He had no screwdriver, no conductor, no metal contacts, nothing. Easy!

In the end he snapped two spikes off a nearby shrub and used them as miniature tweezers to prise out some of the wires from inside the heel. It seemed to take for ever, and as the sun climbed higher he felt the sweat trickling down his forehead, but he didn't stop to rest. Painstakingly he unstitched the inside of the radio beacon and then broke off two lengths of wire, each one barely more than a centimetre long. Did the battery still have any life? He rubbed the wires against it, and to his delight he was rewarded by a tiny spark. So now all he had to do was connect the battery to the watch, using a couple of pebbles to keep everything in place.

There was nothing more he could do. He set the battery next to the watch with the wires touching, feeding precious electricity into the transmitter, and balanced the entire thing on a rock. After that he went and lay down in the shade of a tree. Either the transmitter was working now or it wasn't. He would find out soon enough.

A few minutes later, he was sound asleep.

ATTACK FORCE

Alex was woken by the sound of a helicopter. For a moment, he was filled with dread, fearing the Bell UH-1D had returned. If that were the case, he would let them take him. He simply didn't have any more reserves of energy. He had nothing left with which to fight back. But squinting into the sun he saw at once that this was a bigger helicopter with two sets of rotors: a Chinook. And there was a figure already leaning out of the door.

Dark eyes. Short black hair. A hand raised in greeting. It was Ben Daniels.

Alex clambered to his feet as the Chinook landed on a patch of scrubland a short distance away. He went over to it, taking care where he put his bare feet. It would be just his luck to step on a death adder now! Ben climbed out and stared at him. Then, before Alex could stop him, he grabbed hold of him and pulled him into a crushing embrace.

"So here you are!" he exclaimed, shouting over the noise of the rotors. "I've been so worried about you!" He let Alex go. "What the hell are you doing out here? Where have you been?"

"It's a long story," Alex said.

"Has it got anything to do with the smoke coming from upriver?" Ben jerked a thumb. "We saw it as we flew in."

"That used to be a hospital." Alex couldn't hide his relief that things were finally going his way. "I'm really glad to see you..."

"Mrs Jones has been going frantic. We knew you'd flown to Jakarta, but we lost you after that. She's got people all over Indonesia but she sent me to Darwin in case you made it across. I've been waiting there for three days, hoping you'd get in touch. You look terrible! Like something the cat dragged in."

"That's how I feel." Alex stopped. "What time is it, Ben?" he asked.

Ben was obviously surprised by the question. He looked at his watch. "It's ten past one. Why do you ask?"

"We have to get moving. We've got less than twelve hours."

"Until what?"

"I'll tell you on the way..."

Alex was feeling better than he had in a long time. He was warm and dry and fed, and the dangers of the last few days had slipped away behind him. He was lying on a comfortable bunk in a military compound just outside Darwin, which was where Ben Daniels had brought him earlier that day. He was wearing combats, the only clothes Ben had been able to find for him. For the last few hours, he had been left on his own.

He could see a certain amount of activity taking place outside the window. Soldiers crossing the parade ground, jeeps speeding in and out of the main gate. The helicopter was still sitting where it had landed. Half an hour ago a truck had pulled up and Alex had watched as refuelling began. He wondered if it was significant. Maybe something was happening at last.

Despite everything, he couldn't relax completely. It was half past six and very soon the sun would be setting; at the same time, the earth and the moon would be moving into the alignment that Major Yu had been waiting for. At midnight Royal Blue would be lowered beneath the seabed and detonated. The devastation would begin.

And what were MI6 and ASIS doing to prevent it?

Alex had explained everything, not just to Ben but to a whole posse of Australian army officers. His story was incredible, almost beyond belief, but the strange thing was that not one person in the room had doubted him. This was, after all, the boy who had dropped in from outer space. Alex supposed that where he was concerned, anything was now considered possible. One of the men was a munitions expert and he had quickly confirmed what Major Yu had said. It would be possible to manufacture an artificial tsunami. At midnight the fault line would be in the grip of enormous gravitational pressure. Even a relatively small explosion would be enough to trigger a global catastrophe, and Yu had all the power of Royal Blue at his command.

Of course, in one sense Scorpia's mission had already failed. Thanks to Alex the intelligence agencies knew what they were planning, and even if everyone on Reef Island were killed in a freak wave, nobody would now think it was an accident. Alex assumed that the island would be evacuated anyway, just to be on the safe side. There was no longer any need for Major Yu to press the button. If he was sensible, he'd already be looking for somewhere to hide.

There was a knock on the door. Alex straightened up as Ben Daniels entered. He was looking grim.

"They want you," he said.

"Who?"

"The cavalry's just arrived. They're in the mess…"

Alex walked across the compound with Daniels, wondering what had gone wrong. But at least he was still being included. MI6 had always treated him as a spy one minute, a schoolboy the next, dumping him whenever it suited them. The mess was a low, wooden building running the full length of the square. With Daniels right behind him, Alex opened the door and went in.

Most of the officers he had spoken to earlier that day were still there, poring over maps and sea charts that had been spread out over the dining tables. They had been joined by two men that Alex recognized at once. This was the cavalry that Ben had referred to. Ethan Brooke was sitting at a table, Marc Damon standing just behind him. Presumably they had been flown up from Sydney. Garth – the guide dog – saw Alex come in and thumped his tail. At least someone was pleased to see him.

"Alex!" The blind man had become aware of his presence. "How are you doing?"

"I'm OK." Alex wasn't sure he was too happy to see the head of ASIS Covert Action. Ethan Brooke had manipulated him as cold-bloodedly as Alan Blunt would have done in London. It seemed to him that all these people were the same.

"I know what you've been through. I can't believe the way things played out. But you did a fantastic job."

"Major Yu knew about me all the time," Alex said. Even as he spoke the words, he knew they were true. The fight in Bangkok had been designed to cripple him. And on the *Liberian Star*, Alex had overheard Yu boasting to the captain. He had known Alex's identity before he entered the container. He had simply been playing with him for his own amusement.

"Yes. We have a security leak and it's worse than we thought." Brooke glanced in the direction of his deputy, who looked away, as if he didn't want to make any comment.

"What's happened to Ash?" Alex asked.

"We don't know. We only know what you told us." Brooke fell silent and Alex could see he was preparing himself for what he had to say.

"So what are you going to do?" Alex asked.

"We have a problem, Alex," Brooke explained. "Here's the situation ... I'll give it to you straight. The first thing is, the Reef Island conference is still going ahead."

Alex was shocked. "Why?"

"We told them they were in danger. Obviously we couldn't give them all the details, but we suggested in the strongest possible terms that they pack their bags and get out of there. They refused. They said that if they left, they'd look like cowards. Tomorrow's their main press conference, and how's it going to look if they've all skulked away overnight? We're still arguing with them, but in a way, I suppose they've got a point. Scorpia want them out of the picture. If they simply disappear, they'll be doing the job for them."

Alex took this in. It was bad news – but Reef Encounter was only part of the picture. After the tsunami hit the island, it would continue on its way towards Western Australia.

"Have you found Major Yu?" he asked.

"Yes." Brooke smiled briefly. "He told you he would be on an oil platform in the Timor Sea, and we've gone through all the records, including the latest satellite images. There's an oil rig licensed to the Chada Trading Company of Bangkok. It's a semi-submersible platform moored in twelve hundred metres of water a few hundred miles north of Reef Island."

"Right over the fault line," Damon muttered. It was the first time he had spoken since Alex came into the room. "It's called Dragon Nine."

"So that's it," Alex said. It seemed obvious to him. "You bomb it. Blow it out of the water. Kill Major Yu and everyone who works for him."

"I wish it was as easy as that," Brooke replied. "But first of all, Dragon Nine is just outside Australian waters. It's in Indonesian territory. If we send a strike against it, it'll be like declaring war. We can't even send one man in a boat without written authority, and that could take days. Officially, we're stuck..."

"Why can't you ask the Indonesians for help?"

"They don't trust us. By the time we've persuaded them we're telling the truth, it'll be too late."

"So you're just going to sit back and let him get on with it?" Alex couldn't believe what he was hearing.

"Obviously not. Why do you think we're here?"

Ben Daniels took a step forward. "Why don't you tell Scorpia that you know what they're up to?" he asked. "You said it just now. The plan only works if we all think the tsunami was caused naturally. If we tell them they've failed, maybe they'll back off."

"We've already thought of that," Damon replied. "But Dragon Nine has shut down. It's observing radio silence. And even if we did find a way to contact Major Yu, he might go ahead anyway. Why not? He's obviously mad. And if the bomb's already in place..."

"So what is the answer, Mr Brooke?" one of the other officers asked.

"A small British and Australian task force. Un-authorized and illegal." Brooke turned to Alex. "I've already spoken to your Mrs Jones and she's agreed. We have very little time but I've assembled some of our best people. They're kitting up right now. You and Daniels go with them. We parachute you onto the oil rig. You find Royal Blue and deactivate it. Meanwhile, my people kill Major Yu. If you can locate the whereabouts of Ash, so much the better – but he's not a priority. What do you say?"

Alex was too shocked to say anything, but next to him, Ben Daniels shook his head. "I'm happy to go," he said. "But you can't be serious, asking Alex. He's only a kid, if you hadn't noticed. And I'd have said he's already done enough."

Some of the Australian officers nodded in agreement, but Brooke wasn't having any of it. "We can't do it without Alex," he said simply.

And Alex knew he was right. He had already told them what he had done on board the *Liberian Star*. "I scanned my fingerprints into Royal Blue," he said. "I'm the only one who can deactivate it." He sighed. It had seemed like a good idea at the time.

"I'll expect you to look after him, Mr Daniels," Brooke continued. "But we don't have a lot of time to argue about this. It's already seven o'clock and you've got a long flight ahead of you." He turned to Alex. "So, Alex. What do you say?"

Two men and a woman were watching the sun set on Reef Island.

The island was only a quarter of a mile long but it was strikingly beautiful with white beaches, deep green palm trees and a turquoise sea ... all the colours somehow too vivid to be quite real. Limestone cliffs covered in vegetation rose up on the north side of the island, with mangroves below. Here sea eagles circled and monkeys chattered in the trees. But on the southern side, everything was calm and flat. There was a wooden table and a bench on the sand. But no deckchairs, no sun umbrellas, no Coke bottles or anything that might suggest that, just over the horizon, the twenty-first century was ticking on.

There was only one building on Reef Island, a long, wooden house with a thatched roof, partly on stilts. There were no generators; the only electricity was supplied by wind or water power. A large organic garden provided all the food. The owner of the house ate fish but not meat. A few cows, grazing in a field, were milked twice a day.

There were chickens to lay eggs. An elderly goat, wandering free, was no use at all, but it had been there so long that nobody had the heart to ask it to leave.

In the last few days, the island had been invaded by a press corps, which had established itself in a series of tent-like structures behind the house. The journalists had brought their own generators. And meat. And alcohol. And everything else they would need for the press conference the next day. They were enjoying themselves. It was nice to be able to report a story that people actually wanted to hear. And the weather during the last few days had been perfect.

The woman on the beach was the actress – Eve Taylor – who owned the island. She had made quite a lot of bad films and one or two good ones and she didn't really care which were which. They all paid the same. One of the men was an American multimillionaire – a billionaire, in fact, although in recent years he had given much of his wealth away. The other man was the pop singer Rob Goldman, who had just arrived following his tour of Australia.

"ASIS are still insisting we should leave," Goldman was saying. "They say we could all be killed."

"Have they explained the nature of the threat?" the billionaire asked.

"No. But they sounded serious."

"Of course they did." The actress let sand run through her fingers. "They want us to go. This is a trick. They're just trying to scare us."

"I don't think so, Eve," Goldman said.

Eve Taylor gazed at the horizon. "We're safe," she said. "Look how beautiful it is. Look at the sea! That's part of the reason we're here. To protect all this for the next generation. I don't care if there's a danger. I'm not going to run away." She turned to the billionaire. "Crispin?"

The man shook his head. "I'm with you," he said. "I never ran away from anything in my life and I'm not starting now."

Three hundred miles further south, in the towns of Derby, Broome and Port Hedland, thousands of people were watching the same sunset. Some of them were on their way home from work. Some were tucking children into bed. In pubs, in cars, on the beaches, wherever ... they were simply edging towards the end of another day.

And none of them knew that in a few hours' time, the bomb known as Royal Blue would begin to inch its way down the pipe which would carry it to the seabed and below. That the earth and the moon were moving, inexorably, into an alignment with the sun which wouldn't happen again for another century. And that a madman was waiting to press the button which would unleash chaos on the world.

Five hours until midnight.

And in an army camp south of Darwin, Alex Rider gave his answer and the final preparations began.

DRAGON NINE

Ethan Brooke had hand-picked ten soldiers from the Australian SAS for his assault team and at least some of them needed no introduction. As Alex joined them in the hangar that was going to be used as a briefing room, he saw Scooter, Texas, X-Ray and Sparks waiting for him, and suddenly he was back where this had all begun, in the forest near Swanbourne. He wasn't sure if he should be glad or annoyed to meet up with them again.

Scooter was equally uncomfortable. "I'm really sorry about that trick we pulled on you, Alex," he said. "We all felt bad about it. But we had our orders."

"Colonel Abbott asked us to pass on a message," Texas added. "No hard feelings. And if you ever come back to Swanbourne, we'll throw you a proper Aussie barbecue."

"With no hand grenades," Alex muttered.

"You got it."

Alex looked at the other soldiers. None of them

seemed to be older than twenty-four or twenty-five, meaning there was an age gap of just ten years between him and them. Maybe that was why all of them had accepted him. Like Alex, they had changed into night combat gear. A couple of them carried balaclavas. The rest had painted their hands and faces black.

The hangar was vast and empty. A blackboard had been placed in the middle in front of two rows of metal benches. Alex sat down next to Ben. The others took their places, Scooter facing them. Once again he seemed to be in charge. Scooter was looking tired. He seemed to have grown a lot older since Alex had last seen him – or maybe it was just that he knew how much was at stake.

"We haven't got a lot of time," he began. "But nor do we have much of a plan ... so this won't take long.

"We're parachuting in from about eight thousand feet. I know a boat would have been easier and less conspicuous, but by the time we got there it would all be over. Anyway, it's always possible our friend Major Yu has radar."

He turned to the blackboard. Someone had taped up what could have been an engineer's drawing of two oil platforms – one square, the other triangular, joined together by a narrow bridge. Each of the platforms had three cranes and one had a helicopter pad, represented by an H in a circle. Scooter picked up a stick which he used as a pointer.

"All right – listen up!" He tapped the plan. "This is what we *think* Dragon Nine looks like. We don't *know*, because we don't have any pictures and we haven't had time to take any. All I can tell you for certain is that it's a semi-submersible plat- form, which means that basically the whole thing floats on the surface of the water, connected to the seabed by a dozen steel tethers. In case you're wondering, each one is about two kilometres long."

"What happens if they break?" someone asked.

"Nothing much. The whole thing will float away, like a ship without an anchor. At least that's some- thing we don't have to worry about." He pointed again. "This is the processing platform on the left. Dragon Nine isn't in production so the whole area will be quiet – and that's where we're going to start. We'll land on the helipad, this H here..."

Now Scooter turned his attention to the square- shaped rig.

"This is the drilling platform," he continued. "Once we've assembled and checked that every- one's there, we'll make our way across the bridge, heading for the main derrick – this metal tower over the well hole. And that's where we're going to find Royal Blue. Our friend Major Yu will be using some sort of system – maybe guide wires – to lower it down to the seabed."

"So let's blow it up," X-Ray growled.

"It's our first target," Scooter agreed. "The power unit will be our second. But we can't take anything for granted. Despite what Yu told Alex, he could just as easily be using a submarine to take the bomb down. That's why Alex is here. Our job is to find the control room and get him there. He can deactivate Royal Blue but no one else can – so if he gets shot we might as well pack up and go home. You hear what I'm saying? I want you to watch his back. And his front and his sides."

Alex glanced down. He understood what Scooter was saying and why he had to say it, but he still didn't like being singled out in this way.

"I'm afraid this mission isn't as easy as it seems," Scooter added, although Alex wouldn't have said it looked simple to begin with. "We've no idea where the control room is. There are five different levels, two separate platforms. Yu could be on either. You've got to think of Dragon Nine as two metal cities. They've got their own storage depots, dormitories, messes and recreation rooms, as well as fuel tanks, desalination units, pump rooms, engineering blocks and all the rest of it. Somehow we have to navigate our way through all that until we find what we're looking for. Then we have to deal with Royal Blue. And when we start, it's possible that we're going to be spread out all over the place. We're lucky there's not too much breeze, and no moon. Just try not to fall into the sea."

He paused. Eleven silent faces watched him from the two rows of benches. Alex could feel the clock already ticking. He wanted to be out and away.

"So what do we have on our side?" Scooter asked. "Well, first there's the element of surprise. Major Yu thinks Alex is dead, so he'll have no idea we're on our way. And there's the question of timing." He looked at his watch. "Yu can't detonate the bomb whenever he likes. He's got to wait until midnight. That's when the sun, moon and earth are going to be in the right position. It's nine o'clock now, and we're only two hours from drop-off. That means we'll have one hour to find Yu before he can throw the switch. And there's something else we know, thanks to Alex. The bomb can only remain at that depth of one kilometre below the seabed for twenty minutes. So it's not there yet. And if all goes well, it never will be."

He looked around. "Any questions?"

There were none.

"We've got to move quickly and quietly," he concluded. "Take out as many of Yu's people as we can before they know we're there. Leave the guns and grenades for as long as possible. Use your knives. And find the control room! That's what this is all about."

He put down the pointer.

"Let's go."

Everyone stood up. Ben had Alex's parachute – black silk, for a night drop. He'd packed it himself before the briefing and now he helped Alex put it on, pulling the straps tight across his chest and around his thighs.

"It's probably a bit too late to ask you this," he muttered. "But have you ever parachuted before?"

"Only once," Alex admitted. That had been nearly eight months ago. He had landed on the roof of the Science Museum in London. But he decided not to go into all that right now.

"Well, don't worry if you miss the target," Ben said. "The sea's warm. Conditions are perfect. And with a bit of luck, there won't be too many sharks."

The Australian SAS men were already moving. Ben strapped on his own parachute and the two of them followed the others out of the hangar. There was a helicopter waiting for them on the tarmac – the same one that had picked Alex up in the jungle. The Chinook CH-47 was the ideal machine for this night's work. Often used to ferry troops or supplies, its wide rear exit was also perfect for parachute drops. It would fly them to the target at one hundred and ninety miles an hour and at an altitude no higher than eight and a half thousand feet. That wouldn't leave long to deploy the chute.

Ben must have been reading his thoughts. "We're using static line," he said. The static line deployment system meant that they wouldn't have to pull a ripcord. The parachutes would open automatically.

Alex nodded. His mouth was suddenly too dry to speak.

They climbed in the back. In the jungle Alex had used a door just behind the cockpit, but this time the whole rear section of the Chinook had been opened, forming a ramp big enough to take a jeep. Alex looked in. The pilot and the co-pilot were already in their seats. There was a third man, a flight engineer, checking a 7.62mm M60 general-purpose machine gun which must have been bolted on at some point during the day. Alex hoped it wouldn't be needed.

The twelve of them took their places. Two long rows of seats faced each other on either side of the fuselage. Although they were made of canvas stretched over metal, they reminded Alex a little of dining-room chairs. Normally the Chinook carries thirty-three men, so at least there was plenty of room. Alex sat next to Ben. It was clear that everyone expected them to stick together – although how they would manage that parachuting out into the night was something they hadn't discussed. Scooter leant over and clipped Alex's ripcord to a silver rail running all the way to the cockpit. The pilot pressed a switch and slowly the rear door closed. A red light flashed on, the helicopter lurched off the ground, and moments later they were on their way.

It was dark and there was nothing to see out of the windows, which were too small anyway to provide much of a view. Alex could only tell their height from the feeling in his stomach and the pressure in his ears. The SAS men were sitting silently, some of them checking their weapons – machine guns, pistols with silencers attached and a wide variety of vicious-looking combat knives. Next to him, Ben Daniels had nodded off to sleep. Alex guessed he'd be well practised at taking a catnap whenever he needed it, conserving his strength.

But Alex couldn't sleep. He was in a Chinook helicopter with the Australian SAS, on his way to attack an oil rig and defuse a bomb before it caused a tsunami. And as usual he was the only one who hadn't been given a gun. How had he managed to get himself into this? For a moment, he remembered walking with Jack around the Rocks in Sydney. It seemed a long, long time ago. How could he have allowed it all to happen?

The helicopter droned on through the night. Below them the Timor Sea was black and still. They were rapidly approaching Indonesian airspace.

The light turned orange.

Smoothly, a centimetre at a time, the great door at the back of the helicopter dropped open, revealing the black rush of the night outside. Although it was true there was no moon, the sea seemed to be shining as if with some natural phosphorescence – Alex could see it glinting far below.

He hadn't even thought about the parachute jump until now, but as the reality hit him, his stomach lurched. The simple truth was that he wasn't some sort of daredevil who enjoyed the prospect of hurling himself eight thousand feet from a helicopter in the dark. Right now he would have given anything to be back in London with Jack. Well, all he had to do was survive the next hour. One way or another, in just sixty minutes this would all be over.

The door had gone down as far as it could and clicked into position. It was jutting out of the back of the helicopter. A short walk into nothing.

"I'll be watching you," Ben shouted. With the roar of the wind, only Alex heard. "Don't worry! I'll stick close..."

"Thanks!" Alex shouted back the single word.

Then the light went green.

No time to think. Because of his position, Alex was going to be the first out. Maybe they had planned it that way. He didn't hesitate. If he stopped to think what he was doing, he might lose his resolve. Three steps, trailing the cord from his parachute behind him. Suddenly the blades were right over his head, thrashing the air. He felt a hand on his shoulder. Ben.

He jumped.

There was a moment of complete disorientation – he remembered it from the last time – when he couldn't quite believe what he'd done and had no idea what would happen next. He was falling so fast that he couldn't breathe. He was completely out of control. Then the parachute opened. He felt the jolt as his descent slowed. And then the peace. He was floating, dangling underneath an invisible silk canopy, black against the black night sky.

He looked down and saw the oil rig. He could only make out its vague shape – two geometric islands with a narrow corridor in between. There were about twenty lights, flickering and still tiny on the twin platforms. By joining them together in his imagination, Alex was able to draw a mental image of Dragon Nine.

He twisted round and saw the helicopter, already far away, and beneath it the eleven black flowers that were the other parachutes. It seemed to him that the Chinook was surprisingly quiet. If he could barely hear it at this altitude, perhaps Major Yu would have heard nothing below. Just as Scooter had promised, there was no wind. The sea was utterly flat. Alex didn't need to steer himself. He seemed to be heading in exactly the right direction. He could make out the white H in the middle of the helipad. H for happy landing ... at least, that was what he hoped.

There are three stages to a parachute descent. The raw fear of the jump itself. The sense of calm once the chute has opened. And the panic as the ground rushes up. Alex reached the third stage all too soon, and that was when he realized he had drifted off course after all. Maybe he had been overconfident. Maybe some sea breeze had caught him unawares. But suddenly he found himself with nothing but water below him. He was drifting away from the triangular processing platform. Urgently Alex tugged the two cords at his shoulders, trying to change direction. He was plunging towards the sea. He couldn't let that happen. The splash might give the others away. Worse than that, he might drown.

Alex jerked and writhed helplessly, but at the last minute another breeze caught him and carried him over the lip of the drilling platform and onto one of the decks. He had been doubly lucky. The deck was wide enough to allow him to land safely, dropping to one knee and folding in his parachute in a single movement. And the area was like a metallic courtyard, enclosed on all sides. With a bit of luck he would be completely out of sight. No worries there. He had landed on a bumpy, uneven surface, close to some sort of electrical generator. The noise of the machinery would have covered the crash of his feet as they made contact with the metal surface.

Five seconds later, a figure dropped out of the sky and landed just a few metres away. It was Ben Daniels. Unlike Alex, he had chosen the deck with pinpoint accuracy. He gathered in his chute and gave Alex the thumbs up. Alex twisted round. As far as he could see, all the other SAS men had landed on the processing platform. He looked up. The helicopter had already gone but presumably it would be near by, in case it was needed.

Alex realized that his own inexperience had spoilt Scooter's plan. The whole idea had been to stick together; it was vital that Alex should be protected at all times. Now he and Ben were cut off on the drilling platform. The SAS men would have to make their way across the bridge to find him. And if Yu's control room was on the other side, they would have to take Alex all the way back again.

Not good.

He looked around him. He was standing on a row of pipes. The whole deck was covered with them, cut into lengths of about three metres. A huge metal trough rose up out of the ground, slanting towards the tower that housed the well head. Presumably the pipes would be dragged up and somehow assembled in a straight line before they were lowered all the way to the seabed and beyond. On the other side, a metal wall rose up, like the side of a fortress. There were windows on the third or fourth floor but they were so covered in dirt and grease that surely nobody would be able to see through them. One of the cranes stretched out over the water, its arm silhouetted against the stars and the night sky.

Ben Daniels had taken off his parachute. He scuttled over to Alex, keeping low. He must have already come to the same conclusion as Alex, but he had decided what to do.

"We won't wait," he whispered. "We'll start looking over here. We don't have a lot of time."

Alex didn't have a watch. He looked at Ben's. It was ten past eleven. He wondered how so much time could have passed so quickly.

The two of them set off together, making their way across the pipes, trying to find the entrance into the well head. Dragon Nine was bigger than Alex had expected, and every inch was crammed with pipes and cables, cog wheels, chains, dials and valves. The oil rig was a living thing, throbbing and humming as different machines carried power or coolant to the various outlets. It was a hard, unpleasant environment. Every surface had a permanent coating of mud, oil, grease and puddles of salt water. Alex could feel his trainers sticking to the floor as he walked.

But Yu didn't seem to have posted any guards. Scooter had been right about that. With Alex supposedly dead, why should he have been expecting any trouble, miles from anywhere, in the middle of the Timor Sea? Together they eased their way round corners and between ventilation towers, immediately lost in the great tangle that had been designed to pump oil from the seabed, more than a thousand metres below. Ben was carrying a miniature torch which he kept cupped in his left hand, allowing only a trickle of light to escape. His right hand held an automatic pistol, a Walther PPK with a Brausch silencer attached.

Scooter and the other SAS men had dropped out of sight. Alex could imagine them moving towards him on the other side of the water. In the far distance he thought he heard a sound: a soft thud, the clatter of metal against metal, a stifled cry cut off very quickly. Maybe there were guards after all. If so, one of them might be wishing that he had been a little bit more alert.

Ben was opening doors, peering in through windows. There was still no sign of life on the drilling platform. They climbed a flight of steps that brought them to a metal walkway on the very edge, high over the sea. Alex looked down, and that was when he saw it. The oil rig was actually balancing on four huge legs, like an oversized metal table. One of the legs had a ladder which ran all the way down to the surface of the water and disappeared beneath it. Next to the ladder and tucked away almost underneath the drilling platform was an executive yacht, the sort of thing that would have looked more at home in a private marina in the South of France. The boat was about forty-five feet in length, sleek and white, with several sun decks and a bow that was clearly designed for speed. Alex tapped Ben on the shoulder and pointed. Ben nodded.

It had to belong to Major Yu. It was surely there to provide him with a fast escape, which meant that he had to be close by. If Alex had known the make of the yacht, there would have been no doubt in his mind at all. It was a Sealine F42-5 flybridge motorboat with a unique extending cockpit system. It had been designed and manufactured in Britain.

Ben signalled the way forward. More than ever,

Alex wished that Scooter and the others were with them. They were following a narrow gantry that led to a door set in a circular building, jutting out over the corner of the rig with curved windows that provided views in three directions.

The control room. It had to be.

They crept towards it. Alex didn't know what Ben had in mind. Maybe he was going to wait for the rest of the squadron to catch up. That would have been the sensible thing to do.

But in the end he was never given a choice. Without warning, a spotlight swept through the air, searing its way across the drilling platform. A second later, a machine gun began firing, bullets ricocheting crazily off the railings, slamming into the walls and sparking as they flew off the metal walkways. A siren began to wail, and at the same time Alex heard answering fire from the other side of the bridge. The silence of the night had been shattered. There was an explosion, a ball of flame erupting into the night like a brilliant flower. More shooting. Ben twisted and fired twice. Alex didn't even see his target but there was a cry and a man fell out of the sky, slammed into a gantry and bounced off it into the sea.

"This way!" Ben shouted. He had already started forward and Alex went after him, knowing that Yu would be expecting them now but that there could be no going back. Yu's men would be taking up positions all over the oil rig. They had the advantage.

There were a dozen ladders they could climb, and decks high above from where they could pick off the invaders one by one. He and Ben would be safer inside. The door was ahead of them, leading into the circular room. Ben reached it and crouched down.

"Stay back!" he commanded.

Alex saw him count to three.

Ben slammed the door open and went in firing. Despite what he had been told, and even though he wasn't carrying a weapon himself, Alex followed. And that was how he saw what happened in the next few seconds, even though it would be a lot longer before he took it all in.

There were two men in the control room, surrounded by computer screens, radio transmitters and the equipment that Alex had seen on the *Liberian Star*. One of them was Major Winston Yu. He was holding the pistol which he had just used to gun down Ben Daniels. Ben was lying on the floor in a spreading pool of his own blood. The Walther PPK had dropped out of his hand and lay pointing towards Alex. There was another man lying face down a short distance away, and Alex realized that Ben must have shot him as he came in. Major Yu himself was unhurt. He was staring at Alex in astonishment and disbelief.

Somehow he managed to recover. "Well, this is a surprise," he said.

Alex didn't move. He was less than three metres

away from Yu. He had nowhere to go. Yu could shoot him at any time.

"Come in and close the door," Yu ordered.

Alex did as he was told. Outside, the battle was still going on – but it was happening on the other platform. Too far away. The heavy door clicked shut.

"I knew you hadn't drowned in the river," Yu said. "Something told me. And when we couldn't find your body..." He shook his head. "I have to say, Alex, you're very hard to kill."

Alex didn't reply. Out of the corner of his eye he could see Ben's pistol lying on the floor, and part of him wondered if he could dive down and grab it. But he would never be able to bring it round and fire it in time. He was too easy a target.

"You're finished, Major Yu," Alex said. "And you've failed. ASIS know what you're trying to do. Reef Island has been evacuated. There's no point setting off a tsunami. Everyone will know it was you."

Yu considered his words carefully. Part of what Alex had said was a lie – the Reef Island conference was still taking place – but there was no way Yu could know that. Alex was here. He had brought the SAS with him. The facts spoke for themselves.

Eventually Yu sighed. "You're probably right," he said. "But I think we'll go ahead anyway. After all, it's taken meticulous planning and I'd like to make my mark on the world."

"But you'll kill thousands – for no reason."

"What reason can you give me to spare them?" Yu shook his head. "World chaos does have its uses, Alex. This was never just about Reef Island. The reconstruction of the Australian coastline will cost billions, and I have commercial interests all over South East Asia. The Chada Trading Company has shares in many building firms who will be first in line for the new contracts. Unwin Toys will offer gifts to the many hundreds of new orphans – paid for, of course, by the Australian government. There are all sorts of other interests too. A snakehead thrives on misfortune and unhappiness. For us it just means new business."

He glanced at one of the television screens. Alex saw a white line running straight from the top to the bottom. There was a blinking red square attached to it, moving slowly downwards.

"Royal Blue," Yu said. "In six or seven minutes it will reach the seabed and enter the shaft that I told you about. The shaft continues a further one kilometre down. At midnight exactly the bomb will detonate and my work will be done. By then I will be a long way away, and you will be no more than a fading memory."

Yu raised the gun. The single black eye searched for him.

"Goodbye, Alex."

But then there was a movement, and the man who had been shot by Ben Daniels groaned and dragged himself into a sitting position.

Major Yu was delighted. "How very fortunate," he exclaimed, lowering the weapon. "Before you die, let me introduce you to one of my most trusted and effective colleagues. Although, on second thoughts, I believe you've already met."

The man looked up.

It was Ash.

He had been shot twice in the chest and the life was seeping out of him. Alex could see it in the dark eyes which were filled with pain and remorse and something which was less definable but which might have been shame.

"I'm sorry, Alex," Ash gasped. He had to pause to catch his breath. "I didn't want you to know."

"I'm not sure Alex is surprised," Yu remarked.

Alex shook his head. "I guessed."

"May I ask how?"

This time there was no point in ignoring the question. Yu had been about to shoot him anyway. The longer Alex could keep him talking, the more chance there was that the SAS might finally arrive. Alex could still hear the alarm but there was less shooting and it seemed to be further away. Had the SAS been overpowered or were they already in command and on their way? He glanced at the television screen. The little red square was continuing its journey down.

"Everything went wrong from the start," he said, talking directly to Major Yu. "Ethan Brooke had already lost two agents. Somehow the snakehead knew everything he planned. They knew about me too. Why else was I chosen for that fight in Bangkok? At first it didn't make any sense. But then, when I was in the arena, Anan Sukit said something to me. He said he'd kill me if I didn't take part, and he said it first in French, then in English. Why? If he'd really believed I was an Afghan boy, he'd have known I wouldn't speak either.

"I wondered about that. But it got worse. Ash gave me an emergency telephone number. I called it and it led me straight to you."

Ash opened his mouth to speak but Alex cut in.

"I know," he said. He looked briefly at the dying man. "You made it look good with the fake blood, as if you'd been taken prisoner like me. But then I lost two of the gadgets Smithers had given me and that was when I knew it had to be you.

"I told you about the watch and the belt. Somehow the battery went missing out of the watch. I suppose you must have removed it when I was asleep, that night in Jakarta. As for the belt, Major Yu took that when I was in his house. But I'd never told you about the coins. Smithers had also given me three coins with explosive charges, and they stayed in my pocket. If I'd told you, I guess they would have gone too."

He stopped.

"When did you start working for Scorpia, Ash?" he asked.

Ash glanced at Major Yu.

383

"Tell him – but be quick," Yu snapped. "I don't think we have very much time."

"It was after Mdina." Ash's voice was weak. His face was grey and he could no longer move from the waist down. One hand was on his chest; the other lay palm upward on the floor. "You can't understand, Alex. I was so badly hurt. Yassen..." He coughed and blood speckled his lip. "I had given everything to the service. My life. My health. I wasn't even thirty and I was crippled. I was never going to sleep properly, never eat properly. From that day on it was just pills and pain.

"And what was my reward? Blunt humiliated me. I was demoted, taken out of the field. He told me..." Ash swallowed painfully. With every word he was finding it harder to go on. "He told me what I already knew," he rasped. "I was second-rate. Never as good ... as your dad."

He had almost come to the end of his strength. His shoulders slumped and for a moment Alex thought he had gone. Blood was all around him now. A steady flow trickled from his mouth.

Major Yu was enjoying himself. "Why don't you tell him the rest, Ash?" he crowed.

"No!" Ash straightened his head. "Please..."

"I already know," Alex said. He turned to Ash one last time. He could hardly bear to look at him. "You killed my parents, didn't you? The bomb on the aeroplane. You put it there."

Ash couldn't answer. His hand tightened on his

chest. He had only seconds left.

"We had to test him," Major Yu explained. "When he came over to us, we had to make sure he was telling us the truth. After all, we had just been tricked by one British intelligence agent – your father. So we set him a very simple task, one that would prove to us with no doubt that he was ready to switch sides."

"I didn't want to..." It wasn't Ash's voice. It was just a whisper.

"He didn't want to, but he did. For the money. He put the bomb on the plane and he detonated it with his own hand. Rather more successful than his mission in Mdina. And the start of a long association with us."

"Alex..."

Ash tried to look up. His head fell forward. He died.

Major Yu prodded him with his foot. "Well, as they say, Ash to ashes and dust to dust," he remarked. "I'm glad you heard that from him, Alex. You can take it with you to the grave."

He raised the gun once again and pointed it at Alex.

There was an explosion, loud and near. The entire room shook, and dust and metal filings came showering down from the roof. Alex heard a shearing of metal as the crane overhead broke in half and came crashing down. The shock sent Major Yu reeling back. His arm banged against one of the work surfaces and the gun went off, the bullet smashing harmlessly into a wall. Major Yu was shouting in agony and Alex realized that the impact of the blow had shattered the brittle bone in his arm. The gun now lay on the ground.

Deafened, half dazed, Alex threw himself onto Ben's gun, snatched it in both hands and pulled the trigger over and over again until it clicked uselessly. It was the first time he had fired in anger and with the deliberate intention to kill. But he had missed. The room was full of smoke, and even in his pain Yu had been quick-thinking enough to use it as a screen, crouching down, clutching his broken arm. He had lost his gun. He knew that he had run out of time. The SAS were here. Alex Rider would have to wait until another day.

There was a trapdoor set in the floor with the ladder Alex had spotted earlier leading down underneath. Somehow, using his one good arm, Yu pulled it open and clambered down, dropping into the boat below. But the fall was too much for his bones. Howling with agony, barely able to crawl, Yu groped his way over to the controls. He used a knife to cut through the mooring rope. A second later, he was speeding away.

Meanwhile Alex had staggered over to the controls. On the TV, the little square representing Royal Blue was about two centimetres above the seabed but edging closer all the time. There was the scanner, wired into the computer. Alex slammed his palm onto the glass panel and let out a sigh of relief as a line of text appeared on the computer screen.

> AUTHORIZATION ACCEPTED

There was a pause, then a second line scrolled across.

> OVERRIDE MASTER COMMANDS? Y/N

Alex hit the Y key just as the door crashed open and about half a dozen SAS men burst in, covering every angle with their weapons. Scooter was at the front, Texas and X-Ray right behind him. It looked as if Sparks, the young soldier who had once played a guitar on an Australian beach, hadn't made it.

Scooter saw Alex. "Where's Yu?" he demanded.

"Gone." Alex's attention was fixed on the screen. A menu had come up. He ran his eye down the list of options, looking for the one that said DISARM or DEACTIVATE. But it wasn't there. Instead his eyes settled on the last command.

> DETONATE

"Over here!" It was Texas. He had found Ben Daniels and was already kneeling beside him, tearing open his shirt to examine his wound. One of the other soldiers rushed over with a medical kit.

Alex slid the mouse, highlighting the last command. He looked at the television screen. Royal Blue was still above the seabed but was gradually closing in. He remembered what he had heard. The bomb had to travel one kilometre down into the earth's crust before it was in place. A digital clock read 23:47:05:00, the microseconds flickering and changing too fast for his eye to follow. The bomb still had thirteen more minutes until it was in position. The sun, moon and earth were not quite ready yet.

Could Alex destroy the bomb without accidentally causing a tsunami?

In desperation he turned to the SAS leader, who seemed to understand the stakes almost at once.

"Do it," he said.

Alex double-clicked on the command.

One thousand and fifty metres below Dragon Nine but one hundred and fifty metres above the seabed, the bomb exploded. Alex felt the entire oil rig shudder violently, and the floor veered crazily beneath his feet as five of the steel tethers along with the drill pipe itself were torn apart.

And half a mile away, speeding through the water in his Sealine yacht, Major Yu heard the explosion and knew, with an overwhelming sense of bitterness and defeat, that even his last hopes had been destroyed. Somehow Royal Blue had been detonated too early. There would be no tsunami.

He sat, hunched up in front of the steering wheel, moaning quietly to himself. He had failed.

He didn't even feel the shock wave from the explosion until it hit him, but this of course was the main purpose of Royal Blue, to flatten anything for miles around. The pulse smashed into the boat, destroying the electrics, snuffing out the lights, ripping every fitting apart. Major Yu's bone structure wasn't strong enough to withstand it. Every single bone in his body fractured at the same time. For about two seconds, he remained vaguely human. Then his body, with no frame to support it, crumpled in on itself: a bag of skin full of broken pieces. The boat veered round, a quarter of a million pounds' worth of British engineering with no one to steer it. Zigzagging crazily, it disappeared into the night.

Back on Dragon Nine, Yu's remaining men were being rounded up. The SAS had lost two men dead with three more injured. Ben Daniels was still alive. He'd been given a shot of morphine and there was an oxygen mask strapped to his face.

Scooter had finally noticed the other body lying in the control room.

"Who was that?" he asked.

Alex took one last look at his godfather.

"It was nobody," he said.

DINNER FOR THREE

"It's very good to see you, Alex. How are you getting on at school?"

It seemed a very long time since Alex had last found himself in this room, the office on the sixteenth floor of the building in Liverpool Street which called itself the Royal & General Bank but which in fact housed the Special Operations division of MI6. Alan Blunt, its chief executive, was sitting opposite him, his desk as neat and as empty as ever: a couple of folders, some papers awaiting his signature, a single pen, solid silver, resting at an angle. Everything in its place. Alex knew that Blunt liked it that way.

Blunt didn't seem to have changed at all. Even the suit was the same, and if there was a little more grey in his hair, who would notice when the man had been entirely grey to begin with? But Blunt was not the sort of person to grow old and wrinkled, to wear baggy jumpers, play golf and spend more time with his grandchildren. His job, the world he inhabited, had somehow pinned him down. He was, Alex decided, a twenty-first-century fossil.

It was the last week of November and suddenly the temperature had dropped, as if in response to the Christmas decorations which were going up all around. There had even been a few scatterings of snow. There wasn't enough to settle but it had added a certain chill to the air. Walking to the office, Alex had passed a Salvation Army band playing "Good King Wenceslas". The players had been huddled together as if for comfort and even their music had been cold and mournful – as well as slightly out of tune.

He couldn't hear the music in the office. The windows would doubtless have been double- or triple-glazed to stop any sound coming in or – more importantly – leaking out. He focused his attention on the man sitting opposite him and wondered how he should answer the question. Blunt would know already, of course. He probably had access to Alex's school reports before they were even printed.

Alex had just completed his first week back at Brookland School. Blunt would know that too. Alex had no doubt that he had been under twenty-four-hour surveillance from the moment his Qantas flight had touched down at Heathrow Airport and he had been hurried out through the VIP channel to the waiting car outside. The last time he had taken on Scorpia he had been shot, and MI6 certainly weren't going to let that happen again. He thought he had seen his tail once: a youngish man standing on a street corner, seemingly waiting for a taxi. When he had looked for him a second later, the man had disappeared. Maybe it was; maybe it wasn't. Blunt's field agents knew how to live in the shadows.

And so, finally, he was back at school.

For most kids of his age, it meant coursework and homework, lessons that dragged on too long and terrible food. For Alex it was all that and some-thing more. He had been nervous, walking back into Brookland on a chilly Monday morning. It had seemed a long time since he had seen the famil-iar buildings: the bright red brickwork and the long stretches of plate glass. Miss Bedfordshire, the school secretary who had always had a soft spot for him, had been waiting in reception.

"Alex Rider!" she had exclaimed. "What has it been this time?"

"Glandular fever, Miss Bedfordshire."

Alex's illnesses had become almost legendary over the past year. Part of him wondered if Miss Bedfordshire really believed in them or if she was just playing along.

"You're going to have to drop back a whole year if you're not careful," she remarked.

"I'm very careful, Miss Bedfordshire."

"I'm sure you are."

In Sydney Alex had been worried that he wouldn't fit in, but from the very first moment he arrived it was almost as if he hadn't been away. Everyone was pleased to see him, and he wasn't as far behind as he had feared. He would have extra tuition in the Christmas holidays, and with a bit of luck he would be at the same level as everyone else by the start of next term. Surrounded by his friends and swept along by the day's routine – the ringing bells, the slamming doors and desks – Alex realized that he wasn't just back at school. He was back in normal life.

But he had been expecting Alan Blunt to make contact, and sure enough he had got the call on his mobile. Blunt had asked Alex to come to a meeting on Friday afternoon. Alex had noticed the one small difference. Blunt had asked. He hadn't demanded.

So here he was with his backpack full of books for the weekend's homework: a particularly vicious maths paper and *Animal Farm* by George Orwell. A British writer, he reflected. Major Yu would surely have loved it. Alex was wearing his school uniform – dark blue jacket, grey trousers and purposely crooked tie. Jack had bought him a scarf when she was on holiday in Washington and it was hanging loosely around his neck. Apart from this, he felt comfortable looking the same as everyone else.

"There are a few things you might like to know," Blunt said. "Starting with a message from Ethan Brooke. He asked me to pass on his thanks and his good wishes. He said that if you ever decide to emigrate to Australia, he'll be happy to arrange a permanent visa."

"That's very kind of him."

"Well, you did a remarkable job, Alex. Quite apart from tracking down our missing weapon, you've more or less destroyed the snakehead. The Chada Trading Company has gone out of business, as has Unwin Toys."

"Did you realize it was an anagram?" Mrs Jones asked. She was sitting in a chair next to the desk, one leg crossed over the other, looking very relaxed. Alex got the sense that she was glad to see him. "Unwin Toys. Winston Yu. That was the vanity of the man – he named it after himself."

"Have you found him?" Alex asked. He had last seen Yu climbing down the ladder towards the motor launch and didn't know if he'd got away.

"Oh yes. We found what was left of him. Not a pleasant sight." Blunt folded his hands in front of him. "Yu dealt with quite a lot of his own people before ASIS could reach them," he went on. "I think you know that he killed the captain of the *Liberian Star*: de Wynter. After your escape from the hospital, Dr Tanner committed suicide, possibly following orders from Yu. ASIS did manage to pick up the rest of the staff, though. Two guards – one of them with a fractured skull – and a handful of nurses. They also arrested a man called Varga."

The name meant nothing to Alex.

"He was a technician," Mrs Jones reminded him.

"He helped adapt Royal Blue to work underground. He also organized the detonation procedure."

Now Alex recalled the man he had glimpsed on the *Liberian Star*, setting up the scanner for Major Yu.

"He was a fairly low-level Scorpia operative," Blunt added. "From Haiti, I understand. He's being questioned and may provide some useful information."

"How is Ben?"

"He's still in hospital in Darwin," Mrs Jones said. "He was lucky. The bullets didn't do any serious damage and the doctors say he'll be out by Christmas."

"We'll look after him," Blunt added.

"Better than you looked after Ash." Alex looked Blunt straight in the eye.

"Yes." Blunt shifted uncomfortably. "I wanted you to know, Alex, that we had no idea about Ash's association with Scorpia. Even now I find it hard to believe that he had any involvement with … what happened to your parents."

"I'm so sorry, Alex," Mrs Jones cut in. "I understand how you must be feeling."

"Do you think Ethan Brooke knew?" Alex asked. It was something he had been thinking about on the long flight home. "He knew someone was a traitor. Someone had been feeding the snakehead information all along. He put me together with Ash. Was that what he really wanted? To flush him out?"

"It's quite possible," Blunt said, and Alex was surprised. The head of MI6 wasn't normally so honest. "Brooke is a very devious man."

"It's what makes him so good at his job," Mrs Jones remarked.

It was five o'clock. Outside, it was already dark. Alan Blunt went over to the window and shooed away some pigeons. Then he lowered the blind.

"There are only a couple of things to add," he said as he took his seat again. "Most important of all, we want you to know that you're safe. Scorpia aren't going to have another crack at you." He blinked twice. "Not like last time."

"We've been in contact with them," Mrs Jones explained. "We've made it clear that if anything happens to you, we'll let the whole world know that they have been beaten – for a second time – by a fourteen-year-old boy. It would make them a laughing stock and destroy what little reputation they have left."

"Scorpia may be finished anyway," Blunt said. "But they've got the message. We'll keep an eye on you just to be on the safe side, but I don't think you need have any concern."

"And what was the other thing?" Alex asked.

"Only that we hope you found what you were looking for." It was Mrs Jones who had answered.

"I found some of it," Alex said.

"Your father was a very good man," Blunt muttered. "I've told you that before. You obviously take after him, Alex. And maybe, when you leave school, you'll think again about intelligence work. We need people like you, and it's not a bad career."

Alex stood up. "I'll show myself out," he said.

He took the tube back to Sloane Square and then a bus along the King's Road to his house. He had told Jack he would be late home from school. The two of them would have supper together when he arrived, and then he would start his homework. He was seeing his friend Tom Harris tomorrow. Chelsea were playing at home to Arsenal and somehow Tom had managed to scrounge two tickets. Otherwise, he had no plans for the weekend.

Jack Starbright was waiting for him in the kitchen, putting the final touches to a salad. Alex helped himself to a glass of apple juice and hoisted himself onto one of the bar stools by the counter. He liked to talk to Jack while she cooked.

"How did you get on?" she asked.

"It was fine," Alex said. He reached out and stole a piece of tomato. "Alan Blunt offered me a job."

"I'll kill you if you take it."

"Don't worry. I let him know I wasn't interested."

Jack knew everything that had happened to Alex since she had left him in Sydney, including Ash's final moments on Dragon Nine. He had told her his story the moment he got home, and when he had finished she had turned away and sat for a long minute in silence. When she had finally turned back again, there had been tears in her eyes.

"I'm sorry," Alex had said. "I know you liked him."

"That's not what's upsetting me, Alex," she had replied.

"Then what?"

"It's this world. MI6. What it did to him, to your parents. I suppose I'm scared about what it'll do to you."

"I think I've finished with it, Jack."

"That's what you said last time, Alex. But the question is – has it finished with you?"

Now Alex glanced at the table. He noticed that it was set for three. "Who's coming for supper?" he asked.

"I forgot to tell you." Jack smiled. "We have a surprise guest."

"Who?"

"You'll find out when they get here." She had barely spoken the words when the doorbell rang. "That's good timing," she went on. "Why don't you answer it?"

Alex noticed something strange in her eyes. It wasn't like Jack to have secrets from him. He was still holding the piece of tomato. He tossed it back into the salad, swung himself down and went out into the hall.

He could just make out a figure behind the mottled glass panels of the front door. Whoever it was had activated the automatic light in the porch.

Alex threw open the door and stopped in surprise.

A young, dark-haired and very attractive girl was standing there. The car that had dropped her off was just moving away. Alex was so stunned that it took him a moment to recognize her. Even then, he didn't believe who it was.

"Sabina!" he exclaimed.

The last time he had seen Sabina Pleasure, the two of them had been under Richmond Bridge beside the Thames, and she had told him she was leaving for America. He had been convinced that he would never see her again.

That had only been a few months ago, but she looked completely different. She had to be almost sixteen now. Her hair had grown longer and her shape had changed. She looked wonderful in tight-fitting DKNY jeans and a soft cashmere jersey.

"Hi, Alex." She stayed where she was, as if a little wary of him.

"What are you doing here?"

"Aren't you pleased to see me?"

"Of course I am. But..." Alex's voice trailed off.

Sabina smiled. "That was my dad in the car. We're visiting for Christmas. He's over here writing a story for the paper. Something about some sort of weird Church. He got me out of school early and we're going to stay over here until the new year."

"In London?"

"Where else?"

"Is your mum here too?"

"Yeah. We're renting a flat in Notting Hill."

The two of them stared at each other. There were so many things Alex wanted to say. He didn't know where to begin.

"Are you two going to come inside?" Jack called from the kitchen. "Or would you like me to serve dinner in the street?"

There was a moment of awkwardness. Alex realized that he hadn't even invited Sabina in. Worse than that, he was actually blocking the way. He moved to one side to let her pass. She smiled a little nervously and stepped inside. But the doorway was narrow, and as she came in he felt her briefly against him. Her hair brushed his cheek and he smelled the perfume she was wearing. At that moment, he realized how glad he was to see her. It was as if everything was beginning all over again.

Now she was in the hall and he was the one outside.

"Sabina..." he began.

"Alex," she said, "I'm freezing. Why don't you shut the door?"

Alex smiled and closed the door and the two of them went in.

AN AFTERWORD BY ANTHONY HOROWITZ

NAMES

I spend an awful lot of time thinking up names ... both for the books and for the characters who inhabit them.

Titles, of course, are extremely important. They have to be short, strong, memorable and relevant to the story. They have to be something that my publishers can illustrate. When I announce a new Alex Rider book, it's the first thing that everyone wants to know. In a way, the title is there to sell the book. It's a quick promise of what is to come.

And yet sometimes the titles take me months to get right (and even then I can't be sure that I've cracked it). This book was easy. As soon as I learned that there were gangs in Asia known as snakeheads, there was no need to look any further.

But the one that followed it – *Crocodile Tears* as it eventually became – was a nightmare. This was a story to be set in Scotland, London and Kenya, which involved an international charity and GM crops. I initially wanted to call the book *Endurance*

Point, which, in my imagination, could have been the name of the valley where the deadly crops are grown, but I didn't get a lot of enthusiasm in schools that I visited and anyway I had already used the word "point" both in *Point Blanc* and *Christmas at Gunpoint*, an Alex Rider short story which appears in *The Mission Files*. (In that story, Gunpoint turns out to be a ski resort in America.) Then I tried *Dark Harvest*, which seemed quite powerful and certainly described the poisonous wheat field. But everyone said it sounded too much like a horror story. At different times the book was *Wolf Moon*, *First Aid* (the name of the charity), *Poison Dawn* and *No Spy Like Alex*.

The strange thing is that the actual title had come to me quite quickly and seemed perfect. Crocodile tears are fake or hypocritical tears and Desmond McCain, the villain in the book, certainly sheds plenty of them. They also connected with the Kenyan setting ... if you've read the story, you'll know that crocodiles are very much involved. So what was the problem? Sadly, very few people knew what the title meant. Language is changing all the time and it seems that the phrase – "crocodile tears" has slipped out of use. Well, hopefully by now it's back in business because that was the title I went with. I had to add the definition on the first page.

My favourite title of all the Alex books is probably *Skeleton Key* because those two words say so many different things. A skeleton makes you think of death. A skeleton key is something a burglar or a spy might use to break into a house. A key is also a type of island (I was thinking of Key West in Florida) and much of the story takes plays on Cayo Esqueleto, near Cuba.

For the same reason, I'm also quite fond of *Point Blanc* – which has a double meaning. You shoot someone point blank. And I invented a mountain in the French alps called "White Point". But if I'm going to be completely honest, I got it slightly wrong. If there really were a mountain with that name, apparently it would be called Pointe Blanche. It also worries me that very few English readers would set out to buy a book with a French title ... and I wonder how many sales I've lost because of that!

Stormbreaker, the name of the first Alex book, is a strong title, I think. I needed to work out what a brand new, highly advanced computer might be called, and I thought about the electricity that powered it and the codes that went into it (spies break codes). The book was very nearly called *Stormchaser*. Just a few weeks before it was to be printed, we discovered that another well-known writer had come up with the same name. It was a near miss. I'm not sure what would have happened if two books with identical titles had appeared at around the same time.

Character names are equally important. Often, the

first thing you know about someone that you meet in a book is their name – and it very much helps the opinion you form of them. This is something that my great hero, Charles Dickens, recognized in his books. When he called a teacher Gradgrind, you knew you wouldn't want to be in his class. Or what about Uriah Heep? Someone to avoid, surely!

Alex Rider's name is probably the most important decision I ever made. Would you, for example, enjoy the books as much if I had decided to call him Maurice Thwaite? As a matter of fact, naming Alex was quite easy. The son of a friend of mine came to lunch just as I had started writing *Stormbreaker* (or *Stormchaser*). His name was Alex, he was thirteen, spoke fluent French (he had a French dad) and was learning Tae kwondo. I wouldn't say I modelled Alex on him, but I certainly stole his name. As for Rider, it's a solid, action name. And, by coincidence, it's also the name of one of my favourite characters in the James Bond novels. Honeychile Ryder is the beautiful fishing girl who rescues Bond in *Dr No*.

A lot of the names in Alex Rider have secret meanings and I'm going to finish this afterword by sharing some of them with you. Names can really help a writer. They can act a bit like a pedestal. That is, they put someone or something into my mind which then helps me build the character.

This won't be a complete list – I don't have the space – but it'll give you an idea of how I work:

ALAN BLUNT

The head of MI6 was always going to be an important character because I knew he'd appear in all the Alex Rider books. I named him Blunt after one of the most famous spies in British history. Sir Anthony Blunt was a traitor, an art historian who looked after the King's pictures and secretly worked for the Russians. My own spymaster is a bit cold and untrustworthy and I think the name with its dark history suits him.

MRS JONES

She is, of course, Blunt's deputy and curiously she is named after my agent – Anthony Jones – who handles all my contracts and business deals. I'm not quite sure what made me think of him. I always liked the idea that she had no Christian name, at least in the first four books. Then, in *Scorpia*, we discover that she is called Tulip. No wonder she never uses it!

JACK STARBRIGHT

Alex's loyal friend and housekeeper was originally named after a girl called Jacks who worked at my publishers. I have no idea how I came up with Starbright. Maybe I'd been having too many coffees. I'm afraid this is my least favourite name of all my characters.

DEREK SMITHERS

I've discussed Smithers in the afterword of *Eagle Strike*. The original Smithers is a minor character in Ian Fleming's *Goldfinger* but I liked the name because it was so old-fashioned.

JOHN CRAWLEY

He's another MI6 agent who turns up from time to time. I'm not entirely sure where his name came from but when we were making the film of *Stormbreaker* we were told we weren't allowed to use it. Does this mean that there's a real John Crawley, who really is a spy, somewhere in the world? If so, his cover has been well and truly blown.

YASSEN GREGOROVICH

The assassin who turns up in two of the books and who changes Alex's life, was inspired by a children's book illustrator whom I met in Sweden. I often "borrow" the names of people I meet and the moment he told me his name I knew that I had found my perfect cold-blooded killer. I've never found out if Mr Gregorovich is pleased or annoyed to be a character in my books.

SABINA PLEASURE

A friend of Alex's who appears in three of the books, Sabina has a slightly absurd name (rather like the nurse who looks after Alex in *Ark Angel*, Diana Meacher, and the American agent, Tamara Knight). This is a nod at Ian Fleming, the Bond author, who gave his girlfriends suggestive names such as Plenty O'Toole and Pussy Galore! In *Point Blanc*, I gave the girl that Alex saves the name Fiona Friend, but I'm afraid nobody got it. I was thinking of the television programme *Who Wants to be a Millionaire* and the three choices: fifty-fifty, ask the audience or...

HEROD SAYLE

The bad guy in *Stormbreaker* was inspired by a famous businessman called Mohamed al Fayed. Not that I think that Mr al Fayed is an evil man, although he's certainly larger-than-life and has often been mocked in the British press. Like him, Herod is an outsider, somebody who feels he has been badly treated by the establishment. His name is taken from Harrods Department Store, which is owned by al Fayed. Every Christmas, there's a Herod Sayle.

ALEXEI SAROV

The general who wants to bring back communism in *Skeleton Key* was originally called Skeletov. That was how I got the name of the book. Although he's in many ways the most sympathetic villain, I wanted a name with a hint of death. But Skeletov was more than a hint. It was a dollop. And then I remembered some terrorists who had attacked the Japanese train system with a poison called Sarin and the right name fell into place.

DAMIAN CRAY

I found it quite difficult coming up with a believable name for the mad pop singer who combats Alex in *Eagle Strike*. His surname is taken from the Kray brothers, two vicious criminals who terrorized London back in the sixties. His first name was an echo of Damon Albarn, the lead singer of a group called Blur.

JULIA ROTHMAN

My only female villain, so far, was partly inspired by the Welsh actress, Catherine Zeta-Jones. I wanted her to have a name that was both attractive and yet somehow deadly and I came up with the idea of naming her after a cigarette.

DESMOND McCAIN

The villain of *Crocodile Tears* is an ex-politician who has been sent to jail for fraud and who has seemingly converted to Christianity and now runs an international charity. I chose the first name, Desmond, thinking of Desmond Tutu, the South African cleric and anti-apartheid campaigner who is a bit of a hero of mine. I originally called him Desmond Cain, again thinking of the Bible – Cain, the first murderer. But this seemed a bit obvious so I changed it to McCain and had him found, as a baby, wrapped in a used bag of McCain Oven Chips.

SCORPIA

This is the deadly organization that Julia works for. It stands for Sabotage, Corruption, Intelligence and Assassination, but it got its name in quite a different way. I was at the end of *Eagle Strike*. Yassen was dying on the President's plane and told Alex to go to Venice to search for ... what? I couldn't think of a name and I was in a hurry. I was late delivering the book. As it happened, there was an opera – Puccini's *Tosca* – playing on my iPod. It was the moment when the villain makes his grand entrance and he is called Scarpia. In an instant, Scarpia became Scorpia and I had my next book.

TOM HARRIS & JAMES HALE

Alex's closest friends come from two different sources. Tom is named after an old friend of mine from my university days. But James demonstrates another way you can get into an Alex Rider book: the charity auction. His father paid a very generous sum of money and James's appearance in *Crocodile Tears* was the prize. I was hugely relieved that he had such a simple name. It could have been Polish with seventeen syllables!

There are two more books in the Alex Rider series and I'm still looking for names. Often, when I do book signings, I come across an interesting name in the queue and I always make a note of it. Then, months later, I'll rummage around in my name box and pull it out. Zeljan Kurst, the exotic-sounding gangster who takes over Scorpia, was actually a boy who came to get a book signed. Kolo, the guard who tries to drown Alex in *Ark Angel*, was a perfectly pleasant boy I met in a school in Belgium.

So do watch out if you come to get a book signed. You never know where you might end up.

Anthony Horowitz
January 2010

ACKNOWLEDGEMENTS

As with all the Alex Rider books, I've tried to make *Snakehead* as accurate as possible – and I wouldn't have been able to do this without the generous help of people all around the world. So it seems only polite to mention them here.

Dr Michael Foale at NASA spoke to me at length for a second time, and the opening chapter is largely based on his own experiences returning from outer space. The mechanism by which Major Yu attempts to bring chaos to the world was suggested to me by Professor Bill McGuire at University College London; he also came up with the planetary alignment that makes it feasible.

Panos Avramopoulos at CMA CGM Shipping (UK) Ltd kindly arranged for me to visit a container ship, and Captain Jenkinson allowed me on board. A few weeks later, Andy Simpson of Global SantaFe and Rupert Hunt from Shell gave up a whole day of their time to show me round an oil rig near Aberdeen. Neither of these visits would have been possible without Jill Hughes, to whom I am eternally grateful.

I spent a week in Bangkok, where I was looked after by the author Stephen Leather, who took me to all sorts of locations, many of which I wasn't allowed to mention in the book! He also accompanied me to the Thai kick-boxing fight which is the basis of Chapters 8 and 9. I also want to thank Justin Ractliffe, who showed me round Perth and Sydney during a lengthy book tour.

Joshua King, Alfie Faber, Max Packman-Walder and Emma Charatan all read the manuscript and gave me great notes and advice. Not for the first time, my son Cassian suggested some major changes.

Finally, my assistant Cat Taylor organized everything and then organized it again when I changed my mind. Justin Somper continues to be the guiding light behind much of Alex's success. And my very lovely editor, Jane Winterbotham, spent hours trawling through some of the most complex notes ever to come out of a publishing house to ensure that all the dates and times make sense.

AH

READ OTHER GREAT BOOKS BY
ANTHONY HOROWITZ...

Collect all the Alex Rider books

STORMBREAKER

Alex Rider – you're
never too young
to die…

POINT BLANC

High in the Alps,
death waits for
Alex Rider…

SKELETON KEY

Sharks. Assassins.
Nuclear bombs. Alex
Rider's in deep water.

EAGLE STRIKE

Alex Rider has 90
minutes to save
the world.

SCORPIA

Once stung, twice as
deadly. Alex Rider
wants revenge.

ARK ANGEL

He's back – and
this time there are
no limits.

SNAKEHEAD

Alex Rider bites
back…

CROCODILE TEARS

Alex Rider – in the
jaws of death…

SCORPIA RISING

One bullet. One life.
The end starts here.

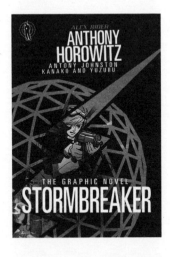
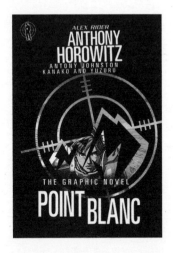

WELCOME TO THE DARK SIDE OF
ANTHONY HOROWITZ

THE POWER OF FIVE

BOOK ONE

He always knew he was different.
First there were the dreams.
Then the deaths began.

BOOK TWO

It began with Raven's Gate.
But it's not over yet. Once
again the enemy is stirring.

BOOK THREE

Darkness covers the earth.
The Old Ones have returned.
The battle must begin.

BOOK FOUR

An ancient evil is unleashed.
Five have the power to defeat it.
But one of them has been taken.

BOOK FIVE

Five Gatekeepers.
One chance to save mankind.
Chaos beckons. Oblivion awaits.

OTHER BOOKS BY ANTHONY HOROWITZ

Heading for an exciting new life in London,
Tom Falconer is ambushed by the murderous
Ratsey. Helpless and alone, the orphan gallops
towards the great city, where a number of mortal
dangers await him. But on the first night of a new play
– *The Devil and his Boy* – Tom discovers that the fate
of Elizabethan England rests in his hands..

"A cracking historical adventure... Thrilling." TES

The Diamond Brothers series

Meet Tim Diamond, the world's worst private detective, and his quick-thinking wisecracking younger brother Nick!

"His first job was to find some rich lady's pedigree Siamese cat. He managed to run it over on the way to see her. The second job was a divorce case – which you may think is run-of-the-mill until I tell you that the clients were perfectly happily married until he came along... There hadn't been a third case."

Collect all 4 hilarious Diamond Brothers investigations!

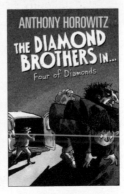

Photograph © Jon Cartwright

Anthony Horowitz is the author of the number one bestselling Alex Rider books and The Power of Five series. He has enjoyed huge success as a writer for both children and adults, most recently with the latest adventure in the Alex Rider series, *Russian Roulette* and his highly acclaimed Sherlock Holmes novel, *The House of Silk*. He has won numerous awards, including the Bookseller Association/Nielsen Author of the Year Award, the Children's Book of the Year Award at the British Book Awards, and the Red House Children's Book Award. In 2014 Anthony was awarded an OBE for Services to Literature. Anthony has also created and written many major television series, including *Injustice, Collision* and the award-winning *Foyle's War*.

You can find out more about Anthony and his work at:

www.anthonyhorowitz.com
@AnthonyHorowitz